I was told that you would help me. If you want to aid your country, meet me in the bakery.

Now, my mama didn't raise a fool. A gnarly guy follows me around the store, leaves this cryptic note in the tomatoes, and I'm supposed to go meet him? Yeah, I don't think so.

But after he followed me to the canned fruit aisle, the spaghetti section and the deli, I caved. Sighing, because I knew I was gonna regret it but my curiosity was killing me, I pulled my cart over and waited.

He stopped his cart by me and whispered, "I'm with the CIA, and my cover's blown. My case involves money laundering. I was told that if I got in a bind, I could trust you."

A large woman with a tiny dog in her bag pulled up her cart. The lady's dog suddenly went nuts, barking its head off. It scrambled out of the bag and took off. The big woman bumped into Mr. Gnarly as she ran after the dog and disappeared down the aisle.

As I watched in horror, Mr. Gnarly fell to the floor. A knife protruded from his chest. I rushed to kneel beside him, yelling, "Call an ambulance! This guy's been stabbed!"

Dear Reader,

What's in *your* beach bag this season? August is heating up, and here at Bombshell we've got four must-read stories to make your summer special.

Rising-star Rachel Caine brings you the first book in her RED LETTER DAYS miniseries, *Devil's Bargain*. An ex-cop makes a deal with an anonymous benefactor to start her own detective agency, but there's a catch—any case that arrives via red envelope must take priority. If it doesn't, bad things happen....

Summer heats up in Africa when a park ranger intent on stopping poachers runs into a suspicious Texan with an attitude to match her own, in *Rare Breed* by Connie Hall. Wynne Sperling wants to protect the animals under her watch—will teaming up with this secretive stranger help her, or play into the hands of her enemies?

A hunt for missing oil assets puts crime-fighting CPA Whitney "Pink" Pearl in the line of fire when the money trail leads to a top secret CIA case, in *She's on the Money* by Stephanie Feagan. With an assassin on her tail and two men vying for her attention, Pink had better get her accounts in order....

It takes true grit to make it in the elite world of FBI criminal profilers, and Angie David has what it takes. But with her mentor looking over her shoulder and a serial killer intent on luring her to the dark side, she'll need a little something extra to make her case. Don't miss *The Profiler* by Lori A. May!

Please send your comments to me c/o Silhouette Books, 233 Broadway, Suite 1001, New York, NY 10279.

Best wishes,

Natashya Wilson

Natashya Wilson
Associate Senior Editor, Silhouette Bombshell

STEPHANIE FEAGAN

$HE'S ON THE MONEY

Silhouette

BOMBSHELL

Published by Silhouette Books

America's Publisher of Contemporary Romance

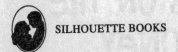 **SILHOUETTE BOOKS**

ISBN 0-373-51369-0

SHE'S ON THE MONEY

Copyright © 2005 by Stephanie Feagan

This edition published by arrangement with Harlequin Books S.A.

® and TM are trademarks of Harlequin Books S.A., used under license. Trademarks indicated with ® are registered in the United States Patent and Trademark Office, the Canadian Trade Marks Office and in other countries.

www.SilhouetteBombshell.com

Printed in U.S.A.

Books by Stephanie Feagan

Silhouette Bombshell

Show Her the Money #40

*The Pink Files

STEPHANIE FEAGAN

planned to be a park ranger, so she could live in the mountains, marry a good-looking guy who likes bears and spend her evenings by a cozy fire, writing novels. But a funny thing happened in college. Instead of a forestry degree, she graduated with a BBA in accounting and became a CPA. Instead of a mountain man, she married an oilman. And instead of living among mountains and bears, she lives in the flatlands of west Texas, amongst mesquites and jackrabbits. That's okay for Stephanie—she happens to love the mesquites and the jackrabbits. She especially loves her oilman. And she does spend her evenings writing novels, although instead of a cozy fire, she opts for an air conditioner. Stephanie would love for you to visit her Web site at www.stephaniefeagan.com.

For Callie, with my love and awe.
I musta done something incredible to earn the privilege
of having you in my life.

Acknowledgments

Thank you, Leslea, for your support and wacked-out
sense of humor! To Mike, for your love and faith and
spot-on oil business know-how. To Natashya Wilson, for
once again proving that you are, indeed, Dream Editor.
To Karen Solem, for career advice and support. Thanks
to Jo George, CPA, aka Mom, who never seems to mind
when I pose bizarre accounting scenarios and ask if
they'll work. Thanks again to the Wet Noodle Posse—the
midwives who helped bring Pink into the world of
publishing. And thanks to Sammy Hagar,
for the spectacular tunes—and the inspiration.

Chapter 1

Wednesday, September 7—5:05 p.m.

There are some days when it just doesn't pay to get up. This Wednesday in early September was one of them. Things had started out lousy and grown exponentially worse with every hour that passed. By late afternoon, I was shell-shocked by just how sucky one day could be, and I'd had enough. I decided to retreat to the sanctity of my small apartment and spend some serious downtime with a pint of Cookies 'n Cream. At ten minutes until five, I left work and headed for the grocery store.

That's how I ended up with a dead guy's blood splattered all over me.

My name is Whitney Ann Pearl, but most everyone calls me Pink. As in Pink Pearl erasers. I live in Midland, Texas, and I'm a CPA, which is an acronym for Certified Public Accountant. Or Constant Pain in the Ass, depending on who you're talking to.

Late that Wednesday afternoon, I pulled in at the Allbright's on Loop 250, and with no list or real idea of what I needed except for the ice cream, I grabbed a shopping cart and began my trek through the supermarket.

I first noticed him in the canned-fruit section while I checked the labels on peaches, looking for something without fifteen pounds of added sugar. The guy was sort of lingering behind me, just to the right. He was tall and kinda gnarly, with a crew cut and work boots, and his skin was a shade darker than mine. It dawned on me, in a weird, lightbulb moment, that he'd been close by on the spaghetti aisle. He'd also been hanging out at the deli when I'd ordered a quarter pound of shaved turkey.

I'm convinced we all have some secret, inner alarm that goes into alert mode whenever something isn't quite right. Mine began to go off, right there in canned fruit. I didn't look directly at him but tossed a can of peaches in my cart and shoved off, headed for the cosmetics aisle. If he showed up there, I'd know for sure he was following me.

A few minutes later, I felt relieved when he didn't appear. I tossed some mascara and a new tube of lipstick in the cart and strolled off toward the produce section to look for salad stuff. I was kinda looking forward to having some real groceries at home. The past few months my diet had mostly consisted of fast food and frozen dinners.

After I nabbed a bag of lettuce, I went to find a decent tomato. There, while I searched for one that wasn't too ripe, the man moved next to me, reached out one tanned, rough hand and grabbed two tomatoes. When he pulled back, turned his cart and left, I saw he'd dropped something in the middle of all that red. With my hair slowly rising, I picked up the small piece of paper and read his note.

I was told that you would help me. If you want to aid your country, meet me in the bakery.

Now, my mama didn't raise no fool. A gnarly guy follows me around, leaves this cryptic note in the tomatoes, and I'm supposed to go meet him? Yeah, I don't think so.

I hauled ass for the checkout counter, convinced he was a bigger nutcase than the wannabe client I'd had a run-in with earlier in the day. Maybe it was National Nutcase Day and nobody told me.

At the front of the store, just my luck, there were only two lanes open and each had at least five people in line. I debated leaving the cart and hitting the road, but I really wanted that ice cream. I also definitely needed the groceries, so I decided to take my chances on the nutty guy finding me. If I was in line, he couldn't do anything, could he?

I had my answer about thirty seconds later. He came right up behind me and said conversationally, "Boy, what's with only two lanes? This time of day, with so many people stopping in after work, you'd think they'd have more checkouts open."

The lady in front of me nodded and added, "Last week, I had to take my own groceries to the car!" She said this as though carrying her groceries ranked up there with superhuman efforts like swimming the English Channel or climbing Everest.

"The bakery's kinda falling off, too, if you ask me," the gnarly man said. He stared at me as he said it and I felt my scalp tingle again. Then he picked up the *National Enquirer* and studied the front page for a time. I kept my focus on the chewing gum selection until he tapped my shoulder and held the paper toward me. "I'm always pretty skeptical about their articles, but they are sort of intriguing, don't you think?"

The lady was still looking at us, and I couldn't ignore the

guy without appearing boorish. Miss Manners took over, and I glanced at the cover. He'd attached another note to it.

I understand you think I'm crazy. Santorelli gave me your name—said I could trust you if I got in a bind. Just give me two minutes.

Santorelli? *My* Santorelli? The senator from California who could kiss like nobody's business, who had an off-the-wall sense of humor and awesome suits? I looked up, into the man's eyes, and couldn't miss the sincerity there. Along with a small amount of fear.

"You know," he said to no one in particular, "it seems to me that with this many shoppers, they'd have more people working. There's a whole crowd over on the pickle aisle watching a demo for a stuff-it-yourself olive gizmo."

"I tried that!" the lady in front of me said. "You can stuff them with garlic and jalapeños and the like." She looked at me. "Did you try it?"

"No, I guess I missed that." But I didn't miss the stranger's point. The store was crowded. I wasn't in any danger, and what could it hurt to hear what he had to say? Sighing because I knew I was gonna regret it but my curiosity was killing me, I pulled back my cart. "I think I'll check it out."

The stranger said, "Yeah, I think I'll stuff some with sardines. Gotta love sardines."

I pushed my cart toward the pickle aisle, überaware of the sardine-loving guy right behind me. I slowed down next to the kosher dills, several feet away from the small crowd gathered around the olive company representative, a short guy who was giving away ceramic olive boats to anyone who tried the olive stuffer. They were pretty cool, and I decided maybe I'd get one, too, as soon as Mr. Gnarly explained how he knew Santorelli and how I could aid my country.

While the olive rep went on about the olives, the mystery man angled his big body toward me, bent his head as if he were studying his grocery list and whispered, "I don't have much time, so I can't give you a long explanation, but I need you to pick up a cake in the bakery and deliver it to someone. It's imperative that you get it to the right person, that you not allow anyone else to take it. Tell everyone it's a birthday cake for a little boy."

I consider myself a quick study, but I was thoroughly confused. What did this have to do with aiding my country? Or Senator Santorelli? Maybe I was having a blond moment, but I didn't think so.

He retrieved a jar of sweet gherkins from the shelf and studied the back while he whispered, "I'm with the CIA, and my cover's blown. I've gotta get out of town immediately, but I have to get the information that's in that cake to the right people. I can't take it myself because I'm being followed."

His tone was serious but calm, not nutty, and I started to believe maybe he was on the level, that maybe he wasn't smoking crack. "Who's following you?"

"I don't know. It could be anybody in this store, or I may have lost him and he isn't anywhere near here. Don't trust anybody and don't give the cake to anyone but the man whose name is on the paper baked into the cake. It'll be ready in half an hour."

"How do you know Santorelli?"

"As the chairman of the Senate Finance Committee, he gets briefed about money laundering. This assignment involves following a money trail. Santorelli said if I got in a bind, I could trust you to lend me a hand."

Before I could ask more questions, a large woman with a tiny dog in her bag parked her cart next to him.

Acting as though we'd been chatting it up all along, he said in a normal voice, "What kind of cake are you picking up for your friend?"

"A birthday cake, for her son. They said it would be ready in about thirty minutes, so I'm killing time."

The man nodded. "My nephew just had a birthday and his cake had a Spider-Man action figure on it. He loves Spider-Man because he always gets the bad guys."

The big woman chuckled. "Spider-Man's not just for boys. My little girl is crazy for him."

The gnarly guy smiled at her, then said to me, "Interesting name your friend's son has. Can't think I've ever heard of a boy named Santa. I bet the kids tease him about that."

Santa? What the hell? Couldn't he have dreamed up a better name for the pretend boy? I cast about for an appropriate comeback. "It's a nickname, actually." Leaning closer to him, I pointed at a block of fresh mozzarella in his basket. "Is that brand any good?" I asked aloud, then added beneath my breath, "Who's laundering money?"

"It's excellent," he replied, "especially with a ripe tomato, fresh basil and a bit of olive oil drizzled on it."

"I like it with balsamic vinegar, as well," Big Mama said.

Mr. Gnarly nodded in her direction, then focused on the olive man. After a few moments, he whispered, "Al Qaeda."

Maybe I sucked in a breath. Or perhaps I actually made a small noise in the back of my throat. I admit, it's all a bit fuzzy now. But I know I must have made my shock and horror known, because the man looked panicked and his expression warned me to be cool. I swallowed back the lump of fear in my throat and began to back away from him.

Al Qaeda? It was so surreal, but this was the second time today someone had brought up the terrorist group. Coincidence? I thought not. Suddenly, the simple task of picking up the cake and delivering it to someone had become very dangerous. Was I up for it? Did I really have a choice? I was keenly curious to know more, and most especially, to know what was hidden inside the cake. Only one way to find out, and that was to agree to deliver it.

"You know, I don't really need more stuff in my apartment, even an olive boat. I think I'm gonna head for the bakery. It was real nice talking to you."

He'd been staring at the big lady, but when I spoke, he turned, and his dark eyes crinkled at the edges as he smiled at me. I had the fleeting thought that he was a lot better looking with a smile on his harsh face. "Hang on and let me give you something." He shot a quick glance at Big Mama, who now appeared to be absorbed in the olive rep's spiel, then reached inside his right jean pocket. Before he could withdraw his hand, the lady's little dog went ape-shit and started barking its head off. Well, barking is a little strong. Did I mention the dog wasn't much bigger than a rat? Its barks were more akin to high-pitched squeaks. In the middle of its conniption fit, it scrambled out of the bag, hit the floor and took off.

Big Mama bumped into Mr. Gnarly as she ran after the dog, her long caftan billowing out behind her. The olive crowd parted like the Red Sea, but the olive rep wasn't fast enough to get out of her way. She upset his tray as she rushed past, and suddenly, olives skewered with toothpicks rolled drunkenly across the shiny linoleum.

Mr. Gnarly leaned down. That's when I saw the logo on the back of his khaki shirt.

North Face. My memory kicked into overdrive and I realized I'd seen this man earlier in the day. Then I realized why he was bent over. The handle of a knife protruded from his chest! While I watched in stupefied horror, his big body crumpled to the floor. I rushed to kneel beside him, yelling at the top of my lungs, "Call an ambulance! This guy's been stabbed!"

Chapter 2

Looking back, it seems inevitable that I'd end up in the grocery store with a dead body at my feet. But early that day, I'd assumed the worst was behind me by nine o'clock in the morning.

"You know how this works, so give it up with that hangdog look. Nobody can stay in business without bringing in new clients, and I expect you to pull your weight around here."

From across the football field that's my mother's desk, I answered automatically, "I don't have a hangdog look."

Mom huffed out an irritated breath, leaned back in her executive leather chair and twirled around to face the east wall of her office, where her diplomas and CPA certificate hung along with a handful of awards and accolades. "I offered you this job because I thought you'd bring in more business."

"You offered me this job because I couldn't find anything else after I got canned for being a whistle-blower."

"That's not true." She twirled to face me again, looking a bit hurt. "Ever since I opened my own CPA practice, I thought about how nice it would be for the two of us to work together. I never thought it would happen because you were on the fast track to make partner at your firm in Dallas. But when you lost your job, I sort of looked at it like fate, like this is the way it was supposed to be. I had high hopes."

"And now you have low hopes? Or no hope at all?"

Watching her pretty face form a frown, I slumped back in the leather guest chair and waited for the guilt trip to begin. The wait was very short.

"It's been a long, hard road to get where I'm at, and all I want is a little effort on your part. Is that so much to ask?"

There are bound to be worse things than working for my mother. Living in Afghanistan would probably be worse. But only if I had to wear one of those funky blue things. Spending time in prison might be worse, because I'd probably get an embezzler cellmate who has issues with accountants. On the other hand, she wouldn't get on my case about bringing in new clients.

That I was getting this lecture at all really bugged me, but the fact that I was getting it from my mother made it a gazillion times worse. My pride had taken a beating during the past few months, so I was a little more sensitive than usual.

At the beginning of summer, I'd been on top of the world, making an awesome salary as a senior manager at one of the best CPA firms in the world and living in a way-cool loft on Central Expressway in Dallas. Then I found out our biggest client was scamming its investors, so I took what I learned to the Securities and Exchange Commission. Turned out my boss was in on the whole thing and he didn't like that I squealed, so my career at Big Important CPAs was over.

While I was testifying to the Senate Finance Committee and becoming a regular news item on CNN, every possible job opportunity dried up. I jumped the rails from the Make Partner fast track to the Make Mac'n'Cheese from a Box Because That's All I Can Afford track. Okay, so it wasn't that bad, but I really couldn't find another job, and things started to look mighty dismal.

Then Mom offered me a position in her newly created forensic accounting department. Granted, I'd had to sell the loft and move back to my hometown of Midland, Texas, where oil is king and June Cleaver is a patron saint, but it hadn't been as bad as I'd feared. So far, I'd sort of enjoyed the job, tracing assets in divorce cases and looking into bad oil deals. I thought things were rocking along quite nicely.

Until Mom called me into her office first thing this morning and raked me over the coals for my apparent failings as a salesman for her firm. I'd like to say I was pissed off at her for being harsh, but the truth of it was, I knew she was right. I hate it when that happens. I sucked it up and gave her the response I knew she wanted. "Okay, Mom, I'll work on bringing in some business."

"How? You spend all your time at the office or in your rinky-dink, tacky apartment. You can't find new clients if you don't get out there and become involved in the community."

"My apartment isn't tacky."

Mom's dark eyes narrowed slightly. "You're right. It's worse than tacky. I was being nice."

I stood and smoothed out the wrinkles in my khaki skirt. "Any suggestions about how to go out there and get involved?"

Mom became interested in her manicure, inspecting her nails closely while she said in a subdued voice, "Actually, I thought you might call Dru and offer to take her to lunch. She's involved in a lot of community activities around Midland, and she might have some suggestions." My mother glanced up at me through her lashes. "And she may have a referral for you. She left a message on my machine yesterday about a gentleman she knows who needs some help with his oil revenue checks."

I sucked in a breath and let it out slowly, mostly to give myself time to corral all the raw expletives that wanted to spew forth. Aunt Dru is at the top of my Relatives To Avoid list. Mom wanted me to take her to lunch on a day that was already shaping up to be awful. Didn't it just figure?

Not that any other day would make it better. Lunch with Aunt Dru is simply an especially gruesome form of torture, regardless of the sort of day I'm having. "Aunt Dru is in her seventies, Mom. Everything she's involved in is chock-full of old ladies, most of whom would have no need for a forensic accountant. And I bet her gentleman is some crotchety old geezer who simply doesn't understand how the oil business works."

"Maybe, but perhaps you'd be surprised. It's a start, Pink." Mom dropped her hands to the desk and folded them primly. "Besides, she's your aunt and it's your duty to look in on her every so often."

Enlightenment dawned and I stared her down. "This has nothing to do with me turning into Cathy Community, does it? What gives?" I should have known her mention of Dru wasn't totally random.

"Lurch called last night."

I sank back into the guest chair, halfway wishing I hadn't asked. Lurch is a behind-his-back pet name we use for my father. And when I say pet, I don't mean it in an affectionate, warm and jolly way. After all, what would most people think of a guy called Lurch? They'd be right. He's arrogant, cold and can be the meanest son of a bitch on Earth when the mood strikes him. When it comes to me, the mood strikes a lot more often than not.

Don't get me wrong. Lurch isn't violent. He didn't beat me or anything like that. Let's just say he didn't get the memo that positive reinforcement is a good thing. In the glass is half full or half empty analogy, Lurch would yell, "I ordered a damn cheeseburger! Can't you morons get anything right?"

I watched Mom fidget with her mechanical pencil, well aware she was stalling. "Why does he still call you? Most ex-husbands don't call."

"Because he's Lurch, and he doesn't operate like normal men." Mom leaned back in her chair. "I think he's lonely, if you wanna know the truth. Nelda dumped him and he's stuck in that house up there in the Colorado mountains. Even if he is more unsociable than Bigfoot, he still needs some human contact."

"He talks to Aunt Dru. She told me that she calls him every Wednesday."

"True, but she's his older sister, and he can't bitch and moan about the sorry state of the world to her because she'll go off on him about Jesus. He'd probably call you, except he knows you're permanently pissed off at him. So he calls me."

"And you're not permanently pissed off at him?"

"Yes, I am, but evidently he still harbors hope that I'll come back to him." Mom let out a chuckle I can only describe as diabolical. "Yeah, like that would ever happen."

"So he calls and you listen to him gripe. Why? You divorced him because he's such a jerk, so why would you let him call and go off on you?"

"Vanity, probably. He's come to realize what a peach of a wife I was, and what a disaster Nelda was." A bit of a sly smile crept across Mom's lips. "She blew through most of his retirement fund. My net worth is bigger than his now."

"And you crowed about it to him, didn't you?"

"Of course. I'm only human, after all. I remember when I told him I was leaving him, he said I'd never make it, that I'd starve or end up having to marry some loser just so I could eat. He never thought I could go to college and get a degree, much less become a CPA."

At fifty-five, with a nice figure, dark hair that gets a little color help from the hairdresser, and lively dark eyes, Mom's still extremely pretty. Not that it matters much, at least where men are concerned. Mom's a barracuda in business, but get her around a potential love interest and she turns into a mealy-mouthed doormat. She knows it, and therefore swore off men after she divorced Lurch, which was while I was in college.

She enrolled in summer school, tested out of her first two years, and finished with her undergraduate degree and MBA in three years, total. That was one year before I finished my five-year plan and got out with a bachelor's degree—and I had a head start on her. Mom's freakin' brilliant. I'd feel intimidated, except, well, she's my mom, and I can't explain it, but our relationship just isn't like that. I'm proud of Mom, who didn't go for the displaced homemaker rap, but reinvented herself instead. In spite of Lurch.

"Hmm, sounds familiar," I said. "He told me I'd be lucky to get a bookkeeping job."

Mom blinked at me. "I'm sorry, Pink. I shoulda left him years ago, when you were still a little girl."

Oh, man. No way did I want to go back in time and let her wallow in regret. I sat up a bit straighter, determined to head her off in another direction. "So he called last night and he must have mentioned something about Aunt Dru."

Still fiddling with the pencil, Mom said, "He's worried because she's getting so involved with Trina Lorenzo, and he's convinced Trina is after Dru's money."

"Trina Lorenzo is thirtysomething and a major babe, on the hunt for a new rich husband. Why on Earth is she hanging out with Aunt Dru?"

Mom slanted me a look. "Trina found Jesus."

"I didn't know he was lost."

Ignoring my irreverent humor, Mom said, "She started going to Dru's church and Dru took her under her wing. You know how she is—always gotta have a protégée."

"I heard that Trina walked away from her divorce with over two million dollars. Why would she want Aunt Dru's money?"

"She wouldn't. This is Lurch we're talking about, don't forget. He thinks everyone's a crook. The point is, he asked me to check up on Dru and I said I would, but I gotta say, I'd rather get a root canal."

"So you want me to do it. I see how it is."

"Well, she is your aunt, after all. Since I divorced your father, she's technically not even my relative." Mom put on her game face and I knew then that I was toast. "And Dru has always favored you, Pink. She's a sweet lady, even if she is a bit overzealous with her religion, and I know she so looks forward to hearing from you. Take her to lunch and you can get the story on Trina, find out if Dru knows of some good contacts and whether her gentleman is a likely client."

Yeah, I was gonna have lunch with Aunt Dru. Mom sealed my fate with the guilt speech. I let out a huge sigh, then stood and walked toward the door. "I'll let you know how it goes."

"Yes, do that. And Pink?"

I stopped with my hand on the doorknob. "Yeah?"

"I expect you to have at least one new client before the end of next week."

I mumbled an affirmative and left her office, futilely wishing I could get out of the lunch thing, and feeling guilty about it at the same time.

Aunt Dru has been a widow since she was thirty. I'm convinced her husband died young just so he could get away from her. They never had any children, and Aunt Dru is the sort who needs people to boss around, so she set her sights on me and my two cousins, the progeny of Lurch's older brother, Robert.

They live out of state, the lucky dogs, and therefore escape the agony of lunches with Aunt Dru.

That's not to say I couldn't weasel out of it. I could. But I wouldn't be able to face myself in the mirror because I'd feel so guilty. Maybe Aunt Dru is boring and bossy, but there's no denying she does everything she does out of genuine love. She really thinks she's helping, just like she really thinks she's interesting. So I suffer the long, boring stories, and the edicts about how I should live my life.

Back at my cubicle in the bullpen, I called and asked her to lunch, and her enthusiasm made me feel like an even bigger heel, so I didn't complain when she suggested Busbee's cafeteria. "Sounds great," I lied. "Is noon okay?"

"Noon is fine," Aunt Dru said. "Funny you should call, Whitney Ann. I was going to call later and talk to Jane about a gentleman from church who needs some help with his oil revenues. I told him all about your mother and you, so he wants to come up and discuss his problem."

"You can tell me more about it at lunch," I said, even though I had a feeling the old man didn't need accounting so much as he needed a lesson about oil revenues. I told Aunt Dru goodbye, then settled in to work.

An hour and a half later, I had a call from the receptionist. "Pink, there's a man here to see you. Says he's a new client."

Great. The old man had come without the okay from Aunt Dru. I got up and headed for the front, deciding to be positive. Maybe he really did have a problem. Maybe he really would turn into a new client. Maybe his account would get my backside out of the sling it was in with Mom.

Regrettably, my positive mood evaporated into thin air when I turned the corner and spotted the "gentleman."

Banty McMeans. No way I could have luck this bad. I wondered if I'd committed some heinous sin as a child and God was paying me back, in spades.

Banty is not a handsome man. He's one of those people whose age is impossible to determine. He could be anywhere from forty to late fifties, but with no sign of gray in his strawberry-blond hair, which leans closer to red than blond, and only the vaguest beginning of a middle-age paunch, I'd guess he's early forties. Personality-wise, he's in his nineties, a wet blanket who most likely hasn't cracked a smile since he emerged from the womb. He never married and still lives with his mother in an old house over in the museum district. For as long as I've known anything about him, he's been called Banty, probably because he's like a bantam rooster, picking a fight with anyone who crosses his path.

He's made a career out of complaining, sending a letter to the editor of the local paper on a weekly basis to piss and gripe about something. There's not a store or restaurant in Midland that hasn't suffered his endless groaning. He's frequently on the evening news programs, and not in a good way. He's also a conspiracy theorist, always tilting at windmills, imagining Big Brother is watching, when really, the government couldn't care less what he's up to.

So maybe Banty would be the kind of client who causes CPAs to live up to their reputation of becoming alcoholics, but I couldn't persuade Miss Manners to tell him to take his business elsewhere. Not yet, anyway. I stuck my hand out and said, "How do you do, Mr. McMeans? I'm Whitney Pearl."

"Morning, Miss Pearl," he said with a trace of a whine in his voice while he gave me a wimpy handshake.

"I understand my aunt, Dru Grimes, gave you our name?" This didn't actually surprise me. Banty might be an odd duck, but he went to church on a regular basis, which made him okay in Aunt Dru's eyes. Anybody who takes church seriously is good and worthy in Aunt Dru World, regardless of the sort of person they are outside of church.

"That's right." He hitched up his green Sansabelt slacks, a nervous gesture, I decided, because he did it several times while he stood there.

"Let's go to the conference room and you can tell me the nature of your problem." I turned to lead the way, and once we were there, I closed the door and took a seat at the head of the long table. Banty took the seat perpendicular to mine and sat with his hands in his lap, looking at me with anticipation.

"Aunt Dru says you're having trouble with your oil runs."

His ruddy face flushed to a brighter shade of red, blending with his red hair and making it hard to tell where one stopped and the other started. "I've got an interest in some wells operated by David Lorenzo's company, and I'm absolutely sure he's ripping me off. I want you to prove it."

Two things came to mind simultaneously: this case would be a bust because David Lorenzo was no crook, and we would play hell ever getting Banty to pay us for our services, especially when he didn't end up with the results he wanted.

"Lorenzo spends a lot of time in Venezuela. Doesn't that seem odd?"

I wondered how he knew where David Lorenzo spent his time. "Venezuela is one of the world's largest petroleum producers, and David Lorenzo owns one of the most successful independent oil companies in America. I don't think his travels there are at all unusual."

"Last month, somebody ripped off a load of oil from one of the Lorenzo wells that I have an interest in. I heard it on my police radio, and verified it with a sheriff's deputy. But when I checked my revenue statement against the Railroad Commission report Lorenzo filed, the produced barrels were the same, which means they didn't report the stolen oil as ever being produced."

"So you think Lorenzo is stealing oil off of the wells he operates, then altering the production reports he files with the Railroad Commission to cover up the theft?"

Banty looked righteous. "That's exactly what I think. By stealing it, he can sell it and get one-hundred percent of the proceeds. He doesn't have to split it up among the other investors or the royalty owners."

"That makes no sense. He's one of the richest men in America. The money he could make doing something like that would be a drop in the bucket to what he probably earns on his investments while he's asleep every night."

"Maybe the money isn't for him. Maybe he's giving the stolen oil to someone else to sell."

Good Lord, the man was absolutely nuts. "Like who?"

He dropped his voice. "Ever heard of Koko Petroleum?"

"No."

"Me neither, and I can't find out anything about them. But as of about six months ago, they bought up all the drilling rights and royalty on a piece of property that's been proved a barren field. Dry as toast. With no other investors to share the risk, Koko drilled a well and it came in like gangbusters. Seems mighty odd for a piece of property every geologist in town said was barren."

"Let me guess," I said, not quite believing the poor man could be so delusional. "Lorenzo steals the oil off the wells his company operates, transports it to Koko's well, fills up the tanks, and they sell it. Is that about it?"

Looking pleased that I'd caught on, he nodded enthusiastically. "That's got to be it."

"If what you're saying is true, what's the motive? Why would David Lorenzo risk getting arrested for oil theft in order to give oil to a petroleum company nobody ever heard of?"

"That's one of the things I want you to find out."

I admit it all sounded very intriguing, but I couldn't get

away from the reality of taking on a man like Banty as a client. I would regret it. I was sure of it. Especially when I considered what I knew of David Lorenzo. He was drop-dead gorgeous, but that didn't actually mean squat when it came to his integrity. Good-looking men are just as likely to be crooks as ugly ones. Lorenzo was generous beyond belief, giving millions to the community for things like state-of-the-art medical equipment and improvements to the local museum. Still, that didn't speak to his honesty. Thieves have been known to be generous.

What made me so sure that Lorenzo wasn't guilty of Banty's accusations was how he'd handled his divorce from Trina, who was evidently the latest in a long line of Aunt Dru's born-again Christian protégées. In spite of a prenuptial agreement, which essentially gave Trina nothing, David settled two million dollars and a host of other assets on her. He didn't have to do that, but he did. And no matter how much mud Trina threw at him during their highly publicized divorce, he never once said anything derogatory about her. I admired that, and thought it said a lot about what David Lorenzo was made of.

Keeping my gaze level and my voice calm, I gave Banty the bad news. "I can certainly appreciate your concerns, but I'm afraid I can't take you on as a client at this time."

He didn't look disappointed. But then, he didn't look like he believed me, either. Leaning forward a bit, he said earnestly, "Aren't you a little curious about what's going on?"

"Maybe a little, but I really think you're wrong, that this is another one of your conspiracy theories."

"Take this job and find out."

A vision of Mom's frown floated in front of me, but I ignored it. Okay, so I needed to drum up some business—I didn't need to make myself miserable in the process. Shaking my head, I gave him the same answer. "I'm sorry, but I simply can't help you. Have you asked your tax CPA for any guidance?"

"I don't have a regular tax CPA. I've found that I get more value for my money if I use someone different each year."

I translated that to mean he never paid his bill, so had to hire a new accountant every year. "There are numerous other CPAs in town. Perhaps one of them might be of some assistance."

He looked exasperated as he leaned back in his chair. "Look, I didn't want to get into this, but I see I have no choice. The truth of the matter is, this is a delicate situation."

"Yes, I can see how accusing Mr. Lorenzo of being a criminal might be a bit delicate."

Totally missing my sarcasm, he rushed on. "I can't go to another CPA for exactly the same reason you're refusing to take me on. This sounds crazy, and let's face it, I have a reputation for sounding crazy. What people don't realize is that I'm almost always right, but some are better at covering their tracks than others, so I'm frequently unable to prove my claims. In this case, Lorenzo has no idea anyone's on to him, so you'd be able to find out what he's up to before he gets wise and hides all the evidence."

"If no other CPA will take this account because it's crazy, what makes you think I will?"

Banty nodded slowly, as though he'd proved a point. "Because you blew the whistle on your company when you found out they were committing a crime. Anybody who would do what you did, putting yourself on the line to expose a bunch of con artists dressed up as corporate executives, is somebody who isn't afraid to look for the truth, no matter how uncomfortable it makes people." He rested his hands on the smooth mahogany tabletop and gave me a serious look. "You're the only one I can trust, the only one who'll keep digging, no matter how many roadblocks Lorenzo puts in your way."

I know a snow job when I see one, and Banty was starting to look like Frosty. "My tenacious personality only applies when I get really worked up about something. No offense, but

I can't get too worked up about your problem, because I don't believe there is a problem. Maybe there is something out of whack, but my guess would be it's a mistake, a glitch somewhere within Lorenzo Petroleum's revenue department. If you'd take your concerns to the revenue manager, you'd probably get a logical explanation. As for Koko Petroleum and their amazing good fortune, it's not totally unbelievable that they'd drill a producing well in a barren field. The oil business is ten percent knowledge and ninety percent luck."

Surprising me, he got to his feet and began to pace back and forth in front of the windows, waving his hands about as he talked. "All right, so I'm going to have to go one step further and tell you some of what I already know." He stopped, hitched up his pants and glared at me. "I need your solemn word that this won't be repeated."

Whatever. I was quickly tiring of his histrionics and goofy theories. I had work to do. "Get to the point."

He resumed pacing. "Almost a year ago, Lorenzo converted to Islam. It's one of the reasons he divorced Trina, because she wouldn't conform to the doctrines of the Koran. Only a very few know about his conversion, and one of his conditions of giving money to Trina was her promise not to tell anyone."

"How do you know all of this?"

For a brief moment, he looked smug. "Trina is in my mother's Saints Above Bible Study. They share a lot of confidences with one another, sort of like group therapy."

I wondered if Trina had any idea how her confidence was being betrayed. I felt sorry for her, even though I didn't personally know her. "Why would he want to keep it a secret?"

Banty stopped again and his expression said loud and clear that he thought I was dumber than a box of rocks. "This is Midland, Texas, where George W. grew up, the last bastion of ultraconservative politics, and one of the few remaining old-boy networks in the country. A man can be Baptist or Presbyterian or Catholic. But no way he can be Muslim and keep any of his business connections. If everybody knew about David's newfound religion, he'd never get anyone else to invest in his wells. Even rich men need investors in the oil business. Costs too much to drill with the possibility of dry holes."

"I don't think people in this town are that narrow-minded."

"Yes, they are, and David knows it."

I was surprised, but it didn't change my opinion in the least. I still thought David Lorenzo was a fine man and Banty was a nutcase. "It looks to me like you're the narrow-minded one. Just because a man converts to Islam, he becomes a crook?"

"That's not why I think he's ripping off the revenue owners in the wells his company operates."

"Then what is the reason?"

Banty came close, glanced around as if to see who might be listening, and whispered, "I think he's the one behind Koko Petroleum. He's stealing that oil and giving it to Koko to sell, and Koko is sending the money to Islamic terrorists."

Lunging out of my chair, I went to the door and said in what I hoped was a firm voice, but probably sounded more pissed off, "There is nothing I can do for you, Mr. McMeans, because the pope will convert to Islam before I'll have any part in a witch hunt like you're proposing."

Darting around me, he put his back against the door and became quite animated in his passionate plea. "I know this sounds insane, but just hear me out!"

I let go of the knob and backed up a couple of steps to get him out of my face, wondering if I'd have to kick him where it hurt in order to make him leave. He was kinda wigging me out, he looked so red-faced and frantic. "You've got one minute, and then you have to go away. Understand?"

He nodded, hitched up his Sansabelt and swallowed audibly. "Before Lorenzo's father started Lorenzo Petroleum and discovered the enormous reservoir in the Pendergast field, he was an engineer for Texaco and worked in Saudi Arabia. A couple of years ago, when Mrs. Lorenzo was in the advanced stages of her cancer, she told David he was actually the illegitimate son of a Saudi man, someone Mr. Lorenzo worked with while they were over there. After her death, David looked up his biological father and discovered he had six brothers and two sisters."

"And he converted to Islam because he wanted to get in touch with his roots. So what? I'm sure other people have similar stories. It doesn't make them terrorists."

"One of David's half brothers is involved with Al Qaeda."

"Yeah, and I'm pretty sure Ted Bundy had a sister. She didn't become a serial killer because her brother was one."

"When David goes to Venezuela, the man he visits is an arms dealer with known terrorist connections."

"Who probably has a lot of oil and gas interests." How did Banty know all this? "Anyone can be made to look bad, if you leave out enough details."

Banty seemed ready to explode with frustration. I suppose I should have cared, but to be honest, he was making me want to go take a shower. I really have a thing for judgmental people who throw stones, and the way I saw it, Banty was hefting a boulder. "Just out of curiosity, did you learn all of this from your mother, as well? Is this more confidential information Trina trustingly provided?"

"You don't have to say it like my mother is a bad person."

"If she broke her promise to keep the group's discussions confidential, then she's certainly not one of the saints above."

"For your information, I didn't learn any of this from my mother. We share a maid with David Lorenzo, the same woman who's been cleaning our home since I was a boy. A long time ago, Mr. Lorenzo and my father were friends, and she began working for both of them. After Mr. Lorenzo struck it rich, he built a huge house with servants' quarters and she moved in with them, but she still comes to our house one day a week."

"And fills you in on all the details of the Lorenzo household?"

"Eleanor considers all of us one big family."

I wondered what Eleanor would think if she knew her innocent gossip was fodder for a conspiracy theorist to hurl the worst of accusations at her primary employer. "Mr. McMeans, you still haven't given me one single piece of information that would convince me that David Lorenzo has any links to terrorists. Even if I did believe it, I wouldn't try to discover what he's doing. I'd contact the CIA, or the FBI, and let them look into it. As for your original request, to see if and how Lorenzo Petroleum is shorting your revenue checks, I'd be happy to check it out, but for one thing."

"What's that?"

"You have a terrible reputation for not paying for services. Your lawsuit record is astonishing. But most of all, I simply won't work with someone who's willing to ruin a man's reputation, and maybe even his life, for the sake of some sick need for notoriety." I reached around him, turned the knob and shoved him out of the way with the door. "This is your exit cue. Goodbye, Mr. McMeans." I waited for him to leave.

He didn't.

"Don't think I won't call security."

As he turned to leave, he said confidently, "Okay, I'll leave, but I'm not giving up. Goodbye, Miss Pearl. Until we meet again...."

Thinking I needed to have a long talk with Aunt Dru about her church friends, I watched him leave, then turned to go back to my cubicle. But before I could walk away, Gert Luebner waved me into her office, which is situated just across the hall from the conference room.

I so didn't need a showdown with Gert right then. The chick Mom has in place as office manager has an attitude that's a cross between Attila the Hun and the defensive line-up of the Dallas Cowboys. She's not much prettier, either. Unable to escape, I stepped to her doorway. "What do you want?"

With a stack of bank statements in front of her, she frowned from behind a pair of gi-normous frames with thick lenses. Did I mention that Gert hates me? She sees me as a loser who couldn't get a job anywhere except with my mommy, and now she thinks, erroneously, that I'm up to make partner, which would bypass her many hours of toil and trouble. I also think she's a little jealous of me because I actually have the ability to attract members of the opposite sex. Not that I'm a hot mama or anything, but at least I can get a date. And I happen to like sex, which makes me a sexual being.

Amoebas are more sexual than Gert.

All the same, I had the brilliant idea of finding her a man, an equally geeky person who might consider her brilliant mind a turn-on. I reasoned that if Gert had a guy to focus on, she'd lay off of me. Thus far, regrettably, I'd had no luck, largely due to Gert's inexplicable resistance to makeup, modern glasses or contacts, and a hairstyle that didn't involve a messy bun. Even geeky guys want a woman who's not scary to look at. But I wasn't giving up. Gert needed to get laid. Soon.

"You should know," she said in her husky, manly voice, "Jane spoke to me about your conversation this morning. She asked me to help you with your search for new clients."

"Thanks for the offer, Gert, but I think I can manage just fine. Was that all you wanted?"

She nodded toward the hallway. "Was that a potential client you just told to leave?"

I knew this would lead to some angle she could use to guilt me into resigning. We'd done this same song and dance during the whistle-blower thing. "No, that was a potential lawsuit."

She gathered herself up and said virtuously, "In this business, and especially in light of what Jane asked of you, I can't imagine how you could turn away a client."

I'd rather talk about insurance or read up on algebra than spar with Gert, but I didn't have much choice, so I slid into my iron underwear and moved farther into her office. "Did you notice that it was Banty McMeans?"

Her bank statements were apparently riveting and she made a big show of stacking them while she avoided my eyes and said, "So? He came here, I assume, to ask for our services, and you told him to leave. You even threatened to call security." She pushed her I-Love-the-80s glasses up on her nose. "Maybe you think you're too good to work with someone like Mr. McMeans."

And maybe Gert was the bitch from hell. "What? You think we should commit business suicide and take on a nut like him?"

"I intend to let Jane know about this and I'm sure she'll be very disappointed to find out we lost a prospective client."

Watching her stack those bank statements, I couldn't help wondering if she honestly thought I was that stupid. That I'd buy into her bullshit and swallow it. It definitely proved how desperate she was to get rid of me. A part of me felt sorry for Gert, because she was so pathetic, but a part of me hated her for being so unfair.

I moved closer to her desk and lowered my voice. "If I call Mom out of the meeting she's at and ask her about Banty, what will she say? Will she concur that she wants him for a client, or will she tell me she'd rather eat shards of glass?"

"I'm sure she'd say she wants him. Even if he is a little thorny, he's got a lot of money. He owns all the Taco Casas in town, a couple of dry cleaners and the EZ Rental Furniture and Electronics store. He also owns some apartments. Mr. McMeans would be a good client for us."

"The man has a lot of money because he squeezes every penny until it screams for mercy." I turned to leave. "I'm not resigning, Gert. Give up and lay off with the whale tales. It's getting really old."

I walked away and made myself put her out of my mind. No point belaboring her hatred of me, because there didn't appear to be a damn thing I could do about it.

By the time I shut down for lunch, I'd scheduled out three investment accounts and kicked some major bank statement ass, so I was in a good place as I rode the elevator from the fifteenth floor down to the basement parking garage.

Unfortunately, my feeling of accomplishment faded as soon as I spied my car. Somebody had written nasty notes on it with a black Marks-A-Lot. Things like I've Got a Hard-On for Pink and Let Me Show You My Pink Pistol.

Dammit, didn't I have enough problems? I peered around the immediate area for suspicious characters, but saw nothing more threatening than a couple of ladies from the bank lobby heading out for lunch. Continuing toward the old Ford—which isn't actually my car but a loaner that belongs to my immediate boss—I wondered when my fifteen minutes of fame from the whistle-blower thing would be over. I was way ready to go back to blessed anonymity.

I also wondered how much a paint job would cost. My boss, Sam, is a pretty nice guy, but he was not gonna be happy about the new decorations on his car. He'd been nice enough to loan it to me after I'd wrecked mine, and I felt terrible that it was now covered in icky words. Granted, it was his extra car, a vehicle he used for trips to the oil field, and possibly the ugliest car in town, painted an awful shade of lavender, but no way could I leave the graffiti on it.

As I got in, I considered calling Aunt Dru to beg off, but I couldn't do that to her. I'd just have to suffer the stares I was sure to get on my way to Busbee's.

Yep, the day was shaping up to be one of the worst on record. And it wasn't even half-over.

Chapter 3

Busbee's is an institution in Midland, at least for the under-ten and over-seventy crowd. For everybody in between, it's someplace to eat when forced to dine with someone under ten or over seventy. At noon, I fell into the latter category.

Aunt Dru was early, of course. She follows the hurry-up-and-wait philosophy. I walked in at three minutes to twelve and she immediately commented about how late I was, and how inconsiderate it is to make someone wait. Miss Manners took over, apologized nicely, and we went to stand in line.

"How've you been, Aunt Dru?"

Patting her dark, silver-streaked hair, which was styled in a heavily hair-sprayed mass of short curls, she pursed her lips and eyed me with a look of pained resignation. "Funny you should ask, because I was just at Dr. Rosser's this morning. I'm having trouble with my back again. When I was a young girl in Comanche County, I had to pick cotton from sunup to sundown, and it was hard on my back. It was hard on everything, but in those days, during the Depression, we were glad to get the work. Not like nowadays. You young people don't know the meaning of hard work. We'd work all day and get paid ten cents."

She slowed down a bit and I was about to comment on the weather, but she geared up again before I could say a word.

"I hope you don't mind, but I asked my friend Trina Lorenzo to join us for lunch. I want you to meet her, Whitney Ann." She turned her bright gaze to mine. "It's a blessing how she has God in her life, and you could learn a lot from her."

Oh, man. I decided to kill Mom just as soon as I got back to the office.

"Poor thing was cast aside and abandoned by that no-good husband of hers. She teaches Sunday school and brings her little boy every Sunday that she has him." Aunt Dru narrowed her eyes, causing her wrinkles to become more pronounced. "It should be every Sunday, but David Lorenzo won't allow her to have Colby more than two weekends a month. That man is a disgrace to decent people."

Aunt Dru obviously considered Trina's ex-husband the spawn of Satan. To my aunt, everything in the world is black or white, right or wrong, and extenuating circumstances are irrelevant. I'd heard through the Midland gossip grapevine that Trina Lorenzo had a drinking problem, along with a shopping obsession and a taste for pool boys named Julio. Maybe I'm a cynic, but I wondered if Trina's amazing transformation from drunken spendthrift adulterer to devoted Sunday school teacher was a ploy to regain custody of her child.

Not that I blamed her, if that was the case. I wasn't sure I even wanted kids, but if I had one, I know that losing custody would eat me alive. I'd probably join a convent and become Mother Teresa, if it gave me a chance to regain my child. Maybe that's hypocritical, but I'd do it anyway.

"There are a lot of people in this town who can't see past

his family's money, but he's not fooling me. A man who inherits that kind of fortune, then doesn't share a penny of it with the Lord—" Aunt Dru sniffed with disapproval "—that man is asking for trouble."

"He gives enormous amounts of money to charity every year. If there was such a thing as a Mr. Midland contest, he'd win, hands down."

"It doesn't change the facts. He won't share his good fortune with God, and that makes him a man with no soul." Aunt Dru raised one brow in obvious censure. "His father was a fine man, a servant to the Lord. Look what his faith did for him."

"Earned him royalties on the biggest petroleum discovery in the past forty years?"

She totally missed my sarcasm. "God rewards the faithful, Whitney Ann."

"Okay, Aunt Dru."

Her thin face took on a slightly softer look, and she said sadly, "After he passed, his beautiful wife just seemed to wither away. When she died a couple of years ago, this town lost a good woman." Her eyes hardened again and fixed a stare on me. "It was after she was gone that himself began his wicked ways, throwing over Trina, taking her son away from her, turning his back on God, descending into a sojourn among the heathens!"

She was starting to get worked up, definitely annoying everyone around us. We caught some dirty looks, or rather, I caught some. Aunt Dru was oblivious.

Then, as suddenly as her diatribe began, it was over. "Lookee there, will you? They're having baked chicken and cornbread dressing. Don't order it. Dressing's not *fit* to eat. By the way, did I tell you…"

And on she went, until we were almost to the tray stacks. That's when Trina showed up, dressed in a hot-pink suit with to-die-for strappy pink shoes and enormous diamond earrings winking from her ears. If I were a man, I'd go for Trina in a heartbeat. She's like a scaled down Pamela Anderson, without the tattoos. I suppose part of me was insanely jealous, standing there in my khaki skirt, white blouse and sensible mules. My only possession that could possibly compete with Trina's was my Kate Spade bag—and wouldn't you know, she had Fendi, which blew poor Kate outta the water.

She floated toward us in a cloud of designer perfume and an ocean of appreciative male stares. "Dru, I'm so sorry I'm late," she exclaimed as she came abreast of us, her wide, green eyes perfectly dressed in subtle makeup. "I confess, I've never been to Busbee's, and I got all confused about where to turn to get here."

Never eaten at the local cafeteria? Go figure. Didn't she ever crave comfort food? I glanced at her perfect legs, which were at least ten miles long, and decided, no, she didn't. Accepting the hand she extended, I returned her smile. "How do you do? I'm Dru's niece, Whitney, but everyone calls me Pink."

Her grasp was firm and her smile friendly. "Oh, my, this is so great! Dru talks about you all the time, and goes on and on about how smart you are, being a CPA and everything. I hope you don't mind me horning in on your lunch."

"Of course not," Miss Manners said politely. "I'm glad to meet someone my aunt holds in such high regard."

Trina looked heavenward and laughed softly. "I've got her completely snowed, and that's the truth." She patted Aunt Dru's shoulder. "But she's a dear, and has been a big help to me since my divorce."

Aunt Dru looked pleased and I grudgingly admitted that Trina was nicer than I'd expected. Maybe her friendship with Aunt Dru was odd, since she was in her early thirties and Dru was seventy-one, but I supposed after all Trina had been through, a solid, kind woman like Aunt Dru would be very appealing. I'd heard that a lot of Trina's friends deserted her after the divorce. As so many of Midland's society wives did after divorce, she fell to the bottom of the food chain, and none but her very best friends stuck by her. That's only one of the reasons I don't want to marry again. I like that my identity is my own, that no part of me is judged on how much money my old man's got in the bank.

We made small talk as we went through the line. Actually, Aunt Dru did most of the talking, while Trina and I contributed the occasional "How interesting," and "Is that so?" and "Hmm, who knew?" Aunt Dru went on and on about the importance of church and Jesus, the practicality of Buicks and the sanctity of George W. Bush, all during the time we sat at a table in the middle of the restaurant so she could see everyone who walked by, and all during dessert and coffee. Well, Aunt Dru had dessert and coffee. Trina had water with lemon. And I drank my iced tea while praying for a bottle of Valium to miraculously appear on the table.

Then, just when I didn't believe it was possible to be more bored, or close to comatose from a constant barrage of dictates about how to live life, things actually got worse. Yes, I know. I couldn't believe it, either. But it was that kind of day.

In the middle of Aunt Dru's slice of cherry pie, which she declared "not *fit* to eat!" but ate anyway because it's a sin against God and a crime against man to waste food, Banty McMeans walked up to our table.

"Afternoon, Miz Grimes," he said with a nod. Then he looked at me but gave no greeting. Like I cared? I damned him to hell and hoped he'd leave.

Of course he didn't. He hitched up his pants and his ruddy face flushed to a brighter shade of red when he looked at our lunch companion. "How do, Trina?"

"Very well, thank you," she said with a warm smile.

"Why are you just standing there?" Aunt Dru demanded. "Sit down."

He pulled out the empty chair and took a seat, staring at Trina while he turned up the wattage on his red face.

Clueless to Banty's obvious fascination with Trina and her very impressive cleavage, Aunt Dru said around a bite of her pie, "Whitney Ann, this is Banty McMeans, a good and dear friend of mine from church. He's the one I was telling you about that needs some accounting help."

"Yes, I know, Aunt Dru. Mr. McMeans stopped by the office this morning."

She looked up from her pie, obviously surprised. "Well, why didn't you say so?"

I shot Banty a quelling look. "It slipped my mind."

He ignored my glance and said in his whiny voice, "She won't help me, Miz Grimes. I'll have to find someone else."

So this was his ploy? To tell on me and get Aunt Dru to guilt me into taking him on? He really didn't want to go there.

On cue, Aunt Dru said, "Whitney Ann, I'm astonished! I specially recommended you to Banty. Why won't you do some work for him?"

I noticed Trina was hanging on every word. Our eyes met across the table and she gave me an imperceptible nod, as if to say, Hey, I know exactly why you didn't take him on, and I don't blame you one bit. Turning my focus toward my outraged aunt, I said simply, "My reasons are my own, and Mr. McMeans is fully aware of them. Don't worry about it."

She looked from my face to Banty's. "He does have a reputation for being hard to please, but he's a good man, Whitney Ann. I can personally vouch for him."

Resisting the urge to ask if she'd pay his bill after he stiffed us, I said, "That's very nice of you, but my reasons are more complicated than that. The sort of work Mr. McMeans wants done is beyond the capabilities of Mom's firm. I think he should probably hire a private investigator."

"Oh," she said, returning to her pie, "well, then, Banty, you should take Whitney's advice and do so." She took a bite and asked around it, "How's your mama?"

"Fit as a fiddle, but she tires easily."

Aunt Dru narrowed her eyes and gave Banty a speculative look. "Are you helping your mama?"

"I try, but it's a burden, and that's God's own truth."

Aunt Dru pursed her lips and I felt a Church Lady sermon coming on.

"Don't you blaspheme, young man. God smites those who sojourn among the heathens. You been sleeping through Pastor's sermons?"

"No, ma'am."

Trina set her glass down and said pleasantly, "I thought Pastor's sermon last Sunday was particularly inspiring, didn't you, Banty?"

He opened his mouth, but nothing came out. He snapped it shut and I thought he might be on the verge of apoplexy.

Turning her pretty eyes toward me, Trina explained. "Pastor talked about the sins of the flesh, that those who succumb to temptation will perish in the flames."

Indeed. I had a feeling Banty would gladly roast, if only Trina would submit to a wee bit of his temptation. She looked across the table at him and maybe I imagined it, but I swear, she gave him something close to a sexy look. What was that about? My respect for her took a nosedive, because even if she did seem fairly nice, I don't think any woman should lead a man on. And the notion that a woman like Trina would give a man like Banty the time of day, much less a sexual liaison, was past laughable. It was ludicrous. But there was no denying the way she looked at him.

While I was speculating about Trina's motives, wondering if she suffered from I Need All Men to Lust for Me syndrome, Aunt Dru remained out in left field, looking pleased as she polished off her pie. I decided I would only be pleased if God came through with that Valium. I'd have settled for a martini.

"Banty, you know of a good exterminator?" she asked out of the blue. "I need a good exterminator to come over and get rid of the no-see-ums in my house."

"No-see-ums? What's that?" he asked.

"Pesky little varmints, like gnats but a lot smaller. That's why they're called no-see-ums—because most times you can't see 'em. My husband, the late Mr. Grimes, complained of them when we lived in Abilene, but since I've moved to Midland, I'd never seen any. Until about a month ago."

"So you *have* seen the no-see-ums?" I asked, absolutely dying laughing on the inside.

"Of course not."

"Then how do you know you have them?"

"Because I've got bites."

"Maybe it's mosquitoes," Banty suggested. "The city of Midland was supposed to spray for mosquitoes, but to date, they haven't. In my letter to the mayor, I pointed out that everyone in the city is at risk for Lyme dis—"

"This is *not* mosquitoes," Aunt Dru insisted. "It's no-see-ums, I'm sure."

Having never heard of no-see-ums, I had to wonder if Aunt Dru was making this up, or imagining an infestation of some insect she'd heard about while growing up on the farm, some sort of old wives' tale or country legend.

"Call Bug Busters," Trina said. She gathered her purse up and said to Aunt Dru, "I hate to eat and run, but I've got some errands to do before I pick Colby up at his father's." She said a polite goodbye to Banty and me, then turned and sailed out of Busbee's, creating a few neck pains for the men who snapped to attention as she walked past.

When she was gone, Aunt Dru continued my shock treatments by saying, "Banty, you should ask Trina for a date and not worry so much what your mother would say."

I didn't think she'd noticed his fascination with Trina, and it blew me away, how up close and personal she appeared to be with Banty. I gauged his reaction and was further surprised when he looked a bit cowed.

"It's not what Mama would think. It's that I'm afraid Trina would turn me down."

"Nonsense. You're a good man and any woman would be proud to have you." My aunt turned a speculative eye toward me. "Whitney is single, and she's a lovely woman. She knows a good catch when she sees one. Perhaps the two of you should go out for dinner or something."

Mother of God, she couldn't be serious! I'd rather move to a mountain in Tibet and give up sex for the rest of my life than spend ten seconds in a romantic interlude with Banty McMeans.

Banty snorted and expelled a harsh noise that I suppose was a laugh. "Maybe I've set my sights too high with Trina, but I'm not desperate."

I wanted to kill him. I really did. It's not that I'm an egomaniac, but honestly, to be insulted like that by a man who'd have to sharpen up to be called a nerd, it went all over me like a cheap suit, and I wanted to kill him. Slowly.

He must have noticed my murderous glare. "I meant no offense. We're just not suited to each other."

But he considered himself suited to Trina? As if.

Aunt Dru pointlessly stirred her coffee again, and shocked me by keeping mum.

Stifling the urge to tell Banty he was a pompous ass with the personality of a brick wall and the body of a pregnant yak, then insist I meant no offense, I managed to say in an even voice, "There's this new thing called tact. Get some."

Incredibly, that didn't faze him. He moved his chair a little closer to the table, propped his arms in front of him and said conversationally, "Speaking of dates, is it true that you had an affair with the chairman of the Senate Finance Committee? What was his name? Senator Something-or-other. Italian from California, with expensive suits."

"You shouldn't believe all you read in the papers and hear on the news. Senator Santorelli and I are only friends."

Although the kiss the senator gave me in my hotel room in Washington, after the last whistle-blower hearing, had definitely not been just a friendly kiss. More in line with a Let's Get Naked and Stay Horizontal for Three Days Straight kind of kiss.

But that wasn't any of Banty's business. Besides, in spite of the senator's promise to call, I'd heard nothing from him in the three weeks since that extremely hot kiss—which was probably just as well. Even though I had fun flirting with him, and there was a certain sexual tension between us, I didn't see any kind of romantic future for us. Mostly because I'm a one-man kinda girl, and at the moment, I was all tied up with somebody else.

"He's rich, and a widower, and a very powerful man. You could do a lot worse. Which reminds me, I heard you've been slumming with that rogue lawyer, Ed Ravenaldt. What's he think about you and the senator?"

I didn't want to answer, so I didn't. I glared at him and wished all over again I hadn't gotten out of bed that morning. Not just because Mom yelled at me, Banty was a giant pain in my ass and Aunt Dru was forcing me to make nice with him, but because I'd just been reminded of something I'd taken great pains not to think about.

Ed. He'd been my lawyer during the whistle-blower thing, but he'd become a lot more than just legal counsel. I had a major thing for Ed, and thought he had one for me, too. But he'd been out of town the past few weeks, stuck down in Sanderson, the county seat of one of the least populated counties in Texas, getting ready to take a huge class action suit to trial. I missed him, and even though we talked on the phone a lot, I wanted to talk to him in person, see how he was, get back to the friends we'd been before he left.

Aw, who am I kidding? I fully intended to jump his bones the instant he came back to Midland. Not that I'm a wild and crazy sex maniac, but there's just something about Ed that could push me over the edge into Nymphoville. It didn't help that we'd yet to do the deed. Long story, but suffice it to say, Lady Fate had effectively conspired against us in the bedroom department. And that old adage about wanting what we can't have certainly held up. I wanted Ed so much I had to put him out of my mind in order to get anything done. Otherwise, I'd sit around and moon over him like an eighth grader with a crush.

"Miss Pearl, you look mighty preoccupied." Banty leaned over a bit and lowered his voice. "Could it be I've found your Achilles' heel?"

For a man who wanted something from me, Banty had an unusual approach. Instead of trying to butter me up, he appeared determined to piss me off. Way off.

"Suppose I agree not to send a letter to the editor about Ed's brother's new restaurant?"

"Why would you do that? Mr. Maynard's is a wonderful restaurant, and he's doing great. There's a line waiting for tables every day at lunch and every weekend night."

"I could change all that with just one letter."

"Banty, you won't send a letter and lie," Aunt Dru said, her face formed in a severe frown. "I know you better than that. Now stop trying to coerce Whitney and mind your manners before I start minding 'em for you."

"Yes, ma'am." He looked at me again, but instead of apologizing, he simply changed tactics. "Suppose I paid up-front for your services. Would you consider taking me on then?"

"No, and you know why. Just drop it, because I'm not changing my mind."

"How about if all I want you to do is find out who's behind Koko and get to the bottom of my reduced revenue checks? That's all I'd ask, and I'd pay a retainer."

I opened my mouth to tell him hell no, and to lay off or I'd make him regret the day he was born, but Aunt Dru spoke up before I could say a word.

"Sounds fair to me, Whitney. You can't argue with his sincerity, can you? I'd consider it a personal favor if you do this for him."

Well, crap. This was shaping up to be a submarine job. Banty knew she'd back him, and he also knew I would never repeat his horrible accusations, which was really the only way I could explain why I didn't want Banty as a client. Then, while I was trying to think of a way out of it, Banty lived up to his suspicious nature.

His pale green eyes narrowed slightly. "Of course, if you do this work, I'd have to be reassured that you won't take any kickbacks or hush money to keep someone's identity a secret."

Aunt Dru, curiously silent again, kept stirring that damn coffee, and I had to hold myself back from grabbing the spoon. Then using it to beat Banty about the head. "Are you saying you think I'd take money from someone to *lie?*"

He nodded a little more enthusiastically. "Exactly."

"I'm certified by the state of Texas to be honest and fair and worthy of the CPA title. If I prove otherwise, they'll take the license away from me and tell the world and the only job I'll be able to get is selling coffee at a convenience store."

"But you could take a kickback, couldn't you?"

"No, because I'm not a crook."

"I'm done," Aunt Dru announced as her spoon clattered against the saucer. "Banty, tell your mama hello, and if you ever again insinuate my niece would do something as slimy as taking a kickback, I'll bring my horse whip over to your house and beat you black-and-blue." She smiled very nicely. "Are we clear on that?"

"Yes, ma'am."

He trailed after us as we headed for the door and walked outside into the sweltering heat. Close to the lavender Ford, we stopped and said our goodbyes, but Banty kept standing there. Aunt Dru waved her hand impatiently. "Whitney, are you going to take Banty on or not?"

"Not."

She looked very disappointed in me. "Very well then." She looked at Banty. "If you'll excuse us, I've got something of a personal nature to discuss with my niece."

"Yes, ma'am. Good afternoon, ladies." He didn't appear at all ruffled by my refusal. In fact, he gave me a sly look before he left, like a warning that he wasn't giving up.

After he was gone, Aunt Dru said, "Have you talked to your father recently?"

"You know me and Lur...uh, Dad, don't get along that well."

"Remember the Ten Commandments, young lady. God says we should honor our father and mother."

"I do honor him. I just don't talk to him."

She sniffed in disapproval.

"He did call Mom last night, however, and wanted her to check on you. He thinks you're getting too close to Trina and that she's after your money."

"Oh, pish! She's got more money than I do. What would she want with mine?"

I was politically correct and simply shrugged, declining to tell her what I thought about Lurch and his paranoia.

"Jim's my brother, and I love him, but I will always wonder if he was hatched or something. He's nothing at all like Robert and me." She shook her head sadly. "Maybe because he was the baby, and came so much later than us. No doubt our parents spoiled him, but Robert and I probably did, too. Now, Mama must be rotating in her grave."

Again I declined to comment. What was the point? Aunt Dru knew all of Lurch's faults, just as I did. No sense in beating a dead horse.

I'd done my duty and checked out the Trina thing, found out about Aunt Dru's gentleman who needed help—fat lotta good that did—which left me with one last item of business. "Aunt Dru, I've been thinking about getting more active in the community, and wondered if you have some ideas."

Looking ecstatic, Aunt Dru beamed and said, "Oh, Whitney Ann, this is such a blessing! I'm a member of the Right Hand of God prayer group, and we're sorely in need of help. We mail Bibles to missionaries and it's gotten to be such a task for us. You being so young and all, well, it would be wonderful if you'd join us and lend a hand. Besides that, you'll benefit from the spiritual guidance we can give you."

Definitely, I was going back to the office to kill Mom. But what could I say at that moment, except, "Gee, that sounds swell, Aunt Dru." I hoped my smile didn't look too wimpy.

She gave me a pat on the arm, then looked at Sam's car and her eyes widened with shock. "Go immediately and get that car a paint job. It's an offense to decent people, all that trash written on it. And that color is nauseating."

"I was planning to do that, Aunt Dru."

She rifled around in her oversize bag for a bit, then withdrew a flat box and handed it to me. "This is one of the Bibles my prayer group sends out. All the answers are in there, Whitney Ann, if you'll just read it." She dived into the bag again and pulled out an envelope. "Here's some money for you. Use part of it to get the car painted."

I could only stare at the envelope, frozen in shock. Since I was a little girl, Aunt Dru has never given me anything but small, cheesy trinkets, all of which are in a box I cart around every time I move because I feel too guilty to get rid of them. But not guilty enough to put them out or wear them, depending on the nature of the trinket.

"Take it," she insisted, shoving it into my hand. "And don't be telling anyone. I'm not giving anything to your cousins, and I don't want 'em getting their noses out of joint."

"Aunt Dru, what's this all about?"

"It's about me getting old and having more money than I know what to do with. God didn't see fit to give myself and Mr. Grimes any children. I have no one to look after, and it pleases me to look after you. Now take the money and don't make a fuss about it. I don't expect anything for it, you understand. It's a gift, given because I love you."

Instantly, tears sprang to my eyes. Aunt Dru has never, my whole life, said she loves me. "Thank you," I managed to murmur, "and I love you, too." It wasn't a fib. I do love Aunt Dru, even if she is a persnickety woman with boring stories.

"Well, I'd best be on my way," she said as she turned to leave. "Got to call the bug people to see about killing off those no-see-ums."

"Bye, Aunt Dru. Thank you for lunch, and the gift."

"You're welcome. Now be a good girl." With that, she got into her late-model Buick, backed out of her space at the speed of metamorphic rock, then inched out of the parking lot.

Fifteen minutes later, I pulled up to Beeps Body Shop and went in to speak to the owner, a lanky guy by the name of Nolan. He took a look at the car and said it would be at least two weeks before he could get to it.

"I can't drive around with it like that for two weeks!"

"Tell you what," he said with a slight nod, "I'll get Ricky to get some steel wool and scrub the hell outta it. Take that garbage right off."

"Won't it take off the paint if he does that?"

"Yeah, but it'd be better than them words. And it'll only be a couple of weeks you have to drive it with some bare spots in the paint."

He had a point. "Okay," I agreed.

"You can wait in my office over there if you want."

I thanked him and headed for the small, cluttered room where I took a seat in a dusty chair and waited for Ricky to work his steel-wool magic. While I sat there watching the hands of an old clock that had a Midas ad on its face, I heard a deep voice from the back of the shop.

"All I want is a fair price, Beeps. This is a late model Suburban with low mileage, and I could get twice what you're offering if I took it to a dealership."

"Then take it to a damn dealership! I sell used to a contact in Mexico, and they don't pay top dollar on account of most of what gets moved through here is probably hotter than a firecracker. I don't ask questions, because I don't want answers. I just move the merchandise, and that's all. So if you wanna unload this baby, fine, but don't expect me to pay anything close to blue book on it."

My curiosity got the best of me, and even though it was none of my business, I stood and moved to the door at the back of the office, which wasn't completely closed, and peeked out to see who Nolan was talking to. All I could see was the man's back, and he had a very broad one, which obstructed my view of Nolan and everything else in the back of the shop. I noticed his khaki shirt had a North Face logo embroidered on the yoke, just above the back pleat. Must be a backpacker, I decided.

"Doesn't look like I have much choice. I'm leaving tonight, and the truck will be parked out at Midland International, with the keys in the glove box. Here's the other set so you can get in, and here's the wiring instructions for the money. Once I have it, I'll send you the title."

"Dude, I could just write you a check."

The man hesitated. "It will be hard to cash it where I'm going, so just wire it."

I wondered where the man was going that it would be hard to cash a check. Out of the country, no doubt. And he was selling his car before he left. Hmm. Curious. Very curious.

But none of my business. I turned back toward the chair just as Ricky came through the front door and announced my car was ready. "Don't look too good, but then it was pretty butt-ugly to start with."

"Thanks," I said, my mind still preoccupied with the stranger who was about to leave the country. I followed Ricky out to the main area of the shop and scarcely noticed the huge gray spots in the lavender paint, I was so intent on catching a glimpse of the stranger.

I was doomed to disappointment. Even though I took my time getting in the car, thanking Ricky, starting the engine and buckling my seat belt, the stranger never came around the corner. With regret, I pulled out of Beeps Body Shop and headed back to the office.

On the way, I passed Bettina's House of Enchiladas, my very favorite Mexican restaurant, and on a whim, I stopped in and bought a package of tamales, thinking how tasty they'd be for dinner. In fact, I decided, I would bite the bullet and go grocery shopping after work. Get salad stuff and some real food, instead of frozen dinners.

When I got back to the office, I was greeted by Mom's receptionist, a perky girl with pouty lips named Tiffany. She's generally one of those bright and happy types, but as soon as I came in, I noticed her lack of a smile and knew something was up. Something very not good.

She stood and said to me in a quiet voice, "Pink, there's a Midland cop in the conference room. He came in just awhile ago and insisted he would wait for you."

Nodding, I turned and headed for the conference room, nervous shivers crawling up and down my back. Why in the world would a Midland cop be here to see me?

I opened the door and a big bear of a man in a uniform stood to greet me.

"Are you Pink Pearl?"

"Yes." I closed the door.

"I'm Sergeant Vandergriff, and I need to ask you some questions about what you saw today at Beeps Body Shop."

The nervous shivers became nervous shakes. "Why?"

"Just after you left, an unknown assailant shot and killed Nolan Beeps."

The day sped past bad and careened toward freakish and weird. After I told the sergeant what I'd seen, which was basically nothing, he asked me to call him if I thought of anything else, handed me his card, then left. When he was gone, Gert waved me toward her office, but I ignored her and went back to my cubicle to get my thoughts together.

Nolan Beeps, shot and killed. I had wondered if the big man I'd seen talking to him was the murderer, even though it didn't fit with what I'd overheard, but Sergeant Vandergriff said no. According to Ricky, just after I drove off, a black Mercedes sped straight up to the shop. Shots were fired from the driver's window, then the car peeled out in reverse and was gone. All of it happened in less than a minute. Ricky never saw who was driving, and the plates were covered. During the shooting, the big man ran through Nolan's office and out the front, jumped in his Suburban and took off. Ricky did manage to get his plates, and the sergeant said they were looking for him. Ricky also told the sergeant about Nolan Beeps's side business of moving hot cars to Mexico through his shop. Vandergriff surmised one of Beeps's customers had a grudge or was afraid of getting fingered for the recent rash of auto thefts, and took him out.

Maybe Nolan Beeps was as crooked as the thieves he did business with, but he was a likeable sort. A while back, he'd bought my car after it was wrecked. Didn't pay me near what it was worth, but I'd had my reasons for wanting to unload it quietly, and he'd helped me do that. Now he was dead, and it really bummed me out. He couldn't have been over forty, and it's always awful to me when people die too young.

The rest of the afternoon I couldn't concentrate. Close to five o'clock, I gave up, gathered my things and headed for the grocery store. In less than an hour, I planned to be in boxer shorts and a T-shirt, plowing through a carton of ice cream, watching a Friends rerun. After the day I'd had, it sounded like a little slice of heaven.

Of course, things didn't turn out that way. Like I said, I never should have gotten out of bed this morning.

Chapter 4

Wednesday, September 7—5:35 p.m.

Shouting that the gnarly guy had been stabbed probably wasn't the smartest move on my part. The small crowd was already jumpy because of the yipping, runaway dog. The minute I said the word *stabbed,* somebody screamed and all hell broke loose. All but the olive rep turned and ran, knocking pickle jars off the shelves in their mad dash to get away.

While the olive rep picked his way through the broken glass to come close, I heard Mr. Gnarly whisper, "Santorelli… tell him I'm sorry. And get the cake. Promise!"

I leaned over farther, completely freaked by the blood soaking his shirt. "Be calm, okay? You're going to be fine."

He shook his head and gripped my hand. "Promise!"

"Yes, I promise. Now relax." The store manager came rushing up behind me, just as the olive rep reached us.

The wounded man jerked me close and whispered fiercely, "Don't tell anyone about the cake, especially the cops." He squeezed his eyes shut and gripped my hand tighter. "Jesus, I shouldn't have brought you in on this."

"Don't worry about it. I'll take care of the cake. Please, don't try to talk, don't think about anything but hanging on." I could hear sirens. Thank God.

I noticed his grimace and reached up to smooth his hair away from his brow.

His eyes opened slightly and he whispered, "Nice girl. Santorelli said so…pretty…and smart. Bad people…stay out of…their way." He swallowed hard and pressed on. "Mc-Means…not so crazy as…" His voice drifted off and his eyes closed again. I kept my hand on his head, murmuring inconsequential things I hoped would give him some comfort, even while I was mega-freaked out by his mention of Banty.

Then, just as I heard the sirens stop, his eyes flew open and he looked at me with full lucidity. "I've screwed up, so bad. God forgive me."

"The ambulance is here," I told him, hoping he'd hang on. The guy couldn't possibly die now, when he'd been so close to making his escape.

But a few seconds later, that's exactly what happened. While I held his hand, the big stranger who'd asked for my help slipped to the other side. Tears welled in my eyes, blurring my vision. Watching another human being pass on was something of a definitive moment, a profound sort of thing that rocked me to my soul. Mine was the last face he saw before he died.

The EMTs descended on us, and once they determined the man was dead, they said they couldn't move him, that the pickle aisle was now a crime scene and we all needed to back off. A few police had arrived and while they were busy bringing some order to the hysteria of the shoppers, I moved away from the crowd, all the way over to the tampon-and-condom aisle, figuring that was the one people tended to stay in the least amount of time. I fished my cell phone out of my purse and dialed Ed's cell number. He answered after two rings.

"Ed, it's Pink."

"Hey, Pink. Why are you whispering?"

"So no one can hear me."

"Yeah, I kinda had that figured out. How about I call you later tonight, when you don't have to whisper? This is sort of a bad time."

"I'll be brief then. I'm at Allbright's and I met a CIA guy who asked me to deliver a cake with some important information in it. Then the guy got stabbed and died and I know the cops will want to talk to me and I'm not sure if I should tell them about the cake because the CIA guy said not to. What do you think?"

There was a long pause before Ed said, "How do you know the guy was with the CIA?"

"He told me. He said his cover was blown and he had to get out of town before somebody killed him, but he needed to get this information to the right person and Santorelli told him he could contact me if he got in a bind."

"Did the dead guy tell you his name?"

"No. But I'm pretty sure he's on the level, because he said he briefs Santorelli about money laundering in Midland. Ed, would you believe that Al Qaeda is here, in Midland?"

I could have sworn I heard him mumble, "Holy shit."

"The cops are gathering up witnesses, so you gotta tell me what to do. Should I tell them about the cake or not?"

"I think you have to tell them, Pink. Otherwise, you can be charged for withholding evidence. If whatever's in the cake has something to do with national security, the Midland police will know what to do with it."

"Do you think I should call Santorelli?"

Another long pause. Then Ed said, "Maybe later. For now, just talk to the police, tell them everything, and be extremely careful when you leave the store. Whoever killed him may think you know something, since he was talking to you before he was stabbed. If the police hassle you at all, tell them you want to call your attorney, then phone me back. Otherwise, call me later tonight and let me know how it went."

I agreed, ended the call and went to see what was developing. The cops had cordoned off the pickle aisle, posted guys at the entrances to keep people inside, and were questioning everyone still in the store. Some were asked a few questions and allowed to leave, but others, particularly those who were in the pickle aisle at the time of the stabbing, were asked to talk with a detective.

After we'd been directed to the hall outside the manager's office, I looked around the small group and noticed the big lady wasn't there. I wasn't surprised. She had to be the one who'd stabbed the man. Undoubtedly she'd left the store before anyone even knew what had happened.

While I stood there waiting to be called, I remembered that Mr. Gnarly had to be the same man I'd seen in Nolan Beeps's shop, the big man with the North Face logo on the back of his shirt. His voice hadn't rang a bell, but maybe that was because he hadn't been facing me when he was at the shop. So Mr. Gnarly was the guy at the shop, which meant the killer in the Mercedes had most likely come to kill Mr. Gnarly, not Nolan. He got the wrong guy. Or *she* got the wrong guy. Maybe the driver of the Mercedes was the big lady.

When the store manager pointed out that I was the one standing closest to the dead man, I was chosen first to be interviewed. A stocky, blond uniformed cop with no neck ushered me into the small, cluttered office and introduced me to Detective Raymond Garza. He waved me to a chair and as I sat down, I noticed the detective's shoes were muddy. That struck me as odd because Midland hadn't had a drop of rain in over a month. Garza was in his midfifties I guessed, a short, heavyset Hispanic man who sported a bushy black mustache. He took the chair opposite mine and asked, "Are you okay?"

"I'm a little shook up, but yeah, I'm okay."

He held a legal pad and a pen. Bending his head, he asked my name, address, etc., and when he was done, he glanced up and said, "You're the whistle-blower, aren't you?"

"That's me."

"People call you Pink. Why is that?"

"Because my last name is Pearl." He looked confused. "Like Pink Pearl erasers?"

"Oh, I get it." He cleared his throat while he smoothed his mustache. "The last homicide in this town was about four hours ago, and as I recall, you left the scene just before the murder took place. Seems mighty odd to me that of all ninety-five thousand people in this city, the one who was standing closest to this victim just happened to be you."

"What are you implying?"

"Nothing at all. Maybe you're just the kiss of death." As if he thought it might be possible, he scooted his chair back a few inches. "Tell me what happened here today."

Choosing to ignore his smartass remark, I told him, including what had happened beforehand—the notes, the guy following me around, and what he'd said about the cake. Then I told him about seeing the dead guy earlier, at the body shop.

Garza wrote everything down, and when he was done, he turned toward the no-neck cop, who was leaning against the closed door. "Go to the bakery and get the cake."

When the uniform was gone, Garza refocused on me. "Do you think the fat lady stabbed him?"

"It had to be her, because he wasn't standing close enough to anyone else."

Garza's dark eyes narrowed. "He was standing close to you."

"Not when he was stabbed. I'd backed up to leave and was behind my cart."

"So after he dropped to the floor, you came to his aid?"

Not liking the inflection in his voice, which seemed to say he thought I was full of it, I tried my best not to get too upset. Wasn't it logical he'd think I was a suspect? "I didn't know the man from Adam, and he was clearly trying to do the right thing before he left town. Why would I want to kill him?"

Garza answered my question with a question. "Do you think whoever shot Nolan Beeps was actually after this man?"

"Has to be. It's too coincidental to be anything else."

Garza nodded thoughtfully. "We matched the license plates the kid at Beeps's shop gave us to a Suburban out in the parking lot here, so there's no doubt it was the same guy. Wonder if the fat lady was the one in the Mercedes?"

"I have no idea. I was already gone when the shooting took place."

The uniformed cop came back just then, a cake box in his pudgy grasp. He set it down on the manager's desk, then produced a cake knife from his back pocket, which he presented to Detective Garza. "The guy's been IDed as Dan Becker."

Garza looked annoyed. "Jesus, man, don't you know you're not supposed to reveal somebody's identity until next of kin have been notified?" He looked at me and raised one black brow. "I hope you'll keep that information to yourself, Ms. Pearl."

Before I could say anything, the cop said quietly, "There is no next of kin. The guy was a cop in Portland a few years ago, and they had all the records. He was married, with a kid, but they were both murdered by a dealer Becker was investigating. He has no brothers or sisters, and his folks have been gone awhile."

"That's so sad," I said, imagining the horror he must have felt when his wife and child were murdered, and thinking there was now no family to mourn for him.

The detective looked thoughtful. "Something like that's gotta make a guy walk a different line. Get Stockton to find out about his psych evaluation. See if he was delusional, if he had episodes or seizures, or anything like that."

When the cop was gone again, Garza said to me, "You need to go downtown and give a description of the fat lady to the police artist. Give him one of the dog, too."

"Okay, but I didn't really get that good of a look at her. She was on the other side of Mr. Becker, and after I backed up, I could only see her from behind."

"You probably remember more than you think. Just do the best you can." He took a drink from his bottle of water, then asked, "Are you absolutely sure no one else could have stabbed him?"

"I'm positive. The three of us were at least five feet behind the crowd."

"And the two of them didn't appear to know one another?"

"Not at all."

"If you were looking right at them, how is it that you didn't see him get stabbed?"

"I was looking at the dog. I think she must have done something to make the dog go nuts so it would create a diversion."

The uniformed cop came back then. He glanced at the cake box and the knife in Garza's hand. "The girl in the bakery confirmed that Becker ordered it, with instructions to put the name Whitney Pearl on the ticket for pickup, but she said he didn't give her anything to hide in the cake."

I expected them to tell me to leave, but they didn't. When Garza opened the box, I peeked over the edge. Inside was a quarter sheet cake, with white icing, trimmed in blue and red, with a big blue spiderweb across half of it and a little plastic Spider-Man figure set in the middle. It read, Happy Birthday, Santa. While the cop and I watched, Garza hacked and sawed into the cake, effectively mutilating it. He inspected the little

Spider-Man figure, then tossed it aside and cut into that part of the cake, but when he was done, there was no sign of anything that could be considered information of any kind. No name and address of the supposed contact. Nothing. Garza looked up at me and shrugged. "I hate to say it, but it's looking like your man was a certifiable wacko. Either that, or he was trying to put the make on you."

"If that's true, how come he was murdered?"

"I don't know, but I intend to find out."

Glancing at the pile of cake, I asked, "Can I have the Spider-Man?"

"What for?"

"I love Spider-Man and I think he's kind of cute."

"Yeah, fine."

After I'd retrieved the small plastic figure, Garza waved his hand at me in dismissal. I turned toward the door, then paused when I caught sight of his shoes again. "How'd you get mud on your shoes? Hasn't rained here in weeks."

He made a face as he raised one foot to look at the heavy, red mud caked on the sole. "Had to meet a Texas Ranger out at an oil spill. Big mess, and muddy because the saltwater tank busted."

"A Texas Ranger came to look at an oil spill?" I thought the Texas Rangers were the guys to call about oil theft, a holdover from the old days, when they hunted down cattle rustlers and horse thieves. Things like oil spills were usually looked at by the Texas Railroad Commission.

Garza put his foot down, shoved his hands in his pockets and jingled coins. "Wasn't just any oil spill. Somebody ripped off a load from the tank battery, then left the damn valve open. Flowed close to twenty barrels onto the ground before a pumper found it. And whoever swiped the oil is a bad driver. Looked like they ran smack into the saltwater tank, which busted it open. Biggest mess you ever saw."

My insides seized up and I had to fight to keep my voice even. "Just curious, but was the well one of David Lorenzo's?"

He narrowed his eyes and gave me a speculative look. "As a matter of fact, it was. How'd you know?"

"I had a guy ask me to look into some oil thefts off of some wells operated by Lorenzo Petroleum. He says the Railroad Commission reports are being altered so they don't reflect the stolen oil as being produced."

"What did you find out?"

"Nothing because I didn't take the account."

"I see. Well, if you change your mind and look into it, let me know what you find. Sheriff's department says there's been a sudden increase of thefts lately. Seen a lot of equipment stolen in my time, but never oil. Not exactly easy to fence." He shook my hand and walked with me to the door. "We may call you in again, Ms. Pearl, and after we find the fat lady, it's a pretty sure bet the D.A. will want you to testify. If you have to leave town, you let me know."

"Yeah, sure." I reached for the doorknob, but stopped when I felt his hand on my arm. Turning my head, I saw something like compassion in his eyes.

"It's tough watching a man die. You might want to contact your priest or minister or whatever."

"Thanks, Detective. Maybe I'll do that."

I left the manager's office and was escorted to the front of the store by another cop. Dodging the news folks who'd congregated outside in the parking lot was something of a problem, but I managed to run the gauntlet without saying much more than, "I don't know," or "I'm not at liberty to say."

Once I was in the car, I decided to go ahead and drive downtown to the police station. The sooner they had a picture of some sort, the sooner they could get other law enforcement people out looking for Big Mama and her little rat dog.

The sketch artist was done fairly quickly, and although I

couldn't be sure the picture actually looked like the woman, he got the dog dead-on. Not that it mattered so much. After all, the dog didn't kill anybody. I'm not so sure that dog was big enough to kill anything at all.

By the time I drove away from downtown Midland, it was almost seven-thirty and the late-summer sun was setting in a blaze of orange and purple. I really miss Dallas with its lakes and trees and gentle, rolling hills, but I have to admit that nowhere on Earth has sunsets like west Texas. I think maybe they're a consolation prize from God, a bit of pity on all of us poor slobs who are doomed to live in the middle of the flattest, most desolate land on the planet.

But my appreciation of the sunset was less than usual that evening. Remembering what the detective said, I considered who I could talk to about what had happened. I wanted to vent, to get righteously pissed off, maybe cry a little. Or perhaps I just needed to put it in perspective. I thought about the minister at church, a nice, older man who'd married me and my ex-husband, George, over eight years ago. But I gave up the idea almost as soon as I thought of it. He was a man of the cloth, a holy dude—and I was a foul-mouthed, hot-tempered woman who always allows Miss Manners to take over in churchy situations. Miss Manners didn't need help—I did.

I couldn't call Aunt Dru. She'd freak out and fret about it, then give me a lecture about talking to strangers in the grocery store. It would all be well-intentioned, but that just wasn't what I needed right then.

Clearly, Lurch wasn't an option.

I could call Ed later, and would, but I needed someone to talk to right then, in person.

That left Mom. Poor Mom. I spent the first twenty-two years of my life as the perfect daughter. Then I married George, whom she despised, and things had gone steadily downhill ever since. That whole whistle-blower thing, which garnered me a stalker, a couple of attempts on my life and a dead guy in my bathtub, had just about sent her over the edge. What happened in the pickle aisle at Allbright's was gonna be hard on her. But she would find out sooner or later, and maybe it was best if I was the one to tell her.

I turned off of A Street and headed toward the gated community where she lives in a zero-lot line house. The gate was open, as it always is. I never can figure out what's the point in living within a gated community if the gate's always open. But I live in an old apartment complex with turquoise appliances, so what do I know?

After I pulled up to the curb, I got out and was about to close the door when I heard running footsteps pounding behind me. Before I could turn around, I felt something poke me in the back and a hand came around my head to cover my mouth. I looked as far to the right as possible, and saw a Spider-Man tattoo.

Maybe I imagined it, but I swear my guardian angel said a cuss word. Poor thing had been working overtime lately. I prayed she wouldn't desert me now.

A deep, guttural voice said softly, "Don't scream or try to run, and I won't shoot you. Got it?"

I nodded and he dropped his hand.

While I sucked in a deep breath, trying to cleanse my nose from the icky, oniony smell of his huge hand, the man said, "I'm here to collect whatever Dan Becker gave you."

"He didn't give me anything. He said there was some information in a cake, but when the police cut it up, there was nothing inside."

"Figures. Becker was a wily bastard. Hand me your purse," the voice demanded.

I did, then watched the entire contents fall to the asphalt around my feet. I said a quick prayer of thanks that I'd had the forethought to put the money Aunt Dru gave me in the car's glove box. Then I sent a prayer asking that the man not search the car.

He stayed just behind me and I noticed his feet were housed in a pair of boots that were caked with red mud. Just like Detective Garza's. How interesting. He shoved my things around with his filthy boot, then stopped with his toe next to Spider-Man. "Gimme that."

"You can't have it."

He pressed the gun harder against my back. I bent to pick up the little toy and held it over my shoulder. "So take it, but I had plans to give it to a very sick little kid who loves Spider-Man." Okay, so I lied through my teeth—not so much because I wanted the plastic figure, but because I didn't want the horrible man with the gun to have it.

I was shocked when he said, "Keep it. Now stand still so I can check you out."

Remembering the gun and figuring from the size of his feet that he had at least a hundred and fifty pounds on me, I followed instructions and stood still so he could run his big, beefy hands along every inch of my body.

Yes, it was extremely creepy and gross. I decided I would be taking a shower in the very near future.

When he was satisfied I wasn't holding any information from Dan Becker in any nook or cranny of my person, I feared he would start on the car, but instead, he leaned against me and whispered into my ear, "Just forget everything Becker told you and you'll live to see your grandchildren. Not one bit of this is any of your business, so keep out of it. Understand?"

"I understand."

"Stay right there until I'm gone. If you turn around, I'll shoot you. And trust me, I'm an excellent shot." I heard his footsteps as he walked away, and it took every bit of discipline I had not to turn and look. An engine started, then accelerated, and in my peripheral vision I saw him make a

U-turn. He misjudged the width of the street, jumped the curb and mowed down the mailbox of the house next door to Mom's. He never slowed down, but sped off into the semi-darkness. I jerked my head around, but it was too dark to see his plates.

When he was gone, I gathered up all of my things, returned them to my purse, then sat back in the driver's seat and took awhile to get myself together. I couldn't go in to see Mom if I was shaking like a leaf. She'd go into Manic Mother mode and smother me to death. And she'd be so scared. I hate it when Mom's scared. Especially when I'm the cause of it. So I sat there until it was completely dark, until I wasn't shaking, then got out and made my way to her front porch.

I rang the bell as I opened the door with my key, to let her know I was there. Once inside, I hollered, "Yo, Mom! It's me!"

She met me at the entrance to the kitchen in a faded sundress and bare feet, her toenails painted fire-engine red. "Hi, baby." She stepped back and waved me in. "I've been cleaning out my closet and just made some iced tea. Want some?"

"Sure, Mom." I trailed after her and took a seat at the wide island bar.

After she handed me a glass, she took the stool next to mine. "You look like hell."

"Thanks." I took a long drink, set the glass on the granite countertop, then sucked in a deep breath and told her, feeling worse with every millimeter her eyes widened. I elected not to tell her about Banty or David Lorenzo or anything at all about what had happened earlier in the day. Except I did tell her about the car and Nolan Beeps, because it tied into what had happened at Allbright's.

Mom didn't say anything. When I was done, she reached her arms out and hugged me so tightly I about lost my breath.

"I dunno, Mom, but maybe that detective is right and I *am* the kiss of death."

With her face over my shoulder, she said, "No, Pink, you're somebody people see as a woman who stands up for what's right, someone who gets things done. That man knew that, just like Santorelli knows it, which is why he gave him your name." She pulled away and brushed my hair from my face. "Are you okay?"

"I'm not sure. Maybe if I'd just been standing there like all those other people who were listening to that guy go off about his olives, I wouldn't feel this way. But I keep remembering how Dan Becker looked at me when we were standing in line, like he was afraid." I looked down at my iced-tea glass and drew figures in the cold sweat. "I never saw that woman as a potential murderer."

Mom crossed her arms on the bar and appeared to give it some thought. "It's always easy to see things in hindsight, but there's no sense beating yourself up about it. Nobody, ever, in a million years, would see a large woman with a teacup Chihuahua as a threat."

We sat there in silence, listening to the ticktock of the kitchen clock. I kept reliving what happened, wondering why Becker had mentioned Banty, trying to convince myself it was some weird coincidence, that Banty really was a paranoid conspiracy theorist and whatever Al-Qaeda-money-laundering scheme Becker was investigating had nothing to do with David Lorenzo. I was dead-dog tired, and anxious to talk to Ed about all that had happened. Ed can put a whole different spin on things and look at it from an angle I would never consider. He was bound to have some insight that I hadn't thought of yet.

I looked at Mom and managed to give her a small smile. "I guess I'll go home now. It's been a long day, and I'm anxious to take a shower. Tattoo Man was a smelly, yucky guy."

"Maybe you should stay here tonight."

"I'll be okay, Mom. Now that they know I don't have what they're looking for, I don't think they'll bother me anymore."

"Just be careful, and make sure you lock up."

"I always do."

Mom pointed toward the hall that leads to her laundry room. "You wanna go through the box I'm sending to the Salvation Army? It's mostly pretty worn stuff, but there's a few blouses in there you might like."

I might like them if I were fifty-five. "No, thanks, Mom. I'm pretty well set for blouses."

"What about the old Ping-Pong table? Do you want it?"

"Mom, I barely have room in my apartment for the bed. I'm thinking a Ping-Pong table might make it a tight fit."

"I wish you'd move, Pink. Those apartments are atrocious."

"They're not that bad. They're clean and neat and the manager is a nice guy who comes right away when I call about a problem. He let me move to a different apartment after they found the dead guy in my bathtub."

"I just don't understand why you'd rather pay rent when you could get a mortgage and own your home. It makes so much more sense financially."

Oh, man. What is it about parents? I'll be sixty-five and Mom will be ninety, rolling around on her walker, dispensing Mom-advice about how I should eat more fiber and invest in T-Bills, and why don't I look through her box of her old dentures to see if I could use some because I'd save a lotta money? "Mom, I've owned two homes since I got out of college, so I'm pretty up on the advantages of home ownership. When it's time to buy another one, I will. For now, I'm saving to buy a new car, which is a higher priority. I can't drive Sam's forever."

Mom looked as if she might get in some practice on her Aunt Dru skills and launch into a lecture, but she refrained and said instead, "Don't forget Spider-Man." She retrieved him from where I'd laid him on the bar and held him out to me.

"I don't really want him, Mom. Just put him in your box of Salvation Army stuff."

"All right." She tossed him into a basket by the telephone, then went to the refrigerator. "Take some of this chicken salad home with you."

That reminded me of my groceries. The ones that were still sitting in a cart at Allbright's. Bummer. "Okay, Mom. Thanks. I bought some tamales today at Bettina's, but they're probably spoiled by now, so long out of refrigeration."

"Nonsense," Mom said. "All that chili powder and cumin is like a preservative. Just put them in the freezer and they'll be fine."

In Life According to Mom, anything can be saved if you just put it in the freezer. Mom freezes everything. Restaurant leftovers, the ends of loaves of bread, milk that's a day from going bad. Even lemons. Mom should get a gig as a Maytag saleslady.

She walked around the other side of the island, headed for the cabinet where she keeps plastic containers, but stopped suddenly, her eyes wide with fear and the blood draining from her face.

Scared to death, I turned on my stool and nearly had a heart attack.

With a pistol in one hand and the little rat dog in the other, Big Mama stood at the entrance to the kitchen.

Chapter 5

I mentally kicked myself into next Sunday for failing to lock the door behind me when I came in. How could I have done that? Especially when I'd just been accosted in the street. Me and Mom were gonna get blown away by a very fat woman, all because I had my head somewhere besides between my shoulders.

"I want the information Dan Becker passed to you."

"Get in line," I said, suddenly wondering why Al Qaeda would have a woman as an assassin. That didn't fit at all. "One of the other minions already hit me up for it, and I'll tell you just what I told him—there's nothing."

"Who hit you up?"

"Some humongous dude with a Spider-Man tattoo. I didn't get a look at his face."

This appeared to freak her out and my curiosity went up yet another notch.

"Competition?"

"Never mind," she snapped. "Where's the cake?"

"In the garbage at Allbright's, I expect. Becker said the cake had something in it, but when the police cut it up, there was nothing."

"You told the police about the cake?"

"I thought it was best."

She stared at me for a moment, then looked at Mom. "I suppose you taught her to always trust cops."

"How did you find us?" Mom asked, her tone just a step shy of pissed off. I said a mental prayer. Hell, I said about ten mental prayers. This was so not the time for Mom to get huffy.

But the woman didn't appear to notice. "In Midland, Texas, if someone's not at home, there are only so many places they can be. Call it a lucky guess that I'd find your daughter here, at your house, after she witnessed a stabbing." She looked at me again. "Are you sure there was nothing in the cake?"

"I was there, and trust me, there was nothing."

Her gaze went to my purse, lying on the bar. "Empty out your purse."

For the second time that night, Kate Spade was dumped.

Big Mama moved a few feet closer and eyed the contents. She nodded toward my miniature Altoids box. "Did Becker give you that?"

"No, I got it at Target."

"Hmm." She cast a roving glance over the remainder of my personal purse stuff, then stepped back. "It isn't like Becker to be so obvious about anything, and all that cloak-and-dagger business about the cake was amateurish and ridiculous. I figured he dropped something in your purse and his contact would show up to get it from you later."

I shot a glance at Mom, who looked like she did the day I told her I was marrying George—as if the end of life as we knew it was near. Looking again at Big Mama, I said, "If it wasn't like him, then why did he do it?"

"I think he set all of us up."

"I don't understand."

She waved the pistol in an impatient gesture and I resisted the urge to duck. "You said there was nothing in the cake, and there's nothing in your purse, which means he managed to hand off the information to someone else, and faked us out by following you. I followed him all day, which means I followed you all day." She stopped and grimaced. "You really should get a new car."

"I'm working on it."

"He probably intended to follow you home and make it look like he handed the information off, then leave town while we switched our attention to you. When you went to the grocery store instead of home, he cooked up the birthday cake scenario, thinking that while we chased you and the cake, he'd hop a plane and be gone."

Becker had been following me all day? I'd wondered about him showing up at Beeps Body Shop at the same time I did, and now it made sense. Becker was most likely the one who wrote all that trash on my car, because he'd figured I'd take it to the body shop right away. But why had he wanted me to go there?

I had a Eureka! moment just then, and it was all I could do not to give away my excitement. The keys! He'd talked to Nolan about wiring the money and leaving the car at the airport. He'd given an extra set of keys to Nolan. I wondered if they were still at the shop, or had Nolan put them in his pocket? If so, where were they now? At the morgue? That had to be how Becker passed the information without his tail being wise. There was probably a microchip in the keyless entry fob.

"Anyway," Big Mama continued, "he knew we had someone following him, he just didn't know who. So he faked us out and used you as bait."

"And you bit."

She frowned. "Yes, dammit, I did, right up until he reached in his pocket."

"Then you killed him."

With a slight shrug, she said matter-of-factly, "Self-defense. He had a gun in that pocket, and the instant he realized who I was, he reached for it."

Since she didn't appear inclined to shoot us, and she was being so chatty about the whole thing, I ventured a question. "Are you doing all this because you think it's right, or are you just in it for the money?"

She stared at me for several pregnant moments, then looked at Mom. "Is she always so nervy?"

"Always." Mom shot me a look that meant *Shut Up!*

Big Mama said, "Who's to say what's right? The men I work for are convinced they're right, just like the men on the other side think they've got all the answers." She waved the gun toward the pile of my purse's guts. "I gotta run, but first, I'll take a souvenir." Lowering her hand to her side, she let the little dog go. He hit the floor, ran to Mom and yipped at her feet.

"Give the Altoids box to Boris."

Mom turned unexpectedly brave. "Or what?"

"Or I'll shoot you."

"You'd shoot me for some breath mints?"

"Well, no, but I really like that little box."

Mom glanced at me with a comical look. Then she leaned down and held out the small, metal box. Boris parked it between his tiny teeth, turned and ran back to his mistress. After he leaped into her hand, she smiled at him from within the folds of flesh lining her face. The woman really was humongous. She must have weighed at least three-fifty. Maybe four hundred. And she was above-average height. In a way, she reminded me of that lady on the *Drew Carey Show,* sans the neon-blue eye shadow and wacky earrings. And she was taller.

She looked at me and said solemnly, "Don't dig into this. Forget all about what happened today. Heed the lesson of the curious cat." Turning, she said over her shoulder, "And thanks for the Altoids."

Then she walked out, cooing to Boris as she went.

We stared at the entrance of the kitchen until we heard the sound of the front door closing. Mom looked at me from across the island bar. "Boris?"

I took off running and looked through the blinds in Mom's dining room to see if I could get a license plate number off of Big Mama's car. Of course I couldn't, because, duh, it was dark outside. But in the dim light of the neighbor's porch lantern, I did see that Big Mama drove a black Cadillac. One of those old ones that are as big as a pontoon boat.

When Detective Garza showed up at Mom's, he took one look at me and said, "You're not having a good day, are you?"

"This one's in the top ten of bad days."

He listened to my story about the tattoo man, then Mom told him about Big Mama's visit. When we were done, I told him my theory about the key fob.

"So you think the information Becker wanted to pass is stored inside the key fob he handed over to Beeps?"

"It makes sense, doesn't it? Becker handed the key to Nolan so he could get the Suburban from the airport after Becker was gone, and Becker's contact probably had instructions to get the key from Nolan. But Becker didn't count on his tail trying to kill him and shooting Nolan instead. After that, he couldn't get the key back, so it's probably at the morgue."

"If Beeps did have the key, it'd be at the station, in the evidence room, along with everything else Nolan had on him when he died." Garza glanced at Mom. "What's your take on this?"

"Makes sense to me, but I wonder how Becker planned to

get the key to his contact after Nolan was shot. If the information is in the key fob, he would have made an alternate plan."

"Maybe he figured, just as Pink did, that the key would end up with the police. His contact would have the ability to retrieve it if he produced the right credentials." Garza gave me a half smile. "Let's put your theory to the test." He took his cell phone out of his pocket, dialed a number, then said, "This is Ray. I need you to take a look at Nolan Beeps's personal effects and see if there's a car key there." He paused for a bit, his gaze traveling around Mom's living room and settling on the portrait above the fireplace. "Nice picture of the two of you. Is that the Great Wall in China?"

"Yes," Mom said a bit proudly. "I had it painted after Pink and I got back from a trip over there."

Garza nodded, and said into his phone, "Okay. Right. A GMC? Got it. Thanks." He ended the call and dropped the phone back into his pocket. "There was a set of GMC keys in Beeps's pocket, and the kid at the shop said Beeps drove a Lexus. Someone from Washington's coming out to take care of details with Becker. I'll hand the keys off to them and if something's inside the fob, great. If not, nothing's lost." He stood and said, "Thanks for calling me. If anything else comes up, be sure and let me know. I'll be taking any and all tips in order to find the big lady and whoever was driving that Mercedes."

Mom and I agreed and waved him off at the front door. After he was gone, I told Mom I was beat and wanted to go home. We hugged a lot and promised one another we'd go on a trip soon, just the two of us, to spend some time together away from the office. I guess we were feeling our mortality that night—and that's not necessarily a bad thing.

Almost six hours since I'd driven away from the office, I pulled into the parking lot at the Windmills apartment complex, anxious to get to my dinky, second-floor place, take a hot shower, then curl up in bed and read something far removed from the day's events. Something that would force all thoughts of Banty, Mr. Gnarly, Tattoo Man, and Big Mama and her gofer dog out of my mind.

Inside the apartment, I moved toward the bedroom. I had a one-track mind about getting in bed as fast as possible. There's no overhead light in the bedroom, so I fumbled in the dark until I found the bedside lamp and switched it on.

Ed was lying across my bed, and I let out a little squeak of surprise. "How did you get in?"

"Your apartment manager. Nice guy, but way too gullible." He rolled over and blinked in the light of the lamp. "Just once, when I come by, could you act like a real girlfriend and maybe have something for me to drink besides Midland tap water?"

"It's good for you. Has lotsa minerals."

"I could mine iron ore out of it." He sat up and reached for me, then pulled me down to the bed. Rolling on top of me, he laid one of his Ed Wonder-Kisses on my lips. Oh, man. My toes curled up inside my sensible mules.

When he raised his head, I stared at his wonderful face for a very long time without talking, without asking why he'd driven more than three hours to come to Midland. I wanted it to be for me, but I didn't want to know if it wasn't. So I chose not to ask. Totally unlike me, but what can I say? It had been a shitty day, and I wasn't taking any chances.

Ed is way hot, with nice brown eyes and dark hair that's always a little too long because he procrastinates about getting it cut. When he's not in court, where he has to wear a suit, his wardrobe of choice is faded jeans and an assortment of T-shirts that have seen better days. On any other man, the clothes would look ratty. On Ed, they magically transform into the sexiest use of cotton on the planet. If Ed lived in the olden days, he'd have made a great pirate. Since he lives in modern times, I guess he picked the next best thing and became a lawyer.

Staring into those dark eyes, I thought of how deeply I'd missed him since he'd been gone. "How long can you stay?" I asked, curious about what he intended to do with the very significant bulge pressed against my thigh and hoping I was part of the solution.

"I have to go back five minutes ago, but I'll be done with the trial by Friday and come home for good."

"How's the trial going?"

"Even better than I expected." He kissed my nose, then rolled off of me and stared up at the ceiling. "I requested a late start tomorrow so I could come to Midland to see you in person."

"Because of this CIA thing?"

"Because you're real bad about jumping into deep water without a flotation device." He turned to look at me. "I had a call from Banty McMeans just after I talked to you today."

I sat up so fast I got dizzy. Or maybe I was dizzy because every drop of blood in my body had rushed to my head. "I'm gonna kill him! I swear to God, I'm going to go over to that little weasel's house and blow it to kingdom come. But first, I'll beat the snot out of him, then max out his credit cards and rearrange his stock portfolio to Titanic Incorporated." I glared down at Ed, so mad I couldn't even hang on to the happiness I'd felt mere seconds ago. "What did the slimy bastard say to you? Did he whine because I won't take him on as a client? Did he threaten you with something so you'd talk me into it? Because if he did, I'm gonna—"

"It wasn't anything like that, Pink. Just hang loose and I'll tell you all about it."

Hang loose? I was being harassed by Midland's resident fruitcake and there didn't appear to be anything I could do about it.

Ed reached for my hand and drew small circles against my wrist with the pad of his thumb. "Are you ready for this?"

Intrigued by the laughter I could hear in his deep voice, I looked at him and nodded.

"Banty wants to retain me to represent him. Seems the King of Lawsuits has had the tables turned, and he's being sued."

"For what?"

"Child support."

My mouth dropped open from shock.

"Amazing, isn't it?"

"You mean there's actually a woman out there who willingly let herself be impregnated by Banty McMeans?"

"It gets better. She goes to his church. Twenty-three years old and a brand-new mama. She swears the baby is Banty's, and he says it's impossible. When I asked why, he said he always used a condom."

"I think I'm gonna hurl." My head was swimming. "Did you take the case?"

"Yes, but I told him he has to deposit a hefty retainer. I figure if the paternity test is negative, the case is over. If it's positive, I'll get him to settle out of court because no judge in the county could possibly be fair and unbiased when it comes to Banty McMeans." Ed sighed and added, "It's true what they say, that you reap what you sow, and Banty's sown a lotta bad feelings over the years. He's bound to get it back in spades one of these days."

"Did he tell you why I won't take him on?"

Ed nodded while his hand circled my arm and squeezed gently. "He said the feds got wind that money is moving out of Midland and going to support Al Qaeda. I have no clue how Banty found out that they're here, although my guess is that he pays off people in the police and sheriff's department to tell him things. What I do know is that once he discovered they're conducting an active investigation, he started pestering them about David Lorenzo. He's convinced the guy is behind the money."

"Just because he converted to Islam?"

"Maybe, but it seems deeper than that. When I talked to him this afternoon, he sounded way too righteous. I think he hates Lorenzo's guts, and anything he can do to bring the man down is worth the effort."

A mental picture of Trina popped into my head, followed by a vision of Banty ogling her, and I wondered if she had something to do with Banty's feelings about Lorenzo. It didn't make sense, however, because she and Lorenzo were divorced. I tried to think of any other reason he might hate David Lorenzo, but came up empty.

"I understand why you refused to help him, but I wonder if you should rethink your decision."

"You can't be serious." Pulling my arm from Ed's grasp, I scooted away from him, which set the bed to squeaking. "Why would I reconsider him as a client when his sole purpose is to malign an innocent man in the worst way possible? Besides, if there was any merit to Banty's theory about the oil field thefts, the feds would investigate it. Since they're not, it's simply a fantasy, dreamed up by the worst conspiracy theorist in the state of Texas."

Ed sat up and faced me, running his hand through his hair. "There are a few things I don't think you've considered, and once you do, maybe you'll change your mind. But first, tell me everything that happened today."

"Everything? Are you sure? Because this day has lasted the equivalent of a month, and this will take awhile."

He glanced at his watch. "I've actually got a half hour before I have to leave, so let's hear it."

I eyed the center of his worn jeans, which was still looking very interesting. "A half hour, huh? And you want to spend it talking about my majorly sucky day?"

"No, I'd much rather take you up on that look, but I want our first time to be more than a hit-and-run. It's important we talk about what's going on. This is some serious shit, Pink, and like it or not, you're in the middle of it now."

I knew he was right, but I didn't have to like it. Why couldn't I just have the life all CPAs are supposed to have? An eight-to-five job, a nice little three-bedroom house, a steady-Eddie guy and nothing more dangerous in my life than a paper cut? Sighing, I kicked off my shoes and crossed my legs. While Ed listened, I gave him the blow-by-blow, starting at the very beginning, with Mom ragging my ass about new clients.

By the time I was finished, Ed looked a bit dazed. "I never give flowers, but damned if I don't wish I'd picked some up on my way over." He reached out and smoothed my hair, his fingers sending shivers down my neck. "Poor Pink. Trouble just seems to find you, doesn't it?"

"Why is that, Ed? Do you think I have bad karma?"

He smiled and dropped his hand. "On the contrary, I think you have the very best karma. People see that and they know you can help them."

"I suppose I have Santorelli to thank for what happened at Allbright's. Imagine him telling a CIA operative to contact me if he had a problem."

"Doesn't surprise me, not after how you handled the whistle-blower thing. Pink, you've become a kick-ass woman."

"Yeah, right. The only ass getting kicked right now is mine, and I'm starting to get paranoid."

"Are you paranoid enough to start doing some checking on those oil field thefts? Maybe Lorenzo isn't behind them, but somebody is."

"Why should it be up to me? Detective Garza told me there's been a rash of them and the Texas Rangers are looking into it."

"Yes, but they're looking for the thief, not the oil. Banty told them about Koko Petroleum, but he says they won't check it out because they think he's a nut."

"He *is* a nut."

"With a fairly logical-sounding theory. Look at it this way, Pink. Your mom's on your ass about bringing in new clients. Banty says he'll put up a retainer. There's no question about the oil thefts being legitimate. If you take the account, you'll be checking into something that may end up thwarting a major terrorist-funding scheme. No doubt the odds of Lorenzo being involved are zilch, and if you find out who is involved, Banty will have no choice but to shut up about it. So you see, you'd be doing everyone a big favor, including yourself."

I stared at him in wonder and awe. "Your logic is so twisted sometimes, you scare the hell outta me."

"I think I was dropped on my head at birth."

"Yeah, well, you can maybe make this sound good, but don't forget I'll have to work with Banty. I'd rather walk across Siberia in the dead of winter in a bikini."

"He's not really so bad. The trick is to talk to him exactly how his mother talks to him. The man's got a major mother complex. Have you ever met her?"

"Not formally, but I know who she is."

"He would do anything for her. When she says jump, he asks, 'How high?' She's very demanding and blunt."

"I'm hearing you say, in a nice way, that she's a controlling bitch."

"Exactly. So when dealing with Banty, be a controlling bitch and he'll fall right in line."

"I'm way too kindhearted and politically correct to be a controlling bitch. My Miss Manners alter ego takes over and I can't be mean, no matter how hard I try."

Ed laughed. He really did. I was about to have my feelings hurt when he said, "Maybe that's true under normal circumstances, but when you get pissed off, I think Miss Manners goes on vacation. You're already pretty ticked at Banty, so it's going to work out fine."

"Okay, I'll take the paranoid little toad's account, and I'll find out who's behind Koko. In the meantime, I'm not so sure you should take on his lawsuit."

"Why?"

"Because I'll need you to defend me when he sues me, and it would be a conflict of interest."

"He won't sue. I promise."

"How can you be so sure?"

Ed shoved me backward and came down on top of me. "Leverage. Mama doesn't know about his sweet young thing. I'm thinking Banty would do anything to keep it from her."

My breath caught in my throat, partly because Ed was squashing me, but mostly because of the implication of his words. "You'd betray a client confidence? For me?"

He lost his smile and stared down into my eyes. "I'm beginning to think I'd do a lot of things for you, Pink."

Then he kissed me senseless and left, and I decided it was a good thing that we hadn't talked anymore. I was way too emotional and didn't want Ed to know.

Several hours later, at ten after three in the morning, the phone rang. I answered with dread curling in my belly because no one calls at three in the morning with anything but bad news.

A nearly incomprehensible female voice replied to my groggy greeting. "I'm sho shorry to call you at this unholy time, but I gotta know shomethin', an' you gotta tell me."

"Trina?"

She sobbed a bit and choked out a yes.

"What do you want me to tell you?"

"Did he…did he shay anything 'bout me? I can't shtand it, Pink, thinkin' 'bout him lyin' there on the floor."

"You knew Dan Becker?" I asked, sitting up in bed, blinking away sleep.

"Knew him?" She laughed through the sobs. "I *loved* him!"

Oh, man. I switched on the lamp and swung my legs over the side of the bed. Trina was in love with Dan Becker? The CIA guy? Too weird. I considered his last words, about being sorry for screwing up, about the cake, about Santorelli. I couldn't remember anything about Trina. In fact, he hadn't mentioned a woman at all. But he was dead, and dead men tell no tales. Who would ever be the wiser if I told Trina a wee fib? She was clearly beside herself with grief. I crossed my fingers and said, "Just before he died, he said, 'Tell her I love her.' I didn't know who he was talking about."

"He said that? Really?"

I sent a fast one to God. Surely a white lie under the circumstances was okay. "Yes, Trina, he really did." I had to wonder if she knew Becker had been on his way out of the country. Then I wondered if she did know and had planned to go with him. "How did you know Dan?"

Lucky for me, she was slap in the middle of the True Confessions of the Truly Drunk stage. "He's with the sh…sh… CIA, an' they shent him here to find out 'bout money for Al Ki…Al Ka…oh, hell, you know, the shonsabitches who blew up New York. He came to see me 'bout David, on accounta he goes over to Shaudi 'rabia so much. An' Ven'zwayla." She giggled. "Ain't it a hoot? Mr. Perfect, shuspected of bein' a terrorist!" She laughed again, then descended back into heavy, heartrending sobs.

"Did Dan find anything?"

"Pink, shugar, you'd be freakin' 'mazed what he found. It was so bad, he planned to leave the Shtates. He was 'fraid they'd kill him."

"Who was he afraid of?"

"Ever'body." Her crying stopped and I heard her blow her nose. Sounding a bit more in control, she said, "Thanks for telling me, Pink. I gotta go, but please, please, don't tell anybody 'bout this. I want my baby back, so bad, an' if the bloody bastard knew about me an' Dan, he'd tell the judge, who already hates me 'cause he thinks I'm a whore."

"Why would they hold it against you? Surely David and the judge don't expect you to become a nun."

I heard the tinkling of ice in a glass, then an audible swallow. "They'd prolly like it better if I was, but that's not it. It's 'cause of Dan and what he was."

"A CIA operative? What's wrong with that? If anything, it's heroic."

Trina laughed again. "Poor Pink. You're a real naive one, ain't ya?"

I asked what she meant by that, but realized I was talking to a dead phone line. Trina had already hung up.

The following morning, after sleep made more sketchy by phone calls from Aunt Dru and Mom, who wanted to make sure I was okay, and woke me up to find out, I dragged myself out of bed and got ready for work.

On the way downtown, I glanced in my rearview mirror and saw a Suburban, which made me think of Dan Becker following me all day without me knowing it. I gave that some thought, remembering what Big Mama had said, that she'd been following Becker while he followed me. I wondered why she'd followed him all day. If her only intent was to get his information and kill him, why didn't she do it right off, first thing in the morning? Why follow him around all day, then kill him in a grocery store, a very public place for murder?

She'd said it was self-defense. Was she telling the truth? Had Becker really been about to pull a gun on her? So many things didn't fit and the more I thought about it, the more confused I got. Why had they sent two different people to retrieve whatever Dan supposedly gave me? Why had Big Mama looked so surprised about Tattoo Man? I considered the possibility that Becker's information concerned someone in addition to Al Qaeda. Maybe he'd found information about another organization, and Big Mama and Tattoo Man weren't working for the same group. That would explain her surprise.

I considered Trina's odd last words about Becker. She thought David Lorenzo and the judge would hold it against her if they knew about her affair. After I pointed out that the man was something of a hero, she'd said I was naive. Why? Something was way jicky with the whole story, and I hardened my resolve to find some answers.

I arrived at the office, and almost as soon as I got settled down with a cup of coffee, my boss, Sam, called and asked me to see him. In his office, he closed the door and waved me to one of the chairs in front of his desk before he took his seat.

Not that it's relevant to anything at all, but I swear, he's a dead ringer for Sammy Hagar. Except Sam's eyes are blue instead of brown. But he's tall and meaty, and wears Hawaiian shirts all the time. His hair is long and blond and wavy, and his skin is tanned to surfer-dude brown. Just like Sammy Hagar.

Today's Hawaiian shirt had blue palm trees on it. In his deep, sexy Sam voice, he asked, "How are you holding up, Pink?"

"Okay."

"Do you mean okay like you're really okay, or okay like you don't want to talk about it?"

"I don't wanna talk about it."

He nodded. "I understand, but let me know if you need any help. Watching a man die isn't easy."

"You would know?"

"Yeah…I know. Happened to me more than once while I was with the Bureau." He glanced at my blouse. "Nice shirt. You look good in pink. Goes with your blond hair and blue eyes."

"Thanks, Sam. Uh, was that all you wanted? I appreciate

your concern, but after the ass-chewing I got from Mom yesterday, I'm kinda anxious to get some billable hours, since my client-recruitment efforts are pretty dismal."

He rocked forward and lost all semblance of a smile. "I'm worried about you, Pink."

Aw, geez. Sam can be more overprotective than Mom. Maybe because he was once with the FBI and hunted down serial killers and rapists before he switched to embezzlers. "I'm fine, Sam. It's all over now, so there's nothing to worry about."

"I'm not so sure. The woman who killed Becker came looking for you. Whatever information Becker had is still floating around out there somewhere, so it's likely someone will come looking for you again, to double-check whether you have what they want."

It occurred to me that *I* hadn't told him about what had happened at Mom's. "Have you talked to Mom this morning?"

"No, why?"

"Then how do you know about Big Mama's visit?"

"Ed told me."

"When did you talk to Ed?"

"Last night. Actually, early this morning. He called and told me what happened. Then he asked me to keep an eye on you, and threatened to castrate me if I put anything else on you."

Ed being territorial toward Sam might have seemed to be a good thing, an indication of Ed's true feelings about me, but I didn't put too much stock in it because Ed and Sam have a long history of despising each other and competing for everything. It all started when Sam had a fling with Ed's ex-wife. Sam claims they were already divorced; Ed claims they weren't. Either way, even though they work together on a lot of mutual clients, they've built up an animosity toward one another that can be intense. I frequently find myself in the middle of things because I work for Sam and am almost sleeping with Ed.

Sam cocked one brow. "If you make up your mind to blow off Ed, be sure and let me know."

"Sure, Sam." I cocked a brow back at him. "You do realize, I could so haul your ass into court for sexual harassment."

He shrugged. "Do what you gotta do, but so long as you're single, hot and mildly attracted to me, I figure you're fair game. Besides, all you have to do is squeal to Mama and I'm toast. It's not as if I could threaten your job for sexual favors."

"How do you know I'm mildly attracted to you?"

"I just know. Guys make it their business to know things like that."

I had no comeback for that, except to say, "Oh."

Sam cleared his throat and got very serious. "Ed told me he encouraged you to take on Banty McMeans. Have you decided to do it?"

"Yes."

"Figures," Sam said with pseudodisgust. "God knows why you always put your faith in Ed, but I guess it's because you're so gone on him. One of these days, you're gonna wake up and realize he's not perfect."

That got my back up, big-time. "Are you insinuating my judgment is impaired because of how I feel about Ed?"

"No, I'm not insinuating. I'm throwing it right out there. Think about it, Pink—before Ed came along and talked you into taking this account, you didn't say no, you said *hell* no." He stopped, I guess because I must have had a questioning look on my face. "Gert told me you sent Banty packing."

"She would."

"Anyway, after you emphatically refused to accept him as a client, Ed shows up and applies his usual convoluted logic to the situation, and voilà! Taking on Banty McMeans and his goofy theory suddenly seems like a real good idea."

I looked at the east wall of Sam's office, at his framed degree from UCLA, his CPA certificate and a smorgasbord of awards he'd received while he was with the FBI. "I really hate it when you're a smart-ass."

"Beats the hell outta being a dumb-ass." He pointed to the west wall of his office, where he keeps a dry-erase board listing all of our current forensic accounting clients and the progress made on their accounts. "Every one of those clients are wealthy individuals who need a service from us and are willing to pay top dollar to get it. Most of them I went out and drummed up, some of them your mom pulled in, and the rest are divorce clients of Ed's whom he referred to us for asset tracing. Not one of them can be attributed to your effort. Now, think about how it's gonna look when I add Banty's name to that schedule."

I stared at the board for a long time before I had to concede his point. "Okay, so he's not a primo client, but he's a start, and he promised to give us a retainer before I began."

"That's all well and good, but what about at the end of the project when you haven't proved that David Lorenzo is the scum-sucking piece of shit Banty wants him to be? What happens then? Do you think Banty will go away and live with it?"

"That's a rhetorical question, and you should know that I hate rhetorical questions. I get the point, okay? Lay off."

He let out a heavy breath and turned to face the window. "If you're hell-bent on taking the account, take it, but don't say I didn't warn you. And be ready for Jane's reaction when she finds out. It won't be pretty."

"I think she has enough confidence in me to trust that I can avoid a lawsuit."

Turning back, Sam gave me a detached look. "It's real cute how you think your mama will accept anything you do because she's so awful crazy about you, but I think you're in for a big surprise. Maybe you're the most important thing to her, but this firm runs a close second, and if you threaten it in any way, I don't envy you one iota. I respect Jane, and she's an amazing woman, but I would never get between her and success."

I'd had enough of his lecture. "Are you done? I have a new client to call."

He scowled at me. "I'm done. For God's sake, will you be careful? Document everything, admit nothing and come up with something. If the cocky son of a bitch does sue, at least we'll be prepared."

In spite of his negativity, I left Sam's office feeling energized. It makes no sense, I know, because less than twenty-four hours ago, I'd told Banty to stick his theory where the sun don't shine. Now I was planning how I'd go about finding who was behind Koko, whether their great run of luck was a hoax, and if their oil revenues were really flowing out of Midland and into terrorist pockets.

Maybe Sam was right and I was easily influenced by Ed, but I didn't think so. It's just that Ed can look at something in a whole other way and make what's illogical seem perfectly rational.

And the truth of it was, I was pissed off. A lot. Somebody in my hometown was supporting the worst terrorist organization in history, and I'd do whatever I could to help find those people. Maybe Koko would turn out to be legit, and maybe Banty would turn out to be just as crazy as I thought he was. But there was the outside chance that he wasn't crazy, and no matter what Sam said, and even if Mom didn't like that I took Banty on, it was something I was bound to do— for Dan Becker, Nolan Beeps and the three thousand people who'd lost their lives because a wacko with evil eyes said they should die.

By the time I got back to my desk, I was leaning toward righteous. I picked up the phone, called Banty and told him I'd be at his office within the hour. He had the good sense not to be smug about it and actually made a pretty good attempt at being nice. He didn't quite succeed, I suppose, because he's compelled to make derogatory comments, but at least he made an effort.

Chapter 6

I was on my way to Banty's office when Ed called my cell phone. "How are you this morning?"

"Good, actually. I'm going to see Banty." I glanced at my watch. "Why aren't you in court?"

"The defense just rested and the case went to the jury."

"Good luck, Ed."

"Thanks. I think I've got a good chance of winning, especially because half the defense witnesses didn't show."

Call me a cynic, but I noticed he said "I," not "we," and this was a class action suit, with at least forty landowners involved. Ed is all about winning, and it has nothing to do with money or glory or anything but a gut level determination to be the best. I suppose a shrink might have a different take on it, but in my own sensible CPA brain, I figure he's that way because he came from such a big family. With six siblings, he'd had to be the best at some things or always get left behind. "Does this mean you'll be home tomorrow?"

"Maybe, but probably not. This is a complicated case and the jury has a lot to go over. Then there are some loose ends to tie up before I can leave."

"Day after tomorrow, then, you'll be back?"

"Definitely. Been thinking about that, and I wondered if you'd like to have dinner out, somewhere nice."

"Umm, no, I don't think so." I didn't think we could get away with having hot sex on a restaurant table. People tend to frown on that.

"Then maybe I should pick up takeout. We can light candles and play some jazz."

"I don't think so, Ed." Candles are a fire hazard, and Mom listens to jazz. She was the last person I wanted to think about while I was in the throes of extremely passionate sex.

"Okay, what *do* you want to do for our first real date?"

"Get naked. I can eat anytime."

He laughed. "I think I'm embarrassed."

"Bullshit. You're never embarrassed, and if you were perfectly honest, you'd admit you only offered dinner and candles and jazz music because it's sort of the expected thing."

"Men are kinda conditioned to that."

"In most circumstances, it's a good ritual. After all, women don't like it when men they hardly know ask for sex. In our case, we've already seen each other naked, so all the bells and whistles of a date are about as necessary as tea and crumpets at a boxing match."

"I've never known a girl like you."

"I've never known a guy like you."

He was quiet for a while, then said, "Where should we get naked?"

"What's wrong with my place?"

"Nothing, really, except your bed sounds like a squirrel calling its mate."

"I know it squeaks, but a squirrel? Seriously?"

"Pink, that bed blows. I don't know why you don't get a new one."

"I can't, because it's a furnished apartment and the bed isn't mine."

"Then maybe you should move to another apartment complex, one where you can have your own furniture."

"Actually, I've been thinking about buying a house."

No response.

"Ed?"

"Yeah, I'm here."

"What's wrong?"

"Nothing," he said. "You haven't mentioned looking at houses. When did this come up?"

"It came up when I had to put my Dallas loft on the market, then move into a dumpy apartment because I was worried about money. I figure it's smarter to pay on a mortgage than pay rent, so as soon as I can, I'm buying a house. Why? Is that a problem?"

"No...no, not at all. Just seems like a big step."

What the hell was going on? "Ed, did you get the memo? I'm a grown woman, and up until I got fired two months ago, I was pulling down over two hundred grand a year. I've bought and sold a house and a loft since I got out of college. For me, buying a house isn't a big step. It's just a step out of that rat hole of an apartment."

Silence fell once again.

"This is bothering you, and I don't get it."

"Maybe."

"What's up with you? If I recall correctly, you told me you never want to get married again, that you don't want kids and all the trappings. Do you want me to hang out in limbo until you decide if you're gonna change your mind?" My heart began to beat faster and I had to make a conscious effort not to speed. "Because here's a news flash, and you can take it to the bank. It won't matter if you change your mind, because I don't want to get married again. Ever. I don't want to live with a man, married or not."

"I know all about you not wanting to get married again, but I've told you, I'm not George. I'm not gonna go cheat on you with a whole stable of whores."

"And I believe you, but what's your fidelity got to do with me buying a house?"

"You're not hearing what I'm saying."

"I guess not. So what are you saying?" My stomach knotted up and actually hurt. *Please, please, don't do this. Don't screw it up for us before we've even gotten good and started.*

"Aw, shit, Pink. You know what? Just forget it." He hung up without waiting for my goodbye.

I drove the remainder of the way in a major funk. Amazing how men can turn a perfectly good mood into the screaming meemies.

By the time I got to Banty's office, which isn't actually in an office complex, but an old well-service building out on Highway 80, I was in control, but wondering what Ed meant when he'd said to forget it. Did he mean forget the conversation? Forget his bizarre reaction to me buying a house? Or had he meant forget us as a couple?

After the disaster of my first marriage, which morphed from really bad to catastrophic because I never expressed how I felt, I'd decided to be more direct in my dealings with men. Instead of sitting around, wondering what they mean or how they feel, I come right out and ask. As soon as I was parked in front of Banty's one-story metal building, which incidentally was painted a hideous shade of green, I punched in Ed's number.

He answered on the first ring. "What is it, Pink?"

Hmm, not a great indicator. "I'd really like to know what you meant about forgetting it. Forget what?"

"Pink, this isn't a good time to get into this."

"You're freaked out just because I want to buy a house?"

"You really don't get it, do you?"

"Clearly, I don't. And I think you should at least have the courtesy to explain why you're dumping me."

"I'm dumping you?" He sounded exasperated. "Look, maybe I said I don't want to get married, or have kids, or whatever, and I'm sure when I said it, I meant it. But don't I have the right to change my mind? Is it completely out of the question that you might change *your* mind? Maybe I might want to get married or explore the possibility of living together sometime down the road. If you buy a house, it's like saying no, that will never happen. I gotta tell you, Pink, I think I'm in this thing way deeper than you are."

"If I buy a house, it's not like I'm shackled to it for all eternity. Aren't you being a bit dramatic about this?"

"It's not the *house!* It's your whole attitude, Pink. Like all you want from me is advice and sex."

"Isn't that what most couples want from each other? What else is there, Ed?"

He was quiet for so long, I thought maybe he'd ended the call. I glanced at the screen and it still said "connected."

Finally, he said in a quiet voice, "If you don't know what else there is, I feel real sorry for you. Maybe someday you'll catch on, but I'm too damn jaded to be the one to teach you."

"If you expect me to beg you to change your mind, you're way wrong. And if you're serious about this, so be it, but I can't believe you're willing to throw in the towel before we've even gotten started."

"Yeah, well, if I thought there was a chance you'd ever get to where I'm at right now, maybe I'd give it a go. But you're so pissed off about what George did to you, it colors your world."

I felt like the bottom had fallen out of my stomach. Maybe

he was right. I didn't know. All I knew was that I'd regret it if I let him walk away. "Ed, don't do this."

"Give me one good reason why I shouldn't."

Damn, I needed to not blow it, but I'm so bad at quick comebacks. I'm one of those people who think of the perfect thing to say about forty-eight hours after the opportunity to say it has passed. But this was important, and if I screwed it up, I might lose Ed forever. I had no clue where I wanted this relationship to go—I just knew I couldn't bear the thought of losing it. Then I thought, hey, that didn't sound too bad. So I said it, or a reasonable facsimile thereof.

He was quiet for a while. In fact, he was quiet so long, I finally said, "Ed, I'm not that great at this, and I'm sorry."

"I'll be home Friday night and we'll talk, and we'll see how it goes. That's all I can offer right now."

"All right, Ed. Call me when you get to town."

He hung up and I stared at the phone for at least five minutes.

It was still blowing my mind, how things had gone from great to weird in a nanosecond. All because I'd said I wanted to buy a house. I wondered if maybe Mom could tell me why Ed had wigged out so bad. Then I thought about it and almost laughed at myself. Yeah, like Mom would have a clue. She'd stayed married to Lurch for twenty years. In the romance department, she needs customer service as much as I do. Maybe more.

I couldn't do much about my love life at the moment, but I could go set the accounting world on fire. Determined to make the best of the day, in spite of how it had gone so far, I shoved the phone into my leather portfolio, strode to the door and went in to meet with Banty. I was loaded for bear, able to be demanding and bitchy without even trying. As Ed had predicted, Banty was agreeable to everything I proposed. He even signed the engagement letter I'd drafted without batting an eye, and handed over a significant check for my retainer.

After he'd loaded a couple of boxes of files into my car as

I was leaving, he asked about what had happened the day before. "That must have been very frightening," he said, looking a little frightened himself.

"Actually, it was more sad than anything else. Dan Becker seemed like a very nice guy."

Banty snorted. "Getting you involved in his schemes wasn't very nice."

I'd read the morning paper's account of the murder at Allbright's, and it was all very vague about Dan and the assassin. Nothing was mentioned about the CIA or Al Qaeda, I'm sure because the police didn't reveal any of it. Looking at Banty in the bright morning sunlight, I remembered what Ed had said about him paying for information from the police and sheriff departments. Made sense. Otherwise how would he know anything about Becker?

I wasn't inclined to tell him more, so I sidestepped the whole thing. "I gotta get back to the office. I'll call you if I have any questions, and I'll issue a report to you at the conclusion of the project."

He clearly wanted to ask me more, but I said goodbye and got in the car before he had the chance.

My first order of business was to find out who was behind Koko Petroleum. I wasn't sure if Koko was a corporation or a partnership, or even an individual using the name to do business, so I called the Secretary of State's office and made some inquiries. It turned out that Koko was a limited partnership, and although the woman couldn't tell me who the limited partners were, she said the general partner was a man named Gus Thompkins, who lived in Midland. When she gave me the address, I recognized the street as one in an older part of Midland, a community of small homes with one-car garages and tiny yards.

As soon as I was off the phone, I left the office and drove

over to visit Gus, to ask him about Koko. On a street full of tidy little houses, Gus's stood out as the neighbor everyone hates, who screws up property values. His yard was overgrown with weeds, and the house paint was peeling so badly it was impossible to tell what color it had been. There was an old beat-up Oldsmobile in the drive. It hadn't been driven in a very long time if the weeds growing around the almost flat tires were any indication.

I guess that's why I wasn't overly surprised when no one answered the door. The whole place had the look of a haunted house. After knocking several times, I gave up and turned to go back to my car, then let out a little gasp of surprise when a woman stepped into my path.

"Lookin' for Gus?" she asked, eyeing me suspiciously.

"Yes, I am. Do you know where I might find him?"

"I don't, but I sure wish I did. The son of a bitch has let this place go to the dogs, and all his damn weeds are comin' over into me and Sister's yard."

"Sister?"

She jerked her head to the east. "Me and my friend live next door, and we kinda took a likin' to keepin' the yard nice." She pointed. "See? We got us one a them windmills and some deer— they're not real, but they sure look it, don't they?" She turned her attention back to Gus's house. "Don't make much difference, livin' next door to this sorry excuse for a man. Sister says he'd like to drive a backhoe over here one night and just tear the bastard down, but I tol' him he'd get run in, and with him on parole, he don't need to be gettin' in trouble with the law. I'm just tryin' to find Gus, so's I can tell him what I think about this pile of shit."

Sister was a guy? That was weird. The woman looked to be about my age with dirty blond hair, a pair of jeans cut so low she had to have shaved to keep her pubes from showing and a humongous tattoo of Tweety Bird on her right bicep. She looked like what Mom would call a skank.

"When's the last time you saw Gus?" I asked.

"Been at least six months. Not sure where he went, or how. Only car I know of is that antique Olds, and as far as I know, the man had no friends, which ain't surprising, since he was mean and grouchy and used to sit out here on the porch and throw rocks at all the little kids in the neighborhood."

"How old is he?"

"I'm not sure, but I'd guess in his seventies."

Oh, man. "I don't wanna be gross, but have you thought maybe he *is* in there?"

"You mean, like dead?"

I nodded.

"Yeah, me and Sister thought maybe that was it, so we broke in one night and had us a look around. He ain't there." She took a step closer and lowered her voice. "Weird part is, everything's there but his papers. His walker's there, and Gus didn't never go nowhere without his walker. Had a stroke a few years back, and he couldn't get around too good. But his bills and papers and stuff is all gone. Me and Sister can't figure out why he'd leave his walker, but take all his papers. Sister thinks somebody came and robbed him, then took him off and killed him and dumped the body. But nobody misses him, 'cause like I said, he ain't got no friends, and I don't think he had any family."

I shivered, right out there in the hot sun because it creeped me out so bad. I glanced back at the decrepit house. "If he's dead, he wouldn't be paying his electric bill, and the porch light is on, so that means somebody's paying it."

She looked behind me and nodded slowly. "You're pretty smart. Didn't even think about that. I gotta tell Sister he don't know what he's talkin' 'bout." She looked at me again. "So whaddya want with Gus?"

"I had a question about a business he began awhile back."

"Well, you ain't gettin' no questions answered today, that's for sure. Tell you what, if you find the old buzzard, tell 'im me and Sister is looking for him. My name's Pauline, but most ever'body calls me Pauly."

I agreed and handed her a business card. "If he comes back or you see anything happening over here, please call me."

"Be glad to." She shoved my card in her pocket and turned and walked away, back to her yard with the windmill and the fake deer.

And Sister. I saw a tall thin man standing in the drive without a shirt, a smoke clenched between his lips.

As I went out to my car, I felt his stare, all the way. It wasn't necessarily a creepy stare. More like a curious one. As if he really wanted to know who was looking for Gus.

On the way back downtown, I called Aunt Dru, thinking maybe she knew something about Gus Thompkins. It was a long shot, but she was in her seventies and so was Gus. When she answered, I explained my dilemma and she said, "Can't say I recall anyone with that name, Whitney Ann. Why are you asking?"

"It's something I'm working on for Banty."

"So you decided to take him on, after all. That's good to know. You just be firm with him and he won't give you any trouble. Some men are that way, you know. They like a woman to have a strong hand."

"Yes, ma'am."

"I'll ask around about this Gus Thompkins fella, and let you know what I find out. Oh, by the way, we're having a Right Hand of God prayer group meeting tonight. It's at Dotty Haskell's house at seven sharp."

I cast about for any reason not to attend, but came up blank. I'm as bad at spontaneous lying as I am with quick comebacks. Still, I did manage to be vague. "I'll try to make it, Aunt Dru."

"You're a good girl," she said just before she hung up.

Okay, so how could I find out anything about Gus Thompkins? If he'd had a stroke, maybe he had another one and they'd moved him to the rehab hospital. I called Information for the number, then called the hospital, but came up with nothing. They'd never heard of him.

Damn. I had to admit defeat, for the time being at least.

I drove through a Taco Casa and picked up some lunch before heading back to the office. While I sat in the break room and scarfed down a couple of tacos, I brainstormed how I could find out anything about Gus's whereabouts. I was sort of at a dead end. I thought some more about Koko, and it occurred to me that if Koko had drilled a well, put a pumping unit on it and were now producing oil, there would be a whole list of vendors who'd done the work. That meant whoever was pulling the strings, whether Gus or someone who had control over Gus, would have transacted business with local oil-service companies.

As soon as I was done eating lunch, I went to my cubicle, got out the phone book and began making calls, starting with the drilling companies, followed by mud companies and chemical companies and wireline companies.

By midafternoon, I'd made a lot of new friends in the oil business, but I hadn't found a single one who'd ever heard of Koko Petroleum, much less done any work for them. It was beginning to look like Banty was right about at least one thing—Koko's gangbusters well was most likely a fake. I couldn't be sure, however, because Koko might have used service companies in other towns in the Permian Basin. There are hundreds, and it would take me three days to call all of them, which didn't seem like such a great use of my time.

Then I thought about the oil marketer. If Koko was selling oil, somebody had to be buying it. I started calling the oil buyers and hit pay dirt when I dialed Boxwood Petroleum Marketing. I spoke to a man named Randy who said yes, Boxwood had contracted to buy the oil off of Koko's well.

"I'm trying to find Gus Thompkins, who's the general partner in Koko, and wonder if you might know where he is."

"I'm not sure where he offices, Ms. Pearl, but I have a phone number and a post-office box number."

I wrote them down, then asked, "When he signed the contract, was he in ill health?"

"Oh, no," Randy said with a note of astonishment at my question. "Mr. Thompkins is a huge man, on the young side, and very hale and hearty. In fact, he looks like a bodybuilder."

I thanked Randy and hung up, then sat back and wondered who was posing as Gus Thompkins. I dialed the phone number and got an answering machine, the greeting made by a man who did not sound old. I didn't leave a message. I dropped the phone back in its cradle and turned to the computer, where I Googled the phone number. I found out exactly what I already knew—the number was for Koko Petroleum, and the address was the P.O. box.

While I was sitting there, plotting my next move, Tiffany buzzed and said I had a call. I should have known from the breathless quality of her voice that it was not an ordinary phone call, but I was a bit preoccupied. I picked up the receiver and formed a greeting from the side of my brain that runs on autopilot. "This is Whitney Pearl."

"Hello, Pink," a deep, serious voice said.

Santorelli. I sat up straighter and my adrenaline kicked into super octane. "Hello, Steve."

"So you do remember me."

"The last time I spoke to you was in Washington, right after you laid a kiss on me that could go down in the You Can Count on Me Calling You Hall of Fame. I'm no saint, but I'm also not the sort of girl who lets a man kiss her that way, then forgets him."

He was quiet for a couple of heartbeats. "You're mad because I didn't call you sooner, aren't you?"

"I don't get mad about things like that. If you wanted to call, you would have. Since you didn't, I assume you didn't want to."

"It's got nothing to do with what I want. I've been tied up with some things that made it impossible to call."

"Lots going on in the finance committee these days?"

"The Senate's been out of session and I've been in California since just after your last hearing."

"I see." He wasn't making a very good case for being tied up, was he? "So there's a lot going on in California."

"I've been having some problems with my dad."

Instantly, I felt bad for doubting him. "I'm sorry, Steve. Nothing serious, I hope."

"Oh, he's not sick. He's just a big pain in the ass."

Wow, I hadn't expected that. "Parents will be that way."

"Yeah, but Dad takes it to a whole new level. He was a POW in Vietnam, and he's about half-crazy. I mean, not actually crazy—just hardheaded and convinced he's always right. He occasionally does some consulting work for the defense department, but he's extreme and manages to stir things up, which doesn't go over well with the top brass. So they banish him back to California until some weird, unexpected situation comes up again, and they call him back."

"What kind of weird, unexpected situation?"

"You don't wanna know. Suffice it to say, I've spent the past three weeks trying to talk him out of helping with the latest crisis, and in the end, I'm faced with either throwing in with him or calling the defense secretary and demanding he stop recruiting Dad. I hate to do that because these projects mean so much to him, but I'm afraid he's gonna get himself killed."

"I'd say unless he's mentally incompetent, you'd be wrong to interfere."

"That's where I'm at right now. The next time he willingly puts himself into a dangerous situation, who knows?"

This was heavy and I didn't want to step over the line with advice, so I took the easy way out. I changed the subject. "Steve, why did you call me?"

He was quiet for a very long time. Finally, he said, "Are you okay?"

"I'm okay. Remind me to thank you for giving Becker my name. And what's with that, anyway? Last time I checked, you're the chairman of the finance committee. You guys write boring, confusing tax law and pester the head honcho over at the SEC."

"The committee chair is briefed about investigations of things like money laundering."

"That's what Becker said. Naturally, my next question dealt with the identity of the local money launderer."

"And he told you," Steve said with a note of resignation in his voice.

"Yes. That was just before Big Mama stabbed him."

"I'm truly sorry about all of it, Pink. If I'd had any inkling things would turn out the way they did, I never would have given him your name."

It wasn't that I was angry about it, because after all, it was something of a compliment that he had that much belief in my integrity. I guess I was just freaked out and angry about Dan Becker's death. It seemed so pointless. "I've got a million questions, all of which I'm sure you'll say you can't answer because of national security, but leading the list is why the CIA is here. Wasn't the CIA formed to spy on other countries? Since when are they spying on their own citizens? And my next question is why Dan Becker was apparently on his own, why he didn't have any kind of backup."

"You're right, I can't answer your questions, mostly because I don't have the answers. I'm a senator, Pink, not the president. Information in Washington is always on a need-to-know basis, and being the boring money guy, I don't need to know about what the boys at the CIA are up to, unless it has something to do with money. Granted, I'd like to know, but it's not in my job description. Does that make you feel better?"

"Not really."

"Would you feel better if I came to Midland and bought you some dinner and we talked about it at greater length?"

"Excuse me?" I wondered if I was having one of those low blood sugar things. I could have sworn he'd said something about coming to Midland. And dinner.

He cleared his throat, but I could tell it was a stall tactic. He was nervous. "If you recall, I asked you to go to dinner with me sometime after the last hearing was over. You said yes."

"I remember." I also remembered that I'd said yes because he was the chairman of the finance committee, holding my fate in his hands. And I suppose a small part of my yes was because I was flattered by his attention. Steve is a young senator, not yet forty, and a widower. He's also very good-looking, in a dark, Italian, rich-guy-from-the-coast-of-northern California sort of way. And he's got a dry sense of humor that definitely grew on me during the multitude of phone conversations we had while the whistle-blower thing was going on. If not for Ed, I might have gone way goofy over Steve.

"In light of what happened, I thought the least I could do is buy you dinner and explain why I gave Becker your name." He cleared his throat again. "And I figure it's time to get out a little and be more, uh, sociable."

Meaning, I assumed, to go on a real date, which he hadn't done since his wife died. Or so he'd said when he originally asked me out. I was inclined to believe him, mostly due to the media. Not that I believe everything I read, but in this case, I believed everything I didn't read. Because he was the youngest senator, and a handsome widower, he was the media's darling. If he'd had any kind of romantic interlude, they would have plastered her picture on every gossip magazine, the pundits would have analyzed her potential as first lady of California, and Dave Letterman would have joked about her.

Instead, all the articles about the spitfire lawmaker from California included something about his single status after the death of his beloved wife, Lauren, and speculated about the current state of his love life, which was apparently dead.

Now he wanted to resurrect it with me, and I honestly didn't know how I felt about that. I wanted to see him, although I wasn't quite sure why. I had it bad for Ed, so why couldn't I shake this attraction I felt for Santorelli? He wasn't even my type. I guess because there's something so tantalizing about him. I wanted to get to know the real guy, the one who hid behind the serious senator. If the way he kissed was any indication, there was definitely somebody extremely interesting in there.

What should I do? If I said yes, I'd be leading him on, and I didn't like that scenario, at all. Also, I'd feel honor bound to tell Ed, and there was no doubt he would *not* like it. Still, the fact that I was even considering going out with Steve said a lot about where I was in the relationship with Ed. Maybe that's what he'd meant and that's what bothered him—that I wasn't ready to forsake all others, and he was.

I gave Miss Manners a chance to speak up, to tell me what was proper form, but the silly twit was out of the building. Eventually, I relied on my integrity to do the talking. Damned integrity—ruins my good times way too often. "Steve, I would love to have dinner, but I'm seeing someone."

"Your lawyer?" he said without hesitation.

"How did you know?"

"I just know. Guys make it their business to know things like that." He cleared his throat again. "When you say you're seeing him, what does that mean, exactly?"

I wished I knew the answer to that. "Well, let's just say he hasn't asked me to go steady yet."

"So, you're not all that serious?" Maybe I imagined it, but I swear I heard him let out a huge breath.

"What do you classify as serious?"

"Sleeping together more than three times, four if one of the times involved alcohol, gifts that cost over a hundred bucks, holding off on major life decisions or changes while waiting to see which way things go."

"Like buying a house?"

"Exactly." He paused and asked, "Are you thinking of buying a house?"

"As a matter of fact, I am."

"Well, then, there you go. Have dinner with me, Pink."

"If I agree, I have to tell Ed."

Santorelli let out a small laugh. "Of course you do. Just curious, but have you ever been able to lie?"

"No, but not from a lack of trying. Thing is, even if I didn't get caught, I'd still pay a high price because something awful would happen to me. Must be a God thing. I finally gave up, and you know, it really does make things simpler. Hard to remember lies, but it's never hard to remember the truth."

"Hey, that's a great line. Mind if I use it in my next campaign?"

"You're kidding, right?"

"No way. My father's words of wisdom are only getting worse. Last week, he gave me the one about saving pennies."

"A penny saved is a penny earned?"

"A penny saved is a penny those damn terrorists can't get their hands on."

"He didn't really say that. You're making it up."

"Swear on my mother's grave, he really did."

"Tell me you have a good speech writer."

"I write my own speeches, and Dad's always been good with one-liners, but lately the old man's wit is on vacation." Steve paused, then said seriously, "Pink, have dinner with me."

Perhaps I should have said no. Maybe I should have told him my feelings for Ed, even if I wasn't sure about them, were a lot stronger than a simple crush. And there's no doubt I should have been up-front about not wanting to lead him on, that even if I was attracted to him, even if I wanted to be friends, I didn't see a future for us. But I didn't do any of those things. Maybe I can't lie, but I did a bang-up job of abandoning the truth. With my heart hammering in my chest, I said, "All right, Steve, I'll have dinner with you."

"Good. Can you make it tomorrow night?"

Man, he really worked fast. "That's fine. Do you need me to pick you up at the airport?"

"Thanks, but no. I'll be coming in on a private plane, and I'll get a friend of mine to pick me up."

"You have a friend in Midland?"

"Yeah, an old college buddy from Stanford. Maybe you know him—David Lorenzo?"

I almost dropped the phone. "I know who he is, but I don't actually know him."

"Good guy. I haven't seen him in a long time, but he's been really supportive of my political career, and my visit to Midland will be a chance to catch up."

"Yes, that will be nice," I said automatically, while my suspicious mind was zooming ahead, wondering if maybe Santorelli had another purpose for coming to Midland besides buying me dinner. Something about the whole thing seemed too coincidental to be random. But I couldn't imagine what the connection could be. In spite of what Trina had told me about Dan Becker coming to Midland to find out who was funneling money to Al Qaeda, that he'd been looking at David Lorenzo as a possibility, I felt confident that Lorenzo had nothing to do with the terrorist money laundering scheme. It made sense Becker would look at Lorenzo, considering his trips to Saudi Arabia and Venezuela, but it didn't make sense that Lorenzo was a terrorist sympathizer. Every instinct I had told me it couldn't be.

All the same, the timing of Santorelli coming to Midland was way too coincidental to be just a weird, freak thing. I decided I would ask him, as soon as he arrived.

"Until tomorrow, then. Bye, Pink."

"Bye, Steve." I hung up and tried to catch the wisp of coincidence again, but it eluded me.

Chapter 7

Late that afternoon, as I was walking out of the office, Aunt Dru called to remind me about the prayer group meeting. I was about to tell her I was too tired to make it, when she said, "Oh, by the way, one of our members says she knows Gus Thompkins. Doesn't know where he is, but mentioned an ex-wife named MayBelle who works at Cheapo Depot. Maybe you should talk to MayBelle and she can tell you where he is."

I was so grateful for her help, I impulsively agreed to go to her prayer group meeting. Her enthusiasm sent my Guilt-O-Meter into the red zone and I made myself respond with an equal amount of gusto. Later, after I'd gone home to change into something more conservative, I went to the meeting and allowed myself to be talked into helping with the Saturday night Bible mailing at Aunt Dru's. I don't know why. Maybe I just felt guilty for taking advantage of their hospitality. At any rate, Saturday night was now taken care of. If

Ed went through with blowing me off, at least I'd have something to do to take my mind off of it.

The next morning, I went through some of the files Banty had given me, and started scheduling out his revenues off of all Lorenzo-operated wells. It would take awhile because he had a lot of interests, especially in the Pendergast field, which was the find that had made David Lorenzo's family rich. I thought it was interesting how many royalties Banty had in the Pendergast, and wondered if his family had owned the mineral rights at one time.

Usually, when someone wants to drill a well, they contact the mineral owner, who may be different from the landowner, and offer money to lease the mineral rights. Once the well is drilled, if it makes a producing well, the mineral owner receives a royalty interest, the amount of which can vary, based on how the mineral rights were set up in the first place. Where it gets tricky is when land has been passed down from generation to generation, or sold with some, but not all, of the minerals reserved. With the minerals changing hands so many times, and different people retaining a piece of them, some wells may have hundreds of royalty owners. And the royalty owners' slice of the whole pie is in the neighborhood of twenty percent. The rest goes to whoever drilled the well and the other investors.

In Banty's case, he had a fairly high royalty interest in the Pendergast field, and he had a royalty on all of the wells, which led me to believe his family had once owned the bulk of the mineral rights. He made a lot of money off those wells, but no royalty was higher than two percent, a drop in the bucket compared to how much Lorenzo probably earned from them. I wondered if Banty resented that, if he was sorry his father hadn't explored that field, rather than signing away the mineral rights to Lorenzo's father. I remembered what he'd said about the housekeeper they shared, that back when she'd started working for them, his father and David's father were friends. He made it sound as if they were not friends later, and I wondered if the Pendergast field was one of the reasons.

At ten o'clock, I gathered up my purse and took off for Cheapo Depot, anxious to see if MayBelle was at work. After I arrived at the store, I looked around curiously. Can't say I'd ever been in the place, because after all, it's called Cheapo Depot. Not that I've got anything against finding good buys, but something in my psyche rebels at shopping in a store with such a name.

All the same, Mom's bargain hunter genes run rampant in my blood, and I sorta got sucked into the place, wowed by all the great deals. There was a lot of cheap, tacky stuff, but interspersed with a bunch of vases shaped like low riders, I found a set of plain white café dishes for ten bucks. A couple of aisles over, I spotted a hammock for thirty dollars, one of those nice, sturdy ones. Not that I had any need for a hammock, but someday I might. How could I pass up a deal like that?

Maybe fifteen minutes into my shopping bonanza, I decided I'd best look for MayBelle. I headed for the front, thinking I'd ask, then get a cart to go back and pick up my finds.

The lady at the register was all smiles, and called me "hon." When I asked about MayBelle, she laughed. "I'm MayBelle, hon! What can I do for you?"

"My name is Whitney Pearl and I need to talk to Gus Thompkins. I was told that you might know where to find him."

Immediately, MayBelle's smile faded. "What do you want with that old bag o' bones?"

"I'm a CPA, working on a client who needs some information about Koko Petroleum. I hoped I could see Gus and ask him some questions about it."

Her expression became almost angry and I hoped I hadn't pissed her off.

"I don't know where the old cuss has got himself to, but it's probably a town called Trouble. As for Koko, that's what caused me to leave him. He swore he'd stop cattin' around, but not even a month later, I ran across some paperwork, and I knew he'd lied to me. Koko was a partnership, and the partners in it, besides him, was three sleazy women he'd been foolin' around with for years. I showed him those papers, and the sorry dog had the nerve to tell me he started Koko for tax reasons, that it was a tax write-off." She harrumphed, looking disgusted. "I told him he could write me off, because I was outta there. My lawyer got me a settlement that said he's gotta pay me five thousand bucks a year, until the day he dies. That's the only reason I keep up with him, so I can make sure he gives me my money. Then the sorry so-and-so disappeared, and I swear I wouldn't be surprised if he did it on purpose, so he could welsh on the deal and not pay me."

"Would you mind telling me who the three women were?"

"Betty Marks, Shirley Howard and Bobo Lansky. Every one of them are white trash, not fit to be called women." She took on something of a superior look. "But God works in mysterious ways, and it's mighty ironic how they all ended up."

"How is that?"

Her eyes practically glittered with satisfaction. "They're every one of them over in the Bluebird Retirement Center, just passing the days making macaroni pictures and waitin' to die. Ain't a one of them's got a pot to pee in, nor a window to throw it out of. Just livin' off the government. That's what comes from being a tramp."

Clearly, MayBelle had issues. Not that I blamed her, having shared my husband with women of questionable morals, but I didn't really hold a grudge against the women. All of my resentment was focused on George for buying their product, which was sex. Lots of it.

I thanked MayBelle and left the store, my mind making

logical steps to further discover what was going on with Koko. If the women who were the limited partners in Koko were living off the government, what was happening to all the money being made in the partnership? Was Gus behind the oil field thefts, swiping the oil off Lorenzo's wells, spiking the tanks at the Koko well, then pocketing the money? If so, where was he?

It wasn't until I pulled into the parking garage of the Old First National Bank building, where Mom has her offices, that I remembered the café dishes and the hammock. I'd left Cheapo Depot without buying them. Dammit. I was pretty bummed, but then I remembered I had no groceries, so the lack of dishes wasn't my main problem.

As I rode the elevator to the fifteenth floor, I resolved to get a life. Soon.

When I got to the office, Tiffany looked freaked out. "What's wrong?" I asked when I came through the door and saw her pale face.

She appeared more nervous than a crook at the Policeman's Ball, her gaze constantly darting toward the hall. "Gert's ex is here!" she whispered.

I moved close to her desk and whispered back, "Gert has an ex?" This shocked me. A lot.

Tiffany nodded. "Blew me away, too, but awhile ago, this guy comes in and says he wants to see Gert. I say do you have an appointment, and he says, I don't need an appointment to see my ex-wife. So I go tell Gert and she freaks out and tells me to tell him to go away. I come back and tell him to go away and he says no, I won't, and then he takes off for her office, and I've heard them shouting and I don't know what to do."

From somewhere down the hall, I heard a male voice that was just a smidge too loud for normal conversation.

"Is Mom in?"

"She's still over in Odessa at that local CPA symposium. She won't be here until later today."

"How about Sam?"

"He's in court all afternoon."

I heard the too-loud voice again. "I'll go check it out." With a mix of dread and acute curiosity, I headed down the hall, turned the corner, then walked toward Gert's office.

When I heard that loud male voice again, he was way past too loud. He was shouting.

"You've got no right to that ring! It was my grandmother's, and I want it back. *Now!*"

I heard Gert's mannish voice. "You'll hock it for a little bit of nothing, and I'm not going to let you do it. When your brother gets married, I'm giving it to him, for his bride."

"My brother isn't gonna get married. He's queer as a three-dollar bill!"

"You'd like to think so, Jacob, because then you wouldn't feel so lonely in the closet."

Holy smokes! Gert married a gay guy?

"Lay off it, Gert. You know I'm not gay."

Okay, maybe not.

"How would I know that? It's not like you ever burned it up in bed."

Eew! Overshare.

"Maybe because you were cold enough to give me frostbite!"

"It's convenient to blame your sexual problems on me, isn't it? I feel sorry for you, even if I do despise you."

Come on, Gert, you can do better than that.

"What the hell's wrong with you? What's with the no makeup, and what'd you do to your hair? You always had nice hair, so whaddya wanna stick it up in that librarian bun for? Your clothes look like something my mother would wear, and your glasses are close to qualifying as antiques. Is this your way of avoiding men? If so, it's workin' like a charm!"

I was close to the doorway, but slowed down, curious to hear how Gert replied. I hoped she'd dish it back to him.

"You're a user, Jake, a pathetic nobody with a twisted little mind and an overinflated ego. The only reason you graduated college was because I carried you. So insult me all you want, but we both know, if not for me, you'd be out there in the oil field, shoveling dirt." She paused for a moment, then added, "As for sexual attraction, I find you equally repugnant. I'd rather crawl in bed with Moby Toby, the fattest guy in Midland."

I reached the doorway and stopped just short of actually entering her office. "Is there a problem?"

Gert glared at me. "This is none of your business."

No good deed goes unpunished. Wasn't that what Mom always said? "Maybe it's none of my business, or Tiffany's or anyone else in this office, but you're making it our business with all this shouting." I looked at Jake. "Either keep your voice down or leave. This is a professional place of business."

He peered at me. "Who the hell are you?"

"I work here."

"Yeah, I figured that out. I mean, what's your name?"

"Pink."

"What kinda name is Pink?"

"A short, but colorful one."

Gert said, "This is Jane Pearl's daughter." She looked at me with animosity glowing in her eyes. "This is Jake Hollingsworth, my ex-husband, who is just leaving."

His hair was dull brown, and it looked as though he'd spent a lot of time in the sun because he had a rough complexion. He sported a spare tire around his middle. "I came up here for my grandmother's wedding ring, and I'm not leaving without it."

"You can't have it," Gert said, scowling at him. "You've got loan sharks after you and you're desperate, so you'll sell that ring for a quarter of what it's worth. Besides, the ring is mine now. You gave it to me when we got married."

"And descended into hell," Jake muttered.

"Is that your final answer, Gert?" I asked.

"I'm *not* giving it to him."

"Well, Jake, looks like you've got your answer. If you wanna harass Gert about this some more, do it on your own time."

He glared at me, then walked out, yelling over his shoulder, "This isn't the last of the subject, Gert!"

When he was gone, she asked in her best Hitler-in-drag voice, "Did you honestly think I'd appreciate interference from *you?*"

"I doubt you ever appreciate anything." I turned around and left.

The rest of the afternoon I worked on Banty's royalty spreadsheets, which were now taking up a big chunk of hard drive. As the afternoon progressed, however, I became more anxious about my date with Steve, and my ability to concentrate eventually fell to somewhere around zero. I finally gave up and knocked off early.

All the way home, I debated about what to wear, and whether I should take off all my makeup and start over, and how I would handle the later part of the date. I hadn't been on an official date with a guy I actually had some level of attraction to in ages. Ed and I hadn't managed an honest-to-goodness date so far. The last few dates I'd had in Dallas were with men I'd met through my job, and I only accepted because I was beginning to get the urge to wear a wimple—and I'm not Catholic. All of those dates had ended with a sterile kiss, and no one was surprised, or disappointed.

With Steve, I had no idea how it might play out. Would he expect something besides a kiss? I kinda didn't think so because he's sort of conservative, but his wife had been dead almost three years, and he hadn't been out since then. The setup made me a little nervous, because if he got a little too over the top, I wasn't so sure I'd be able to resist. After all, I was pretty love-starved myself. But if I did anything like that, I'd blow it with Ed forever, and no matter how attractive I found Steve, I knew it would never be like it was with Ed.

The latter part of the drive home, I thought about Ed, and felt guilty for going out with Steve, even though Ed and I were technically broken up. Our earlier conversation replayed in my head and I came very close to being a crybaby about it. I wondered if some major part of my psyche was screwed up and that's why I didn't understand what he meant.

I remember seeing on *Oprah* that people learn love lessons by watching their parents, and there is no doubt my education was severely lacking. I can't remember Mom and Lurch exhibiting any affection for each other. I mostly remember Lurch carping and bitching about everything from how much the electric bill was to how lousy Mom is at painting. Which incidentally is bullshit. Mom can do most anything. She never fought back, but meekly took his criticism and allowed him to be a jerk. I dunno, but maybe I want to be independent because I'm so hell-bent not to let a guy treat me like that. I'm sure an analyst could set me straight, but who's got the time? Or the money?

When I pulled into the parking lot at the Windmills apartments, it was just after five. Tromping upstairs with my audit bag, which was stuffed with some of Banty's well files, I felt a trickle of sweat roll down my back. It's so damn hot in Midland, even in September, Pizza Hut could save big bucks on their electric bill by turning off their ovens and just sticking the pizzas outside for a few minutes.

Thinking about the air-conditioning in my dinky, tacky apartment, I groaned. It works about as well as a garden hose at a forest fire. Maybe for some people that wouldn't be such a problem, other than discomfort. For me, a woman who always indelicately sweats buckets, this is a major bummer. My makeup usually tries to melt off before I can even finish applying it.

Still, I was glad to get home a bit early. I'd have time to take a cool shower and fix my hair and redo my makeup before I met Steve for dinner at seven. I set the audit bag down and slid the key in the lock, but the door came open without me turning the knob. It swung inward slowly, creaking and groaning. I stared inside at the small living area, and my heart fell into the toes of my sensible mules.

The place had been ransacked. My gaze swept from the books littering the floor, to the magazines and photographs strewn across the icky couch with half wagon wheel armrests. In the galley-style kitchen, all the cabinet doors were open and my paltry supply of dishes were on the floor, in about ten bazillion pieces.

Listening intently, I didn't hear any sound at all coming from inside. Whoever had been there was long gone. I stepped in and picked my way through the rubble, made my way to my closet and checked my jewelry box. About the only thing I own that's worth more than diddly squat is a pair of ruby earrings I had made in China. Well, and my wedding ring, but I don't really count that, because even if it's worth something monetarily, it's got negative value to me.

The earrings were still there, nestled in their nice little Chinese silk box. I noted that my television and laptop computer weren't gone. Neither was my small Bobcat pistol, though it had been pulled out from its hiding place beneath the mattress. Definitely, whoever was in my apartment came looking for something specific and not to steal anything.

Glancing at the tea set I'd brought home from China, the one made with clay from the Yellow River, the one I'd especially coveted and gained a lot of satisfaction from owning, the one that was now lying in pieces on the floor, I felt vaguely queasy. And I randomly wondered why somebody looking for something feels compelled to break everything. Couldn't they just move things around a little?

So much for my leisurely shower and primp session. I went back outside and had a seat on the top step of the concrete stairs, fished my cell phone out of my purse and called Sam. I'd call Detective Garza in a little while, but first I wanted Sam to take a look and apply his magic FBI skills. He didn't answer at home, so I dialed his cell.

"Weston here," he said in a military-style bark.

"Sam, can you come over to my apartment?"

"Did you blow off Ed?"

"No."

"Then I'm afraid I can't make it." He hung up.

Damn, I hate it when he does that. I dialed again.

"Stop teasing me, she-devil. Whaddya want?"

"Somebody broke in and ransacked the place. I kinda wanted you to check it out before I call Garza."

"Did they take anything?"

"No, not that I can tell."

"Aw, hell, Pink, I have a date at seven. Why do you have to be such a pain in my ass?"

I started to protest, but he'd already hung up.

Less than ten minutes later, his late-model Beemer pulled into the parking lot. Watching him walk toward the stairs, dressed in a black suit with a white dress shirt and a colorful tie, his long hair bound at his neck, I decided maybe I would give Sam a call if me and Ed didn't work out. Not that I'd ever, in a million years, consider a relationship with him. But satisfying my curiosity about what he'd look like naked would be mighty nice.

Sam had on a pair of shades, those cool kind that surfer dudes wear. Guess it fits, because Sam is a nut for surfing. He told me once that he wants to retire at age fifty and open a surf shop in Hawaii. I watched him climb the stairs and come to a stop on the step where my feet rested, which put his crotch right at eye level.

"Are you gonna move and let me see what's up in there, or stare at my crotch? Makes no difference to me, but I gotta warn you, things can start to happen if you keep staring."

I stood and waved toward the door. "Be my guest, and I wasn't staring. Much."

He took off his shades and gave me a look. "Guess you must not be too scared if you've got sex on the brain."

I shrugged. "Guess so. I'm mostly just pissed off because whoever did this broke everything. They even tore up my books. What's up with that? Why rip the pages out?"

Sam walked in, wandered around awhile, picked up a few things, looked them over, then came back to where I was standing close to the door. "I think Tattoo Man is your guy."

"Why?"

"Ed told me the guy had oil-field mud on his boots." Sam held out his hand and displayed a small clod of reddish dirt. "This was on the floor in your bathroom. My guess is they haven't been able to locate Becker's information and he came to see if you have it, after all."

"But I don't have anything!"

"Are you sure Becker didn't hand you something, or slip something into your bag?"

I went to my purse and dumped it out on the kitchen counter. "This is the third time I've done this drill, but I'll look again, just to make you happy."

Sam watched me rummage through the contents. "Why do women always have fourteen thousand coins in the bottom of their purse?"

"Because it's a lotta trouble to get out my wallet and open the little zipper every time I get some change."

"Oh." He reached for the envelope of money Aunt Dru had given me, which I'd stuck back in my purse, intending to deposit it at my bank. "This is a lotta cash, Pink. You been dealin' again?"

"Very funny. My aunt gave it to me. Kinda blew my mind, because she's never done that before." I picked through a wad of Kleenex and some old gum wrappers and random receipts for everything from coffee to tacos, but didn't see anything I hadn't put in the purse myself. "There's nothing, Sam."

"Think hard, Pink. Whoever was here today is missing something, and they think you have it. Are you sure there wasn't something in the cake that maybe Garza missed? Maybe Becker really did put the information in it."

"I'm sure. Garza mutilated that cake and went through every crumb. There was a little plastic Spider-Man on top, but no way would somebody tear up my house to find a goofy toy, worth about twenty-five cents."

"Maybe he had something inside, a message or something."

"How? The lady at the Allbright's bakery said Becker didn't give her anything to put in the cake. There's no way he could have hidden something in Spider-Man."

"Are you sure the store has plastic Spider-Man figures for their cakes? Maybe the girl didn't understand why the cop was asking, and she knew she didn't put anything in the cake, but Spider-Man didn't register as the same type of thing." Sam obviously thought he was on to something. Before I could respond, he dialed Information, got the number at the store and called. "I'm supposed to get a Spider-Man cake for my kid, and I wondered if you guys do that." He paused, his blue gaze fixed to mine. "I see. So you actually put Spider-Man on there with icing. You don't have a little action figure or something like that?" Again he paused. "Oh, so if I wanted a three-D figure, I'd have to go get one on the toy aisle. Thanks." He hung up and gave me a triumphant smile. "There you go.

Becker went over and bought a Spider-Man, somehow used it to hide his information, then handed it to the bakery chick for the cake."

"This is blowing my mind."

"Becker was resourceful. So where is Spider-Man?"

"Mom kept it." My heart stood still and I felt dizzy. "Oh my God! Mom! If they did this to her house, she'll have to be committed."

Sam lifted his cell phone again and called. "Jane, everything okay at your place?"

I could hear Mom's voice from where I stood. She sounded hysterical—or pissed off.

"I'm at Pink's, and they did the same thing over here. Have you called the police?" He looked at me and shook his head. "Just got home? Okay, listen, Jane, don't call the police. We'll call Garza from here and then be over in a bit." He snapped the cell phone closed and looked at me. "You should go with me. She's crying."

Oh, man. "Is she crying like scared crying, or mad crying?"

"A little of both, I think."

"I'd like to get whoever did this and beat the snot outta them. Mom's worked her whole life for a nice house, and now, when she finally has one, somebody trashes it." Way more pissed off than frightened, I dialed Garza's cell number. As soon as he answered, I launched into a tirade about Tattoo Man.

When I wound down, he said quietly, "I'm not really surprised because Becker's car key fob had nothing in it. There's bound to be some other way he handed off the information, and they probably think you have it, even though you don't know it."

"Great. Just great." I looked around the apartment. "Do you wanna come look at this?"

"I'll send a couple of guys to collect evidence and write up a report for your insurance, but I don't think I need to be there."

"Tattoo Man did this to my mom's house, too."

"That's a shame. Your mother has a nice home." He sighed heavily. "I'll send some guys to her house, as well."

"Thanks, Detective."

I was about to tell him what we'd discovered about Spider-Man when he said, "You should know that before I could return the key to the evidence room, it disappeared."

I let that soak in for a moment, wondering why he'd told me, and wondering who would have lifted Becker's key while it was at the police station. Who *could* have lifted it at the police station? Who had access? "Garza, are you telling me there's a mole in the ranks?"

"I don't know. I really don't. Internal Affairs is looking into it, but in the meantime, if you come across anything else that might be of interest to the CIA, you need to call Washington and ask them what you should do with it. I'd rather you didn't pass this along to anyone, but I thought you should know, since they're targeting you."

I thanked him again, ended the call and told Sam what he'd told me.

His face formed into a frown while I talked, and when I finished, he said, "It's always a pissing contest between different agencies over jurisdiction, and local law enforcement never, ever wants to let go of something that happens on their turf. If Garza is passing you off to the CIA, it means he has orders from way up to stay out of it. Otherwise, there's no way he'd tell you something like that."

"What are you saying? That there is no mole?"

"Oh, I'm sure there's a mole, and that's part of the reason they're making Garza back off. They can't afford to lose sensitive information that may pass through the police station. Good thing you didn't mention Spider-Man."

The cops showed up just then, and we waited while they poked around. Then we answered some questions and I signed the report. After they were gone, I called the apartment manager and asked him to fix the busted door lock. As soon as he showed up, I grabbed my purse and followed Sam to his car. "Didn't you say you have a date at seven?"

He nodded as he started the engine. "I can still make it, so don't worry about it."

"I'm not worried. But I'm supposed to meet someone downtown at seven myself, and wondered if you'd drop me off before you go to your date."

He glanced at me from across the front seat as he slid his shades on. "Sounds mysterious."

"It's not. I'm having dinner with a friend."

"Male or female?"

"Male."

He pulled out of the space and drove away from my apartment complex, his hands on the wheel in his usual ten-two position, traveling at one mile an hour below the speed limit. "Is he gay?"

"No." Definitely not.

"Then he's potentially more than a friend, and Ed's gonna be pissed. Are you sure you want to do this?"

"Why would you care? You hate Ed."

"True, but it's a guy thing. If he can't be here to look after his interests, it's my duty to do it for him."

"You're kidding. Tell me you're kidding."

He stopped at a red light and glanced at me. "Have you and Ed done the big nasty more than three times?"

"Is that any of your business?"

"Of course not. Answer the question."

"Actually…no. In fact, we haven't done it at all. But not because we haven't tried. We have bad karma."

"It's gonna get worse if you go out with somebody else. Who is this guy?"

"Steve Santorelli."

"The senator?"

"The same."

Sam shook his head and drove through the intersection. "Did he call you up and ask you out?"

I gave him the history behind the date, and added, "I said yes when he asked several weeks ago, so I feel honor bound to go out with him."

"Does it strike you as coincidental that he called the day after the thing with Becker went down?"

"Yes, but I'm having a hard time matching it up in any way. Maybe he's just worried, and feels bad because he's the one who gave Becker my name." I didn't mention the part about Lorenzo. I don't know why. Maybe I just didn't feel like getting into it. I was worried about Mom, and anxious to get to her house so I could see how she was holding up.

"Something about this is making me nervous. Maybe I should cancel my date and go with you."

"Maybe I should jump off of a cliff onto jagged rocks." I turned my head and looked at him. "With bees on them."

"Okay, so I won't go. Just don't be blinded by the senator thing, Pink." He pulled up to the curb in front of Mom's house, killed the engine and looked at me. "It's clear the guy's after you, and until you make up your mind about Ed, anything's fair."

"What do you mean, make up my mind about Ed?"

Sam gave me one of his funny, lopsided smiles. "You're such a girl."

"Yeah, I was born that way."

"Don't you know, after you've had sex with a guy three times, you've made up your mind and you can't go back?"

Three times. Hadn't Steve said something about three times? I blinked at him. "Clarify 'going back'."

"It's the sex rule. This isn't the same as a one-night stand, or one of those two-week flings that fade away as quickly as they came up. If you start hanging out with a guy, get to be friends with him and have sex more than three times, it's a commitment. You can't go hang out with other guys until you break it off and stop having sex with him. Since you and Ed haven't…" He shrugged. "I guess it's up to you, Pink. I bet Ed's about to lose his mind, being stuck down there in the middle of nowhere while you're up here, unattached."

I didn't mention that Ed had dumped me that morning. I definitely, big-time, didn't want to get into that with Sam. Instead, I focused on his completely macho-man statement. Maybe this is the modern age, a time when women can do just about anything they set their mind to, but beneath it all, things must still be almost the same as they were a hundred million years ago, when Mr. Caveman dragged his woman back to the cave by her hair. "You're stone cold serious, aren't you?"

"Absolutely. Maybe I hate Ed, but I like you, and I can tell you got it bad for the guy. I don't want you to screw it up for yourself." He reached over and brushed my hair away from my face. "Just be careful, Pink."

What could I say? I said, "Okay," and got out of the car.

The police hadn't arrived at Mom's yet, but she must have been looking for them because she met us at the door. She wasn't crying anymore. She was furious. When she wants to, Mom can cuss like a sailor, but that afternoon, I heard her say some things that would make a sailor blush. After Sam checked out her house and found more of the red dirt, he sat her down and told her he suspected Tattoo Man was the culprit. Then she stopped cussing, looked at me and started crying again.

"Mom, come on, it's all going to be okay. Just tell us where you put Spider-Man, Sam will see that the CIA gets him and that'll be an end to it."

She cried harder and I became alarmed. "Mom?"

"I can't give him Spider-Man! I put it in that box of stuff

I left out for the Salvation Army. They picked it up when they came to get the Ping-Pong table. What on earth is this all about?" She looked around the living room, at the remnants of her Limoges collection, scattered in pieces across the dark hardwood floor, at the five hundred dollar elephant lamp she'd talked herself into buying out of the Neiman's catalog, his trunk and ears broken, and finally, her gaze landed on the portrait of me and her on the Great Wall. The painting had a gigantic gash running right through the middle of it, between us. I'm not gonna lie, it really creeped me out and sent my superstitious side into an uproar.

Staring at the painting, Sam said in an even voice, "It's almost like he wanted to send a message."

Mom and I jerked our attention back to him and she asked in a tight voice, "What kind of message?"

"If you have something, they want it, but at the same time, they want you to stay out of it." He stood and walked around the room, stepping over Mom's vases, her potted azalea and the porcelain foo dogs she'd bought in Xian. "I'll go to the Salvation Army first thing in the morning and get Spider-Man back."

"Sam, have you ever been in a Salvation Army store? Finding a little toy like Spider-Man would be close to impossible, they have so much stuff. Besides, it will probably be next week before they get him priced and out in the store."

Turning to face me, Sam said, "Well, then, I'll go round to the receiving dock and tell them your mother inadvertently left something sentimental in a box, and I need to get it back."

"There's no guarantee they'll be able to find it."

"Trust me, they'll find it." The doorbell rang and he went to let the cops in. They were the same ones who'd been at my apartment, so they didn't have to ask as many questions, and it didn't take them very long to scope out Mom's house, collect fingerprints and write up their report. When they were gone, Sam walked toward the foyer, stopped at the entryway and said, "Jane, I suggest you stay somewhere else tonight. This is going to drive you crazy, and right now, there's nothing you can do about it. Besides, although it's unlikely, someone may come back." He looked at me. "Same goes for you, Pink. Now, if you're ready, I've really gotta go."

I stood and went to Mom. She hugged me and sniffed a little, still weepy.

"Maybe I should cancel my plans for tonight."

"I'm fine," she said with a nasal voice from so much crying. "I'm going over to your aunt Fred's for the night." She let go of me and glanced toward the kitchen. "And first thing tomorrow, I'm hiring a new security company."

I knew she was even more upset than she let on because she never asked me about my plans for the evening. I hated to leave her, but if anyone could make Mom feel better, it was her baby sister, Fred.

Feeling torn, I finally followed Sam out to the car. As we drove away, he said, "I really do want you to keep away from your apartment. You can come over to my place."

Having stayed in Sam's cushy, comfortable guest room before, this was not an invitation I was tempted to turn down. "What about your date? Suppose you get lucky?"

He shrugged. "Don't see what that has to do with anything. We won't be in the guest room."

I made a face. "No way am I staying over while you're in bed with some chick. That's just icky."

"Suit yourself."

"But call me if you strike out, willya? I hate hotel rooms, and if I stay with Aunt Fred, she and Mom will give me lectures. It's entertainment for them."

"You don't have to sound so hopeful that I'll strike out. Give a guy a break. Since you won't have sex with me, I gotta go beg somewhere else."

"Is this supposed to elicit sympathy from me?"

"Yes. Did it work?"

"Sorry, but no."

He pulled up to the curb in front of the Stock Exchange, a downtown eatery that's enormously popular because they're the only game in town for fresh fish, flown in every day from the Gulf of Mexico. I'd suggested it to Steve because it's just down the street from the Hilton, where he was staying, and because it's one of Midland's better, nicer restaurants. I glanced at Sam as I reached for the door handle. "Thanks for coming over, and for the lift."

"Sure, Pink." He waited until I was out of the car, then rolled down the passenger window. "Remember what I told you."

I bent low and looked in at him. "I remember."

His gaze went over my shoulder. "Isn't that Santorelli?"

Glancing around, I saw Steve standing on the sidewalk outside the restaurant, his hands in the pockets of his suit trousers as he looked in the window of the closed barbershop next door. I turned back to Sam. "That's him."

"I don't like this, Pink. Got a bad feeling. Let me go get my date and come back and we can all have dinner together."

"Let me jump over a cliff, onto jagged rocks. With bees on them. With laser beams on their heads."

"All right, already. I get your point. Just call me if you have any trouble."

I stifled a smile. He was worse than any anxious father. "Okay, I'll call. Later, Sam." I turned and walked toward Steve, doing my best to ignore the fact that Sam still hadn't driven away.

Stepping up behind him, I met his eyes in the reflection of the window. "Hello, Steve."

He kept looking at me in the window. "Hi, Pink. Who's the Sammy Hagar lookalike?"

"My boss, Sam Weston."

"Any reason why he brought you down here tonight?"

"I'll tell you all about it over dinner."

Finally, he turned and looked at me directly. "If you don't mind, I found another place for dinner. One that's not quite so public."

I couldn't answer right away because I was too busy staring at him. Dressed in a charcoal-gray suit, he wore a pale-pink dress shirt and a beautiful silk tie that probably cost more than my monthly grocery budget. His coal-black hair was cut short, like I remembered, and the hot breeze ruffled it on top, making it a little messy. He stared back at me with those big, dark Italian eyes and I really had no problem at all guessing exactly what he was thinking.

Swear to God, it made me blush.

And I forgot what he said. "Did you say something?"

He took a step closer. "Lorenzo has a place south of here, a hunting lodge in an old ranch house, and he made arrangements for us to have dinner there."

I thought it sounded great, but rife with dangerous possibilities. Alone in an old ranch house with a guy like Steve—a widower who hadn't had sex in three years. And me, a divorcée who hadn't had sex in a year and a half. I kinda thought it would be like throwing a match on a puddle of gasoline and expecting it not to catch fire.

Still, what could I say? I couldn't very well come out and tell him I was scared to death to be alone with him because I didn't trust myself. So I said, "That sounds great," and followed him to a black Mercedes parked at the curb, about thirty feet in front of Sam, who was stopped in the no-parking part of the street.

With the car door open, I stepped closer to the curb and finally gave in to the temptation to look at Sam. He was scowling so hard he had a crease in his forehead. I ignored him and got in the car. Steve closed the door and went around to the driver's side.

Then Sam went commando on me, I guess because he saw I wasn't entering the crowded restaurant, but was getting into a car to be taken away to an unknown location. Just after Steve got in the driver's side, Sam opened my door and said gruffly, "Pink, I need to see you."

I glanced at Steve, who looked ready to die laughing, and said, "If you'll excuse me?"

"Certainly," he said, waving to Sam.

Sam glared at him, then stepped back so I could get out of the car. As soon as I was on my feet, I started to tell him just what I thought about his behavior, but before I could say a word, his expression changed to one I can only call scared shitless.

"Santorelli! Get out of the car! It's gonna blow!"

Steve came out of the car like a shot and we all ran back toward Sam's car farther down the short block. Just as we reached the cross street, the Mercedes exploded with a deafening boom and a blast of heat.

Chapter 8

Not only did Sam not get lucky, he didn't even get to go on his date. But then, neither did Steve and I. At least, not the sort of date we'd envisioned. Within minutes of the explosion, every fire truck in the city of Midland, along with at least six ambulances and a regular convoy of patrol cars, convened on Wall Street.

While Steve lingered toward the end of the block, talking on his cell phone, Sam and I waited for Garza to finish questioning the restaurant staff inside the Stock Exchange. The patrons were questioned by uniformed cops, then escorted out the back door, until no one remained in the building. Garza waved me and Sam and Steve inside, and told us to have a seat while he asked a thousand questions.

Detective Garza had hit the mother lode of cases that week, but this was the kind that could pave the road to the police chief's office. Once he realized he was dealing with the possible assassination of a United States senator, he went into hyperactive overdrive.

While he paced back and forth in front of us, he smoothed his bushy mustache, over and over. "You say you noticed a black box in the back seat, Mr. Weston, but how did you know it was a bomb?"

"Whoever made it is either an amateur or sloppy, because they left wires in view. I was with the FBI for a long time, and while I never worked any bomb cases personally, I had a lot of training. When I spied that box, and the wires hanging from the side, I just knew it was a bomb."

"How was it timed to go off at just the moment Pink and the senator got in the car?"

Sam leaned back in a chair, his weight resting on the back legs. "Most likely it was remotely controlled. Someone was watching and sent the charge when they were in the car. It must have had a long fuse because it didn't go off until we'd gotten away from it."

"Thank God for that," Garza said. He looked at me and smiled crookedly. "Your week's just not shaping up, is it?"

I returned his smile and shook my head.

He straddled a chair and leaned his forearms across the back. "Senator, why are you in Midland?"

"I came to take Pink out to dinner."

"You came all the way from Washington for a date?"

"Actually, I came from California. I'm on my way to Washington tomorrow."

"Who was aware of your visit?"

"My staff, my pilot, Pink and David Lorenzo."

I saw Sam's eyebrows shoot up and he gave me a quizzical look. I shrugged in answer.

"We'll question everyone, of course, but I don't see Mr. Lorenzo blowing up his own car, with a senator inside. The man's not stupid, after all." Garza looked at me. "Seems clear that Pink couldn't have done it because she was with Mr. Weston." He looked again at Steve. "I'm inclined to doubt your pilot would have done it, so that leads me to wonder if the bomb was intended for you at all. Maybe it was placed there for Lorenzo and the bomber didn't know you'd be driving the car."

"Could be," Sam agreed, "but the timing is crucial. If someone was observing the car, waiting for just the right moment to blow it up via remote control, and their intended victim was Lorenzo, they wouldn't have detonated it, because Lorenzo wasn't in it. If the senator was the intended victim, why wait until he drove downtown, parked, got out, then got back in? Why not blow up the car as soon as he pulled out of Lorenzo's compound?"

While I was pondering the obvious logic of what Sam said, they all three turned to look at me. Moving my gaze from one man's eyes to the next, I realized what they were thinking. "You think *I'm* the intended victim? Why would anybody want to blow me up?"

"Maybe they don't like you checking into those oil field thefts," Sam suggested.

"I thought you didn't take that client," Garza said.

"After Becker got murdered, I changed my mind."

Steve asked, "What sort of client are you talking about?"

I briefly explained, although I left out the part about Banty thinking the culprit was Lorenzo.

"What makes you think the money from the stolen oil is going to terrorists?" Steve asked.

"Actually, my client suggested it as a possibility, and maybe it's a long shot, but the money has to be coming from somewhere, doesn't it? And with the investigation going on down here, I imagine they've checked all the financial institutions for large cash outlays. They haven't found anything yet, or they wouldn't still be here."

Garza said, "We'll know more after the bomb guys and the fire department finish their investigation and we find out what kind of bomb it was. I hate to say it, Pink, but if it does turn out to be a remote-controlled device, it's looking like you were the one they meant to hit."

I shivered, thinking about someone out there who would kill me. It took me back to how I'd felt during the whistle-blower thing—threatened, because I was doing the right thing and the right thing was going to ruin someone very bad. But this was different. Greed is one thing—pure evil is another.

Steve stood and reached for my hand. He pulled me up and looked at Garza. "I think you've got everything you need from us, Detective. If you have any further questions for me, I'll be back in Washington by tomorrow afternoon."

Garza got to his feet and shook Steve's hand. "We'll do our best to find out who did this." Then he turned to Sam and shook his hand. "Thanks for the explanations about the bomb, and I have to commend you for saving two people's lives."

Sam looked halfway embarrassed. He nodded and moved toward the door. We all went out into the cool night air, which had cleared of smoke, even though the destroyed car still emitted small puffs.

Steve said to Garza, "Until you're done with this investigation, I think it would be best if no names show up in the media."

Garza looked at the local news vans parked half a block away, behind the fire engines, and said, "I'll do my best, Senator." He gave us all a nod, then turned and headed off toward the fire chief.

After the detective was gone, Sam said, "Pink, you better come home with me."

Steve said quietly, "I'll see she gets home."

"She can't go home. Someone trashed her place today."

With an expression of surprise and worry, Steve looked at me. "Was anything taken?"

"Nothing. They trashed Mom's house, as well."

"What do you suppose they were looking for?"

"I'm not sure. The only thing left from the cake, besides actual cake, was a small Spider-Man figure."

"Was it taken?"

"No, because Mom put him in a box that went to the Salvation Army."

"Wonder what's up with Spider-Man?"

Sam explained about the key lacking any information, and how it had disappeared from the police station. "That means the information is still out there, somewhere. It's possible that Spider-Man doesn't have it, but all the same, I'm going to retrieve him, first thing in the morning."

Steve turned to me again. "Do you have a gun?"

Great. I was back to the gun issue. "Unfortunately, yes."

"Got her a Beretta Bobcat," Sam said proudly, as if buying me something that can kill was a good thing. "Needs some practice, but she does okay."

Steve stared at me for a bit, a small smile playing around his lips. "Wonder why that doesn't surprise me."

Sam withdrew his keys from his pocket. "I'm beat, and I'm ready to go home. Do you need a ride?"

"No, thanks. If Pink's up for it, we'll walk over to Mario's and have Italian."

"Sure, Steve," I said, although I wasn't the slightest bit hungry. Narrowly escaping death by a bomb hadn't been great for my appetite. Still, I wanted to talk to him, face-to-face, and if he was leaving in the morning, this might be my only chance.

Sam rested his hand on my shoulder. "When you're ready, call me and I'll come pick you up. You're staying with me tonight. Understand?"

"You're the boss."

He turned and walked away, toward the Beemer. As soon as he stepped across the police line, a reporter stuck a microphone in his face. Sam brushed past, got in the car and drove off.

I felt Steve's hand wrap around mine and tug. When I turned to look, he whispered, "Let's sneak around the back before they can catch us."

I nodded in agreement and we took off. We crossed three empty parking lots and didn't slow down until we were on the street behind Midland Center, which is Midland's answer to a convention center. There was no traffic, not unusual for downtown Midland on a weeknight. Other than Mario's and the Stock Exchange, there's not much to do within the few square miles of tall buildings that make up the city core. No shops, no bars, no life. Just a lot of sleeping Xerox machines.

"Well, this has been an unusual date so far."

"Yeah, Steve, you really know how to blow a girl away."

He laughed. "I should stop and call Dave. He'd probably like to hear about his car before the cops show up at his door."

"Go ahead," I said, heading for a park bench in the plaza next to Midland Center. After we sat down, he pulled a cell phone out of his pocket and made the call. While he told Lorenzo what had happened, I couldn't help listening, and it occurred to me that they seemed like better friends than just old college buddies.

"Come on, don't tell me you failed to take out the optional bomb-in-the-back-seat coverage?" He paused. "They canceled it after the last bomb? Bummer." In the dim glow from a park light filtering through the tree above us, I saw him look at me and smile. "Thanks again, Dave. I'll be in touch tomorrow." He ended the call and slipped the cell phone back into his pocket.

"Didn't sound like he was too worried about it. How is it that a guy isn't worried about a bomb in his back seat?"

"Trust me, he's worried. It's just easier to deal with creepy, scary things by laughing about them."

"I see what you mean." I took a breath and ventured the question I'd been dying to ask since his phone call the day before. "Steve, do you know that Dan Becker was investigating David Lorenzo?"

He stared off across the street for a while, then said, "I know, but it was pointless. There is no way David would be behind any kind of terrorism, much less an organization like Al Qaeda." He glanced at me with a hard look in his dark eyes. "Becker lost his focus, Pink. He got caught up in the fact that Dave converted to Islam."

"Did he have any other prospects?"

Steve turned his full attention to me. "I don't know."

"Maybe Spider-Man will know."

"Maybe."

I looked down at his hands resting against his thighs, and noticed he had on his wedding ring, on his right hand. I remembered reading once that widows and widowers change their wedding rings from the left to the right hand. At the time, I thought it was sweet, but looking at that ring on Steve's hand made me want to cry.

Why was I there, with him? What could he possibly see in me that was remotely close to what he'd seen in his wife? From all accounts, she was amazing and brilliant and beautiful. I bet she never sweated so bad her makeup melted.

"I'll take it off if it bothers you."

I looked up, into his handsome face, and before I could tell him that I liked that he loved her so much he still wore her ring, he pulled me into his arms and whispered, "Pink, there's something about that near-death experience that's sending me into overdrive." Then he kissed me, and I kinda knew what he meant because my libido jumped off the page and ran around the block three or four times.

That kiss may have been the longest in history. Before it was over, we'd managed to get to our feet, with his hand inside my blouse, inside my bra. I'm not sure how I did it so fast, or why, but I'd loosened his tie and unbuttoned his shirt.

He was warm and solid and very slightly hairy. And our heights were close enough that his erection pressed against my hootus in just the right place. A couple more minutes and I'd have climaxed, fully clothed, right there in a public plaza. It was blowing me away, the intensity of it, and nothing short of lightning striking me dead could have made me stop.

Maybe Steve felt that way, too, and maybe it freaked him out as much as it did me. He broke the kiss and stared at me, his breath coming fast and hard.

The spell was broken and I stepped back to hurriedly button my blouse, embarrassed beyond belief over what I'd just done. Good God. Talk about desperation. "I'm sorry, Steve. I can't believe I got that carried away."

He didn't say anything. I watched him button his shirt, then slide the tie from around his neck and stuff it into his pocket. He held out his hand and said, "Let's eat."

We walked to Mario's in silence because try as I might, I couldn't find the right thing to say. And maybe I was a little afraid that if I opened my mouth, I'd say to hell with eating, let's go make out some more. I don't know, but maybe that's the same reason he didn't talk.

Once we got to Mario's, we'd both cooled off enough to make small talk. At a back table in the dark restaurant, with a red checkered tablecloth and a candle in an old Chianti jug, we talked, sidestepping any mention of what had happened in Midland Plaza. But it was there, tension humming through the air in great waves. We both had lasagna with a nice bottle of wine, and finished by splitting a slice of cheesecake. Then it was time to go, and all I could think about was him leaving the next day and I'd probably never see him again.

Outside, we started walking back to the Hilton, where I would call Sam to come and get me.

We were almost there when Steve stopped me in the middle of the sidewalk and said, "Look, Pink, I understand you're going out with the lawyer, but you said yourself it's not serious yet. I don't know how you feel, but I gotta tell you, I've never, my whole life, had anything happen to me like what happened over there in the park an hour and a half ago. Maybe it's because of the bomb, but I don't think so. I hate it that we wasted time talking about bullshit, when we should have been talking about what matters to us, and getting to know each other."

"So what do you want to do?"

"I want you to come upstairs with me."

My fear of being alone with him must have shown because he quickly added, "You're not ready and I know that, so how about we lay to rest any thoughts of sex and just go up and talk?"

Okay, so I'm probably the most naive woman on the planet, but I believed we really could go up there and just talk.

And we did, for a very long time. But then he kissed me again, and one thing led to another, and I will always wonder if I'd have lost my head enough to go all the way with Steve Santorelli on our very first date. Guess I'll never know, because just about the time he had my blouse off, and I had his shirt off, with his trousers half unzipped, my cell phone rang.

It took a superhuman effort to pull away from him and answer it, but I had to. With Mom all upset, and Tattoo Man on the loose, along with Big Mama and her rat dog, I didn't think it was prudent to miss any calls.

Sure enough, it was Mom. "Pink, where are you?"

Lying is not an option with Mom. Never has been. I could be around the world, in freakin' Australia, do something she didn't approve of, then lie about it, and she would instantly know I was lying. I'd tried to perfect my technique, but it didn't help. So I'd given up, years ago. They should probably hire Mom to interrogate suspected spies. "I'm at the Hilton."

My hope that she'd assume I got a room there because my apartment was unsafe was dashed instantly. "Are you alone?"

"No."

"Who's with you?"

"A friend. Someone you don't know."

"For heaven's sake, Pink, don't be coy. It doesn't suit you at all. I talked to Sam after I saw the news, which incidentally scared the hell out of me and thanks for calling your poor, old mother and telling me you're all right, and he told me you were out with Santorelli."

Poor? Old? Whatever. I mumbled an affirmative.

Mom sighed, one of those long-suffering, I Did My Best and I Don't Know Where I Went Wrong sighs. "Oh, Pink."

"Was that the only reason you called, Mom? Because I'd really like to have the Oh, Pink conversation later on in life. Like never. Is never good for you?"

"Fine. That's not the reason I called, anyway."

Shocked and awed, I sat up straight. "It's not?"

"You're a big girl, and if you wanna sleep with a senator, who am I to say you shouldn't? I'm only your mother."

"We came here to talk in private." Among other things.

"Right. Just do me a favor and say no if Barbara Walters calls for an interview."

"Mom! I'm serious!"

"Okay, okay. I don't wanna know, anyway. There are some things in life a mother shouldn't know."

"So why are you calling, if not to check up on me?"

"Pink, I have an idea. I've been thinking all night about that little Spider-Man toy. Fred says they won't give stuff back, no matter how hard you beg. With all the garage sales she has, she gives a lot of stuff to the Salvation Army, and she's accidentally given them a few things she didn't mean to. Said they made her wait until they'd priced it and put it out in the store, and she had to buy it back."

"Sam will make them give it to him, Mom."

"Suppose someone else gets to it first?"

"No one knows about Spider-Man except us. Stop fretting."

"Nobody knew about those keys, either, but they're gone, all the same. Sam says we need to get Spider-Man to the CIA as soon as possible. Then, if anybody asks, we can say they have it. So, here's what I'm thinking. Every cop in town is over there on Wall Street, working that explosion. Let's go tonight and find Spider-Man on our own."

"Break into the Salvation Army? Have you lost your mind?"

"Have you forgotten what they did to our homes today? And can you honestly think that car explosion doesn't have something to do with all of this? I'd say it's worth the risk. Besides, what cop is gonna arrest us for breaking into a store with a lot of old junk in it?"

"I can think of one," I said, remembering my humiliating arrest several weeks earlier, when I was neck deep in controversy over the whistle-blower thing. "That cop would arrest his mother for jaywalking."

"If we get nabbed, we'll call Garza."

"No, Mom! It's too risky, and you don't even know if the stupid toy is what they were looking for."

"Pink, I'm going, with or without you."

I had a sudden mental image of Mom in jail with a group of tough women. She'd kick their ass. I owed it to all those women to keep Mom out of the slammer. I took a deep breath, glanced at Steve, who was lying there, without his shirt, staring at me. "Aw, hell, Mom. Pick me up in thirty minutes." I closed the phone and tossed it onto the bedside table.

"Off to do a little breaking and entering?"

"What choice do I have? She says she'll go, with or without me."

Steve reached up and traced circles against my back. "I'll go with you."

"No, you won't. If Mom and I get caught, we can most likely weasel out of it. If you get caught, it's a national scandal."

"You're right, but I feel like a wimp, staying here while you go commit a felony."

I glanced at his hard, lean body. He was no wimp. I'd wondered how he stayed in shape, and he said he worked a lot on the farm. Steve Santorelli was the furthest thing from a farm boy I could imagine, but he really had grown up on a farm. It happened to be the largest privately owned farming operation in California, but it was a farm, nonetheless.

"If you get arrested," he said, "call me and I'll come bail you out."

"Thanks. It would be a perfectly bizarre end to a perfectly weird date, wouldn't it?"

He sat up and nuzzled my neck. "Maybe it's been weird, but it's been remarkable. I don't usually get blown up on a first date. Of course, I haven't had a first date since I asked Lauren out, at least eight years ago."

I turned slightly and came almost nose-to-nose with him. "You probably think I'm the worst tease on Earth, but it's not intentional. I have to be honest with you, Steve, and the truth is, I'm awesomely attracted to you, but I can't turn my back on Ed. Sleeping with you would mean the end of any possibilities, and I'm not ready to give that up. Do you understand?"

"You're not coming back, are you?"

"No."

"Suppose I told you I really want you to, because there are a lot of things I think we should talk about."

"Like we were talking just before Mom called?"

"No, Pink. Like two adults who share a mutual attraction that deserves exploring."

"I like you, Steve. A lot. But there are things you don't know about me, and I'm afraid you have an impression of me that's not wholly accurate."

"Is this the part where you try to talk me out of wanting you, so you can walk away and not feel guilty?"

"No. This is the part where I try to make you see that I'm not who you think I am."

"Explain it to me, Pink."

Pushing away from him, I sat on the edge of the bed and stared across the room, at the cheesy painting of a west Texas sunset with a pumpjack. "I've only ever been seriously involved with two men. The first was my high school sweetheart, and the second was my ex-husband. I threw over my high school sweetheart for the ex-husband when I was in college at UT Austin. They were polar opposites, and I realized recently I was attracted to each of them because they appealed to different sides of me. Problem was, they didn't complement all sides of me. Does that make sense?"

"Does to me. Go on."

"I also realized, the reason I couldn't make it with either of them was because I just didn't love them enough. I don't think I have it in me to love someone the way I'm supposed to."

"How do you think you're supposed to love someone?"

Turning back toward him, I lay down and propped my head in my hand. "Wholeheartedly, with no reservations. Maybe I'm too much of a perfectionist, or maybe I expect too much, but with both of them, I found myself wishing they'd be different."

"Is that why you divorced your husband?"

"Actually, I divorced him because he cheated on me with prostitutes, but the real truth is, we hadn't been happy for a long time."

Steve turned his head and looked up at me. "Do you think Ravenaldt can be what you want?"

"I don't know, and that's why I don't want to get seriously involved with anyone. It's not fair to him, or you."

He returned his gaze to the ceiling and smiled wryly. "Are you up for getting slightly involved?"

"What do you mean?"

"Will you see me again? Can I call you?"

I reached over and smoothed the hair on his chest. "Is that really what you want? I don't think so. I think you want someone to fall in love with, the way you loved Lauren. You want to build a life with someone, have kids and grow old together. I want that for you, Steve. I just don't think I'm the one you're looking for."

He captured my hand in his and squeezed tightly. "How can you be sure? You barely know me, just like I barely know you. Suppose we should be together? What if we could be great together? If you walk away now, we'll never know, will we?"

Why did he have to go and make it so much harder? Why did he have to dangle that damn carrot in front of me? Why did I have to want it all, then be too cynical to go look for it?

"All right, Steve, if that's what you can be happy with for now, I'm up for being friends."

"Don't take this the wrong way, but I'm a guy, so cut me a break. Any chance of me seeing you naked in the future?"

I gave him a stern look. "According to the male rules of sex, I could only have it with you three times, and after that, I have to make up my mind if I'm in or out."

He gave me a cocky smile. "Just gimme those three times and you'll be putty in my hands."

I rolled my eyes as I stood and buttoned my blouse. "If men could do half the things with their penises they claim they can, we'd have world peace."

He sat up and grinned at me, and I swear, I wished I could snap a picture, just so I could take it out later and remember how unbelievably hot he looked. And kinda cute, in a sexy, sensual way. His black hair was way past messy, which for some reason I always like on a guy. He had a bare hint of a five o'clock shadow, which made him look a little dangerous. The light sprinkling of black hair on his chest sloped down to the waistband of his trousers. He was leaning back against his arms, which made the muscles stand out.

"You're staring."

"Men stare. Why shouldn't women?"

"Because it sends a signal to the harbinger of world peace and things get complicated."

My gaze dropped to his trousers. "I see."

"Are you sure you don't want to come back?"

"It's not a question of wanting to. I have to go do something illegal with Mom, then I need to get some sleep, and then I have to go to work in the morning."

He got up and came around to me. He closed his hands on my shoulders, drew me near and kissed my forehead. "I'll call you. Please be careful, Pink."

"All right, Steve." I raised my face to his and kissed him. "Thanks for…everything." I pulled away and walked out of the room, slightly freaked by how hard it was to leave. In spite of what I had to qualify as an unbelievable evening, I was almost bummed about it. I'd thought it would make it easier for me, might get rid of this nagging attraction I felt for Santorelli. Instead, all it did was confuse the issue. I thought about Ed, and what his reaction would be when I told him I'd gone out with Steve.

It wasn't going to be good. Even though I'd resisted sleeping with Steve, it probably wouldn't matter to Ed. He'd see it as another indication of my lack of commitment, and that would be the end of it.

I was a bit panicky, thinking about it, but I told myself that I shouldn't allow myself to be coerced into anything, and if Ed wanted to lay down an ultimatum—throw in with him and only him, walk down the road to permanent commitment, or lose him for good—then I'd have to tell him I was okay with calling it quits. I just wasn't ready to jump off into a long-term thing, even with Ed, as crazy about him as I was.

At the end of the hall, I punched the elevator button, then waited for what seemed an inordinate amount of time for the car to reach me. Finally, the ding sounded and the doors opened. I heard voices, so moved aside to let the people out. A man and a woman stepped off, their arms twined around one another, and their focus on each other so complete they never noticed me standing there. It was a safe bet they would be getting to know each other in the biblical sense within the next three minutes.

The elevator door closed before I could get on, but it barely registered. I was too busy staring in wide-eyed shock. From my spot there by the elevator, I watched Gert trip down the hall with her ex-husband, Jake Hollingsworth. The man she said she found so repugnant, she'd rather sleep with Moby Toby.

I punched the button again, the doors opened, and as I got on the elevator, I couldn't help a chuckle. By the time I reached the ground floor, I was laughing.

Thirty minutes later, after Mom drove me to my ransacked apartment so I could change into dark clothes and retrieve my little Bobcat, we parked a few blocks from the old building that houses the Salvation Army. I'd been there lots of times to drop off old stuff. The building is on the southeast edge of downtown, just south of the railroad tracks, in a warehouse area that's completely deserted at night. Except for the occasional vagrant.

"I'm hoping my box of stuff is still in the back so we don't have to go inside. Picking locks isn't my forte."

"Me, neither. But Mom, won't the stuff all be inside the building? They wouldn't leave it outside, would they?"

"I don't know, but every time I come down here, there's an enormous amount of stuff on that loading dock, and the receiving room inside is always crammed full. I can't imagine they move the stuff in every night."

"Wouldn't it get wet when it rains?"

Mom slanted me a look. "This is Midland, remember? Average rainfall of ten inches, and we get it all in three days. But there is an overhang above the dock, if it makes you feel better. Anyway, I thought we'd look there first, and if we can't find the box, then we'll figure out how to get inside."

"It's a lame plan, Mom. Sam would fire you at the FBI."

"Yeah, well, this is sort of spur of the moment. If I plan a bank heist, I'll give it a little more forethought, okay?"

At the back of the building, we hesitated around the corner because a light illuminated the loading-dock area. "Uh, Mom, we could probably get a tan, that light's so bright."

Without saying a word, Mom reached down to the ground, picked up a golf ball-size rock, aimed and hurled it at the light. I couldn't believe it then and I can't believe it now, but she nailed that sucker dead-on. With the soft sound of lightbulb glass hitting the pavement, the loading dock was blanketed in semidarkness, now just dimly lit by a streetlight some twenty yards away. "Whoa, Mom! How'd you do that?"

"Used to have to chuck rocks at snakes when I was a kid growing up on the farm where my dad was a hand. Daddy wouldn't get me a slingshot, because I was a girl, so I learned how to hit 'em without one. You didn't get a second chance with rattlers. If you missed, all it did was piss them off, and they'd bite you for sure."

"Wow, Mom. You rock." I grinned at her.

"If there was a law against bad puns, you'd be doing time."

We moved toward the dock and stopped at an eight-feet-tall chain-link gate. "Mom, how long's it been since you climbed a fence like this?"

"Not long enough." She slipped her hand into the pocket of her denim jacket and withdrew a pair of wire cutters.

"My, my, aren't you the well-prepared burglar?"

"Gimme a hand, will you?"

I bent each section back as she cut through, managing to nick my hand in several different places in the process. "Mom, do you remember when I had my last tetanus shot?"

"Three years ago, right before we went to China."

"So I'm not going to get lockjaw and die?"

"Not tonight, no." She slid the wire cutters back into her pocket, then withdrew a small flashlight and handed it to me.

"Who are you? Mary Poppins? Have you got a flower arrangement and a hat stand in that pocket, too?"

"Go on through the fence, Pink, and stop kidding around."

"Okay, Ma." I did as she said, then waited for her to join me. We crept toward the loading dock, which was littered with boxes and miscellaneous furniture and odds and ends such as a lawn mower and a tricycle, all protected from the elements by the extended overhang. I'm always amazed they can make any sense at all of the awesome amount of stuff they get. That night, I wondered how we'd ever find a three-inch action figure in the mountain of clothing and boxes and old appliances.

Part of the dock was a wooden platform, and when I walked across it, I felt it sag beneath my weight. I decided I'd make a donation to the Salvation Army, a monetary one, so they could get a new platform. That would be in addition to the money we needed to give them to repair the fence we'd annihilated.

Mom shone her flashlight around the area, searching for the box she'd left on the curb that morning. After about five minutes of stumbling about, stubbing our toes on things, she declared, "The damn thing's not here! Wouldn't you just know it? Now what are we gonna do?"

"Hit the road before we get caught?"

"We have to break in."

"I don't think so, Mom. Let's just leave now, and Sam can get Spider-Man tomorrow, like we planned in the first place."

Ignoring me, she spied the white Salvation Army truck,

parked just to the side of the dock, and even in the near darkness I could see the gleam in her eye.

"Mom, we can't break into the truck. Wire cutters won't break a lock."

She jumped down to the ground and walked around to the back of the truck. I heard her whisper, "Pink! Come here!"

I went round and saw her point to the handle on the door. "It's not locked. Raise it up."

"I'll do it, but this is making me nervous. Bad karma."

"You and your karma. Just open the damn thing, will you?"

I hoisted myself up to the truck's bumper, reached for the handle and tugged with all my strength, which isn't much because I'm a CPA and don't do a lot in the way of physical labor, unless sharpening pencils counts. Still, weakling though I am, I managed to lift the heavy door and it rolled back on its tracks, much like a garage door.

After Mom climbed up and joined me, we made our way to the front of the truck, poking in boxes, looking inside a washing machine, turning over rugs and clothes. We were encouraged when we saw the old Ping-Pong table, and hit pay dirt about two-thirds of the way. "Here it is!" she exclaimed. I moved close and shone my flashlight in the box while she dug around.

"Hey! Isn't that my Stevie Ray Vaughan T-shirt?" I reached to get it, but she slapped my hand.

"It's not good for anything but a rag. There's a hole in it big enough to drive this truck through."

"You're harsh, Mom. I loved that shirt. It was from his last tour before he died."

Mom made a weird noise that indicated she didn't give a flying rat's ass about my T-shirt. Then she pulled her hand out of the box and held it up with a look of triumph on her face. "Spider-Man is back."

I took it from her and inspected it closely, looking for any indication that it was anything more than a cheesy little plastic figure. I didn't see anything that would lead me to believe he held any sort of state secrets. "Mom, I hate to say it, but I think this is a bust. Nobody's searching for this, because he's got nothing to say."

"*Au contraire*," a voice said from outside the truck, startling me so badly I jumped.

I shoved Spider-Man into the left front pocket of my jeans, then hastily pulled the Bobcat out of the right.

"Who is it?" Mom whispered.

"Unless I miss my guess, it's Big Mama."

We heard a high-pitched yip.

"And Boris."

Once again, that bad-karma premonition had been right on the mark. Maybe one of these days I'd pay attention to it.

Chapter 9

It took all of five seconds for Big Mama to relieve me of the Bobcat. As soon as she stepped around to the back of the truck, I pointed the pistol at her and she pointed hers at Mom. "They told me you can't shoot, and I'm a sharpshooter, Pinks. If you don't toss that gun over here, I'll have no choice but to shoot your mama. Don't make me do that. I'm getting down-right fond of her."

Hating to give up our protection, lousy shot though I am, but seeing I had no choice, I tossed it toward the end of the truck and it landed next to a vegetable crate filled with very ugly hats.

She set Boris down on the truck's wide loading platform and reached for the gun. "Nice weapon." She glanced at the hats. "Who gives this kind of garbage? Do they think poor people have no taste?" Then she looked up at me again. "Give Boris the toy."

The tiny dog picked his way through the truck and stopped

at my feet. He yipped and I took Spider-Man out of my pocket. I looked at it again, ignoring Boris. "What's so special about this?"

"His eyes. One of them is a computer microchip. Very clever of Mr. Becker, wasn't it?"

I inspected the eyes and could see that one was slightly different. Yeah, it was clever of Dan Becker. It was freakin' brilliant. I remembered how passionate he'd been about me getting the cake, and had wondered why he'd continued the lie, even when he knew he was dying. Now I knew. It wasn't a lie. He'd died trying to get Spider-Man into the right hands.

I looked at Big Mama, who stood there waiting for Boris. "How'd you figure it out?"

"I heard there was nothing in the key fob, and Spider-Man was the only other possibility. Problem was, I had no clue where he might be."

"So you trashed our homes to find him?"

She shook her head. "Tattoo Man did that. In fact, he showed up at your place just as I was finishing my look-see." Appearing smug and superior, she said with disdain, "Most men simply don't have the finesse women have."

"How'd you know we'd be here tonight?"

"That's for me to know and you not to know. Now hand Spider-Man to Boris and we'll be on our way."

I bent down, Spider-Man in my outstretched hand, but something wouldn't let me do it. Whatever was on that computer chip was important enough that a man had died trying to pass it to people who could use the information to keep America safe. I had a mental vision of those towers crumbling, of a fanatical man with evil eyes, and God. I know it's weird, and I was probably delusional from stress, but I swear I could see God, in my mind, sitting up on a big chair, with long white robes and a long white beard, pointing His finger at me, demanding I refuse to hand over Spider-Man.

In a moment of blind impulse, I faked a stumble and allowed the small toy to fly out of my hand, hoping he would land in the middle of all the junk and it would be impossible to find him without emptying half the truck's contents.

Unfortunately, I missed the mark. As if I'd aimed, the damn thing shot through the air and bounced off Big Mama's extremely humongous breasts. So much for obeying God. No doubt He was hugely disappointed in me.

Mom grabbed my shirt and hauled me up next to her. "Nice try, but no cigar," she whispered while Big Mama bent to retrieve Spider-Man. "What should we do?"

I shrugged in answer.

"Thanks, ladies. I really wondered where you put the little guy." She made a kissy noise and Boris leaped into her hand.

We watched her turn to leave, but at exactly that moment, a shot rang out. Mom and I started violently, then sank to a crouch, hiding behind the boxes. I heard a man yell, "Drop to the ground, *now!*"

I peeked over the box and saw Big Mama take off, but I couldn't tell where the man was, so I crawled to the back and poked my head out, ignoring Mom, who was hysterically whispering for me to come back.

Big Mama looked to be cornered up on the loading dock. The doors into the warehouse were locked, and the gate at the other end of the dock was blocked by a refrigerator. The faceless man yelled again, "Drop to the ground!" Several more rounds were fired, but the guy was either a really lousy shot or the big woman was the luckiest broad in the world. After all, her wide bulk made an easy target.

I turned and saw two dark shadows moving along the outside of the fence. Then I saw one of them raise his arm and fire at the other. No wonder the first guy couldn't hit Big Mama. He was too busy dodging bullets from the second guy. Who was he? Big Mama's backup?

Eventually, the first guy gave up trying to dodge the second guy's bullets, and fled. I kept my eye on Big Mama, and held my breath when she ran across that wooden platform. Maybe it would collapse and she'd be hurled to the ground. Me and Mom could take her, and I could grab the Bobcat and shoot her backup.

But the platform held, barely sagging when she ran across it. Damnation. While I watched helplessly, she sprinted down the asphalt drive, then nimbly slipped through the hole Mom had made in the fence. Man, a big woman can run like the wind when someone's shooting at her.

The second guy ran with her. Then the first guy reappeared, chasing them, firing off rounds as he went.

I jumped to the ground and turned to help Mom down, but she jumped just behind me. "Let's get outta here, Pink."

She didn't have to say it twice. I ran with her, followed her through the hole in the gate after I insisted she go first, and hauled ass down the street, in the opposite direction from Big Mama and the mystery men. We were almost to Mom's car when I heard a man yelling for us to stop.

"You think he's gonna shoot us?" Mom asked breathlessly, never slowing down.

"Are you gonna shoot us?" I yelled over my shoulder.

"Pink! Stop running, dammit! Of course I'm not going to shoot you."

I put the skids on and turned around, my shock complete. "Steve? What are you doing here?"

He caught up to us and stopped just in front of me, breathing hard. "Did you seriously think I'd let you come over here by yourself?"

"Well, yeah, I guess I did." I glanced at Mom, who was bent at the waist, dragging wheezing breaths into her lungs. "Mom, this is Senator Steve Santorelli. Steve, this is my mom, Jane Pearl."

"Nice to…meet you," Mom said, finally raising up, shaking his hand. "Too bad you didn't get…Big Mama."

Steve's eyes widened. "*You're* Pink's mom?"

"Damn straight," she said, dropping his hand. "Got the stretch marks to prove it."

He kept staring at her, until I finally asked, "What's up? You look like you're about to be sick."

He shook his head as if to clear it, and said, "Nothing. It's nothing. Are you both all right?"

Mom and I nodded.

"I'd have gotten here sooner, but the car I borrowed from the hotel was blocked by a beer truck and I couldn't get out." Turning to look over his shoulder, he said with an element of disbelief in his voice, "I can't figure out how they knew about Spider-Man. Did you tell anyone besides Detective Garza?" He looked back at me and Mom.

"I didn't even tell him. After he said Becker's key was missing from the evidence room, I thought it best to get Spider-Man on my own, then hand him over to the Feds."

Mom pulled a face in the semidarkness. "Best laid plans, right?" She dabbed at her forehead with the hem of her jacket, which she'd taken off and tied around her waist. "Now we'll never know what Dan Becker found out."

Steve continued to stare at Mom, and I was dying to know why, but I wouldn't ask him in front of her. I'd have to wait until later.

"Didn't you pay a lot of money for that gun, Pink?" she asked.

"Yes, and now it's gone."

"No, it's not," Steve said, reaching into the pocket of his black pants and withdrawing the Bobcat. "She tossed it over her shoulder while she was running."

"Thanks." I took the gun and stuck it in my own pocket. "Where did she go?"

"She got in a big Cadillac and took off. The other guy ran off behind those warehouses across the street and I lost him."

Mom yawned. "I'm outta here." She glanced at me. "Are you coming with me to Fred's?"

"No, thanks, Mom. I told Sam I'd stay over at his house tonight."

"You can't go wake him up at one-thirty in the morning, Pink. It's rude."

"I won't wake him up. I know where he keeps his key."

"Suit yourself," she said, turning away. "I won't be in the office until nine. I suggest you do the same." With that, she got in her car, started the engine and drove off.

Steve said in a low, even voice, "Pink, you won't believe this, but your mom is a dead ringer for my mom."

"Hmm, that is odd. But they say everyone has a twin, somewhere in the world."

"My dad would…"

"What? What would your dad do?"

He smiled then. "Does your mom date anybody?"

Understanding dawned and I immediately held my hands up, warding off any romantic ideas he might have. "Oh, no, don't even think it. Maybe your mom and mine look alike, but any similarity ends there, I promise you. No woman, anywhere, is like Mom. She's so bad at romance, Cupid had to go into therapy. Trust me, your dad would regret the day he ever met my mom."

Steve was staring at me the whole time I spoke, and when I finished he didn't say anything at all.

"What? Why are you looking at me like that?"

"I'm just surprised at you. I never would have pegged you for the jealous-daughter type."

"I'm not. I just know how she is with men, and it's not a pretty picture. Keep your dad away from Mom. He'll thank you for it."

Steve didn't believe me, I could tell. And he looked so enthused at the prospect of getting Mom and his dad together, I knew he'd wrangle it somehow. Fine. He'd learn pretty quick that Mom has her own ideas about romance, and they lean toward the international symbol for no. A big heart in a red circle with a line through it.

"Steve, I'd really appreciate a lift over to Sam's, if you don't mind."

"Suppose I do? Suppose I ask you to come back to the hotel and spend the night with me?"

"I'd say yes, but it's too dangerous."

"Me? Dangerous? You're kidding, right?"

"Steve, we can't be alone together in a hotel room. Besides, I'm so tired, I can't see straight. And I'm starving to death. Chasing Spider-Man worked up an appetite."

"I won't kiss you, I promise. And I can get you something to eat."

"The Midland Hilton has all-night room service?"

He grinned. "For me, they do. I'm a powerful man, and I'm willing to abuse that power for a ham sandwich."

"Okay," I agreed, walking with him toward his borrowed car. "Since you're playing the despot gig tonight, how about you abuse that power enough to get me a slice of chocolate cake?"

"No problem." He grabbed my hand and didn't let go until we got to the car.

I went back to the hotel with him and it was really, *really* nice to be treated like a Queen Bee. By Steve, that is. After I'd eaten and taken a quick shower, he insisted I take the bed and he stretched out on the couch across the room. While I drifted off to sleep, I had the random thought that I could get used to the Queen Bee thing.

My little happy place didn't last long. The cell phone rang at seven o'clock in the morning and Sam went off on me about never showing up at his house the night before, about staying all night with Steve and about taking on Banty McMeans as a client. When I asked what he meant by that, he said in a pained, irritated voice, "Because the idiot called me at the ass-crack of dawn to find out where you were. Pink, I cannot believe, of all the potential clients in west Texas, you took on a goofball like McMeans."

"He did give us a hefty retainer, Sam. I thought you'd be glad about that."

He let out a huffy breath. "Pink, this is like when my cat drags a dead bird up to my back door and gives it to me, then expects me to be enthused about it."

"Am I the cat in this scenario?"

"Yes, and McMeans is the dead bird. Only worse because I can't pick him up and toss him in the garbage, as much as I'd like to."

"He's not that bad."

"Okay, fine, so keep your dead bird. Just don't come crying to me when he starts to stink."

"I never cry about business."

"After working with this joker for a few days, you may change your tune. And speaking of jokers, how's Santorelli this morning?"

Raising my head, I looked at his peculiar position on the couch and immediately felt guilty. No way did that seem comfortable. "Asleep on the couch, probably dreaming about getting a massage."

"Late night?" Sam asked with a whole lotta sarcasm.

"As a matter of fact, yes, but it's not what you think."

"I wasn't thinking anything at all, so tell me about your late night."

As briefly as possible, I told him about Big Mama and Spider-Man. Sam got pretty worked up about it, and I wasn't sure who he was more angry with, me or Mom. There was some mention of female high jinks, and he may have said something about walking disasters, but I can't be sure. I pretty much tuned him out. When he was all done, he offered to pick me up later. I accepted, said goodbye and hung up.

I slipped back into sleep, and when I woke up again, Steve was talking on the phone to someone named Charley. After he hung up, he ordered breakfast, and while we had bacon and eggs and fresh-squeezed orange juice, we talked about inconsequential things. I think we were avoiding talking about the inevitable goodbye.

While I went in the bathroom and tried to make some order to my hair, I became a little dejected. I'm not inclined to be depressed, but everything was a mess, and I had no clue how to untangle things. Because Mom and I were inept at espionage and theft, we'd bungled the Spider-Man thing. I couldn't help thinking about Dan Becker, about his ultimate sacrifice for America, and how I'd negated it by losing the toy. Then I thought about Ed, who was due to arrive back in Midland early in the evening. My feelings for him had run the gamut since the minute we'd met, and I was so confused at that moment I wasn't sure how I felt about seeing him again.

As I stepped into my tennis shoes, I glanced at Steve, who sat at the table, reading the morning paper. Could I have a long-term relationship with this man? Could I hang out with someone whose personal life was held up for inspection and criticism on a daily basis? Could I ever love him?

He glanced up and smiled at me. "Give me a minute, and I'll take you home."

"It's okay," I said, bending to tie my shoes. "Sam's coming to get me."

"Bummer. I was looking forward to taking you."

"Thanks, but Sam insisted. Besides, you need to get back to Washington."

"True, but it's still a bummer." He laid the paper aside.

"Sam's an interesting guy. He left the FBI and went to work for your mom, right?"

"Yeah. He's way too macho, and something of an autocrat, but he's a good guy, and becoming a good friend. Can't say I've ever had a boss quite like Sam."

I was done. It was time to go. Walking toward Steve, I did that goofy, immature thing most women do, and tried to memorize him. I wanted to remember just how his dark brows lie above his dark eyes, how his chin has a shadow of a dimple, how his strong, farm-boy hands have a sprinkling of black hair on the backs.

As I came close, he stood and wrapped me in his arms. "This isn't goodbye, you know."

"I know, but it sure feels like it."

He kissed me then. Nothing like that kiss in the plaza the night before, but oddly more passionate. It truly was so emotional, I couldn't speak after he let me go.

Turning away, I walked toward the door. When my hand was on the knob, I heard him say, "Thank you, Pink."

The knot in my throat grew twice as big, and I could only nod as I walked out.

After Sam dropped me at the apartment, with a surprising lack of lectures, I showered, dressed and drove back downtown. I got to the office a few minutes before nine, just enough time to print out my current client-project list for the staff meeting.

On my way to the bullpen, I passed Gert in the hallway and she gave me the hairy eyeball, then made a big show of looking at her watch, getting in a dig about how late I was. I didn't pay her any attention, mostly because I couldn't look at her without remembering the night before, and just thinking about it made me want to die laughing all over again. Why? I have no idea. Maybe because she's such a nonsexual being, and made such a big deal about how disgusting she found Jake, but the two of them had come off that elevator like a couple of parolees just sprung from twenty-year sentences.

I practiced mind-control techniques in a desperate attempt to rid myself of the image, but it was no use. The whole incident had colored the world around Gert in a new shade of passion-pink, and there was no way I'd ever be able to look at her in quite the same way.

Unfortunately, I had a problem with my printer, which meant I was the last one to get to the conference room, which meant I had to sit directly across from her, which meant I couldn't wipe the grin off my face. Not even her pointed glares did any good. If anything, they made me want to laugh even more. I was finally forced to turn my chair at an angle so I could avoid eye contact and concentrate on Mom's usual staff-meeting spiel.

When it was my turn to give a client update, I went through the list, noting the clients who'd been wrapped up, progress ongoing and new work I'd started, which included Banty McMeans.

Then the shit hit the fan, and all traces of a grin, and any accompanying humor, were gone from me. Real gone.

"Whitney Ann!" Mom said in a voice that was damn close to a shout. "Have you completely lost your mind? That guy has single-handedly bankrupted the Midland County budget and backlogged civil court for the next hundred years because he has a lawsuit against every man, woman and child in town!" She got up from her chair and paced around the table, waving her hands about, getting more worked up as she went. "Not only that, it's an insult to stingy skinflints everywhere to call him a tightwad. He'll never pay us!" She stopped at my chair and glared down at me. "What the *hell* were you thinking?"

I looked away from her enraged expression and glanced

around the table. Sam was slowly shaking his head, as if to say, See, I told you it was a terrible idea. The other seniors and managers were completely captivated by their own client lists, and wouldn't meet my eyes. Gert looked as if she'd just won the lottery. And she'd had the gall to tell me how wrong I was to refuse Banty, that Mom would be upset. Yeah, right. I really did hate her guts in that moment. What a bitch.

And I wasn't real keen on Mom, either. I looked up at her and said as calmly as possible, "I've had some experience dealing with difficult clients. He gave us a retainer, and he won't sue."

Mom let out a huge breath and I could tell she wanted to really lay into me, but she realized we had an audience, so she refrained. Not that it mattered. She'd already pretty much humiliated the hell outta me.

Turning around, she went back to her chair, sat down, cleared her throat and asked the chick next to me, a tax senior, about her clients. I had a hard time sitting through the rest of the meeting, but I managed. As soon as the last person was done, and Mom had given us her standard Good Job speech, I hightailed it back to my desk in the bullpen.

I half expected her to call me to her office and continue yelling at me, but she didn't. So I spent that morning working on Banty's revenue spreadsheets, which were beginning to take over the world. While I worked, inputting the numbers, my mind was occupied with other things. I had to wonder where I was going in life, had to consider how I'd gotten to such a sorry pass.

It would be convenient to blame it all on what had happened in Dallas—finding out one of my firm's biggest clients was scamming its investors, then blowing the whistle and losing my job. Enough time had passed that I could most likely find another position now, a good one, with any number of accounting firms, or even in private industry.

But every time I thought about it, I cringed and made up lame excuses about why it was a bad idea. I'd lost my competitive edge, the bulldog determination that had gotten me through eight years with a huge firm, the drive to be the best, the brightest and the youngest female to make partner. It seemed I was content to drift, to work in a job for Mom that didn't tap into my real capabilities. I wanted to blame it on loss of faith in myself, brought on by getting canned from my dream job, but I knew that wasn't it.

I had to face the fact that my complacency was only a symptom of a bigger issue. Since I'd jumped on the fast track for partner at that firm, I'd given every ounce of myself to it and all but ignored the rest of my life. My marriage had died, I hadn't kept up with my family as well as I might, and I'd allowed myself to be consumed with ambition. Now, I realized the job had been an escape. I could blame all of my shortcomings on the job. Gee, I don't have time to do that because I'm too busy. No, I can't make it to Cousin Susan's wedding because I've got to work. So sorry, George, but I'll have to miss our anniversary dinner because I've got a client function.

Then, when the job was taken away, all my excuses were gone. I had to face the woman I'd become, and I wasn't all that crazy about her. I knew, deep down in my soul, that if I went to work for another firm, or took a controller-type job with a corporation, I'd get sucked in again. I'd abandon my personal life. I'd wind up like Gert, bitter and angry, blinded by ambition, my only companionship a cat and late-night sex dates with my ex-husband, whom I despised.

Jesus God, that scared me to death.

At the same time, working for Mom was killing my ego. It was bad enough that the level of work wasn't anywhere close to what I was used to doing, but having Mom chastise me in front of other people was painful. Very. She didn't do that to her other employees.

So my options boiled down to staying at Mom's firm and losing every shred of self-respect I had, or getting another position and losing my soul.

By noon, I was done with Banty's revenue spreadsheets, but I was still in a deep funk over where I was going in life. There just didn't seem to be anywhere to go but down.

I left the office, went to Rosario's and drowned my sorrows in a gi-normous fajita plate. While I sat there in a corner booth, eating my lunch alone, I saw an army of soccer moms stream through, picking up lunch for their kids. I thought of all the times I'd looked down my nose at soccer moms, thinking they'd sold out, given up their lives for a Volvo and laundry. But watching them closely, I saw smiles and contented faces. I didn't see anyone who looked like I felt.

When I got back to work, I attacked Banty's case with a vengeance, determined to shove all thought from my mind. It didn't work. I just couldn't shake the icky feeling I'd gotten when Mom yelled at me in front of the staff.

I spent the next two hours analyzing my spreadsheets, and at the end of it all, I concluded that Banty had indeed been shorted. Someone had changed his royalty interests in all the Lorenzo operated wells. Not much, mere fractions of a percentage point, but enough to cheat him out of several thousand dollars.

More than likely, someone in the revenue department was embezzling. They had probably set up a shell company and added it to the revenue system, giving it tiny, unnoticeable fractions of the royalty owners' interests.

Deciding to go directly to the person who could check into it, I called the controller at Lorenzo and explained the discrepancies. She seemed genuinely surprised and concerned by my questions, and assured me she'd get back with me as soon as she located the problem.

I left the office then and headed for home. I wanted to clean up the apartment and get ready for Ed. On the way, I stopped and bought a bottle of Jack Daniels whiskey, just like a real girlfriend would do.

At half past seven, I'd just finished picking up all the books and magazines in my living room when someone knocked on the door.

Ed.

Nervous and anticipatory, I swallowed hard and opened the door. Not Ed.

"Banty, what are you doing here?"

"I came to see how your progress is coming."

He didn't wait for an invitation, but stepped inside, took the door out of my hand and closed it behind him.

"Banty, this is highly irregular, you showing up at my home like this. We have an office and office hours for a reason."

He hitched up his pants and said, "I'm sorry, but I just couldn't wait until Monday."

I know it's bad of me, but I lied so I could get rid of him. "I don't know anything yet, but you'll be the first to know when I do."

He was hugely disappointed, I could tell, and I almost felt guilty for lying. Almost.

His gaze moved to a spot behind me and he said, "I like that couch. The armrests look like half of a wagon wheel."

I wasn't surprised he liked the couch. Banty was just the sort who'd like a wagon wheel couch. "Thanks for dropping by, Banty, but I've got to get ready for a date."

"You've got your radio tuned to jazz music. Does that mean you're going out with the senator again?"

"No, and how did you know about that?"

"My buddy at the police department told me about what really happened with that car bomb. I'm glad you're okay."

"Thank you."

"So, if you're not going out with the senator, that means you must be going with Ed."

"That's right, and he's due here any minute."

"Did he tell you I just hired him to represent me in a child support case?"

I didn't think Ed would like me saying anything about that, so I played stupid. "No, he didn't. I didn't know you had children, Banty."

He frowned. "I don't, but this woman swears her child is mine, so I've gotta prove she's lying—hopefully without my family finding out about it. The whole thing will upset my mama something terrible."

"Yes, I can see how it would."

"Mama had an illegitimate baby before she had me, and she says it's a high sin she's always regretted."

"I thought you were an only child."

"Most people think so. My father never liked my brother, I guess because he was a constant reminder of Mama's high sin, so he lived with her parents in San Antonio. She was a Dinkle, from the San Antonio Dinkles."

Apparently, this was supposed to impress me, so I nodded thoughtfully, as though I had a frappin' clue about the San Antonio Dinkles.

I was just about to open the door and show him out when he crossed the small living room and peeked out the curtains. "Unless I miss my guess, someone's following you."

"What?" I went to the window and looked out, but didn't see anything except one of my neighbors smoking a cigarette. "That's just a guy whose wife makes him go outside to smoke."

"Not him," Banty said impatiently. "Look over there, next to your car."

I did, and felt my heart do a double half gainer. In the pale light of rapidly encroaching dusk, Ed leaned back against

Sam's Ford, with one booted foot crossed over the other and his arms folded across his chest. He wore a pair of faded jeans, the ones with a hole in the right leg, and a white T-shirt that stood out in the gloom. His head was tilted back at an angle, and his eyes were trained on my window. "Banty, that's Ed."

He sighed dramatically. "Are you blind? I don't mean Ed! Look on the *other* side of the car. Well, not right by your car, but one over. See the guy with his head under the hood of that El Camino? The one Ed is talking to? He's watching this apartment."

I shifted my gaze and studied the guy for a while. Sure enough, he looked up at my window every so often, quickly, as if he didn't want to get caught. He was clearly trying to appear nonchalant, acting as though he was working on the car while he talked to Ed. "I know that guy."

"Do you know why he's checking out your apartment?"

"No, but I know how I can find out." Why was Gert's ex hanging out in my parking lot with an El Camino, glancing up at my window? That was really weird. I looked again at Ed, and wondered why he was standing there, by the car, instead of coming up to my apartment.

I slipped into a pair of flip-flops and opened the door. "You should leave now," I said to Banty. "I'll call you as soon as I have a report ready."

He hitched up the Sansabelts and walked toward the door. "I'll see you Monday," he said rather autocratically, "and check your progress." Surprising me when he didn't insist on seeing who was watching my apartment, he strode out the door, down the concrete stairs and disappeared around the corner of the building.

Anxious to find out why Jake was stalking me, I tromped down the stairs and walked across the parking lot. When I was even with the El Camino, which was turquoise, and actually uglier than Sam's old Ford, I looked over at Ed. "Hi, Ed."

"Hi, Pink."

"Did you win?"

"Yeah, Pink. Big win."

I focused on Jake and asked, "What are you doing out here?"

He fumbled a wrench and dropped it. "I, uh, well, I'm just out here workin' on my car. What's it look like I'm doing?"

"It looks like you're lying. That's a plumber's wrench. And there's that pesky detail that you don't live here. So give it up and tell me why you're checking out my apartment."

"It's a free country and I guess I can be out here if I wanna be."

"Sure you can, and since it's a free country, I can tell anybody who's interested how you spent last night, and who you spent it with."

His eyes widened in shock and his mouth gaped open. "How would you know?"

"I saw you. And Gert. Room ten-o-four, wasn't it?"

His surly mood turned downright nasty. He brought the wrench down on the edge of the El Camino, leaving a pretty good dent. "I told her this was never gonna work, but she had to have her way." He looked at me with anger sparking from his eyes. "She told me I could have that damn ring if I'd follow you around."

"Why?"

"She wants to catch you at something she can hold over your head, to force you to resign. Something you wouldn't want anyone to know."

"Like what?"

Ed's deep voice rumbled close behind me. "Like what you were doing on the tenth floor of the Hilton last night. Would you resign before you'd let Gert tell me about that?"

I kept my gaze on Jake, whose blue eyes were fixed on a spot just above my shoulder. "No, I wouldn't resign."

"You'd let her tell me?"

"She'd never get the opportunity because I'd tell you first."

No response. We all three stood there for several tension-filled moments. Then Jake reached up, lowered the hood of the El Camino and said, "I'm outta here. Let's just forget it, okay, Pink?"

"Sure, Jake. I'll forget it." Not.

"Nice to meetcha, Ed."

"See ya, Jake."

As soon as he drove away, I turned to face Ed. "Just tell me right up front, did you come over here to get in an argument?"

"I came over here to get laid."

"Is that all?"

His hands wrapped around my upper arms and he held me there, his brown eyes staring into mine. "No, that's not all. I came to find out why you'd sleep with Santorelli the night before I was due to get back to Midland. Because that seems very, very weird to me, Pink."

"I didn't sleep with him, Ed. If I did that, you'd never get past it, and any chance of you and me would be toast."

"You went out with him. You stayed all night in his hotel room. And you expect me to believe you didn't have sex?"

"Yes, I expect you to believe me. If I had slept with him, I would tell you."

"Why did you go out with him?"

"Because he asked, way back during the whistle-blower stuff, remember?"

"I remember you said you'd beg off when the time came."

"Maybe I would have, if you hadn't dumped me two days ago."

"I didn't dump you, for God's sake!"

"If you didn't, why don't you clarify what you meant when you told me to forget it?"

Ed dropped his hands from my arms and turned away. "Let's go inside."

I followed him up the stairs and into the apartment, fighting down the very worrisome queasiness in the pit of my stomach.

Ed walked straight to the bedroom, then came right back out. "Love what you've done with the place. It's got that just-searched look."

"So you know about that?"

His expression was unreadable. "I know about everything. Talked to Sam early this morning."

"For a couple of guys who hate each other, you sure do talk a lot."

"It's business. We share many of the same clients. You know that."

"Did you talk about business this morning?"

"No. We talked about you."

That's how he knew about Santorelli. Sam ratted me out. Oh, man. "You want a whiskey?" I don't drink whiskey, but I wondered if maybe I should have one, too.

He narrowed his eyes. "You bought whiskey?"

"Yeah, but I have no glasses. You have to use the top of the mouthwash."

"Minty fresh whiskey? I don't think so. Just gimme the bottle."

I did and watched him take a drink. He looked like a guy in a western. When he was through, he set the bottle down and walked around the small living room. "Well, this is awkward, isn't it?"

"Yes."

"I'm so righteously pissed off, I'd like to indulge myself in a jealous rage."

"So why don't you?"

"Because I know it wouldn't do one damn bit of good." He moved across the room until he was right in front of me. I mean *right* in front of me, so close my boobs were smashed against his chest. "The way I see it, I have two options. I can leave or I can stay."

"What do you want to do?"

"Both. I want you so bad, it's like a disease. But I feel as if I've been sucker punched."

"This from a guy who told me to forget it?" Thinking about what he'd said bugged me all over again. "What did you mean about the house? Why does it bother you so much?"

"Because it locks you into something that doesn't have anything to do with me." His hands caught my upper arms and he squeezed tightly. "You wanna know a little secret about men? Men get married because they see it as the only way to keep a woman to themselves."

"Women have affairs, same as men."

"If you were living with me, or married to me, would you go out with Santorelli? Would you even consider whether or not you should sleep with him?"

"No."

He stared down at me for the longest time. "Does he know about me?"

"Yes, but he said we fall under the three-times rule."

"So you told him we haven't slept together yet?"

I nodded.

"Well, then, I have no excuse to kill him." His hands loosened and one slid upward, to wrap around the nape of my neck, and the other slipped around my waist. "I've never felt like this, Pink. Ever. And I don't like it."

We stood there for a while and stared at each other, and I cast about in my mind for the perfect thing to say. Just my luck, I couldn't think of anything witty, or clever, or even very sophisticated. Instead, I said, "Ed, I really don't want you to leave."

Behind him, a jazz tune wound down on the radio.

"You're listening to jazz," he said with a half smile.

The radio blared out three very annoying beeps, then a detached man's voice announced an emergency-response alert. I was scarcely paying attention, except to think it was aggravating, when I heard the name Trina Lorenzo. And Colby Lorenzo. Followed by a description of them, and what they were wearing when they were last seen, which was that morning.

"An Amber Alert on Colby?" I said to Ed. "Oh my God! Trina kidnapped him!"

Ed dropped his hands from my arms and went to my phone. I watched him dial, and wondered who he could be calling. After a few seconds, it was obvious. I sat down on the couch and waited until he was done. Then I asked, "Since when are you so tight with David Lorenzo?"

Looking at me with those big brown eyes, Ed answered slowly, as though it pained him to tell me. "Since he hired me to take Trina back to court and get her visitation rights suspended. She was served papers this morning, and I'm sure that's why she ran."

"How could you do that? Maybe she's not a saint, but she's that boy's mother!"

"I can't tell you why, but would you just believe me when I say this is for the best? The fact that Lorenzo posted a half million dollar reward should give you a clue how serious this is."

"Unless she's abusive, I can't see any reason to take a woman's right to visit her child away from her."

He jingled the coins in his pocket, I suppose because he was uncomfortable with the conversation. "There are things you don't know about Trina, or you wouldn't say that."

"If you're talking about her affair with Dan Becker, you'll have to do a little better. How could anyone hold that against her? The man was a hero, for God's sake!"

Ed stared at me with the weirdest expression. As if I'd mutated into an alien with five heads. "Who told you she was having an affair with Becker?"

"She did, the night he was killed. She called and wanted to know if he'd mentioned her before he died."

Ed turned and paced around the small room, mumbling a lot of cuss words I won't repeat because they were pretty vulgar.

"What's the matter, Ed? Are you embarrassed for me to know you'd sue to take a woman's child away from her, just because she chose to fall in love with someone and start a new life?"

He glared at me and said, "How a woman as smart as you are can be so totally naive is beyond me."

I was deeply insulted. "How a man like you, who I thought was honorable, could take a case like this is beyond me." I turned to switch off the radio and the repeating, freakish alert. "I don't really know you at all."

When I turned back around, he grabbed my arms again. "Dammit, Pink, why do you always doubt me?"

"Maybe for the same reason you never trust me."

"It's got nothing to do with trust. I'm an attorney, and there's such a thing as client confidentiality."

"I'm not a moron, and I know this doesn't qualify as priv-ileged information. You just don't want to tell me because you don't trust me. You think I'll say or do something to taint your case, and that might make you lose, and more than anything, you hate losing."

With an angry, frustrated expression, he stared down at me for several heartbeats before he said in a tight voice, "She faked you out, Pink. She wasn't in love with Becker. About three months ago, she started an affair with a Venezuelan named Juan Miguel de Santa Morena."

"I don't understand."

He actually shook me a bit, but I hardly noticed, I was try-ing so hard to figure out why Trina would lie about being in love with Becker.

"She was fishing! It's the oldest trick in the book, and you fell for it. Trina knows something, or has something to do with what Becker was investigating. She wanted to know what he said to you, if he mentioned her name."

Well, hell. And I wasted a lie to make her feel better. I felt stupid and highly manipulated. "Are you sure?"

"She's probably on a plane to Venezuela as we speak, on her way to meet her lover, Santa Morena, who just happens to be an arms dealer with known connections to terrorists. Put yourself in Lorenzo's place. If that boy was yours, wouldn't you do everything possible to keep him away from a man like that?"

I nodded slowly, wishing I hadn't jumped to conclusions.

"And if you were me, wouldn't losing mean a little bit more than just a bad deal for your ego?"

I nodded again, and whispered, "I'm sorry, Ed."

His hands loosened and he wrapped his arms around me. "If you were any other woman, I'd be out the door."

"Why?" I asked, my face pressed against his shoulder.

"Because I hate being second-guessed, and you've done it over and over, ever since we met."

"Then why are you still here?"

He held me closer and sighed against my hair. "Because you're not any other woman."

Chapter 10

I kind of thought Ed and I would patch things up, that we would talk it out and make some kind of a plan for the future. Set some ground rules.

Unfortunately, it didn't happen that night. About the time I said something about ordering a pizza, the phone rang. It was Dotty Haskell, from Aunt Dru's prayer group.

"Pink, have you heard about Trina?"

"Yes, it's frightening. I hope it all is resolved soon."

"I hate to be a busybody, but I'm worried that the older woman with them is our Dru. I've been looking all over for her, and she's nowhere to be found."

"Older woman? I didn't hear that."

"It's on the alert. Trina and Colby are traveling with an older woman. I called you to see if you know where she is."

"I don't, Dotty. I haven't spoken to her today at all."

"Me neither, and we were supposed to have lunch at the

country club. I figured she just got tied up, but when she never called, I though it was very odd. What should we do?"

"Have you called the other ladies in the prayer group?"

"No, I didn't want to alarm them. Do you think I should?"

"Not yet. I'll try to find her, and get back to you."

"Yes, that would be wonderful. Thank you, Pink."

I hung up and relayed the conversation to Ed.

"Is this something your aunt would do?"

"Definitely. She thinks Lorenzo is the devil."

"Then we'd better find her before the cops do. Otherwise, she can be charged with kidnapping, same as Trina."

In order to save time and be more efficient, Ed and I split up. He went to check all of her usual haunts, while I went to get a key to her house. I knew Mom had one because Aunt Dru usually asks her to stop by and water the plants whenever she's out of town.

When I got to Mom's, I went up to the front door and did the same thing I've been doing since I was in college. I unlocked the door, opened it and yelled, "Hey, Mom! It's me!" When there was no answer, I went in, disengaged the security alarm and walked to the kitchen, thinking I'd look in the drawer by the telephone, where she keeps all the keys.

But I never made it to the drawer. A man with a slight paunch and thinning brown hair stood in the kitchen, drinking a beer and watching CNN—in his tighty whiteys. Oh, shit. I turned to leave, but didn't make it before he saw me. "Hey, Pink," he said, turning forty shades of red.

"Hi, Harry. I'm gonna go out on a limb here and assume you're not here to fix Mom's air conditioner."

He took a huge swallow of beer, set the can down and looked up at the crown molding. "Would you believe I came over to help her clean up the mess the burglar left?"

"I'd really like to believe that, Harry."

"Good, then it's all settled." He darted a glance toward the back hall. "She's in the shower, so if you were to go out and come back, she'll never know about this unbelievably embarrassing incident."

"Works for me," I said, turning and hauling ass for the front door. But I didn't stop there. I went ahead and got in the car and headed for Aunt Dru's. I'd break in or something, but no way I was going back to Mom's.

I'm not gonna lie. I was shocked, even though I'd suspected for some time that Mom was playing patty fingers with the air-conditioner man. What shocked me was her choice. Harry's a very nice guy, and an ace air-conditioner dude, but he's probably ten years younger than Mom, a real man's man who loves to hunt and fish and ride a Harley. I always thought if Mom got involved with another man, she'd pick an intellectual she could have serious discussions with, who would travel all over the world with her, who would help allay her self-consciousness over her background. Mom's family would need to step up in the world to be called white trash, and she's always considered her upbringing a dead weight around her neck.

Not that Harry was anywhere close to white trash. He just wasn't anything like what I imagined for Mom.

I was still shaking my head in disbelief when I pulled into Aunt Dru's driveway. She lives in an older part of Midland, in a house built in the forties, after the war. It's small, but neat, nestled in a short block of equally neat and well-kept houses, all of them with large, mature trees in the yard. I got out of the car and walked around to the back of the house, looking for an open window. No such luck.

On the back porch, I scouted for a hidden key, even though I knew there wouldn't be one. Aunt Dru is way too careful to leave a key outside. While I stood there, thinking of a way to get inside, Ed came around the side of the house.

"Any luck?" I asked.

"None." He glanced at the back door. "No key?"

I shook my head.

"Wait here," he said, then took off toward the front. Within a few minutes, he was back, a small tool in his hand.

While I watched, Ed picked the lock in less than thirty seconds.

"You're an old pro, aren't you?" I asked.

He shrugged. "I wasn't always a lawyer." He swung the door open and waved me in.

On the inside, Aunt Dru's house is nice, and surprisingly modern. She's just as anal about her home as she is about everything else, and it didn't take long to go through the papers and files in her small desk. Other than a brochure about visiting the Holy Land, which appeared to be outdated by at least ten years, there was nothing at all related to travel.

We looked in every room, but found nothing. Except in the laundry room, where there were two large boxes. I peeked inside and saw more of the flat Bible boxes like she'd given me.

"What's up with the Bibles?" Ed asked.

"Aunt Dru and her prayer group ship them all over the world, to missionaries."

He looked skeptical.

"Hope springs eternal," I said. "I'm going to go call all the other ladies in her group and see if they know where she might have gone."

An hour later we were no closer to finding Aunt Dru, and I was starting to believe the "older woman" with Trina was indeed my zealous aunt. Faced with my last option for hunting her down, I called Lurch from Ed's house. Alone in Ed's bedroom, sitting on his bed, I dialed the number and told myself I would not let my father get to me, no matter what. It took five rings before he answered, which only prolonged the tension. "Dad, it's Whitney."

"Whitney Ann. Huh."

Great start. "How are you, Dad?"

"Makin' do."

"I'm looking for Aunt Dru. Have you heard from her?"

"Of course I've heard from her. She's my sister. Calls me every Wednesday before she goes to church. Good woman."

"I meant, have you heard from her today?"

"It's not Wednesday, now is it?"

"No, Dad. It's Friday." I wasn't going to pay any attention to his rude, rhetorical questions. "She could be in some trouble, so it would be very helpful if you'd tell me when you spoke to her last, and if she mentioned anything about going on a trip."

"Whitney Ann, why don't you listen? I told you, I talk to her every Wednesday."

"Did she say anything about going on a trip?"

"Said she was coming up here."

I felt a huge amount of relief. "Is she there now?"

"Of course not. She'll be here in November, for Thanksgiving."

My frustration level climbed several degrees. "She's in serious trouble, and I'd like to know if you intend to help."

"Your aunt couldn't be in trouble. She's a good woman."

"Yeah, Dad, she's so good she helped a woman abduct her kid and run away. The police are looking all over for them, but as it stands now, they don't know who Aunt Dru is. If I can find them first, I can get her out and avoid an arrest."

He didn't respond for the longest time. Finally, he said, "Is this a friend of yours? Because this sounds just like something one of those silly twits would pull, running off half-cocked, conning a good woman like Dru into helping her."

Amazing. Abso-fucking-lutely amazing. He really had managed to make this my fault. He'd actually figured a way to criticize me. I hadn't planned to tell him, but I was compelled to say, "It's Trina Lorenzo."

"Figures," he said, then abruptly changed the subject. "You still got a job?"

"Yes."

"Workin' for your mama, I guess you don't have to worry about getting fired. She can't get rid of you, no matter how bad a slacker you turn out to be."

"That's right, Dad. I'm the same old bloodsucker I've always been."

"Didn't the state of Texas take your CPA license after that fly-by-night firm you were with went belly-up? How are you working without that?"

"No, they didn't take it."

"Huh. I see here on the caller ID you phoned from Edward Ravenaldt's house. He one of the Ravenaldts there in Midland?"

"Yes."

"Why the hell you wanna mix it up with any of those people? Damn Catholics, with fourteen kids and the daddy didn't do much but work welding jobs."

"Seven. They have seven kids, and they're Methodists. And their father is a manager at an oil service company."

"Oldest boy went to the pen for holding up a store."

"That's right. Now he lives in Big Lake and owns a machine shop."

"Which one are you mixing it up with? Is it the fat kid who had stupid hair?"

I know, I *know* I shouldn't have told him anything else. But I did, because I still have a juvenile wish to win his approval. "It's the one who's a lawyer."

"Hell, I guess one of 'em needed to be a lawyer, to keep all the others outta jail. Never thought you'd get mixed up with an ambulance chaser, Whitney Ann."

I had to mentally beat myself up to keep from telling him to go straight to hell and never come back. "Me neither, Dad."

"'Course I never would have expected you to marry a goddamn mechanic. The very idea, I buy you a college education and you marry a lousy mechanic. Showed his true colors, though, off shacking up with whores."

"Yes, Dad. True colors."

"You oughtta get rid of this ambulance chaser. Worst people in the world to be involved with. Only money they make is because somebody died."

I wanted to tell Lurch about the fee Ed earned when he sued a large oil company that licensed his client's invention, then stiffed him for it and stole the patent rights. I wanted him to be impressed with Ed, to agree that he was a smart man, and that five million bucks was awesome. I wanted him to pat me on the head and say he always knew I'd wind up with a smart, honest man, then ask how soon he could meet him. Of course I didn't do anything like that. I just sat there and felt my stomach churn with the pain of unrequited father love.

"Best thing you can do is find an engineer. Need to settle down and have a family. Women want that."

I really couldn't think of anything to say.

"It's not like you've got any kind of career, working for your mama. That's just a big joke. Need to find a man to take care of you, a God-fearing, decent one who doesn't chase ambulances for a living."

"Dad, I have to go. I need to find Aunt Dru."

"That's right. Least you can do, since it's your fault she's in a bind."

"Bye, Dad."

He hung up without a goodbye and I sat there for a full three minutes staring at the receiver in my hand, wondering how a human being could have a child and hate her. How did a person do that?

Ed came in and stood at the end of the bed. "Don't be pissed, but I listened in."

"Why?"

He shrugged. "I could tell you were wigging on it, and I was curious." He moved around the bed, took the phone and hung it up, then sat beside me. Circling me with his arms, he pulled me close. He didn't say a word. Just sat there and held me.

I didn't cry. I'd spent half my life crying about it, and I was all cried out. Still, no matter how prepared I am, how much I tell myself I won't let him get to me, he never fails to cut deep. After a long time, I whispered, "Thank you, Ed."

He kissed the top of my head.

"What are we gonna do? I'm all out of ideas."

"If you want to know the truth, I think Trina is probably long gone, and your aunt is in a motel somewhere, planning to head back home tomorrow."

"You're probably right, but I'd like to know for sure. I've been thinking. Aunt Dru gave me one of those Bibles yesterday at lunch. She said all the answers were in there, if I'd just read it."

He stopped rubbing circles on my arm. "Maybe she was giving you a hint?"

"Doubtful, because she's not the least bit mysterious, but it could be."

He pulled away from me and stood up. "Let's go to your apartment and take a look."

"Okay, but can we get something to eat on the way? I'm starving."

"Actually, I've got something cooking right now. We'll go get the Bible and come right back."

I stared up at him. "You're *cooking* something?"

"Why so surprised? Remember my brother is a chef. Cooking runs in the family."

"What are you cooking?"

He waggled his eyebrows at me. "Asparagus, with oysters?"

I couldn't help smiling. "Ed, the last thing I need around

you is an aphrodisiac. Total waste of time on your part, because no way I could want you any more than I do already."

"Good to know, since what I stuck in the oven is a frozen casserole my mom made for me about three months ago."

Fifteen minutes later, we went into my apartment and I got the Bible off the bed, where I'd tossed it earlier. I opened the box and noticed there wasn't any plastic wrap on the book, encouraging me to think there might be a note. Ed took it out and flipped through the pages, but there was nothing. "Bummer."

I closed the Bible, put it back in the box, and just as I got the lid on it, the phone rang. Figuring it was Mom, I answered with an automatic, "Hey."

"What the hell kinda way is that to answer the phone?"

Lurch. More browbeating was in store. "Dad, what's up?" I saw Ed's eyes widen.

"Dru just called. Said she's been calling you the past two hours and you weren't home. Like I said, if you weren't running around with a damn ambulance—"

"Where is she?"

"Abilene. Here's her number. Three-two-five—"

"Hang on and let me get a pencil."

"Hurry up about it. I gotta get to bed."

It was just past ten, which meant it was nine in Colorado. On a Friday night. Lurch was an old man about forty years too soon. I dug in my purse and got a pen, then looked for a scrap of paper. All I found was the envelope Aunt Dru had given me with the money in it. "Okay, shoot."

He gave it to me, then said, "Need to call her right away. She's upset. I'm holding you responsible for this, Whitney Ann." He hung up.

I immediately dialed the number, telling Ed about it at the same time. Aunt Dru answered on the second ring. "Aunt Dru? Are you okay?"

"Whitney Ann!" Her voice was laced with relief. "Lordy, I've been through it, and that's the truth. I'm in a motel on Interstate 20, close to Abilene, with no car, very little money and this child."

"Where's Trina?"

Her voice dropped to a whisper. "I'm not sure. She was set to get on a plane, one of those little ones that crash all the time. I asked where it would take them and she said South America. Made me nervous, I tell you, and I said maybe she should think about just taking the boy somewhere in the States. But she insisted she had to get him out of the country to get him away from his father. Since David converted to one of those Allah people, it's killing her to see Colby raised like that, to abuse women and blow people up."

Aunt Dru's narrow mind was showing again. "Is that why you helped her? Because David Lorenzo converted to Islam?"

Ed's eyebrows raised a notch.

"Of course! The child needs to know Jesus."

"Okay, so what happened after you got to the airport?"

"We weren't at an airport. We were out in the middle of nowhere, at a landing strip, waiting on this plane that was supposed to come and get her. All of a sudden, a car drove up and a bald man with a tattoo jumped out, waving a pistol. He grabbed Trina and shouted for us to get in the car."

A shiver went up my back. "How'd you get away?"

"I prayed for guidance, and the Lord provided wings to my feet, Whitney Ann. I grabbed up the boy and ran into the brush, and I didn't stop running until we reached the highway. Then I prayed for help, and a nice truck driver stopped and gave us a ride to this little motel. I can't go back for the car in case the man's still there, waiting for us. And my purse is in it, with my money and credit card."

No wonder she hadn't answered her cell phone. "How did you get a room without any money?"

"I always keep a hundred dollar bill in my bra, just in case. Thank God for that, right? Oh, Whitney, I need help in the worst way."

"Hang on, Aunt Dru." I covered the mouthpiece and told Ed all that Aunt Dru had said. "What should we do? If we call the cops, they'll arrest her for sure, but she and Colby could be in danger, don't you think?"

Ed held his hand out. "Let me talk to her." I passed him the phone. "Mrs. Grimes, this is Ed Ravenaldt. Here's what you need to do. Get the boy to bed, turn out all the lights, and no matter what, don't open the door. I'm going to make some calls and a state trooper will be there soon to stay with you until we can get there. Don't answer any of his questions. Tell him you're waiting until your attorney shows up."

I watched him listen for a while, wondering what Aunt Dru was saying, wishing I had a second phone.

"Mrs. Grimes, by helping Trina take Colby away from his father, you could be charged with kidnapping." He stopped and made a face. "I advise you not to repeat that to anyone else. A man has the right to raise his child the way he sees fit, and your opinion doesn't mean squat. The way it stands now, I can probably keep any charges from being brought against you, but if you keep up that kind of talk, I can't help you."

My heart was beating double time and I wished Aunt Dru would lay off. She would never last in prison.

"Sit tight, and everything will be all right." Ed handed the phone back to me.

"Aunt Dru, you need to do what Ed says. He's a very good lawyer and he knows what he's talking about."

"Can I really be charged with kidnapping?"

"There's an Amber Alert out on Colby. David Lorenzo put up a five hundred thousand dollar reward for him. Yeah, they can nail you to the wall if they choose. You need to play up that you saved him."

"He's such a sweet boy, and it turns my blood cold to think about him worshipping a heathen, pagan god."

"It turns my blood cold to think about you in prison. Just sit tight, and do what Ed says."

"All right, Whitney Ann. You're a good girl. When I called your father and he said you'd called, looking for me, I told him what a good girl you are."

I had to ask. "And what did he say?"

She huffed out a breath. "He agreed, of course. Jim's very proud of you."

Yeah, right. I gave her my cell-phone number and reminded her again to be careful.

"Thank you," she said, with just a trace of tears in her voice. "I'll see you soon."

I ended the call, hoping and praying that she was right and I would see her soon.

Ed turned toward the door. "Let's go, Pink."

"Where?"

"Lorenzo's. I'll call the state troopers on the way."

In Midland, there's wealthy, and there's rich, and there's wretched excess on a scale unparalleled in the world. David Lorenzo lived in a house that was bigger than a Holiday Inn, set on one hundred acres of land with a stable, a pond, a waterfall and a three-hole golf course, all enclosed by an eight-foot-high brick fence. That's a lotta bricks. The house itself is awe inspiring, a rambling structure of limestone and rustic wood, like something in the Texas hill country. The front foyer was twice as big as my apartment.

The Hispanic woman who answered the door asked us to wait, then disappeared up the wide staircase. Within two minutes, Lorenzo came bounding down. "You've found him?"

Ed said in a calm voice, "He's fine, Dave." He nodded his head toward me. "This is Whitney Pearl. Colby is with her aunt, Dru Grimes, in a motel close to Abilene."

David shot me a look that was somewhere between hostile and pleading. "We'll take the helicopter," he said, reaching in his pocket for a cell phone. He made a call, to the pilot, I supposed, then dropped the phone back into his pocket. "He'll be here in ten minutes."

While we waited, Ed explained the situation, and I looked around the front of David's house, trying not to be obvious. To the right was a doorway into what appeared to be a library, with hundreds of books in shelves that reached the tall ceiling, accessible by a rolling library ladder. That was way cool. To the left was some sort of a living room, but smallish, and I imagined that's where David met people who came to his home that weren't there for social reasons. Like insurance salesmen.

While I was scoping things out, a little bitty dog crossed the floor of the library, then came out into the foyer to yip at us. I stared at the thing as though it was Godzilla because I was absolutely positive its name was Boris.

Holy shit! I darted a look around, in search of Big Mama. If Boris was here, she had to be close by, didn't she?

David reached down, picked up the dog and held it in the crook of his arm.

"Cute dog," I lied, amazed I could be so freaked out by an animal that weighed less than a toaster.

"This is Natasha," he said, his other hand rubbing the dog's head. "She's a little wary of strangers."

Not Boris. Natasha. Again I had that odd feeling and tried to pin it down. Boris and Natasha. They were the dastardly spies on the *Rocky and Bullwinkle Show*. The names went together like Laurel and Hardy, or Mary Kate and Ashley. I eyed the little dog and wondered if she had a brother named Boris.

And I wondered if Boris was hanging around somewhere in Lorenzo's compound, along with his mistress, Big Mama. If the woman was here, it seemed likely that Lorenzo was involved with the money-laundering-terrorist scheme, which would blow my mind, but I had to face the possibility.

I know it was an incredibly stupid move on my part, but I couldn't stop thinking about Big Mama, and wondering if she was there, and thinking about that eight-foot wall and the bonanza of security cameras around the property and how I'd never get another chance to snoop around David Lorenzo's house.

So I interrupted Ed and asked David, "Would you mind if I step in the bathroom before your pilot arrives?"

He gave me a terse nod and pointed behind him. "Go to the back of the stairs, turn into that hallway, and there's a powder room on the left."

I took off, went directly past the powder room and on toward the very back of the house, glancing into every room I passed, totally intrigued by the amazing place.

Long after I passed the kitchen, I came to a narrow hallway that opened up into a large room with two long pine tables and what appeared to be a sitting area with two couches, a few chairs and a big-screen television. Was this the servants' quarters? Was this where they took their meals and spent their evenings? Too weird, I thought, to have live-in household help.

I hurried through the big room, winding around the tables, and took off down another hall, this one with lots of doors— three on either side. Figuring I'd tell anyone I met that I'd gotten lost looking for the bathroom, I glanced inside the rooms that weren't locked, but never saw anyone. Maybe because it was Friday night, everyone was off duty and out for the evening.

At the end of the hall was a door with a small window set into it. Damn. Nowhere else to look in this part of the house. I was wondering if Big Mama might be upstairs, or in the west wing, and cursing my shortage of time to continue the snoop job, when I peeked out the window and saw a small parking lot, I supposed for the staff vehicles. The only car there was a black Cadillac, the size of a small yacht. It looked exactly like the one Big Mama was driving the night she came to Mom's house.

I knew it could be a coincidence, but add up Natasha the dog and the big black Cadillac, and it was looking like Big Mama was somewhere in the vicinity.

Which meant David Lorenzo must have something to do with what was going down in Midland. My mind didn't want to accept it, but logic told me it had to be.

By the time I got back to the foyer, the helicopter was just arriving. David set the dog down, and on the way outside, he said to me, "I won't press charges against your aunt if you'll promise to keep her away from my son. People like her are only one of the reasons I'm not public about my faith."

"I'll do the best I can."

He shook his head, clearly disgusted. "She helps Trina take him away to live with a ruthless arms dealer, because she thinks it's better than being raised Muslim."

I was inclined to wonder if it was better than living with a terrorist sympathizer. "To be fair," I shouted over the noise of the helicopter, still fifty yards away, "she didn't know about the arms dealer. Just that Trina was going to South America, and she tried to get Trina to stay in the States."

He looked at me in the half light of the grounds around the house. "Don't work me for sympathy, because it won't happen. Most of the problems in this world are due to people just like your aunt."

I glanced at Ed. He had zero expression, giving me no clue as to his thoughts. Then I looked back at David. "You're right, but she's family, and I love her."

"I don't particularly care," he shouted in my direction.

"The only reason I'll refrain from pressing charges is out of respect for Steve Santorelli. He's a good friend, and he would care because he cares so much about you."

The noise from the helicopter was so loud by then I don't think Ed heard that last part, for which I was enormously grateful.

Chapter 11

The ride to the motel was made in silence because we couldn't talk above the sound of the helicopter. Once we got there, we found Aunt Dru in the room, chatting it up about no-see-ums with the state trooper, who looked ready to commit suicide. His relief was obvious when he was able to go out to his car and call in a report.

Colby was sound asleep, and only woke enough to snake his arms around his father's neck when David snatched him up. I swallowed back a lump of tears and turned away to hug Aunt Dru.

She looked none the worse for wear, back to her feisty self. "Trooper Smedley says he'll take us back out to the car. There's a whole bunch of troopers out there right now, looking for clues so they can find Trina. But you'll have to drive back to Midland, Whitney Ann. These cataracts make it hard for me to see at night."

"I'll drive," Ed said, and I didn't argue.

Aunt Dru eyed him up and down. "Edward Ravenaldt, you've grown into a handsome boy. And a lawyer to boot."

"Yes, ma'am."

David moved toward the door and she started to say something, but I held my hand over her mouth and said, "Unless you're going to apologize for helping Trina steal his son, you need to keep quiet." She nodded and I dropped my hand.

"Mr. Lorenzo," she called after him.

He stopped and glanced back at her.

"Your son was very brave. You should be proud of him."

"Mrs. Grimes, he's five years old, and the scariest things he should have to deal with are the wind in the trees at night and the dark shadows next to his toy box. Running from a lunatic who abducted his mother at gunpoint is not the sort of thing he should have to be brave about." He turned a bit more and looked straight at Aunt Dru. "Suppose I abducted your child, because I believe your religion is wrong?"

"God didn't see fit to give me children."

His eyes narrowed and his arms visibly tightened around the boy. "Then you can't possibly know how I feel right now. I thank you for saving him, Mrs. Grimes, but at the same time, I curse you for putting him in harm's way." He nodded toward me. "I've explained to your niece, I won't press charges if you'll stay away from me and my family." Then he turned and walked out.

I looked at Aunt Dru and was amazed when she made no comment. For once in her life, she appeared to be speechless.

By the time Aunt Dru was finished giving her statement to the state troopers, with Ed right there to help so she didn't say exactly the wrong thing, it was four in the morning. In her Buick, we started back to Midland with coffee and a bag of fried pies we picked up at a convenience store.

Aunt Dru ate one, even though she pronounced it "not *fit*

to eat!" then promptly nodded off and snored the rest of the way, while Ed and I talked and ate the pies.

Somewhere between Colorado City and Big Spring, I finally told Ed about what I'd done at Lorenzo's house.

"So let me get this straight," he said when I was done. "You think the big lady is working for Lorenzo because you saw a Chihuahua named Natasha and a black Cadillac at his house. You realize, I hope, how completely lame this sounds. You're grasping at straws, Pink, trying to make something fit that won't. David is not your man. Trust me on this."

"How can you be sure?"

"Don't you ever have a gut feeling about someone?" He saw my nod and continued, "I think David Lorenzo is one of the best men I've ever known. He's got integrity, and he always deals aboveboard. Look at how he handled his divorce from Trina."

"Yes, I know. I thought the same thing."

"And he let her get away with a lot before he finally made the decision to take away her visitation rights."

"I've been wondering about her affair with the Venezuelan arms dealer. How did she meet him?"

"David has some business interests in Venezuela, and due to the guerilla activity there, he has to hire a lot of security, which he does through the dealer. When he and Trina were still married, she went with him. About three months ago, she took a trip to Venezuela by herself, and stayed a couple of weeks. Since then, she's gone back twice. The last trip, she took Colby with her and it freaked David out so much, he decided he had to take her to court."

"How did he happen to hire you? Why didn't he use whoever handled his divorce?"

"To tell the truth, I wondered that myself. He called me just a few days ago while I was down in Sanderson, and said he'd been told I was a stand-up guy, and would I like to do some legal work for him. I asked who referred me and all he'd say was 'a mutual friend.'"

"Doesn't that strike you as…odd?" Once again, the coincidence thing was floating around, begging me to catch it.

"Yes, but I never look gift horses in the mouth, so I said okay, and here we are."

"Still, don't you think I should tell Detective Garza about the Cadillac? Maybe the big lady works at Lorenzo's, or she comes there to visit a relative. Garza should know, I think, and make up his own mind if I'm totally lame."

"I suppose, but be careful, Pink. Don't cast a bad light on David, because the man doesn't deserve it. And he's kind of been through it the past couple of days, with you and Santorelli almost getting blown up in his car, and now this kidnapping."

Just under three hours after we left Abilene, we were back in Midland. As soon as we hit the city limits, I dialed Garza's cell phone and told him what I'd seen at Lorenzo's house. He pretty much agreed with Ed's opinion, but said he was following all leads, so he'd check it out.

I thanked him and ended the call just as Ed pulled into the Lorenzo compound. He got in his old 4Runner, then followed me to Aunt Dru's, where we helped her into the house and got her to bed. She cried a little and wouldn't be consoled, which broke my heart. I called Dotty to come over and stay with her, although I warned Aunt Dru not to tell her any of the details of what had happened. As soon as Dotty arrived, she took charge and I felt okay to leave. I hugged and kissed Aunt Dru, then followed Ed out to his car.

In the front seat, he looked across at me. "Hungry?"

"Not anymore."

"Good thing, because I'm sure the casserole is disgusting at this point. I called my brother to go turn off the oven, and knowing him, he left the casserole in there."

"Not really up for a casserole at eight in the morning, anyway."

He pulled out of the driveway and turned toward his house. I didn't argue. I didn't want to.

It's odd, the way things turn out so different than we imagine. I'd always pictured me and Ed's first time as wild and crazy, and so hot we'd steam up the windows. Maybe because the three separate times we'd come close, it had been like that.

But the time we finally managed to make love to each other without interruption wasn't anything like that. It was slow and sensuous and soulful.

He undressed me, and it took at least twenty minutes because he stopped after each article of clothing and laid one of his Ed Wonder Kisses on me. Ed is, hands down, the best kisser in the universe. It's like his lips were made for mine, a perfect fit, and he has a certain smell that fills my head and makes me dizzy with an indescribable longing. It's not a definable scent. It's just Ed. And it makes me want him with a potent blend of hormones that could be used for mind control if they were bottled and unleashed on unsuspecting females. They'd do anything, say anything, go anywhere, powerless to resist.

When I was naked as the day I was born, I was vaguely disappointed to realize he was, too. Well, not disappointed he was naked. Just disappointed I didn't get to do that whole slow-undressing thing to him. I'd been so wrapped up in what he was doing to me, I'd failed to notice he was shucking his own clothes at the same time.

I got over it. Ed is something amazing to see, akin to looking out over the Grand Canyon, or standing on the beach and watching the ocean. He's a natural wonder.

"Pink," he whispered, just before his hand closed over my breast, "you are beautiful."

I leaned into him, and my voice came out rough and smoky. "So are you."

He kissed me again, and with nothing between us but the vaguest of doubts about where the relationship was going, I could feel the blood pulse through his thick erection. It was immensely erotic.

I have no clue how long we stood there in his bedroom, kissing and touching and inching our way toward the bed, but it was long enough to bring me to the brink several times. And that's sometimes pretty long. I used to wonder if there was something wrong with me, because it takes me so much time to get there, but the older I get, the less I worry. Maybe because I've talked to so many women who never get there. And that's way too sad, because going over the edge is definitely one of the highlights to life on this planet.

We finally made it to the bed, and he laid me down and slid inside of me in one fluid movement. Watching him there, just above me, his too-long, dark hair curling a little at his neck, and his nice brown eyes growing darker with the climax shuddering through his body, I let myself go. And go. It was the most incredible orgasm of my life, and the longer it lasted, the more intense it became.

When I was done flying around the moon, Ed relaxed against me and mumbled into my neck, "It's gonna piss me off no end if I have a heart attack and die right now, but I just might."

My female ego stood up and sang the Hallelujah Chorus. "Thank you, Ed."

He turned his head until his lips were close to my ear. "We never did have that talk, did we?"

"Do you still want to?"

"No." He held me tighter, squeezing so hard I almost couldn't breathe. "Stay with me all day today."

"I will, if you'll do that thing you do again."

"What thing?"

I smiled at him and said something very mushy, which isn't

like me at all, but it was that kind of moment. "Make me feel extraordinary."

He kissed the edge of my ear. "That's easy, Pink, because you are extraordinary."

We lay like that for a while, until we were breathing normally and too sleepy to stay awake. Rolling farther into the middle of the bed, we slipped under the covers, wrapped up in each other and drifted off to sleep.

Over the course of that Saturday, I learned every inch of Ed's body. I learned where he likes to be touched, and where he's ticklish, and where he hides scars.

I also learned a few things about myself. Like, my belly button isn't an erogenous zone, but my ankles are. Figures. How sexy are ankles, as compared to a belly button?

We woke up, made love again and went back to sleep. At five o'clock, he ordered a pizza delivered and we ate it in bed. Then we fooled around in the shower, watched the tail end of a Rangers game on television and went back to bed.

It was while I lay there, fading into dreamland, that I thought of Steve. I was overcome with a great sadness because I knew, no matter how it all turned out with Ed, I could never feel the same intensity of passion for Steve. Yet, oddly enough, I could more easily imagine myself loving him. Maybe because he was safe. Or maybe because we were so alike in so many ways. Loving Ed, I was afraid, would never lead to anything but pain. He was too complicated, and I was too simple.

Didn't matter, I told myself, because I was bound to be alone the rest of my life. It was easier that way. Less messy. And after the horrendous catastrophe of my first marriage, I was very keen on keeping things clean and tidy.

Ed's phone rang early Sunday morning. Reality was back in town. He answered, then immediately handed it to me.

With my leg twined around one of his, and one hand captured beneath his thigh, I managed to wake up enough to say, "Hyello."

"Pink, have you been over at Ed's all weekend? I've been trying to reach you since Friday night."

"I've been here since yesterday morning. Have you talked to Aunt Dru?"

"I just did. I had no clue about any of it until your father called at five o'clock this morning. He was cussing and carrying on because he's been calling you all weekend and you didn't answer, at home or on your cell phone."

"I was pretty tired, Mom, so I turned off the cell."

She was quiet for a while, then gave me that sigh I hate so much. "Oh, Pink. How can you go out with two different men within the same week? I raised you better than that."

"Leave it alone, Mom. Really. Just leave it alone."

"I swear, I don't know what's gotten into you. You've always been so sensible, but lately, you've been making some very poor choices."

"Which you were kind enough to point out in front of God and everybody."

"What are you talking about?"

"The staff meeting. Do you realize how humiliated I was?"

"For heaven's sake, Pink, don't be so dramatic."

Listening to her favorite comeback to any complaint I ever have against her, any attempt I make to point out that maybe, just maybe, she stepped over the line from Good Mom to Queen Bitch, I felt my blood heat up. "You don't do that to anyone else, Mom. Just me. Maybe because I'm your daughter, you think it's okay to point out how stupid you think I am, but it's not."

"You're way overstating this. It wasn't that bad."

I would never, in a million years, convince her that she was wrong, that she'd stepped outta line and needed to be more even-tempered toward me at the office. Ed was rubbing circles against my belly with one hand and playing in my hair with the other. It would be a much better use of my time to fool around with Ed than try to convince Mom to back off.

So I did what any self-respecting only daughter with a powerhouse mother would do. I gave up. "Okay, Mom. You're right and I'm wrong. Now that that's settled, was there some other reason you called?"

"I called to invite you for dinner tonight. Bring Ed, if you like. Your aunt Fred and uncle Alvin will be here."

Sliding deeper under the covers, I wrestled with guilt, and for the first time since I'd moved back to Midland, I won. I stared guilt in the face and told it to take a hike. "Thanks, but I've got a lot to do before work tomorrow. I'm gonna pass."

Dead silence.

"Mom?"

"I can't believe you'd be that small and petty, Whitney Ann. If you're pissed off about something, have the nuts to stand up and say so. Don't play little games."

Extricating myself from Ed's arms, I got out of bed and paced around the room, so angry I could feel the pulse in my neck throbbing. "Yes, I am way beyond pissed off, Mom. You humiliated me in front of the staff, and instead of apologizing and assuring me you'll never do it again, you turn it around on me, as if I'm hysterical and overdramatic. As for dinner, it has nothing to do with being pissed off. I spent Friday night saving Aunt Dru from prison, I spent yesterday hanging out with Ed, and I need to spend today doing my laundry and cleaning up the rest of the disaster Tattoo Man left in my apartment. So, Mom, I don't have *time* to come to dinner, which is altogether different than not coming over because I'm pissed off. Are you following me here?"

She sighed.

And I wanted to throw my head back and scream until my throat hurt.

"Very well, then. I'll see you at the office tomorrow." She hung up.

Ed sat up, his dark hair messy and his eyes still swollen with sleep. "Come back to bed, Pink. Don't let her get to you."

"It's hard not to, Ed."

"I know. I really do. Come on," he invited, tugging back the covers, "get in."

I slid back in and snuggled up next to him. "I love her, Ed, you know I do. But I have to wonder if I can live in the same town."

"Of course you can. You just need to attend and graduate from the Ravenaldt School of Parental Dealing."

"Okay, so matriculate me."

He squeezed me tighter and said over my head, "Our first lesson deals with dinner, since this is your first crisis. It's a known fact that parents will call you to come over for dinner at the worst possible time. If you say no, because it's the worst possible time, this can have two adverse affects. First, they might assume your life's in the toilet and immediately begin to lecture you about how to get it out of the toilet. Second, they may take the reason as an excuse, in which case they will pull out the Martyr Party hats and break into song, which resembles a funeral dirge. At this point, you have no choice but to recant, accept graciously—or ungraciously, it doesn't actually matter—and get in the shower so you can head over for dinner."

He had me grinning, which was undoubtedly his objective. "Okay, so honesty is the wrong way to handle the dinner invitation."

"Yes, which means the best way to handle it, when you can't go because it's the worst possible time, is to lie. You don't even have to be particularly creative. A simple 'I have other plans' will do. If you're afraid they'll press for details, or try and get you to change your mind, you say you're taking someone out for their birthday. Later doesn't work for birthdays, you see, so it's the perfect excuse."

"Mom would ask whose birthday, and where I was going, and who all was invited and what sort of card I got."

"Hmm, well, then in your case, which is extreme, you'll need to pull out the big guns. When you say you have plans and she presses you for details, you should lob a couple of sex bombs her way. Every parent, regardless of how close they are to their children, or how open, will run like hell in the other direction before they'll discuss adult sex. Tell your mother you'd love to have dinner, but you have a date. Before she can ask who with, mention something about needing to get a bikini wax beforehand. Or ask her if she remembers how long you've been off birth control, because you just can't. I guarantee, she'll give you a rain check for dinner."

"How'd you get to be so smart, Professor Ravenaldt?"

"Years of study. And I have six subjects close to me, to add to my research. We've compiled a body of knowledge unequaled in the world of Parental Dealing."

With my cheek pressed against his shoulder, I asked, "What was it like, growing up with six brothers and sisters?"

He didn't answer for a long time. "This isn't going to come out right, so let me say first that I love all of my siblings, a lot. As adults, we're good friends and we enjoy each other. But growing up, with only two bedrooms and an attic between the seven of us, it was pretty awful. I resented the hell outta my folks for having all those damn kids they couldn't afford. My sister didn't get braces until a year ago, when she was twenty-five, and my youngest brother, who broke his leg in football and needed surgery to fix it, still walks with a limp because the parents couldn't afford to get him proper medical attention."

"Did your parents not believe in birth control?"

"They did, but they actually wanted that many kids. God knows why, because every day was a struggle. It wasn't like corny television shows about giant families, where everyone's supportive and helpful and giving and sharing. It was a fight, every day, and a battle to survive. All those scars I showed you are from fights I had with my brothers." His arm tightened ever so slightly, clueing me in that we were heading into infrequently traveled territory. "Of all my brothers and sisters, only one has kids. My sister Maggie, and hers aren't biological. She married a widower with two small children."

"Is that why you don't want any children? Because of how you grew up?"

He sighed and wrapped me up a little tighter. "I'd make a lousy father, Pink. It's not something I'm proud to admit, but I have to be honest. I spent most of my life doing without, and a large part of it taking care of the younger ones because Mom always worked. It's not that I don't like children. I do. I just like being selfish, and once you have a kid, you can no longer be selfish. Even if I ever changed my mind, I'd only want one."

I rubbed my cheek against his shoulder and smiled. "Funny the differences. Being an only child, if I ever had kids, I'd have at least three, real close together, so they'd have company. I was always away from home because I had no one to play with." I stopped and thought about that for a minute. "And I guess I was gone a lot to get away from Dad."

"Do you think you'd be a good mother?"

"Probably not. And it says something that my clock's not ticking. I feel no urgency to have a child, and whenever I give it serious thought, I always think up forty reasons why I don't want one and only one reason why I do."

"What's that?"

"Because I think about getting older, like Aunt Dru, and having no children, and it makes me sad. Makes me want to have a child, so I won't be lonely in my old age. And that's a really dumb and selfish reason to have a kid. That's why I'm not having any. At least, not for a long time."

Ed kissed my forehead. "Maybe we're not up for making babies, Pink, but it's sure as hell fun to practice."

Making love to Ed that morning was different somehow. It was more serious. More weighty or something. And even though I liked it, a lot, it made me extremely anxious. Just like I felt after he went wacko about me buying a house. This bummed me out, because I wanted to go home all starry eyed and thinking about the next time we would be together, as everyone does in the first blush of a romance. Instead, I went home with a vague sense of dread in my heart, as if I were doomed.

After he dropped me off, I went upstairs, and with every step, I cursed my father for screwing me up so much.

Later that night, I'd finished cleaning, folded the last load of laundry and was looking over some of Banty's well files when it hit me; I should go check out the Koko Petroleum well and find out once and for all if it was a fake. I wasn't precisely sure how I was going to do this, but I know a little about how oil wells work, so I thought I could wing it.

I figured nighttime was the best time to go take a look because the chances of anyone being out there were slim to none. If someone was spiking the Koko tanks with stolen oil, they'd do it in the wee hours, when they could almost certainly escape notice. It was barely nine-thirty when I decided to go.

I loaded up with a flashlight, a thermos of coffee and a machete, to kill any rattlers that got too friendly.

At a few minutes before ten, I left the apartment and drove to the north side of town. Out of the city limits, on Telephone Pole Road, I watched for lease road turnoffs and slowed down at each one, looking for Koko Petroleum on any of the well signs. I was almost fifteen miles out of Midland before I found it. Turning onto the caliche road, I hoped Sam's car could take the bumps and ruts.

The road seemed to go on forever, but I thought that might be because I had to drive ten miles an hour to avoid bottoming out the car. It was quiet and scary out there, far from anything, so I switched on the radio to keep me company and chase away any thoughts of turning back.

Finally, I saw the well sign and pulled off the road into the location area around the pumpjack. I saw no one, and wasn't worried about anyone seeing me. In west Texas, out in the oil field, it's a similar feeling to landing on another planet and being the only human on it. The land is flat, choked with scrubby mesquites and yuccas, and it stretches for mile after mile with nothing to break it up except the horse heads of pumpjacks, and narrow roads lined with caliche rock to absorb rain during the few and far between rainstorms, so the pumpers can make it out to the wells.

Every well has a pumper, usually employed by the company that operates the well, and he's responsible for looking after things around the site, making sure the pump is operating, calling service companies out to haul off the accumulated saltwater and generally make sure the well stays productive. He also gauges the tanks every day to see how much oil the well is producing. If the production drops sharply, it's a good clue there's something wrong. Maybe a casing leak in the hole, or a broken sucker rod. The pumper figures it out and hires a service company to come fix it.

Looking over the Koko well, I thought it looked like every other well location I'd ever seen. The ground around the pumpjack was free of debris or plant life. The tank battery was set ten or fifteen yards away, hooked up to a separator that literally separates the oil from the inevitable saltwater, and sends each to its respective tank. I thought about pulling behind some mesquites over by the tank battery, but decided I was being paranoid. Nobody was going to show up, and if they did, I'd park the car close enough that I could jump in and get away.

I pulled around the pumpjack and parked on the other side, with the car pointed toward the lease road, just in case. Grabbing my machete and flashlight, I got out, but the instant I heard the rhythmic sound of the pumpjack as it moved the horse head up and down, up and down, I wondered if I could really do this. Up close, pumpjacks are surprisingly quiet, the only noise made by the hum of the electric motor that drives it, and a distant, eerie, echoing sound of metal on metal, made by the rods in the hole. Pumpjacks are unbelievably creepy, reminiscent of childhood monsters because they're so huge. Since I was a little girl, I've been freaked out by them.

Standing next to the car, I shone the flashlight on the massive thing and watched for a while, talking myself into moving close enough to check out the sucker rods that the pumpjack moves up and down in the well bore, sucking the oil up and into the line that takes it to the tanks. Okay, I could do this. It was just a very large piece of equipment.

I gingerly made my way toward the front, and forced myself not to think about the giant horse head coming down at me while I shone the flashlight on the rods. Looked just like a set of sucker rods should look, so no clue there. Hastily backing up, I decided the pumpjack appeared as real as any other.

Letting out the breath I'd been holding, I turned away and walked toward the tank battery, shining my flashlight along the ground, looking for evidence of a buried line between the pumping unit and the two five-hundred-barrel tanks. The ground on either side of the pumpjack, all the way to the tanks, didn't appear disturbed at all. It looked as dry and hard-scrabble as the rest of the land. That was certainly interesting, especially when I considered that it hadn't rained significantly in forever, which is the only thing that would smooth the ground back to predigging appearance.

At the tank battery, I looked for the attached metal ladder so I could climb up, unlatch the thief hatch and lower a stick inside to see if the tanks had oil in them. The tank on the right had a ladder just to the side. After I cut a slender, five foot branch from the closest mesquite, I laid down my machete, stuck the flashlight in the waistband of my jeans and climbed up the ladder with the stick in one hand. When I reached the top, I carefully laid it on the slightly domed tank top and climbed up another step to get some leverage on the hatch.

I remembered asking Lurch about the thief hatch once when he took me out to a well with him. I imagined a thief could climb in and hide, and that's why they called it that. Naturally, being the old grouch that he is, Lurch told me I was goofy, because why would a thief want to hide in a tank of oil? Besides, he'd die if he got himself coated in oil. Turned out, the thief hatch was nothing so dramatic—just a hole with a lid on it, which the pumper uses to drop his gauge in and measure the level of oil inside.

I tugged at the metal handle, but the thing was jammed or something and I couldn't get it open. Not to be deterred, I climbed down and retrieved the machete, then climbed back up and worked on prying it open. It still wouldn't budge, and okay, so I was frustrated—I started banging on it with the machete and cussing at it at the same time.

While I stood there, twenty-five feet in the air on a metal ladder, debating what to do, I saw headlights turning into the well location. Son of a bitch! I'd made all that noise and hadn't heard a vehicle approaching. Which meant I had no time to make it to my car and haul ass. All I could do was hide, and hope whoever it was wouldn't come looking for me. Maybe they'd think someone had abandoned their car at the location. It wasn't a stretch because Sam's car was pretty sad looking with all the gray spots.

Dammit! What the hell was someone doing out here at this time of night?

I realized I didn't have time to climb down, so I went the other direction, scrambling onto the top of the tank, to the rear of the slight dome, and sprawling on my belly. I figured if I lay flat and didn't move, I might not be noticed. People tend not to look up, unless a movement catches their eye.

From my perch on the back of the curve, I watched a small SUV pull into the well area. I thought it would come to a stop, but the driver went wonky, and instead of braking, must have hit the gas. I cringed when the SUV hit the pumpjack, cracking one of its headlights and smashing in part of the grill. Then I thanked God I hadn't parked on that side of the well, because Sam's car would now be very expensive to fix.

The SUV backed up, turned slightly and stopped again. With the car lights still on, reflecting back from the pumpjack and the mesquites beyond, I could easily see the door open. A big man got out, moved into the light from the beams, and peered into the surrounding brush.

I nearly jumped out of my skin and rolled off the tank when he yelled, "I know you're here, Pinkie, so you may as well come on out and let's get this over with."

Get what over with? I squinted to see him better and noted that he was bald and wore a leather vest. Then he turned the other direction and I saw the tattoo. Spider-Man.

I think my guardian angel whispered, "I took you on because you were supposed to be a boring CPA. I'm putting in for a transfer."

Tattoo Man was also not happy with me. "Okay, have it your way, but it's gonna be a lot more painful when I find you." He took off through the brush, a hefty Maglite in one hand and a very nasty-looking pistol in the other.

From my perch on top of the tank, I watched him wind his way through the mesquite, then lost him when he moved out of the light from the car and into the brush behind the tanks. I could still gauge his direction, however, because I heard him cussing as the mesquite thorns scratched his bare arms. I was so glad I'd gone back down for the machete, because if he saw it there by the tank, it would be a dead giveaway.

I'll never know if he would have continued looking, or eventually found me, because during his search, a god-awful squeal came from the direction of the pumpjack and he hurried back into the clearing to check it out.

Looking toward the pumpjack, I swear, I almost had a heart attack and died, right there on the top of that tank. While I watched in dazed confusion and terror, the entire thing heeled over and fell to the ground in a groaning, metal-on-metal, thunderous crash. The back half of Sam's Ford was a pancake.

Well, at least I didn't have to get it painted.

Tattoo Man looked about as freaked out as I was. Almost as if he'd forgotten I was around somewhere, he ran to the back of the SUV, lifted a large bundle and heaved it away from him. It hit the ground and rolled a bit. After that he went to the driver's door, paused to look at the cloud of dust settling back to the ground, then climbed in and peeled out.

I stayed where I was for a long time after he'd gone, for a couple of reasons. I was afraid he'd come back, and I was still shaking with terror. One of my worst childhood fears was now lying on the ground, on top of Sam's car. It freaked me out in a way I can't really explain.

Maybe thirty minutes after Tattoo Man had split the scene, I made my way back to the ladder and slowly climbed down to the ground. I wanted so badly to run away, but that would only get me a lot of blisters and maybe a few snakebites. I had to go to the car and see if my cell phone was in one piece. I needed to call Ed to come and get me from this real live nightmare.

It took awhile, but I finally skirted the dead pumpjack and made it to the front of the car. The massive crash had shattered the windows, so I was able to look in the front seat, which was now level with the ground.

Lucky for me, Kate Spade had survived and my cell phone was intact. Unlucky for me, I couldn't get any reception out there in the middle of nowhere. I'd have to walk to Telephone Pole Road and hope a cell tower was somewhere close.

Turning away from the car, I started across the clearing and was close to the spot where the SUV had stopped when I stumbled across Tattoo Man's bundle.

Trina Lorenzo.

Oh, God. The poor thing was wrapped in some kind of plastic tarp, and I guess when Tattoo Man dropped her, she'd come partially undone. Her lovely face was visible, along with one slender arm. I couldn't leave her exposed like that, lying on the ground like so much garbage where wild animals could get to her. Since she'd obviously been killed somewhere else, I didn't consider this a crime scene, and I set about moving her to the front seat of the car. I'm not gonna lie—it was the most grotesque thing I'd ever done. And even though it saddened me that she'd been murdered, and out of respect I felt compelled to move her dead body, it gave me the willies like nothing ever had.

When I was done, I walked away from the car, and the pumpjack, and Trina's dead body, headed for the lease road and a very long walk out to Telephone Pole Road. I was almost across the location clearing when my flashlight illuminated something shiny in the dirt. I bent to look closer and saw that it was a ring. A man's ring. I picked it up with a small stick, to avoid screwing up any fingerprints, and felt so nauseous, it was all I could do not to hurl. A class ring, from Stanford University, and inside, engraved in pretty cursive script, was a name. David Lorenzo. The bastard had killed her, then had his goon haul her out to the middle of nowhere and dump her.

I took the ring to the car and left it there, with Trina, then turned and hurried out to the lease road.

Not even five minutes into my walk, which was the scariest of my life, I saw a light far ahead of me. Because I was in the middle of nowhere, I knew it had to be headlights. Tattoo Man was coming back? I stopped cold and looked around for any possible place to hide besides the dark and creepy mesquites. Of course there was none, so I sucked in a couple of deep breaths, gripped the machete more tightly and plunged into the brush. I promised God I'd help Aunt Dru with a thousand Bible mailings if he'd just keep the rattlesnakes away from me.

Too bad I didn't mention coyotes. While I was in there, shivering with fear, I felt something cold against my hand, and when I switched on the flashlight to see what it was, a coyote darted away from me. Maybe coyotes are kinda cute and cool when they're on a restaurant sign, or starring in an *Animal Planet* special. In the wild, up close and personal, they are not cute. They have pointy teeth.

The lights were coming closer and I had to turn off my flashlight. I waited and stayed as still as possible, then peered out at the car as it passed. I nearly wet my pants when I saw that it was not Tattoo Man's SUV, but a black Cadillac the size of a pontoon boat. Big Mama! What the hell was she doing out here? Looking for me?

Deciding to stay put until I figured out an alternate plan, I stood there in the mesquites and listened to her car engine fade in the distance, then stop altogether. While I waited for inspiration of some kind to tell me what to do, the wind picked up. Fast. In west Texas, storm fronts move in at the speed of light, and within five minutes, the wind was blowing so hard, the mesquites around me took on a life of their own and attacked me. Then the sky lit up with a flash of lightning and rolling thunder crashed through the night.

Great. I'd escaped Tattoo Man and it looked as though I was going to avoid Big Mama, but it didn't matter because I was about to be struck by lightning. Or pelted with hail. Knowing my luck, a plague of locusts was en route to my hiding place, as well.

Maybe it was the wind, or maybe it was my overactive imagination brought on by nerves and fright, but I swear I heard my name, from way far away, long and drawn out, without the *P*. I strained to hear, but all I could catch was, "Ii-iiiiink!" Was Big Mama yelling for me? If so, was she an idiot? Or did she think I was an idiot?

Finally, just about the time the sky opened up and hard rain began to fall, I saw headlights coming back down the road toward me. The Cadillac slowly passed my hiding spot and I let out the breath I'd been holding.

Curious to see what she'd done at the location, I headed back toward the well instead of the highway. I pointed the beam of the flashlight around, but couldn't see anything different than when I'd left, fifteen minutes ago. Soaked to the skin by then, I walked closer to Sam's demolished car, and realized something was different. Way different.

Trina Lorenzo was no longer in the front seat.

It took me half an hour to get back out to the highway, even half running, but it was primarily because I stayed in the mesquites, off the road. I was paranoid at that point, scared of the lightning and afraid Big Mama or Tattoo Man might be lurking around.

As soon as I had even the tiniest indication of reception, I dialed Ed's number. No answer. I tried again. And again. I called his cell and got no answer. It was after midnight. Where the hell was Ed? I tried the cell again. I tried his home number again. I even called the office. No answer. From the shelter of the mesquites lining the highway, I stared at the rain and lightning and pondered the significance of his absence.

Okay, I gotta be honest. After what I went through during my marriage to George, I'm all out of faith and trust. The first inkling of doubt and I went over the edge. While I lay low from the lightning, I imagined Ed with any number of women. It was ugly, and awful, and I knew it was wrong to immediately assume the worst, but I swear I couldn't help it. All those dark, depressing feelings came back in full force and I knew they'd never left—they'd only been waiting for something like this to break out through every pore and make me miserable.

By the time I had Ed sleeping with every remotely attractive woman in Midland, Texas, I knew I had to get a grip and focus on getting back home. I called Sam.

He was asleep. "Weston here," he semibarked.

"Sam, I am really, *really* sorry to wake you up, but can you come and get me?"

"Pink?"

"I found Trina Lorenzo, and she's dead. And your car is totaled."

"Did you have a wreck, with Trina?"

"No. Tattoo Man dumped her body out at this well location, and that was after he ran into the pumpjack and the whole damn thing fell over and landed on your car. Then Big Mama showed up in her Cadillac and must have taken Trina's body, because when I went back to look, she was gone."

"Pink, stop crying and get a grip."

I hadn't realized I was crying. "Sam, this is so creepy, being out here all alone in a thunderstorm, and there are coyotes out here." *And Ed is cheating on me!*

"They won't hurt you."

Maybe not, but I decided having a bite taken outta my leg

by a coyote would be less painful that what I was going through over Ed. Where the *hell* was he? "I know that, but it's freaking me out, anyway. Sam, please, just come and get me."

"Tell me where you are."

I managed to give him directions, and he said, "Okay, Pink. Just relax. Tattoo Man and Big Mama won't come back."

"How do you know?"

"I don't. I just said that to make you feel better." He hung up and I wished he was still on the line.

Five minutes later, he called back from his cell phone. "You okay?"

"No. That pumpjack freaked me out bad. They've always given me the creeps, but watching one fall over like that—it was scary as hell."

"I've never heard of a pumpjack falling over. For one thing, they weigh several tons. And they're attached to the rods in the hole."

"I've never heard of it, either, but swear to God, that's what happened."

"And the Ford was underneath it?"

"Yes. I'm so sorry, Sam. I'll pay you for it. Blue book value, or whatever."

"Don't worry about that right now. I'm just glad you weren't in it."

Remembering what it looked like, I shuddered. "Me, too."

"What were you doing out there, anyway?"

I told him and waited for a lecture, but none was forthcoming. Instead, he asked, "Why did you call me instead of Ed?"

"Actually, I did call Ed, but he never answered." *Because he's off screwing some other woman.* Shit! I wanted to curl up on the ground and scream and cry. Maybe I would have, if I hadn't been afraid of snakes. And tarantulas.

"So, Mr. Wonderful let you down. And look who's coming to save your hide. Why don't you go ahead and admit it, Pink? You picked the wrong guy."

"You can say that again," I mumbled.

"Hey, what's this? Is the bloom off the rose?"

I stared up at the stormy sky. "Sam, if Ed was fooling around and you knew it, you would tell me, wouldn't you?"

"Damn straight. You'd be upset and I'd be right there to take advantage of your vulnerability."

"No you wouldn't."

"Maybe not right away." He was quiet, then said softly, "He's not cheating, Pink."

"How would you know?"

"Because there are guys who cheat and guys who don't. Ed's definitely in the don't category. Trust me on this."

By the time Sam arrived, I was way beyond being a basket case. Between fear and paranoia, I was not in good shape. After I took off my muddy boots and tossed them in Sam's trunk, I scrambled to get into the passenger side. "Let's go."

"Not so fast. I need to check this out before I call the sheriff." He took off down the caliche lease road and I clenched my hands and teeth.

When he pulled into the clearing, he got out and I watched him walk around the location in the driving rain with my little flashlight, then climb the tank ladder and look in the thief hatch, which I noticed he opened with almost no effort. Go figure. He used my stick and checked the level, then climbed down and came back to the car. "That pumpjack is so corroded, I have no idea how it was standing to begin with. Somebody coated it with paint, so it looks okay, but all around the bottom it's rusted out. When the SUV hit it, whatever was holding it together cracked through and it caved. It's also without any purpose whatsoever because it's not connected to the well. The sucker rods were just hanging there, not attached to anything but the horse head."

"Is there oil in the tank?"

He looked at me in the light from the dash. "It's chock-full."

I gazed out across the location, toward the car and the pumpjack, and the tankful of oil off of somebody else's well. "Looks like Garza and the Texas Rangers have an answer to where all the stolen oil is going." I turned to Sam. "And it looks like Banty isn't such a nutcase, after all."

Sam nodded solemnly. "Now all you have to do is figure out who's pulling the strings at Koko. How do you plan to do that?"

I told him about the limited partners, the old ladies at the Bluebird Retirement Center that MayBelle had told me about. "I'm hoping I can find out from one of them where Gus Thompkins is, or who's taking care of the partnership in his absence."

"Don't forget, Pink, somebody out there wants you dead."

"Tattoo Man?"

"And whoever blew up Lorenzo's car. You need to be extremely careful, and don't go anywhere without the Bobcat." He glanced at my purse. "Have you got it with you right now?"

I didn't answer.

"You have to get over this fear of guns, Pink. Next Sunday, I'm taking you out to the range and we're going to practice."

Maybe because I was just scared enough, I said with a tired sigh, "All right, Sam."

Chapter 12

At first, the Andrews County sheriff thought I was the bomb.
Even though I was soaking wet and freaked out about Ed, I
took a small amount of personal satisfaction from his glowing compliments about my discovery of Koko's fake well. He
was so enthused, he called the Texas Ranger who'd been investigating the oil thefts and told him all about it.

It was still raining, though the thunder and lightning had
moved on, and I could tell the sheriff was anxious to wrap it
up and get back to dry land. Maybe that's why he wasn't all
that interested in a disappearing dead body. But I suspected
his lack of concern was largely because he thought I was a
hysterical female. He as much as said so. After all, he explained slowly, as though I couldn't follow his line of thinking, why would someone come out and pick up a dead body?
He apparently never got around to wondering why Tattoo
Man came out to the location in the first place.

Sam gave me a look that said I should leave it alone. I knew he was right, and it was obvious the sheriff wasn't going to believe me, so I gave up.

Then he said they would find out who was behind Koko and I should stay out of it. Still wanting to be helpful, I tried to tell him what I'd discovered thus far, but the man was way too busy talking to Sam about the corroded pumpjack and marveling that someone could rig it up to look so real. Even after I managed to get him to listen, he rather arrogantly told me there was a much simpler way to find out who was running Koko. Then he winked at Sam, one of those "Hey, we've got a penis and she doesn't, so clearly she's a moron" sort of winks. My mild pleasure over his compliments evaporated, along with any confidence I had in his abilities. If the fate of the free world depended on the Andrews County sheriff, we'd be speaking Arabic and shopping for burkas in the near future.

In the car on the way home Sam said, "I'm getting to know you pretty well, Pink, and I can tell you're way pissed at the sheriff, that you think the guy's a moron."

"So?"

"So I know you have no intention of backing off, but I'm ordering you to do what the man says. Leave it alone, Pink. As soon as you hear from the controller at Lorenzo Petroleum and find out why Banty's royalties were reduced, write up a report for him and call it a day."

"Sam, do you seriously think the sheriff can figure out who's behind Koko?"

"Eventually, yes." He glanced at me before refocusing on the rainy road while driving five miles below the speed limit. "Don't forget, the CIA has another man in Midland. He was supposed to be Becker's contact. Whoever he is, he's working this thing, as well. You have to let it go, Pink, and let the authorities do their job."

"Of course you would say that, seeing as you're Mr. FBI."

"I'm also saying that because you work for me. You're my

responsibility and if anything happens to you, I'd take it to my grave." He shot me another look. "Where I'll be going a lot sooner than I expected, because your mother will send me there."

I wanted to lay into Sam, but I knew it wouldn't do me any good. I was getting to know him fairly well, too, and he wasn't going to budge.

I grudgingly agreed and he looked pleased at my acquiescence.

When he pulled up at my apartment complex, I impulsively kissed his cheek. "Thanks, Sam."

He gave me a solemn look. "I'd feel a lot better if you'd pack a few things and come stay with me tonight."

"I'll be okay. As soon as I'm upstairs, I'll pull out the Bobcat." I got out of the car, retrieved my muddy boots from the trunk and waved goodbye before I started up the stairs.

It was almost three o'clock in the morning and I was wet, exhausted and ready for a hot shower. Inside, I dropped the boots and headed for my bathroom, but stopped short at the telephone on my nightstand. I picked up the receiver and punched in Ed's number. No answer. He didn't pick up his cell phone, either. I slammed down the phone and went to get in the shower, vowing that I would never, ever, so long as I lived, get involved with another man. Life was way too short to spend even one minute of it feeling that miserable.

By the time I got out of the shower, I was in a rage. It's probably a good thing I didn't have a car, because I'd most likely have gone out looking for him, which would make me worse than pathetic. It would take me right back to my marriage, when I'd turned into a compulsive spy.

I got in bed, but couldn't sleep, my mind conjuring up disturbing images of Ed's large, tanned hands running up and down soft, female skin that wasn't mine. I wanted to cry, but wouldn't let myself. Instead, I just got more angry.

Along about four-thirty, someone knocked on the door and I sat bolt upright in bed, my heart racing and my palms turning clammy. I retrieved the Bobcat from the nightstand and tiptoed to the door to look through the peephole.

It was Ed.

I swung open the door and pointed the Bobcat at him. "If you take one step toward this door, I'll blow a hole in you."

He ignored me and came right on in, crowding me backward until he was all the way inside. He kicked the door closed without ever taking his eyes from mine. "You've got a lotta nerve, threatening me."

"You've got a lotta nerve to show your face over here. Where the hell have you been all night?"

"Where have *I* been?"

I realized then he looked as pissed off as I was. He was wet and muddy and his jaw was locked so tightly I could see a pulse beating in his cheek. I remembered how George used to act mad, trying to get his bluff in before I could ask him who he'd been doing the night before. "Yes, Ed, where have *you* been? Was it your ex-wife, or somebody I don't know?"

"You think I've been with another woman? Is *that* what you think?"

"That's exactly what I think. Where else does a man go until four-thirty in the morning, where he doesn't answer his phone?"

He looked ready to come apart at the seams. If I hadn't been so righteous myself, maybe I'd have noticed he was definitely not playing at being mad.

"Are you sure you want to know? Are you absolutely *positive* you want to know?"

"Absolutely positive." I hoped I didn't throw up right there in front of him, but it was starting to look like a real possibility.

"I was driving a black Cadillac out on Telephone Pole Road." Oh, shit. Stepping back, I dropped my arm and let the

Bobcat dangle from my fingers. I opened my mouth to say something, but nothing came out. I was too stunned to speak.

"I'm gonna be an old man, long before my time, all because of tonight, which I did because of *you,* and now you're standing there accusing me of fucking another woman? I swear to God, Pink, this is it! Either you're in or you're out, but *no way* can I live like this."

"What else would I think? I called all night and you never answered."

"Couldn't I have the benefit of the doubt? Maybe I was sick. Maybe I was stranded out on the road somewhere. Maybe I was beamed up by Martians. Could you have considered *any* other option? Did you have to immediately jump to the conclusion I was with another woman?"

"I can't help it, Ed. I'm conditioned to react that way."

"How many times do I have to tell you, *I'm not George!*"

He looked so pissed, so hurt, that all my rage flowed out of me, leaving only a hollow, empty feeling. God, I was a screwup, wasn't I? "I'm sorry, Ed."

"What you are is a hypocrite. I'm out of pocket for a few hours and you paint me out to be a cheating scumbag. You go out with another guy, then spend the night with him, but I'm supposed to just take your word for it that you didn't sleep with him. I'm freakin' sick of being a chump, Pink." He pushed past me, headed for the kitchen where he opened cabinets until he found the Jack Daniels. He unscrewed the top, tossed it aside and took a long drink, straight from the bottle. Still holding it, he began to pace around the living room. "You owe me a blow job for putting me through seeing Sam's car underneath that damn pumpjack. I hope you never, ever feel like that, because it sucked worse than anything I've experienced in my lifetime. I thought you were inside, beneath..." His voice trailed away, leaving a deathlike silence.

No wonder he was so pissed off. He'd been scared out of

his mind. For me. And I'd met him at the door with a gun in my hand. I was afraid I'd used up all my chances with Ed, and it made me far more unhappy than I ever could have imagined. "Why were you out there?"

"Looking for you. And picking up Trina."

"I don't understand."

"About eleven o'clock, I got a call from Jake Hollingsworth." Ed took another drink and paced to the window, where he opened the drapes and stared out at the rain, which was still coming down in sheets. "He wasn't lying about following you, but he was lying about Gert putting him up to it. Jake's with the CIA. After Becker was offed, he had instructions to follow you, to make note of who you saw and what you did." Ed looked over his shoulder at me. "Evidently, the CIA has a lot of faith in your abilities." He turned back to the window and added quietly, "Santorelli is in the middle of things now, whether because of you or Lorenzo, I have no idea. The weird part is, Jake says he's not involved through the CIA, or even the finance committee."

I laid the Bobcat on the turquoise Formica table and took a seat on one of the vinyl chairs. Ed was blowing my mind and it was a huge effort to take it all in. I randomly wondered if Gert had a clue that her ex worked for the CIA.

"I think there's something extremely weird about that guy."

"Jake?"

"Santorelli." He took another swig. "When Jake called, he said he followed you out to the Koko well, but his car broke down just after he turned onto the lease road. He pushed it into some brush and walked to the location, where he found your car and Trina's body, but not you. He called his supervisor, who told him to hide Trina for the time being. Keeping all of this under wraps is becoming more difficult, and they're afraid it'll start widespread panic if the public becomes aware of terrorist activity in the area. There's a mole somewhere in the police department, so the supervisor said to keep Trina hidden until they're closer to finding something."

"Assuming Trina was killed by terrorists."

"I don't think there's any doubt about that. She was abducted by the tattoo guy, and he's the one who dumped her body."

"Do you think he's the one or is he just a goon?"

"Just a goon, a lackey who does all the dirty work."

"Did you see Lorenzo's Stanford ring with Trina?"

"I wrapped it in a piece of paper." He reached for the drapery cord and swung it to and fro. "Lorenzo didn't kill her, Pink. He's not behind the Al Qaeda funding. Whoever did kill her left that ring to make Lorenzo look guilty. That's obvious because he left it right on top of her body."

"No, he didn't. I moved Trina to the car, then found the ring by accident, close to where Tattoo Man parked the SUV. I think it fell from the car when he pulled the body out."

"I'm not saying it's impossible, but I don't think Dave did it."

I disagreed, but I wasn't going to get into it with Ed about David Lorenzo. "How did Jake call from the location? I couldn't get a signal out there."

"He's with the CIA. They have communication equipment that would probably work from the bottom of the ocean."

I watched him at the window, his broad shoulders silhouetted against the parking lot light. He told me everything in a dull, passive voice, as though all of this was mundane.

Ed took another drink of the whiskey, then wiped his mouth on the back of his hand. "Jake's car broke down so he couldn't transport Trina. He has a number he can call if he gets up against it, a last-resort contact. He says no one knows who it is, but the operatives call him Santa Claus, because technically, he's nonexistent. Santa told Jake to call me."

I could see the Spider-Man birthday cake in my mind and a lightbulb lit it up to blinding white. "Now I know why Santa was the name Becker put on the cake. That's who I was supposed to get the information to."

"I think you did get it to Santa, in a roundabout way."

"What do you mean?"

"Santa instructed Jake to tell me to use an old Cadillac that would be parked on the lot at Wal-Mart. If anyone followed me for any reason, they couldn't trace the plates."

"So that's how you ended up in Big Mama's car. I thought it was her out there."

He glanced over his shoulder again. "Think about that, Pink."

It took a minute, but it was five o'clock in the morning so I have an excuse for being a little slow. When it did finally hit me, I couldn't quite reconcile the idea that Big Mama wasn't a bad guy. "Big Mama isn't on our side."

"Are you sure?"

"If she is, why did she kill Becker? Why did she rip off Spider-Man?"

"If she's not on our side, why did Santa instruct me to use her car to go out and pick up Trina? If Becker was a good guy, why was he leaving the country? Did you ever wonder? As for Spider-Man, when that key fob turned out to be a dead end, I think Al Qaeda sent Tattoo Man to search your home, then watch you to see if you'd lead them to Becker's information."

"And I did."

"If the big lady hadn't been there to take him away from you, Al Qaeda would have gotten Spider-Man."

"Okay, so let's say she is on our side. That would mean the Feds now have Spider-Man and his microchip, so they'd know who's behind the terrorist funding. If they know, why is Hollingsworth still following me around, why keep Trina's death a secret, and why hasn't the man behind the funding been arrested?"

"If Becker was a traitor, if he was selling information to

Al Qaeda, Spider-Man would have information they could use—not the Feds."

"Ed, he couldn't be a traitor. He looked so sincere, so scared. Besides, if he was a traitor, why did he put Santa's name on that cake?"

"He was sincerely scared the Feds were on to him. As for putting Santa's name on the cake, maybe he was sending a message to Al Qaeda, something that pointed to Santa's identity."

If anyone else had suggested it, I'd have called them crazy, but with Ed applying his weird brand of Ed-Logic to it, I had to concede that he could be right. I recalled the big woman's surprise about Tattoo Man the night Becker was killed. She was genuinely shocked when I said he'd gotten to me before she did. I'd wondered why she'd waited all day to kill Becker, and whether she'd been telling the truth that Becker was about to pull a gun on her. *He reached for the gun the instant he knew who I was.* Hadn't she said that? Somehow, Becker realized she wasn't just a big woman with a tiny dog in her purse, and he knew the jig was up. She'd stabbed him before he could shoot her.

"What about that night at the Salvation Army? Steve was there, shooting at her. Wouldn't he know if she's one of the good guys?"

"There was another guy. Maybe it was Santorelli who was shooting at the other guy, who was shooting at Big Mama."

A headache was coming on. Lord, it was confusing. "Okay, so maybe you're right and Big Mama really is on our side. Why didn't Santa tell Jake to call her? Why do you suppose he gave Jake your name?"

"I don't know. I didn't ask why they picked me."

That struck me as very odd. Ed wasn't one to do anything if there wasn't a solid, logical reason behind it. "Santa told Jake to tell you to use the Cadillac, so no one could trace the license plates to you, but it's weird to me that you'd go out and get Trina. Isn't it illegal to remove a body from the scene of a crime?"

"Of course it's illegal! And I'm a fucking lawyer!"

"But you did it, anyway. Why?"

He was quiet for so long, I wondered if he hadn't heard me. I was just about to ask again when he said softly, "He said you were out there. He said he lost you, that he didn't know where you were. He said the tattoo dude drove past him on the lease road and he was afraid maybe he'd gotten you."

"So you changed your mind about getting Trina because of me?" I wasn't sure anyone, ever, had done anything like that for me. Ed had broken the law, broken his own code of honor—for me.

"Yes, for *you!*" He stalked toward me and set the bottle on the table with a bang. "Jake said you were out there. Do you have any idea what that meant? What I imagined could be happening to you?"

While I looked up at his wonderful face, my whole body became a low pressure system and I braced myself for a torrential downpour, biting my lip as hard as I could to keep from crying.

"I went out there wondering where you were, and saw your car beneath the pumpjack, and went over to it and saw a body in the front seat and for just a few seconds that lasted a million years, I thought, that's why Jake couldn't find her. She was in the car when the pumpjack fell. Swear to God, I lost ten years off my life, and I'm ashamed to say I was glad it was Trina, only because it meant the body wasn't yours."

Impulsively, I stood and reached out to him, but he turned away and walked to the door.

"I've gotta get some sleep, but first, I have to go see my

brother Maynard and explain why there's a dead body in the walk-in freezer at his restaurant."

"Ed, I'm sorry."

He turned the knob and said quietly, "Yeah, I know, Pink, but I have to be honest and say I'm not up for a sorry relationship. Sorry gets to be kinda worn-out, you know?" He opened the door and walked out.

I didn't bother going back to bed. No way could I have slept. After I made a pot of coffee, I sat on the couch and gave a lot of thought to why I'd gone off the deep end over Ed's absence. Definitely, I would have had to feel better to get to rotten. But my lousy emotional state wasn't for me so much as for Ed. I'd hurt him, and that bugged me on a level I didn't know I had, way down deep. I couldn't get the image of his face out of my head, or the tone of his voice. Maybe we were over, but I couldn't let it go like that. I had to tell him how I felt.

The problem was, I wasn't sure how I felt, other than wretched.

While I sat there, wondering what to do about Ed, my cell phone rang. It was Steve.

"I'm sorry to wake you up, Pink."

"You didn't. I'm up."

He cleared his throat. "I got a call from David on Saturday, and he told me how you helped him recover Colby. I wanted to check on you and see if everything's all right with your aunt. And with you."

"It's fine. Well, sort of. I called Aunt Dru yesterday afternoon and she's having some trouble with guilt."

"I guess it's natural to feel guilty, but she did what she thought was right."

"She's also beside herself with worry about Trina." Now, all of her worrying wouldn't change a thing, because Trina was dead. I thought of her, lying out there in the dirt, and squeezed my eyes shut to block out the image. Didn't work.

"Actually, Trina is another reason for my call. Have you talked to Ed Ravenaldt?"

"He just left."

"I'm calling from a secure line, just so you know. I need to know what happened while you were out there, Pink."

Remembering what Ed had said about Steve, that he was now in the middle of things, I didn't consider it an odd statement. I told him, and when I was done, he said, "This is classified information, but I'm going to tell you some of it, because if I don't, you're going to get yourself killed. First off, Dan Becker was working for the other side."

"Ed suspected as much. He wondered why Becker was leaving the country."

"Becker was CIA, but he turned because the Al Qaeda network offered him enough money to sell out other operatives. When the agency lost four overseas operatives within the same week, they knew somebody had turned traitor. They sent someone to Midland to check it out, and he confirmed what they suspected."

"Is that why Becker was killed?"

"Pink, the government doesn't kill its citizens, no matter how bad they are. He was to be arrested for treason at the airport, but he never made it."

I wondered if Steve would tell me anything about Big Mama. "Did Al Qaeda kill him?"

He answered without hesitation. "The big lady isn't Al Qaeda. She's with a vigilante organization that operates undercover as another terrorist group."

"So technically, she murdered Becker."

"Technically, legally, yeah, she did, although she wouldn't have stabbed him if he hadn't been about to pull a pistol on her. Her job was to make sure he didn't pass off his information to Al Qaeda before he got to the airport. The agency needed him to get to the airport and attempt to board a plane to Venezuela before they arrested him."

"You just said Big Mama's a vigilante, but it sounds like she's working for the CIA."

"Let's just say she can do things they can't, because she's willing to bend the rules a little. But she has friends in places where it matters. No one will be arresting her."

The significance of that bit of information was staggering. "Did Becker know the agency was on to him? Is that why he was leaving the country?"

"I think he suspected, but he wasn't sure. He did know his local Al Qaeda contact planned to kill him after he handed over his last report. That's why he wanted to hand it off to you, to divert their attention long enough for him to get away."

"If he was working for them, why did Al Qaeda want to kill him?"

"So long as he was alive, he was a liability to them. It's their way. You're either with them or against them, and nobody gets out alive. Becker knew that, but I guess he thought he could beat the system. For him, it was all about the money."

"So that night at the Salvation Army, it wasn't you shooting at Big Mama, was it?"

"No, Pink. I came to make sure you and your mother were safe, and when I got there, I saw another man shooting at the big lady. I tried to help her out."

"If she's on our side, why did she threaten me and Mom? Why point a gun at us and threaten to kill us if we didn't hand over Spider-Man? And what's with the holdup, anyway? Did she think we were incapable of getting Spider-Man to the right people? And speaking of which, where *is* Spider-Man?"

"To keep herself and the others in her organization safe, she has to maintain the illusion of being a bad-ass member of another terrorist group, out for the same kind of information

Al Qaeda wants. That way, she's merely competition, not a threat. She took Spider-Man because she's trained in espionage and is a skilled marksman. What he had to say was way too important to let it get away. As for the man himself, all three plastic inches of him turned up in Washington, where he's been analyzed. The information on the microchip would have meant certain death to several more operatives. Becker was about as low as a man can get. The sick thing is, there are others in Midland who are helping Al Qaeda, who are diverting money to them. How an American citizen can do that, I don't know. All I know is that we have to find these people and stop them."

"I was trying, up until about four hours ago. The sheriff told me to back off, and Sam ordered me to mind him."

"Probably just as well, Pink. There's too much at stake. Under normal circumstances, I know you could find out who's behind all of it, but after what happened last night, it's too dangerous."

Part of me agreed, because after all, I wasn't real hip on winding up like Trina. But another part of me hated that I was out of the loop, that I couldn't follow up on all the leads I'd made. "Steve, do you know why they killed Trina?"

"Same reason they wanted to kill Becker. She knew too much and she was trying to bail out by escaping to Venezuela."

"So you think she was involved with Al Qaeda? For real?"

"I can't say for sure, but her relationship with Santa Morena doesn't look good, and the fact the tattoo guy grabbed her and killed her leads me to believe she was involved."

I hated to ask because it was beyond awkward, but I had to know. "I know he's a good friend, but do you think Lorenzo had anything to do with her death?"

Steve didn't answer for such a long time I was about to back up and apologize. But then he replied in a solemn voice, "It would take a lot to convince me. I've known David a long time and been through a lot with him. But my years in the Senate have taught me that otherwise good people are capable of very bad things."

Instinctively, I knew how hard it was for him to admit the possibility aloud. "The big lady drives an old black Cadillac, and I saw it parked at Lorenzo's house. If she's one of us, what was she doing out there?"

"Must be coincidence, Pink. Dave has an old black Cadillac his mother used to drive. Now, he keeps it for the household staff to use."

I thought that was too off-the-wall to be coincidence, but I didn't pursue it. "Steve, I hope it isn't Lorenzo."

"Me, too, Pink. Me, too." He sighed into the phone. "What are they going to do with your car?"

"It's totaled, so I guess I'll pay Sam for it and go get a new one."

"If you need any help, would you let me know?"

I was unsure if he meant help as in monetary help, or help as in manly, help me pick out a car help. I supposed it didn't really matter. I'm a big girl. I can buy a car, all on my own. "I will, but I think I can handle it," I said diplomatically.

He cleared his throat, a sure sign he was nervous about what he was about to say. "As long as I've got you on the phone, there's one other thing I have to ask."

"Okay."

"In a few weeks, my father's hosting a birthday dinner for me, here in Washington. I'd like for you and your mother to come."

An hour earlier, I'd have begged off because I wouldn't have wanted to upset Ed. But it was an hour later. An hour after Ed had walked out with a finality I was trying like hell not to cry about. What did it matter who I saw, or where I went, or what I did? D.C. in the fall was bound to be nice. "I can't speak for Mom, but I'd like that, Steve. How old will you be?"

"Actually, I turned thirty-seven last Wednesday, but his

schedule wouldn't allow him to have a party then. He'll be sending an invitation, but I thought I'd go ahead and mention it. Please convince your mother to come. I'd really like her to meet my dad."

"I can't make any promises, but I'll try." I paused. "Even though I know it will be a disaster."

"What's so wrong with getting my dad and your mom together? He's lonely since Mom died, and since your mother's single, maybe she'd like to hang out with a guy like him. He's fifty-eight, and most people consider him a good-looking man. I wouldn't know, because he's my dad, and I'm a guy, but I do know he's interesting, and educated, and he tells great jokes, and he likes walks on the beach and world peace."

I was almost laughing. "Just curious, Steve, but would this be a ploy on your part to get your dad interested in something besides you?"

"Actually, it's a ploy to get him interested in something that won't kill him. Ever since he lost Mom, he keeps volunteering for these crazy defense-department jobs."

"I'll ask her, Steve, but I just don't see it happening. Mom has issues with men."

"That's okay. Dad has issues with women."

"Like what?"

"Let's just say he'll never be a sugar daddy."

"Got a few running after him for the money?"

"All the time. But for all that he can be a lotta fun, he's pretty conservative, and there's no way he'd hook up with a younger woman. I'm telling you, he will really like your mom."

"How do you know?"

"She runs her own CPA firm, she breaks into the Salvation Army because she thinks she can save the world and she raised you. Besides that, she's damn good-looking. Come on, what can it hurt? If they don't hit it off, it's not a big deal. But at least we tried, right?"

I didn't mention that Mom was involved with the air-conditioner man. Mostly because I apparently wasn't supposed to know, in light of the fact she never told me, but also because I wasn't sure exactly how they were involved. I decided to go with the I Don't Know Policy. "All right. We'll both come to your dinner party."

"Good. I'll look forward to it. Plan on staying here, with me. We can go up to the Hill one day and I'll give you the behind-the-scenes nickel tour."

"Thanks, Steve. I'd like that."

He cleared his throat and said quietly, "Pink, be careful. Don't take any unnecessary risks. After losing Lauren, I don't think I could take losing you. Promise me you'll be careful?"

Whoa. He was including me in the same sentence with his dead wife, the one he'd mourned for three years before he asked another woman out on a date—namely, me. Oh, Lord. "I promise."

We said our goodbyes, I hung up and went to get dressed. I went through the motions and made myself not think about Ed.

At seven-thirty, Sam picked me up on his way to work. We came into the office together and as we passed Gert in the hallway, she exhibited her split personality by smiling nicely at Sam and scowling at me. What a hag. Something compelled me to follow her into her office.

She looked mildly surprised to see me there when she turned to sit down at her desk. "What do you want?"

"I want to know why you hate me so much."

She looked me up and down. "Because it's always been easy for you. Everything you have came to you easy."

"What would you know about it? You don't know me at all."

"I don't have to know you. You're like a cartoon, a completely predictable cliché. Even your name is like something in a cartoon."

"I'm no more of a cliché than you are, with your workaholic life that doesn't do anything to mask the absolute emptiness that invades your bitter soul."

That wiped the smug expression off of her face.

And something made me say, "You thought I'd hurl an insult about how you look, didn't you?"

"Most people do," she whispered.

I turned toward the doorway. "Maybe I'm not most people. But you wouldn't know that, would you? You're too narrow-minded and small to see beyond your own hang-ups." I walked out and went to my desk to gather my notes for the report I was going to write for Banty.

The only thing left to do was talk to the controller at Lorenzo, to find out why the stolen oil wasn't being reported on the Railroad Commission reports and why Banty's royalties had been reduced. I called to check the status and she asked me to come over at nine, to meet with her about what she'd found.

Barely fifteen minutes later, while I was looking up the number of a rental car agency, Tiffany buzzed me. "Pink, your aunt's on the phone, and when you get done talking, there's a delivery here for you."

A delivery? Hope springs eternal, I suppose, because my first thought was, Ed sent me flowers. I picked up the phone and said hello to Aunt Dru, even while my mind was skipping ahead to pink roses.

"Whitney Ann, I'm calling to remind you about the Right Hand of God prayer group meeting tomorrow night. We moved the Bible mailing to then, since we had to cancel Saturday night, on account of me being so out of sorts. And we're going to pray special for Trina, that God will bring her home soon."

I sidestepped that subject and asked, "How are you today?"

"This whole thing has upset my colon, and Dr. Rosser says he'll have to do that colonoscopy sooner. Besides that, I'm just covered in bites from the no-see-ums."

"Didn't Bug Busters get rid of them?"

"*Humph!* Spent a lot of money for nothing, because not thirty minutes after the man sprayed and left, I was bitten. But I've got a plan to get rid of the little suckers, once and for all."

"I'll see what I can do about the meeting, Aunt Dru, but I'm covered up in work right now."

"Do try. And while you're at it, I need a favor."

"A favor?" I said, forcing a whine out of my voice.

"Well, since we're not sure when Trina will be back, or what will happen to her once she gets back, we need a new sponsor for our Bibles."

"Trina provided all the Bibles?"

"Oh, yes. In fact, when she joined our group, it was her idea to start the program. Now, even though she's not with us, we'd like to continue. But we don't have the money to do it all on our own, so we thought we'd seek a new sponsor."

"I'd love to help, but I don't have that kind of money."

"Yes, I know. I was thinking maybe Edward would be interested since he's a rich attorney. It would give him grace to share his money with the Lord."

Oh, man. I didn't want to know how Aunt Dru knew Ed was having a very good year. And I could just imagine asking him for money to buy Bibles to send around the world. "I don't know about Ed, but I'll see if I can find someone who'd like to sponsor you."

"Ask Ed. He needs to do this. If he's going to court you, he needs to have grace."

Good grief. "He's not courting me. We're just friends."

"In my day, we didn't call it friendship."

"What did you call it?"

"A shotgun wedding."

How on earth did Aunt Dru know about me and Ed? That was way more freaky than I was comfortable with. "I'll ask him about the Bibles, I promise. Now, I really have to go and get some work done."

After the call, I wasted no time putting her out of my mind and heading to the reception area with high anticipation, but slowed down as soon as I rounded the corner. Instead of a flower guy holding a vase of pink roses, a short lady in a gray courier-service uniform, holding an ordinary manila envelope, chatted with Tiffany. I signed for it and thanked the lady, then looked down to see the return address. There wasn't one.

Curious about the small lump in the envelope, I ripped it open and looked inside. A key. A car key, with the remote entry attached. When I reached in to get it, a piece of copy paper fluttered out and I caught it in midair. It was a fax.

Since I can't fulfill the requisite three times before Ed beats me to it, and since you're probably going to buy a house before I have the opportunity to talk you out of it, here's a gift that's over a hundred bucks. Just so you know, even if you're not serious, I am. A lot. And don't go off on me and say you can't accept it. I'm rich, Pink, and it makes me happy to do this for you. So keep the damn car, okay? No strings. No promises. Just an extra nice gift from the friend with whom you're "slightly" involved. S2

P.S.—It'll be the one on the curb that honks.

"What is it?" Tiffany asked, her pretty blue eyes wide with curiosity.

"A car. I, uh, got a new car, and they just delivered it."

"Cool! What kind did you get?"

I hurriedly glanced at the key. "A Mercedes." Oh, my God. The car I'd wrecked during the whistle-blower thing was a Mercedes. I'd loved that car because it represented all I'd accomplished in my old job. I'd bought it the day I was promoted to senior manager. And wrecked it a month after I was fired.

"Are you gonna go check it out?"

A Mercedes. Hot damn. My avaricious side went wild and I nodded. "For sure. Right now. Be right back." I went out and down the elevator and into the bright September morning. Standing by the curb, I looked up and down at the cars parked there. Because Mom's office is in the Old First National Bank Building, along with some of Midland's wealthiest, there were four different Mercedes parked by the curb. I hit the alarm button and the one at the end, the one the color of a pearl, the one that wasn't huge, but wasn't tiny, began to honk, and its lights flashed.

I hit the button again and it stopped. Walking toward it, I was so caught up in the moment, I failed to notice that I wasn't alone until I got even with the car. Then I saw someone move into my field of vision and I stopped cold. Big Mama faced me with a pair of Ray-Bans covering her eyes, a bag over her arm and Boris peeking out. Her head jerked toward the Mercedes. "Is this your car?"

I nodded.

"Let's get in so we can visit, shall we?"

I saw the glint of steel from the pistol she held within the folds of her caftan. "Is this the part where you tell me to drive, we go out to the country and you shoot me? Then leave the gun and take the cannoli?"

Again she smiled. "I love that movie, but no, this isn't that part. This is where you get in the car so we can chat about some things."

I got in the driver's side while she got in the passenger side and set Boris's bag on the floor. Then she inhaled deeply. "New car?"

"Yes," I replied, thinking how soft-spoken she was, and how it was incongruous with her personality. And her size.

"Nice. Beats the hell outta that Ford." She talked while she poked at the multitude of buttons and checked out the sunroof. "You were out at a well last night. Why?"

"To see if it was a fake."

"Why does it matter if it's fake?"

"Because it means someone's using it to store stolen oil."

"Why should you care?"

"I was hired to care, and to find who's behind it if it turned out to be fake."

She stopped playing with the buttons and looked across at me. "Why don't you leave that up to the cops?"

"As of last night, that's exactly what I'm doing."

"Because you're afraid to keep digging?"

"Because they told me to back off, and my boss agreed."

"Don't you work for your mother?"

"Yes, but my immediate boss is a man named Sam."

"Hmm, yes, I know who he is. Sam Weston, previously with the FBI, who went into the CPA business to make his fortune so he can retire and open a surf shop in Hawaii."

"I don't even wanna know how you know that."

"The devil's in the details, Pinks, which you know, of course, because otherwise you wouldn't be a CPA. A nosy CPA." She took off the shades and fixed her dark gaze to mine. "It isn't that you don't think they can find out. It's just that you think you can do it better, smarter and faster. And you're also insanely curious."

"All true, but moot at this point."

"Maybe not." She reached for Boris's head and stroked between his ears. Boris looked ecstatic. "You can come to work for me. I find myself in a bit of a dilemma and I could use some help. The pay's lousy. Nonexistent, actually. But you'd be doing your country a great favor."

"I could also get fired, or arrested."

She looked at me again. "Nothing worth having comes cheap. You were willing to lose your job in order to blow the whistle, weren't you? This is much more important to the welfare of the citizens of this country, so how can you say no?"

I've never considered myself a thrill-seeker, but it occurred to me to wonder if I was maybe an adrenaline junkie. The anticipation was killing me. "How indeed?"

"It's all settled then. You'll keep digging and find out who's the dirty, rotten asshole funneling dollars to Al Qaeda."

"Why me? Aren't there operatives who could do this?"

"It would take several months to get someone in here, get them in a job, acclimate them to Midland and its unusual business climate and give them time to build a network of friends and contacts. In short, it would take months to get someone even close to where you are at this very minute. As for the local law enforcement finding out what's going on, they simply don't have the finesse for this kind of work. Whoever's behind the money going out of here has planned it down to the smallest detail, covered every base. To find them, it will take intuition and smarts and a certain instinct I believe you have in spades."

"You don't have to snow me. I already said I'd do it."

She flipped the visor mirror down and applied pink lipstick to her rather thin lips. "Not much for ego-stroking, are you?"

"Depends who's doing the stroking."

She dropped the tube of lipstick back into her bag and looked at me. "This car is something of an ego stroke."

"I beg your pardon?"

"Come on, Pinkie, don't be coy. A man gave you this car, didn't he?"

"Maybe."

She stared at me for a while, then slowly smiled. "It's Santorelli, isn't it?"

"What would you know about that?"

"I know everything. Don't forget it. So was it Santorelli who gave you this nice ride?"

"Yes."

She nodded, as though she'd known it all along. Then she

held up one fat hand and looked at her ring, a collection of diamonds and rubies. "A very rich man gave this to me. It doesn't suck to get expensive gifts, does it?"

"Uh, no."

"Mr. Senator is a nice guy. You could do a lot worse."

"How do you know Steve?"

"Now that's kind of a long story. I'll save it for later." She gathered up Boris's bag and opened the door. He yipped excitedly and she soothed him. "Right now, I have to be going. I'll be in touch to check your progress. If you need to get hold of me, call Jerry at Bingo Bonanza and he'll let me know."

I watched her leave, intrigued and amused all at once. Bingo Bonanza? Then I realized she'd never said her name.

I didn't have time to call Steve and thank him before I had to be over at Lorenzo Petroleum for my meeting with the controller. So while I sat in the reception area of the very posh offices, I gave some thought to what I would say when I did have time to call him. *Gee, thanks, Steve,* was so inadequate. I know how to be gracious. I know how to be considerate, and polite and generally socially acceptable. But I had no idea how to thank a man for a car. Especially when that man wasn't my father or my husband. He wasn't even my lover. Yet.

While I stared at the collection of exquisite art on the walls, I thought about Ed and wondered how he'd react to the car. At this point, he probably couldn't care less. Nevertheless, it wasn't going to help the situation, if I had any prayer of fixing things. Maybe he'd like it better if I gave it back. Maybe I should.

But I didn't want to. Not so much because of the car itself, but because it meant something. Somebody thought enough of me to buy me a car. A car! I suppose that makes me a shallow person who puts too much emphasis on material things, but get real. In our world, people express affection for one another with things. Whether it's flowers or jewelry or real estate. If Steve thought enough of me to buy me a car, it meant something. It meant he wasn't after me for a one-night stand. Or two or three of them. And maybe I was love starved, but that felt damn good.

I was still trying to decide what to say to Steve when the controller, an attractive brunette named Zelda, came to get me. She looked frazzled and anxious.

In her office, she said the failure to report the stolen barrels of oil as produced barrels of oil on the monthly reports to the Railroad Commission was due to ignorance on the part of the production department, who were responsible for the reports. "We've had a lot of turnaround in employees lately," she said, "largely due to Mr. Lorenzo's recent conversion to Islam. Amazing how many people have resigned because of it, especially considering he hasn't been public about it."

"Seriously?" I knew Midland could be a little backward about some things, but that really did blow my mind.

"Seriously," she said with a tight smile. "So we have quite a few new people, and some of them are pretty green. I'll make a note of this and pass it along so they can make adjustments in the future." She shuffled some files around and withdrew a sheaf of papers. "It appears you were correct about Mr. McMeans's royalties, and after some tweaking I did to the revenue program, along with some research into the land files, I found where the interests were transferred." She peered at the paper in her hand for a moment, then looked up at me. "Koko Petroleum."

I won a thousand-dollar jackpot in Vegas once, and I swear, when Zelda said Koko, it was the same rush. It was so unexpected, and yet, after she said it, the logic was all there. Especially if it was in fact David Lorenzo who was pulling the strings at Koko. How easy for him to change the royalties within his own company revenue system.

"After I figured it out, I had our tech department take a look at the computer logs. Just this morning, they told me someone hacked into our system and made these changes. Naturally, we're concerned about the breach in security and I can assure you we're going to do all we can to rectify it. In the meantime, please tell your client he will be reimbursed for the amounts he was shorted."

Hackers. Uh-huh. Maybe she was telling the truth, but maybe not. If Lorenzo was behind the switches, no way she'd say so. "Yes, I'll tell Mr. McMeans. Thank you for your help."

"Thank you, Miss Pearl, for bringing this to my attention."

After saying goodbye, I headed for the front door. As I stepped outside, Jake Hollingsworth materialized. "Have coffee with me, across the street."

"All right," I agreed, noticing he looked extremely nervous. As we crossed, I said, "Still on orders to follow me?"

"Until further notice." He pointed to the coffee shop, which looked like a Starbucks wannabe. "Here it is."

We went in and ordered, then sat at a corner table. He looked even more nervous, darting his gaze about and tapping his fingers on the table. "If you're trying to look casual, it isn't working."

He drank a bit of his coffee, then set the cup down carefully. "I'm not very good at this, to tell the truth. They only asked me to come here because I know the area."

"You're from Midland?"

"Yes. I went to private school, though, so I never knew many of the kids at public school. I met Gert in college, then found out she was from here."

"Does Gert know who you work for?"

He gave me a wry smile. "She wouldn't believe it if I told her. Gert's a weird duck, and she's got a lotta baggage." His smile faded. "She's just so screwed up she could never believe my interest in her was real, that it wasn't fueled by some ulterior motive. I graduated with a four point from Texas Tech, and she's convinced it was because she helped me." He shook his head. "Coming here has been hard, because as much as I want to, I can't stay away from her. And as you no doubt figured out, ours is a pretty dysfunctional relationship."

"Yeah, I kinda noticed that." I sipped the dark brew and set the cup aside. "What do you want with me, Jake?"

He gazed at me through narrowed eyes. "Do you know why I'm here?"

"You came to figure out if Becker was a turncoat. After he was killed, you started following me around, waiting to see what I come up with."

"All true, but I'm running out of time, which means you are, too. I'm undercover as a pharmaceutical salesman. Last week, somebody broke into my hotel room and ransacked the place, which led me to believe someone was on to me. Later that night a guy in a ski mask, with a gun, broke in and said he knew I was a Fed, that if I didn't fork over five grand, he'd squeal to his boss and I'd be dead by morning."

That's about the point where I began to shake, way deep down in my bones. "What did you do?"

"You mean after I pissed myself?" he asked with a smile.

I couldn't help smiling a little. "Yeah, after that."

"I said he was wrong, that I'm a pharmaceutical rep, not a Fed, but I figured no one would bother to ask before they killed me, so I'd give him five grand. He said to put it in a hymnal at First Presbyterian Church by noon the next day. I intended to follow through and find out who the guy was."

"So that's why you wanted that ring from Gert."

He made a face. "I figured she'd help me out when I told her I was in trouble, but she said she just knew I was in debt to a loan shark, and refused."

"Doesn't the agency cover you for things like that?"

"They'll reimburse me, but when an agent's in the field,

we're pretty much on our own. Contact with the office is strongly discouraged because we can't be sure who's listening or watching. I needed the cash right away, so I ended up selling my car to get the money. That's why I'm now driving a turquoise El Camino that breaks down almost daily."

"Did you find out who the man was?"

"I hid a micro-camera in the balcony at First Pres to see who took the money, but when I retrieved the camera, it hadn't gotten a clear view of the man's face. I'm pretty new at this, and I set the damn camera up wrong. I could see him take the money out of the hymnal, and just after, the Spider-Man tattoo guy showed up, they argued and the tattoo guy took the money away from the first man. I know they're suspicious of me, even if they're not one-hundred-percent sure."

"And you're thinking they'll be one-hundred-percent sure when they realize you're following me."

"Exactly. They know you're looking into the Koko thing, and after last night, it's only a matter of time."

"Before what?"

His eyes widened, as though I surprised him. "Before they kill both of us."

Oh, man. "So what do you want me to do? Or should I say, what does the agency want me to do?"

"Officially, they don't want you to do anything. They don't even acknowledge they have the slightest amount of interest in you, other than you happening to be standing next to Becker when he was killed. Unofficially, they want you to keep looking and report to the fat lady. I'm supposed to be keeping an eye on you, to verify what you're doing and make sure you don't get sucked into the other side."

"That's the very last thing I'd ever do."

He drained his coffee and tossed the empty cup toward the garbage can. "Right now, I think following you around is wasted energy. Not to mention it increases the danger to both of us. I'd rather be doing something that could help find these people, so I'm proposing a compromise. You keep me apprised of what you're doing so I don't have to follow you around, and let me help you with some things."

"Won't you get in trouble for disobeying orders?"

"Not if we can find the connection to Al Qaeda. That's all that really matters, after all."

I didn't have to give it much thought. "Okay, Jake. I'll catch you up to where I'm at."

After I said goodbye to Jake, I got in the Mercedes and headed for the north side of town, to the Bluebird Retirement Center. I intended to visit the limited partners in Koko and see if the ladies had any clue who might be in charge of the partnership.

I pulled into the parking lot of the complex, parked and walked through the xeriscape garden toward the extra wide, automatic double doors beneath the portico in front. Inside, I went to the reception desk and asked to see the first woman on the list, Betty Marks.

The lady at the desk looked at me above the top edge of her skinny reading glasses. "I'm sorry, sugar, but Betty's not able to receive visitors. She's mighty sick, about to go home."

Being a born-and-raised Bible Belt kid, I knew she wasn't referring to Betty's house. Betty was about to check out of life on Earth.

"I see. How about Shirley Howard?"

The woman reached for a tissue and dabbed at her nose. "Shirley's got Alzheimer's, advanced stage. Not much point visiting, but you can if you like."

"Then let me see Bobo Lansky."

She narrowed her eyes as she looked up at me. "Bobo passed on a week ago. Why do you want to see these ladies?"

"It's about an investment they're in, a partnership."

"Well then, you should speak to their conservator. All our residents without family have a conservator to look after their interests when they become unable to do it for themselves."

"I see. Who would that be?"

She nodded toward a hallway with a sign that read Administration. "Man by the name of Bob Fishburn. He's also the bookkeeper, and he pitches in with kitchen duties sometimes, so if he's not there, go on around to the kitchen."

A conservator who helped in the kitchen? Not a good omen. I walked down the hall and stopped at the door with Bob Fishburn on the nameplate.

"Come in," a man called when I knocked. I opened the door and stepped inside a small, cluttered office. Bob was an ordinary-looking, middle-aged man with a wrinkled, short-sleeved shirt and a tie that went out of style so long ago it was on its way back. He sat behind a metal desk, punching holes in a stack of papers as tall as the dead plant at the corner of the credenza behind him.

He looked up as I came in. "Can I help you?"

"My name is Whitney Pearl, and I'm here to visit with you about Koko Petroleum. It's a partnership that I believe some of your residents own an interest in."

He set aside the hole punch and leaned back in his chair, waving me to a seat in front of the desk. I stepped over a pile of file folders, moved a stack of papers and sat down.

"Whitney Pearl," he said thoughtfully, just before recognition dawned across his face. "Say, aren't you the whistle-blower?"

"Yes."

"So you're a CPA, are you?"

"That's right."

He sniffed, and when I say sniffed, I mean he sucked in a gust of air that could have slammed a door. "I didn't bother taking the CPA test. Waste of time, if you ask me. Just another way for the government to look over our shoulder, don'tcha think?"

I thought he was a moron, but I didn't say that. In fact, I didn't say anything.

"Seems to me it's mostly wimmen who go for that CPA, and it makes sense, because they need extra confidence when they get jobs. Betcha it makes you feel better, having that big certificate hangin' on the wall, doesn't it?"

Good grief. My certificate was in a storeroom in Dallas, but nevertheless, I said, "Yes."

He pointed at his empty wall. "See, I don't need anything like that to prove I know my job. But you wimmen, well, you gotta have that, don'tcha?"

I wanted to jump over a cliff onto jagged rocks. With bees on them. "Mr. Fishburn, I need some information about some of the residents whom you serve as conservator."

"Now what would a pretty thing like you want to know about a bunch of old wimmen?"

"They each own an interest in a partnership, Koko Petroleum. I need to know where the general partner, Gus Thompkins, is conducting business."

"Can't see that it matters, because they're all so old, they don't know the difference. What's this for? Why do you wanna know?"

"It's for a client of mine. He's interested in buying the partnership assets."

Bob rocked farther back and his chair screeched annoyingly. While he slid his tie between his fingers, he smiled and pulled another condescending remark out of his chauvinistic repertoire. "Mebbe you should bring your client with you, so we can talk man-to-man about this. Partnerships and the like are complicated animals." His smile became a grin. "Kinda like wimmen."

I stood. "Mr. Fishburn, can I assume from your total lack of anything remotely close to a logical answer, that you are unaware of your residents' interests in this partnership?"

"Now there's no need to get huffy. Just simmer down. Don't need an hysterical female on my hands, that's for sure."

He stood and hitched up his pants. "Wait here and I'll go see what I can find out for you."

He left me there, all alone, with stacks of files and piles of paper and the dead plant.

I made short work of the stacks of files and piles of paper. Within three minutes—miraculous, I know—I had my hand on a file folder labeled Koko P. Without the slightest amount of guilt, I stuffed it in the waistband of my skirt, buttoned my jacket and walked out of his office.

Just as I reached the front door, I heard him call out to me. I watched him saunter closer, and decided I'd like to throw *him* over the cliff onto jagged rocks. With *killer* bees on them.

"I told you to wait, now didn't I? Can't never explain things to wimmen enough, I reckon. You just don't *comprende*." He stopped in front of me and shook his head slowly, as though he was sorry to impart bad news. "Afraid you're looking in the wrong place for any info on that partnership. None of the residents here have an interest in anything like that."

He had the remnants of doughnut glaze on his thin lips, and a new addition to the pattern on his tie in the form of a grease spot. While he'd left me in his office, to wait while he supposedly searched for information, he went to eat a doughnut.

I pointed to his mouth. "You missed some." Turning, I left the building, and my wish for a child came back to me. One who would take care of me when I got old, so I wouldn't have to count on a numbnut like Bob Fishburn to do it.

Chapter 13

It had been at least a week since I had a Mexican food fix, if I didn't count Rosario's from Friday, and I didn't, because Rosario's makes fajitas, which in west Texas doesn't qualify as Mexican food. Fajitas are American food, invented by somebody to fill the need for everyone who doesn't live in west Texas to pretend they're eating Mexican food. To be Mexican food, there has to be a corn tortilla involved, along with lots of cheese, onions, sauce so hot it'll put hair on your chest, and in some cases, a little ground beef. That's on a taco. Or a beef enchilada or a tamale. Wussy flour tortillas, with marinated chicken or steak, also known as fajitas, as tasty as they are, don't make the cut in real Mexican food.

I was on my way to Bettina's House of Enchiladas, already anticipating the Mexican Flag plate, when my cell phone rang.

I answered and Ed said, "How about Bettina's for lunch?"

"Why? So you can officially give me the heave-ho?"

"I want enchiladas and I hate eating alone."

"Sure, Ed," I agreed, wondering what was up.

Ten minutes later, we were seated in a booth, the one below a piñata shaped like a cactus, munching chips and hot sauce.

"Talked to Sam awhile ago. He said you were pretty shaken up last night." He stirred his iced tea.

Checking out his white dress shirt and red silk tie, wondering why I have a thing for men in suits and ties, especially men named Ed and Steve and Sam, I said, "Why don't you and Sam just go ahead and be best buddies? If you'd admit it, you could hang out and go to football games, and play poker and go fishing and scratch and spit and do other guy things together. You may as well, because you talk on the phone more than a couple of junior high girls."

"No way. I hate that guy."

"Whatever."

He took a long drink of his tea. "Just curious, Pink, but what is it that compels you to do something like go out in the oil field in the middle of the night? Do you think maybe you have a death wish? Is it because your dad's an ass? Do I need to spring for some counseling?"

"You're not funny."

"I'm not trying to be. I really want to know, because most people, girls in particular, would never do something like that. You, on the other hand, run at it with all the enthusiasm of a kid at Christmas. Like you can't wait."

I shrugged and kept eating chips.

"You're in denial."

"I'm in business, and that business is uncovering facts, and that entails doing things that will uncover the facts. How can I know if Koko has a fake well if I don't go out there and see?" In spite of myself, I began to get irritated. "I'm all grown up now, perfectly capable of making informed decisions about how to go on in life."

"That sounded like a stick-it-up-your-ass speech."

He was right. What was I doing? If this lunch was an opportunity for me to extend the olive branch, I was screwing it all to hell. I started to say I was sorry, then remembered his parting words from earlier. So instead I said, "I didn't mean it that way. Maybe I'm just a little sensitive lately."

About that time, David Lorenzo walked into Bettina's with a very distinguished man in a dark suit. "Who's with Lorenzo?"

Ed glanced toward the two men as they took a seat at the booth beneath the piñata shaped like SpongeBob SquarePants. "Looks like Santorelli's father."

"Why would Steve's dad be hanging out with Lorenzo?"

Ed ate another chip. "From all that David's told me, their families have been friendly since Santorelli and Lorenzo were at Stanford. Mr. Santorelli is Colby's godfather."

I was surprised. In fact, I was almost shocked. Steve had made it sound as though he hardly ever saw Lorenzo. "Muslims don't do godfathers, do they?"

Ed shrugged. "Once a godfather, always a godfather."

I looked at David and thought all over again how good-looking he was. And he seemed like such a stellar human being. How could he be behind anything as horrible as terrorist financing? But how could I ignore all that I'd learned? How could I forget it was his class ring out there by Trina's dead body? "Does he know about you going out to pick up Trina?"

Ed nodded. "I went by last night, after I took her to my brother's restaurant. David was very upset."

Yeah, I'll just bet he was. On an impulse, I told Ed what I'd discovered that morning, about the switched royalties.

All of a sudden, Ed's semiserious mood turned überserious. "Be careful, Pink. Lots of things are not the way they seem, and lots of people are not who you think they are."

"I hate it when you do that."

"What?"

"Speak in riddles, make it all mysterious, like there's some huge secret you know but won't tell me. Don't you see that's exactly what gets me going?"

He stared at me. "That's it, isn't it? You go chasing after things like last night because you're nosy. You have to know everything that's going on, who's involved and what they were wearing."

"Yes, Ed, so it's cruel of you to say things that make me wonder, then tell me I shouldn't go find out what it is."

"Pink, you really do scare the shit outta me."

"You're way too macho to be scared."

"When it's me on the line, you're right. But when it's you, when I think of all the things that can happen to you, it's scary as hell."

He was practically grim, I realized with a bit of a catch in my breath. I looked at him there, across from me in the orange vinyl booth, and I know it was a bit cosmic of me, but I had something like a flash-forward, to what it could be like if I loved him. If he loved me. If we were together the way a man and a woman are meant to be together.

"Ed, why did you ask me to lunch?"

Our food came just then, and I had to wait for an answer.

While he cut into an enchilada, his eyes not meeting mine, he said quietly, "Sam dared me to. He said I couldn't see you again and stick to my guns."

I decided I loved Sam. "So this is all about a dare?"

He looked up then and I sucked in a breath. Swear to God, I could have been stark naked and not felt so vulnerable.

"I wish I'd known you a long time ago, before George did such a number on you."

"What are you saying? That now I'm damaged goods?"

"Everybody's damaged, one way or the other. Life doles

out nicks and dents to all of us. I imagine that, growing up with your old man, you were already pretty dinged by the time you left home, but knowing you like I do, I'd bet money you didn't let it hold you back. You jumped into it with George and gave it all you had."

Which I assumed was what he wanted me to do with him. And I wouldn't. Or maybe I just couldn't. "You'd lose the bet. Sure, George was the one who went looking for something else, but I have to take some of the blame. If I'd been there, maybe he wouldn't have done it. But I wasn't there, physically or mentally."

"It takes two, Pink. If George was there, you would have been there."

"How do you know?"

He smiled then, sort of sadly. "The same way I know David Lorenzo is not the man you're looking for."

"Gut instinct?"

"I'm never wrong, Pink. Never. So it's like I said. I wish I'd met you before George."

"And since you didn't, you're all done with me?"

He shook his head slowly. "Not yet. Sam was right, the bloody bastard."

We sat there and stared at each other until the waitress came and handed Ed the check. He reached for his wallet.

"Ed?"

"Yeah?"

I'm still not sure what I intended to say. I only know I was drowning in an emotion that was equal parts elation and pain. It was maybe the strangest feeling I'd ever had, and I wanted so much to express it, to understand it. But I couldn't. I opened my mouth and said lamely, "Thanks for lunch."

He looked at me for the longest time, as if he knew what I wanted to say, even if I didn't. "You're welcome."

After he got up to leave, I followed, then felt an enormous rush of adrenaline when David Lorenzo and Mr. Santorelli came to stand behind us at the cashier's stand.

I felt a tap on my shoulder and turned. David said, "Pink, Ed, this is Steve Santorelli's father, Lou."

We all shook hands and I tried not to stare. Lou Santorelli was an older version of Steve, and just as good-looking. He was one of those vibrant men, the kind women fall head over heels in love with and other men want to emulate. With a designer suit, dark hair that was barely silvered at the temples, and a wide, white smile, he looked rich and polished, but real. Like he'd be equally at home in the White House or a pool hall.

They all exchanged idle bullshit while we waited to pay, but I didn't say anything, feeling enormously awkward. Lou kept meeting my eyes and I wondered if he was checking me out, to see what sort of woman his son would give a brand-new Mercedes to. When it was Ed's turn to pay, Lou reached inside his suit jacket and pulled out a miniature Altoids box, reminding me of the one I'd had that Big Mama swiped from me. Lou offered me one and I accepted. Lorenzo declined, appearing completely at ease. I had to admit, he didn't look like a man who'd had his ex-wife murdered less than twenty-four hours earlier.

I realized with a start that he was staring at me, as if he expected me to say something. "I hope your son is doing okay."

"He's having nightmares, and asking about his mother, wondering when she's coming back. It's hard on Colby, not knowing where she is. Your aunt's handiwork will last awhile."

No way I was letting him get by with that. "Weren't you suing to take away her right to visit him? Wasn't that what precipitated her taking the boy?"

"You can't possibly feel sorry for her," he said with disbelief. "I gave her every chance to do the right thing for Colby, but Trina was always all about Trina."

Ed said quietly, "Pink, let's go."

I turned to walk out with him, but stopped when Lorenzo asked, "You saw her last night, didn't you?"

My heart skipped a couple of beats and I shot a questioning look at Ed.

"Dave knows you were out there," he told me.

I looked up into Lorenzo's eyes, and expected to see anything but sorrow. That's why I was so off balance, because his look of grief was so unexpected. "Yes, I saw her."

He came a bit closer. "Did she look—"

"She looked peaceful, and beautiful." If you didn't count the odd twist of her neck. Jesus.

Ed tugged my arm. "Come on, Pink."

I followed him out of Bettina's but I couldn't shake the look on David Lorenzo's face. His grief confused me.

As if he could read my mind, Ed said, "I guess people can hate each other and still be stuck on each other."

Thinking of Gert and Jake, I understood what he meant.

Because I was preoccupied with David Lorenzo's unexpected reaction to his ex-wife's death, I hadn't prepared for the unveiling of the car. It wasn't until we stood beside it that I realized I had some explaining to do.

While Ed stared at it, I did that. I explained how Steve gave me a brand-new Mercedes.

"Are you going to keep it?"

"If somebody gave you a Mercedes, would you keep it?"

"Does this mean you've made up your mind?"

"It means he gave me a car and said no strings, and I need a car, and I'm keeping it."

"So you can use the money you've been saving to put a down payment on a house?"

"That's right."

He shoved his hands into the pockets of his navy suit trousers and walked around the car, inspecting it, kicking the tires. "Nice car."

"Hmm."

"Just for the sake of argument, if I'd given you a car, would you keep it?"

"Depends."

He came close and narrowed his eyes. "On what?"

"On whether I liked it or not."

Leaning down, he brushed his lips across mine. "You're a heartless, money-grubbing female."

I kissed him back. "You're opportunistic and overbearing."

Stepping away from me, he pulled his keys from his pocket and tossed them in the air, catching them with the other hand. "Maybe Mr. Moneybags buys you a new ride, but I bought you the Mexican Flag plate at Bettina's, and I happen to know you could live without those wheels, but you can never live without great Mexican food."

"It's not a contest, Ed."

He stopped tossing the keys. "Wanna bet?"

Then he walked away and didn't look back, didn't say goodbye, didn't even wave as he drove out of the parking lot.

Back at the office, I was waylaid by Mom as soon as I came in. She waved me back to her office.

Not liking the expression on her face, I dreaded following her, but she's my mother, and she signs my paychecks, so it's not like I had a choice. We made it into her office and she closed the door. After she walked toward the window, then walked back, her hands on her hips and her black, pointy-toed pumps making tracks in the carpet, she said, "Why didn't you tell me we've been invited to a party in Washington?"

No way had I expected that. "I only heard about it late last night, and this is the first time I've seen you. Besides, I thought we'd get an invite in the mail."

She went back to the window, tapped her toe for a minute, then swung around and came back. "What am I supposed to think when a man like that calls and asks me to accompany my daughter to his home for dinner?"

"A man like what?"

"Like Steve's father."

"*He* called? I thought Steve called."

Her dark eyes were wide with nervous anxiety. Mom was wigging out and I prayed for patience. She takes goofiness to new heights when it comes to men. I'll even go so far as to say I don't like her very much when she comes under the influence. Much like an alcoholic, those types who take on an alternate personality when they're drunk, Mom becomes a stranger when she thinks a man is interested in her.

All Steve's dad had to do was call and ask her to a party.

I was so not in the mood.

"I just don't know why you wouldn't tell me."

"Mom, would you calm down? It's a dinner party for Steve, and he invited me. Then he invited you, and if you want to know the truth, I think it's for appearance' sake, so I can stay there with him and it won't look bad."

"So this isn't some kind of a setup?"

"No, Mom," I lied quite nicely.

She looked so relieved, I felt guilty. Poor Mom. I really wished she'd see a shrink about the man thing.

I had so much to do, I hurriedly made my escape. "I've got to get to work. Let's talk about this later."

"Fine, but make it sooner than later."

Sam was out of the office for the afternoon, down at a client's office in Marfa, so I decided to use his office to call Steve. Making a call in the bull pen is like making a call with a bullhorn.

I was nervous about it, and sat at Sam's desk and took a few deep breaths before I picked up the phone and dialed. Like always, he answered his own phone, which still amazes me. I mean, he's a senator, an important man, and he has an entire staff of people working for him, but he always answers, "Hello, this is Senator Steven Santorelli."

"Hello," I said, matching his formal tone, "this is Certified Public Accountant Whitney Pearl."

"Are you mocking me?"

"Definitely."

"Don't you realize I'm a dignified lawmaker who commands respect and subordination?"

"I've seen you practically naked."

"And I've seen you—"

"Careful, sir. I'm at work."

He laughed at that. "So, what's up?"

"I had quite the surprise this morning. Thank you."

"Do you like it?"

"Only a lot. It's beautiful. But you shouldn't have."

"Does it make you feel obligated in any way?"

"Not exactly."

"Damn! The old Give Her a New Mercedes So She'll Feel Obligated ploy isn't working. I'll have to go to Plan Two."

"Which is?"

"I don't actually have a Plan Two. I was so convinced Plan One would work."

"I'm not sure I should ask, but what sort of obligation were you plotting for?"

"The kind where you lose interest in Ed and focus entirely on me, become my exclusive sex partner, and generally worship the ground I walk on."

"If I give you a Mercedes, will you do that for me?"

"Gladly. Losing interest in Ed would not be a problem since there's none to begin with, I'm pretty much already exclusively yours because I can't get enthusiastic about anyone else, and maybe I'm not at the worship-the-dirt-beneath-your-feet stage, but I could get there."

"Too bad it's a moot point. I can't afford a Mercedes."

"Maybe I'll convince your mother to give you a raise."

I was smiling the whole time we talked, but after he said that, I began to sober. "It really is a beautiful car, Steve. I can't even begin to tell you how much it means to me, and not just because I need a car."

"Good. That's exactly what I wanted to hear. And you know I'm kidding about any obligation?"

"I know."

"Still, if you get to that point, when you think you're ready to go somewhere else with this, you'll let me know."

"You'll be the first to know."

"I have to go to a meeting now. I'll call you later."

"Thank you again," I said, wondering why I felt at loose ends, wishing I knew what to say, and what I wanted him to say.

"G'bye, Pink."

I heard him hang up, but I sat there with the receiver in my hand for a long time before I laid it back in its cradle.

Eventually, I made it to my cubicle and had a chance to look in the Koko P. file I'd ripped off from Bob Fishburn. But I didn't quite hit the jackpot of answers, because the file was mostly a lot of scribbled notes. Some of them were unreadable, the handwriting was so awful. The ones I could read didn't make a lot of sense and I was close to chucking the whole thing and calling it a bust when I came across a note in different handwriting. The paper had Lorenzo Household Memo printed at the top. Coincidence? Farther down in the note, which had something to do with the medical care of an elderly man, I saw it was signed by Beth Glenn, R.N., who appeared to have worked for the Bluebird Retirement Center at one time.

I grabbed the phone book and looked up Lorenzo's number. It blew my mind, but he had four numbers listed. I dialed the one for household staff and asked for Beth Glenn.

Within a couple of minutes, a soft voice answered, "Hello, this is Beth Glenn."

"Beth, I hope you don't mind me calling, but I was given your name in reference by Bob Fishburn at Bluebird."

"Yes, of course. What can I do for you?"

"I'm looking for home health care for my grandfather and wondered if you might be available."

"I'm sorry, but not at this time. I'm surprised Bob gave you my name. I'm currently working full-time for Mr. Lorenzo."

"Perhaps I misunderstood Bob and he meant you would know of someone else to recommend."

"Maybe so. Try Tender Care. They're very qualified."

"Yes, I will. Thanks so much." I paused, then casually said, "I wasn't aware Mr. Lorenzo had elderly relatives. He used to attend my church, and I know his parents have passed."

"Oh, this isn't Mr. Lorenzo's relative. My patient is the housekeeper's uncle, Mr. Thompkins."

I almost vibrated off my chair, I was so excited. I'd found Gus Thompkins! At last! And he was living under Lorenzo's roof. Coincidence? "How nice of Mr. Lorenzo to hire health care for his employee's family."

"Yes, he's a very kind man. My patient is incapacitated and his niece couldn't bear to put him in one of those state homes, so Mr. Lorenzo hired me to take care of him here."

I prattled on a bit longer, then thanked her and hung up.

Sitting back in my chair, I was wondering what to do next when Sam came by and asked about Banty's report. I told him what I'd learned at Lorenzo Petroleum, and he said firmly,

"Write the damn report, take it out to Banty, then leave it alone. Swear to me you'll leave it alone."

For the first time in my life, I lied like a champ. Maybe because I felt justified. "I'll leave it alone, Sam."

Chapter 14

To maintain the appearance of following orders, I did write up Banty's report, which took up a chunk of the afternoon. It was just as well because Banty started calling at three and continued to pester me until I told him I was done. I agreed to meet him at his office and go over it with him at five o'clock.

When I got there, he was beside himself, and I had to pull out the demanding-bitch hat to get him to settle down. At a small table in his office, which held a mishmash of old, used furniture, I went through the report.

He didn't look too surprised when I told him I'd discovered the Koko well was indeed a fake, but he was disappointed I hadn't figured out who was behind Koko. I didn't mention that I'd found Gus Thompkins, or that he was living in Lorenzo's house. Banty was a loose cannon and he was likely to rush in and screw it all up before I could find further information.

Unfortunately, when I got to the part about the royalty interests, I realized he could still screw it all up.

"I knew it!" he cried as he stood and paced around the room, waving his hands dramatically. "I knew the slimy bastard was ripping me off! It wasn't enough his father stole the Pendergast minerals out from under us? God, I hate him!" He stopped and looked at me, his face so red I was afraid he might have a stroke. "He's behind Trina's disappearance. I just know it. The selfish son of a bitch always has to have everything! Couldn't even share his own son." He began to pace again. "All I have to do is prove he's giving the money to those terrorists and he'll get his, won't he? Then Trina can come back and have Colby, and everything will be good."

I knew Trina wasn't coming back, but I didn't say so. Instead, I tried to douse his enthusiasm for bringing down David Lorenzo. "Banty," I said as I gathered up my files and slipped them back into my audit bag, "you need to be careful about making accusations. He could sue you for libel and slander, and you're already in the middle of that child support case. You don't know that David's the one who changed the interests, and without evidence, you can't openly accuse him of it."

Didn't matter what I said, Banty was on a roll. When I left, he followed me out to the car, still carrying on.

On the way home, I weighed my options and wondered what I should do next. Remembering my promise to Jake, I called and updated him and asked his opinion.

"Maybe the housekeeper knows something," he said. "How about I go to Lorenzo's under some pretense, and talk to her?"

"I'll go with you."

"He knows you, Pink, so you can't. Let me check it out and I'll call as soon as I'm done."

I agreed, wished him luck and headed for home to wait.

It turned into a very long wait. While the hours dragged by, I sat on the wagon wheel couch and watched television, but didn't actually see anything. My mind kept running around in circles, going over all I'd learned so far, looking for something concrete we could get to prove Lorenzo was our man.

Close to midnight, the phone rang and I snatched it up, expecting Jake on the other end. But it wasn't. Believe it or not, it was Gert.

"I need your help," she said in her manly voice.

Slightly dazed because Gert Luebner was on the phone, asking for *my* help, I managed to say, "What's going on?"

"I wish I knew. Jake called awhile ago and said he was in trouble and could I pawn the ring and bring him the money."

"And you said no."

"Of course. He got mad and said I should call you, that you'd know what to do. Then he said the weirdest thing. Something about the ski-mask guy being up to old tricks and the housekeeper biting the big one."

I sat down, hard. Lorenzo had offed the housekeeper to keep her quiet? The man was a monster. "Okay, I got it covered."

"Wait!" she yelled before I could hang up. "What the *hell* is going on?"

"Kinda late to be asking, isn't it? I gotta go save Jake before he bites the big one, too."

"Pink, no! Don't hang up! What kind of trouble is he in?"

"The worst kind, and if I don't go get him, he'll be dead."

"I wanna come, too."

I gave it exactly three seconds of thought and decided she'd maybe be some help. "Fine. Be here in five minutes." I gave her directions, then asked, "Would you happen to have five grand on you?"

"I've got ten bucks and some change."

"Never mind. Just come on."

She got here while I was getting dressed, and I told her to wait, then went back in the bedroom to get the Bobcat. After I stuffed it in my jeans, I grabbed my purse and joined her in the living room, where she was staring at the couch.

"That couch is hideous. I thought you had better taste."

"Right now I can't afford better taste."

Her gaze moved around the room and I could tell she was shocked. Beginning to feel very inadequate, I moved toward the door. "Let's go."

"We'll take my car," she insisted. "You drive too slow."

There was no time to argue, so I agreed and got in her late-model Nissan. "Go to First Presbyterian."

"Are you serious?"

"Completely."

She put the car in Drive and peeled out of the lot, throwing me against the door when she took the turn on two wheels. She wasn't lying about being a fast driver. James Bond's got nothin' on Gert.

"Who's the guy in the ski mask?" she asked as she took a turn at forty. "And why are we going to church?"

"I don't know who he is, but he's blackmailing Jake, and First Pres is the drop-off place for the money."

"Why would anyone blackmail Jake?"

"You'll have to ask him." And oh, how I wished I could be a fly on the wall when she did.

"Since we don't have five thousand dollars, and Jake probably doesn't, what are you planning to do?"

"I'm not sure. Lemme think about it."

Ten minutes later, when she pulled into the parking lot, I still had no idea what to do. And I wasn't sure what was going down.

The church was deserted, because, duh, it was twelve-thirty at night, and people don't hang out at churches at that hour. There was one car in the lot, a turquoise El Camino, which indicated Jake was still there. I got out of the car and said to Gert, "I'm going around the building to see if there's a light, and if I can get in through a window or something."

She opened her door. "I'm going with you."

"Fine by me, but no whining if we get shot at."

Her hand disappeared into the pocket of her khakis, then reappeared with a small pistol.

"You've got a gun?"

"This is west Texas. Of course I have a gun."

Who knew? And there I was thinking I was walking the edge with my little Bobcat. I turned and headed for the west side of the building, Gert on my heels. We made our way around, and when we came to the east side, I noticed an open window on the second floor, in one of the Sunday school rooms. A set of stairs went up to a wide landing, and the open window was just there, easy to climb through. Within a minute, we were both inside the building.

Creeping around a church late at night is weird, maybe because it feels so illegal and wrong, and hello, it's church. But we did it anyway, peeking in rooms, searching for a light, or voices, or anything to indicate where Jake was.

Naturally, he was in the last place we looked, in the old part of the building, in the music room. Gert spotted him first when she looked through the window in the door. "Hey!" she said in a stage whisper they probably heard over at the police station, "there he is!" She reached for the knob, but I stopped her with one hand on hers.

"Hang on and let's see if he's alone."

We both looked in the window. There was one light on, leaving most of the room in shadows. Jake was sitting in a folding chair, his hands and feet tied to it, with a gag in his mouth. Bobcat in hand, I opened the door and looked to see if anyone was next to the wall with the door. They weren't.

Gert hurried toward Jake and took the gag out of his mouth, then began to untie him.

"Man, am I glad to see you two," he said in a hoarse voice.

"What happened?" I asked, still darting nervous looks over my shoulder.

"The housekeeper had gone to visit friends at the retirement center, so I went looking for her. Turned into a wild-goose chase and I went all over town, always just missing her. When I finally caught up to her, she was dead, shot and killed in the mall parking lot by a mugger."

"A mugger?" Gert asked incredulously. "In Midland?"

Jake slanted me a look and continued, "I was on my way out of the lot when I got a call from Mr. Ski Mask, demanding another five grand. Of course I didn't have it, Gert wasn't budging, and I couldn't sell the El Camino and raise that much, especially in an hour, which is all the time he gave me. So I decided to come down and grab the guy, haul him somewhere and ask some real pointed questions."

He rubbed his wrists while he talked, and Gert stood back and stared at him as if he was speaking in tongues.

"Clearly, that's not what happened," I said.

Jake shot me a wry smile. "Clearly. When I got here, I was met in the parking lot by the dude with the Spider-Man tattoo. He brought me up here and said he'd be back later, after he was given instructions about what to do with me."

"What about the guy who called you? Did you see him?"

Jake shook his head as he stood. "Never did. I think maybe the tattoo dude intercepted him before I got here. We need to get out before he comes back."

Turning, I walked toward the door, anxious to get out of the room and the building. Maybe it was sacrilegious, but I could feel bad karma coming at me like a hurricane.

We went back out through the window, down the stairs and around the south side of the building, where the cars were parked. I was in the lead, with Gert and Jake just behind me. Strange, but getting out of the building had done nothing to alleviate the sense of dread hanging over my head like a shroud. I almost ran that last little way toward the cars.

It wasn't enough, and it didn't matter. Just as I got to Gert's car, a man popped up from the back of the El Camino and pointed a gun right at us. I heard Gert breathe, "Holy shit!"

"Going somewhere?" the man asked, his words muffled by the ski mask covering his face.

"Home," I said. "We're going home."

"Not yet. Mr. Hollingsworth hasn't paid his debt."

Jake stepped up and said, "About that money, there's a little problem. I don't have it. I don't have it now, and I won't have it tomorrow. So you're gonna have to do what you have to do."

The gun went off with a loud crack and I started so violently, I bit my tongue. Jake shot me a startled look, then slowly crumpled to the ground. Gert sucked in a deep breath, no doubt to scream, but the gunman said, "Scream and you're next."

Gert snapped her mouth closed and began to cry.

"What do you want?" I managed to ask in a semblance of a normal voice.

"Money. I need five thousand dollars."

I noticed he said he *needed* five thousand dollars. Not I want five thousand, but I need it. "Me and Gert could go to an ATM, but I don't think we can get more than five hundred bucks."

"You can have a ring I have at home," Gert said in a shaking voice. "It's worth at least five thousand."

He waved the pistol around wildly. "I said I want five thousand bucks, and I don't want any goddamn ring! Jake came up with it before. He can do it again!"

"He's dead. How can he get it now?"

He looked down. "Guess I shouldn't have shot him."

"Guess not."

In a move so fast he was blurred, the ski mask guy jumped down and grabbed Gert, his arm circling her throat, the gun pointed at her head. "Listen up, Pinks. I gotta have that money, so you need to think fast before your friend gets it."

My friend? I looked at the sheer terror on her homely face and knew, even if we weren't friends, I'd do anything to save her. That's when, out of the blue, I remembered the money Aunt Dru gave me. I had no idea how much was in the envelope because I had yet to take it out and count it. But he would, if I handed it to him.

"Okay, look, I've got some money in my purse. You can have it, but you have to take it and let her go."

"That was the general idea," he said sarcastically.

I bent and grabbed my purse through the window of the car, withdrew the envelope and handed it to him.

"Is it five grand?"

"If you don't believe me, then count it."

He took it, shoved Gert to the ground, then opened the envelope. I took the opportunity of his loss of focus, grabbed the little Bobcat out of my waistband and shot him.

Well, I didn't actually shoot him. I wanted to, and intended to, but I'm really not good with guns, so my shot went wide and broke a window. But it startled him enough that he darted a look toward the breaking glass, and that's when I fired my second round.

The envelope slid from his fingers, as did the gun, and he looked at me with wide eyes inside that ski mask. "They said you couldn't shoot." Then he dropped to the ground and rolled back, his arms flung wide.

Gert scrambled to her feet. "You shot him!"

"Yes, I know. Have you got a cell phone? Because we need to call an ambulance for Jake."

She grabbed one out of her back pocket, and while she called, I bent to see if Jake was alive. I felt a pulse, and an enormous sense of relief.

Then I went to the guy with the ski mask and pulled the thick knit away from his face.

Lying there, with his face to the stars, was Bob Fishburn,

the numbnut conservator bookkeeper kitchen boy from the Bluebird Retirement Center. He opened his eyes and whispered, "Tell Mama I'm sorry." He swallowed hard while he looked up at me. Then he frowned. "Wimmen!" His head lolled back and I knew he was dead.

Detective Garza was confused, and I was so not in the mood to set him straight. I'd killed a man, and that sat heavy in my soul, making me unable to be much help at all. Gert told him what had happened, including Fishburn's previous demand for money from Jake. Still unconscious, Jake wasn't able to shed any light on the reason for the blackmail, and I knew I wasn't supposed to be involved, so I kept mum. Jake had been taken to the hospital, and we'd heard through Garza that he was in surgery to remove the bullet from his stomach.

Finally, after two hours of questions, the detective said we could leave. Gert drove me home and we didn't talk all the way. When she pulled up to my apartment, she said quietly, "Thank you, Pink. I'm going up to the hospital, but I can come back, if you want, to make sure you're okay."

Maybe if I hadn't been so bruised, more emotionally than physically, I'd have been amazed by her compassion. As it was, I could only murmur, "Thanks, but it's not necessary."

"Are you gonna be okay?"

I opened the car door. "Yeah, I'll be all right." I got out, closed the door and headed upstairs to take a very hot shower. But oddly enough, I didn't cry. I just stood there beneath the running water and prayed a lot.

The next morning, I went against everything I stand for and called in sick to work. I lay in bed most of the morning and pondered life. Not what I should do with my life, but an existential sort of pondering, about what it meant to be alive. Mom called and fretted, because by then the news was all over. Sam called, but instead of the lecture I expected, he went all mushy on me and said he considered me a friend and he wanted to help if he could.

Ed called, and so did Steve. I assured them I was fine and they shouldn't worry. They both said they'd worry, anyway.

I had no clue what to do about Lorenzo. I was convinced he'd had the housekeeper killed, and had staged it to look like a mugging. I was convinced he'd had Trina murdered. All in all, I was convinced Lorenzo was behind the terrorist financing. But what did I have that was solid proof? I needed a paper trail, like check copies and bank statements. I needed an eyewitness that could point to Lorenzo as the man posing as Gus Thompkins.

But I had to face the inconsistencies. Like why Big Mama's car had been at his house. Like his character, as proved over and over by his actions. And there was still that stealthy whisper of coincidence I couldn't get my mind around.

When my head began to hurt from concentrating on so many pieces of information, I opened the drawer of the cheap, fake-wood nightstand beside the squeaky bed, and pulled out the Bible Aunt Dru had given me. I'm serious when I say it was that kind of day. Nothing made sense, and an incredible feeling of loneliness echoed through me. Not the kind you feel when you're alone and wish you had someone to talk to. I'm talking about the kind that makes you feel completely disconnected from humanity. I guess taking another human being's life, even in self-defense, will do that to you.

I sat in bed and read the Bible for a while, sort of amazed all over again by what an interesting book it is. Aunt Dru was right, because there were a lot of answers in there.

I'd just finished reading a Psalm when I found maybe the greatest answer of all. And I'm convinced it was a God thing. I went to the kitchen to get more coffee, which I had to drink out of an old paper cup from McDonald's because I'd yet to get some new dishes, then returned to bed. As I reached for the Bible, the bottom of that cup came apart, sending steaming hot coffee all over the bed and the Bible. I snatched it up and started to wipe it on my T-shirt, then went for a towel and tried to dry the thin pages. In spite of my efforts, they were wrinkled and practically ruined. I turned to the front, to catch extra drips, and saw that it had soaked up a lot of the coffee—which made the white backing almost see-through.

There was money behind it. I ripped it away and found five hundred dollars. Five bills, one hundred dollars each.

I'd just discovered how the funding group transported the money to Al Qaeda. Ironically, in Bibles, sent by a group of well-meaning Christian ladies who had no clue they were aiding the most horrific terrorist organization on the planet.

God does indeed work in mysterious ways.

I immediately called Aunt Dru. As soon as she answered, I said, "You need to cancel the Bible mailing again."

"Whitney Ann! Lord, child, are you all right? I've been watching the news, and it's just awful, that man trying to mug you down there at the church, and right after poor Eleanor was shot at the mall. What's the world coming to?"

"I'm fine, Aunt Dru, but I really need to know you'll cancel the Bible mailing tonight."

"But the ladies are all set to come over this evening. I'm making lemon bars. You know, I bought some lemon bars at the grocery and they're not *fit* to eat, so I'm having to make some from scratch. Have you had my lemon bars? Because they are wonderful. It's an old recipe my mother had, and—"

"I'm sorry to interrupt, but this is very important. I want you to hide those Bibles, and if anyone comes looking for them, say you already sent them. Call your friends and tell them the mailing's off until further notice."

"Whitney Ann, I'm surprised at you, asking me to lie. Why on Earth would I hide Bibles, then lie?"

I couldn't tell her. I just couldn't. There was simply no

knowing what she would do. Whatever she did, there was a good chance she'd tip off the funding group, and that would be a disaster. "Aunt Dru," I said as calmly as possible, which wasn't very, "there's something wrong with the Bibles. There's a, uh, a misprint, and in a few passages, God is spelled with a *C,* so it says 'Cod.' Now I know you don't want all those missionaries passing out Bibles with Cod in them instead of God, so please, hide the Bibles and don't let anyone have them unless I say it's okay."

"Why would anyone want them?"

"Because…uh, because they'll be a collector's item. Someone could sell those on eBay and make a lot of money, and don't you agree, the best thing to do is destroy them?"

"I've never heard of such a thing as a misprint like that. Trina said she got them at a discount, and I guess this proves you get what you pay for."

"So you'll hide them, and call off the mailing?"

"I suppose, but what can I do with these lemon bars?"

"I'll come by later and bring Ed, and we'll have coffee and lemon bars."

"Oh, that would be nice. Then I can ask him about being our new Bible sponsor."

"Thanks, Aunt Dru. Now hang up and go hide the Bibles."

"Okay. I think I'll put them under the Buick."

As soon as I hung up, I called the Bible publisher and started a long process that ended with a book distributor out of Dallas named Mohammed. Go figure. Mohammed was a wealth of information, mostly because he was so pissed off.

"Three invoices, and all unpaid!" he exclaimed righteously. "Mr. Lorenzo, he is a cheat and a disgrace to Allah. His beautiful wife, she said she would make sure her husband paid, but still no money!"

He went at me for a while, and I finally managed to get off the phone by promising to speak to Mr. Lorenzo myself.

But I was no longer so sure Mr. Lorenzo was the man I needed to speak to. While I was listening to Mohammed piss and moan, a horrible thought had taken root, and once there, it wouldn't go away. That whisper of coincidence became a shout, and it screamed an entire laundry list of reasons why Lorenzo could *not* be funding terrorists. Steve Santorelli, who I'd swear was the most honorable man in America, was his long-time friend. Lou Santorelli, a highly decorated war veteran, a POW, was Colby's godfather. And there were so many things about Lorenzo that all spoke to his innocence. His character, evidenced by his patience with Trina and his gentleness with his son. His intelligence, which would never allow him to buy the Bibles using his own name. His generosity and his reputation for fair business dealings. David Lorenzo paid his bills, on time. He was not a tightwad. If he owed Mohammed for Bibles, he would pay the man. He was no Banty McMeans, always chiseling invoices, or outright ignoring them. Banty was the tightest man in Midland.

Bells started going off in my head and I almost passed out when realization hit me like a stack of Bibles. David Lorenzo was the guy Banty had pointed the finger at from the get-go. The one he'd hired me to get the goods on. And I'd damn near done it, because Banty had laid out a trail of crumbs for me to follow, all the way to David Lorenzo's door. I thought about Gus Thompkins. The nurse had said he was the housekeeper's uncle, and the housekeeper was Eleanor, who was also Banty's housekeeper. Gus just happened to have a dormant partnership with a trio of elderly, clueless women as partners. How easy it must have been for Banty to take it over, with Gus out of commission, conveniently housed under David Lorenzo's roof.

And there was Trina, who Banty clearly had it bad for. He undoubtedly supplied the Bibles for her to hand over to the prayer group, who dutifully mailed them off to "missionaries," all of whom I'd bet were fronts, linked to the Al Qaeda network. I wondered if Trina had been in on the whole scheme, as well. If Lorenzo was sent to prison for treason, there she'd have been, ready to be granted full custody of Colby. But she must have gotten squeamish about it, or realized it wouldn't work, after all, and made the break for her lover in Venezuela. She didn't make it, because Banty's goon caught up to her, and Banty probably had her killed to keep her quiet. Or because she pissed him off so bad for leaving him.

Banty had extreme motive. In his own mind, Lorenzo's family had stolen his birthright, the minerals off the Pendergast field. Never mind that Banty's father could have developed the field himself. In Banty's conspiracy theorist, paranoid mind, he'd been ripped off.

It was sick and twisted and criminal, but in Banty World, it made sense. Still, there were a lot of questions such as, who'd set the car bomb? Did Banty do it, intending to get Lorenzo because he hated him so much? If it had been intended for me, why? He'd hired me to find out about Lorenzo, which I could hardly do if I was dead.

Then I thought about Bob Fishburn, and the way he'd hitched his pants up, the same way Banty did. And his last words had been about his mama. Was Bob the long-lost brother? The illegitimate son Mr. McMeans despised, who had to go live with the San Antonio Dinkles? Banty's mama's "high sin"?

The thoughts went round and round in my mind, until I hit on an idea that would flush Banty out, if he really was the one behind the money flowing out of Midland to Al Qaeda. Just as I couldn't openly accuse Lorenzo without solid proof, I couldn't point the finger at Banty without hard evidence.

Reaching for the phone, I called his office and said, "I just spoke to Aunt Dru, and she's planning to hold her prayer group's Bible mailing tonight at her house. Could you lend a hand, Banty? A lot of the ladies can't make it and Aunt Dru is beside herself, anxious to get those Bibles out."

His whiny voice replied, "I've got a lot going on, so I have to say no. Tell Miz Grimes to wait until more can come."

"I did, but she's all fired up about this because she has a new list of missionaries to ship the Bibles to. With Trina out of pocket for the time being, Aunt Dru decided to change the list from the one Trina provided."

He was quiet, then said in a low voice, "I'll be there."

As soon as I hung up, I called Jerry at Bingo Bonanza and asked him to tell Big Mama to meet me, then gave him the address. Oddly, Jerry didn't ask me to clarify "Big Mama." He simply said, "Git 'er done!"

I put the Bobcat in my purse and headed for Aunt Dru's.

Chapter 15

When Aunt Dru didn't answer my knock, I peeked through the front window and could see the television was on. That meant she had to be home, because no way would Aunt Dru leave the TV on when she left the house. It would be a sin against God and a crime against man to waste electricity. Taking off around the house, I thought I'd knock on the back door and she'd hear me over the television.

She didn't, but the door was unlocked, so I went in and hollered, "Aunt Dru! You here? It's Whitney Ann!"

That's when I heard a muffled sound and I immediately feared she had fallen. Probably while she was hiding the Bibles, I thought guiltily. Moving across the den, I went toward the sound and ended up at a closet, but before I could open the door, I heard a man's voice, coming from down the hall.

"Dammit, Miz Grimes, why do you have this stuff all over the place?"

"Banty?" Okay, I needed to just stay calm. He didn't know that I suspected him—yet.

He appeared in the hall entryway and stared at me as though I'd risen from the dead. "Pink! What are you doing here?"

"I came to see Aunt Dru. Where is she, and why do you have that black stuff stuck all over you?"

Trying to shake it off of his arms and legs, he looked comical. "It's flypaper. She's got it everywhere."

"Must be for the no-see-ums." I heard the muffled sound again and reached for the closet door. Inside, Aunt Dru sat on the floor, a gag in her mouth and her hands and feet trussed up like a Thanksgiving turkey.

"Close the door, Pink."

Oh, shit. I closed the door after shooting an apologetic look at Aunt Dru, and saw Banty pointing a pistol at me. My guardian angel whispered, "That's it. I'm outta here."

"What's going on, Banty?"

"I came for the Bibles, but Miz Grimes won't tell me where they are."

"Are the Bibles with the money in them your way of lending aid to the oppressed?"

He narrowed his pale green eyes. "So you found the money. I suspected as much when you called about the new list of missionaries. Obviously, I couldn't let Miz Grimes mail all that money to real missionaries."

"Especially as they're Christians and the money's earmarked for Muslims."

He snorted with disgust. "You think I care about Muslims? The whole lot of 'em should be wiped off the planet."

A voice drifted over my shoulder. "It will happen, eventually."

Tattoo Man. I remembered the voice. And the odor of onions.

Banty rolled his eyes. "Carl is rather passionate about Muslims. His twin brother was killed on nine-eleven."

"Did I miss something? How is justice served by helping the terrorists who killed him?"

Carl's voice came closer. "The terrorists will eventually kill all the other Muslims, and when they're done, we will kill them. The world will be free of heretics."

I eyed Banty, who seemed impatient with his goon's passion. "Carl's in this to rid the world of Muslims, but I don't see it making any difference to you, Banty. What's your angle?"

He looked smug. "As soon as Lorenzo is convicted of stealing oil, murdering his ex-wife, funding Islamic terrorists and trying to blow up a United States senator, I'm moving to Pakistan. Maybe I'm nobody here, but over there, I'll be treated like royalty."

And this was important to him, I could see. The misguided, delusional fool. He'd gone to such great lengths to frame Lorenzo, to discredit him, all because he wanted the same respect and admiration Lorenzo enjoyed. He just didn't get it. "You've got it all figured out, don't you? Very clever, Banty."

He was clearly pleased with my assessment. "Being a San Antonio Dinkle, I come from a long line of intelligent men."

"Yes, I see, but one thing still confuses me. If you're the one who set the bomb that almost killed me and Steve, how did you know we'd be in that car?"

"The housekeeper, Eleanor, told me, just like she told me everything that goes on in Lorenzo's house." He frowned. "Shame we had to kill her. It's so hard to find someone who'll do windows."

"Why did you wait until I was getting in the car? Did you want to kill me, too?"

"I handpicked you as the CPA for this job because of your friendship with Santorelli, which I figured would give you an inside track to uncovering Lorenzo, because of your notoriety as a whistle-blower, and because your aunt was already involved. But I questioned your loyalty when Becker chose you to follow around and hand off the information intended for Al Qaeda. I was afraid you'd gone to the other side, like he did." Banty shrugged, as though it was really of little consequence. "Had the bomb done its job, I'd have hired another CPA. You're a dime a dozen. As it happened, you lived, and proved your patriotism by breaking into the Salvation Army to get Spider-Man."

Maybe I would have taken offense, but I couldn't care less what Banty thought of me or CPAs in general. He was dirt. "Was Bob Fishburn your brother?"

"Unfortunately, yes. He was a moron and a thief, but Mama made me include him. After he stole five thousand dollars, I made him pay it back and the idiot hit up the CIA op for it. Never one to learn his lesson, he did it again and got himself killed. I should thank you for shooting him."

My blood turned to ice. I was facing a machine, a man with no soul. Or was I? "Why did you kill Trina? I thought you had it bad for her."

"Trina was a whore who liked to play Mommy, but her biggest problem was that she still loved Lorenzo. She carried around a ring of his and tried real hard to prove herself, but some mistakes just can't be erased, can they?" He glanced at Carl and nodded slowly, as though agreeing with himself. "People will do most anything you ask of them, if the reward is important enough." He looked at me again. "If Trina couldn't have Lorenzo, she wanted his son, and short of murder, there was only one way she could get Lorenzo out of the way. Hell hath no fury like a woman scorned. But she lost her nerve after Becker got it."

"How did you know Becker?"

"He investigated me because I have a lot of cash-intensive businesses. Of course he didn't find anything, so I offered to help him find what he wanted. I thought he'd catch on that it was supposed to be Lorenzo, but he never did. When I realized he was in love with Trina, I made him an offer he couldn't refuse." Banty's expression became disgusted. "Less intelligent men always think with their little head. He thought if he had enough money, she'd fall for him."

I could feel Carl breathing down my neck and I knew it was getting close to time to die. I really didn't want to die. I wanted to make up with Ed. I wanted to see Steve again. And I wanted to take that trip with Mom. Poor Mom. She'd never get over it if I died, but how much worse would it be if I was killed by a loser like Banty? I thought of Aunt Dru, and how she thought I was a good girl. I wasn't, really, but I couldn't let her down and allow Banty to kill her. I decided to move things along. "Why won't Aunt Dru give you the Bibles?"

"She says they have a misprint in them, and she intends to destroy them. I explained that she's wrong, and discussed the consequences if she doesn't hand them over, but she's a strong woman, your aunt, and she refused."

I glanced over my shoulder at Carl and his Spider-Man tattoo. "They're in the garage, under her Buick."

Banty waved him away, and like the obedient dog he was, Carl took off for the garage.

Turning back to Banty, I said easily, "Well, Aunt Dru is a Pearl, from the Midland Pearls, and we have a long line of kick-ass women in our family. Take me, for instance. You're pointing that gun at me, but I'm not worried."

"Because you think you can kick my ass?"

"No, because the gun isn't loaded."

A worry wrinkle appeared on his forehead, and I could see the thought process as it moved through his brain. *I know I loaded it. Didn't I? What if I didn't?* Sure enough, he disengaged the magazine to check, and in those few seconds, I jerked open the closet door and nailed him, square in the face. His nose began to bleed profusely, and it surprised him so much, he dropped the gun. I grabbed it before he could get to it, then turned it on him. "Get your hands way up, Banty."

He didn't get his hands up. One of them was stuck in the flypaper, attached to his leg. With the other, he lunged for the gun, so I shot him.

Well, I didn't actually shoot him. That gun had a way worse kick than the Bobcat, so I actually shot Aunt Dru's television, which made a very loud noise when the tube shattered. Just like his brother had looked when I shot out the window at the church, Banty had to look when I hit the TV. And that's when I really shot him, but I aimed for his leg because I didn't want another man's death on my conscience.

Unfortunately, the gun kicked so hard, I hit him in the shoulder instead of the leg. It also had a hair trigger, and before I knew what was happening, I'd fired three more rounds, all of which hit Banty in various extremities. As he fell to his knees, he looked at me with confusion on his face. "You shot me! They said you can't shoot."

I wondered who kept telling people that. "They lied. Sort of."

He wasn't dead, but he was out of commission, on his knees, one hand still stuck in the flypaper and the other clutching his shoulder. I grabbed the Bobcat out of my purse, turned and ran to the garage, praying all the way that God would help me shoot straight. I saw Carl's boots, poking out from beneath the back half of the Buick. Hurrying out, I aimed and concentrated, then fired, twice. Only twice. And I hit both tires on the driver's side, which dropped the car enough to pin Carl and his tattoo to the concrete floor. Hot damn! I ignored his shouts and curses and went back in the house, where I took the gag out of Aunt Dru's mouth and started to untie her.

"I can't believe you shot me!" Banty cried, then he groaned as a pool of blood formed around him. "What kind of a CPA are you, that you'd shoot your client?"

"You're kidding, right? Was I supposed to let you get away

with sending thousands of dollars to a terrorist group, just because you're my client?"

"I thought you understood. This is about justice, Pink!"

"No, Banty, this is about revenge, and hate, and probably some envy and sloth and whatever those other deadly sins are. Is one of them being stingy? Because you should rethink your policy of never paying people what you owe them. Mohammed the Bible salesman is so pissed, he gave me the best clue to finding you. Ironic, isn't it, that your own pathetic personality became your downfall?"

His eyes dropped to the blood flowing through his fingers. "Mother of God, call an ambulance! This hurts like the devil, and I'm bleeding to death!"

"Aw, that's a shame, Banty. Maybe you should think about how it feels, and imagine all the innocent people who will bleed to death because they were unfortunate enough to stand next to a suicide bomber whose equipment was bought with *your money*."

That really sent him off, but I had a very hard time mustering any sympathy.

"Banty!" Aunt Dru yelled while I was untying the knot around her ankles.

"Yes, ma'am?" he asked in between his blubbers.

"I told you not to sleep through Pastor's sermons, but you didn't listen. Now look at you! Sojourning among the heathens!"

His answer was another keening wail.

I crossed the room, picked up the phone and called 911. Just as I hung up, Ed came through the back door, his eyes wild and his face pale. "Pink!" He came at me, then saw the gun, stopped on a dime and jerked his head around to look at Banty. "You shot your client?"

"Can you believe it?" Banty asked, still sniveling.

"What is that stuck all over you?"

"Damn flypaper for Miz Grimes's no-see-ums."

Ed's gaze traveled to Aunt Dru, then back to me. "When you didn't answer my calls, and you didn't answer your door, I kinda freaked out and broke into your apartment. I found the Bible, realized what you figured out, then came over to your aunt's to get the rest of them."

"You can't have them!" Banty shouted. "They're mine! I paid for them, and they're mine!"

"You didn't pay for them," I corrected him. "You stiffed the Bible salesman."

"He's on a ninety-day rotation. He'll be paid in October."

Ed reached for the gun. "Maybe you should let me have that. I know you can't shoot." He glanced at Banty, then said under his breath, "Much."

A shadow fell across the floor and I looked toward the door. Big Mama stood there, dressed in an orange caftan, Boris peeking out from his bag. "Look what we have here," she said, moving her bulky body toward Banty. "The big, bad terrorist, taken down by a CPA who runs like a girl and can't shoot."

"Edward?" Aunt Dru hollered from the hallway.

"Yes, Mrs. Grimes?" he asked, his gaze still fixed on mine.

"Do you know a good exterminator?"

"No, ma'am, but I know a damn good CPA."

Chapter 16

A few days later, I received an e-mail from Steve. Pink, it read, look at this photo and tell me if you don't agree that my mom and yours look alike.

I opened the file and checked out the picture. Steve's mother did look a lot like Mom, with dark hair and eyes, and very pretty features, and something in the set of her chin, as if she was a determined woman. That was definitely like Mom.

For whatever reason, I couldn't stop looking at that picture. I retrieved it several times that day, and finally, about four in the afternoon, I figured out why it intrigued me so much. I zoomed in on her hand, resting on her thigh, and inspected her ring. It was a collection of rubies and diamonds, an unusual setting, and probably very expensive.

It looked just like Big Mama's.

Then I noticed something else. In the background, behind the chair where Mrs. Santorelli sat, a very small dog looked toward the camera. A teacup Chihuahua.

I e-mailed back and agreed that our mothers looked alike, then wrote, Cute dog. What's its name?

Within a few minutes, I had my answer. Bullwinkle. He was my mother's favorite dog. I have one of his offspring, Natasha, and Dad has her brother, Boris. There was another one from Bullwinkle's litter named Rocky Squirrel, but he died a few years ago.

I remembered seeing Natasha at Lorenzo's house. Had Steve been there then? I sat back in my chair and made a few conjectures, most of which I knew Steve would never verify. Was Big Mama his dad, in disguise? Lou Santorelli was a POW in Vietnam, and Steve said he took on crazy assignments from the defense department. Somehow, it fit. I've heard it said a lotta guys came back from Vietnam a little off the wall. Dressing as an enormously obese woman and going around saving the world was pretty off the wall. There was also the coincidence of the Altoids box. Big Mama had swiped mine, and Lou had one. Steve had said his dad was being a pain in the ass, putting himself in danger, and Steve was to the point of throwing in with him.

Maybe they'd both stayed at Lorenzo's, somewhere in the giant house, all during the past week. Steve could have forwarded his calls from D.C. to his cell phone, which would explain why he answered instead of an assistant. Hmm. Maybe David Lorenzo was in on the whole thing as well, never suspected of funding anything more sinister than a new hospital wing.

I wondered if Steve chose that picture of his mother for a reason. Maybe he wanted me to know. I wrote, How's Big Mama?

Within a minute, I had an answer. Still a pain in the ass, talking incessantly about a good-looking CPA in Midland.

Mom. No wonder Steve had pressed the party invitation for Mom. I almost laughed out loud at that thought. Mom would die and go to heaven to know a man like Steve's dad was attracted to her. Then she'd blow it by wigging out about what she should wear, and what she should say and how she should

act. I decided I would never tell Mom that a handsome man
that sometimes went around disguised in a fat suit had a crush
on her. I'd take her to Washington and see what happened.

Rocking back in my chair, I stared at the screen for a long,
long time. Then I heard the familiar sound of a new e-mail
received. I clicked to open it. Another one from Steve.

Expect a call from Lorenzo. He thinks Boxwood Marketing is playing funny money with oil prices, and he wants
to hire you to get to the bottom of it. Dave's a good guy,
Pink. He's also a very gracious host—if you ever need a
place to stay.

All along, I'd wondered about Santa, and why Becker put
that name on the cake. A birthday cake he happened to order
on Steve's birthday. Santorelli, which wasn't so far from
Santa. Jake had mentioned there was someone involved with
the project who was completely anonymous. Someone with
the code name Santa Claus, because technically, Santa Claus
didn't exist. Without allowing myself to chicken out, because
I *had* to know, I leaned over and typed, Would Santa agree?

I waited and waited, but there was no reply.

Mom came by my cube then, and I wasn't able to watch
or listen for a new e-mail. "Pink, let's go shopping for new
dresses to wear to that party. I'll buy you one."

"It's okay, Mom. I'm not destitute, you know."

"I know. Consider it a gift, since we've been a little out of
sorts lately."

That was Mom's way of saying she was sorry, and I accepted it as such. To expect anything more would only cause
a lot of frustration on my part. That she hadn't mentioned anything about my very first acquired client turning out to be a
terrorist financier, coupled with the offer of a new party dress,
would be all I'd get in the way of an apology. But from Mom,

that was enough. I wondered how she'd react when she found out I'd landed David Lorenzo. I liked the idea that she'd eat a little humble pie, but that's not her way. "Okay, Mom. Let me get my stuff together and we'll go."

"Good. Then we'll stop at Ed's brother's restaurant for dinner. I've got something to talk to you about."

"What is it?"

Mom assumed a very innocent look. "My air conditioner."

Oh, man. It was going to be a long night. I watched her walk away, then noticed a new message on the computer.

There's no such thing as Santa, but just in case, you'd better be good. Later, Pink. I'm going to California for a few days. I'll call you. S2

I gathered up my things, then followed Mom to the parking garage. We took the Mercedes, and while Mom played with all the buttons, I drove down Big Spring Street, out of downtown, toward Loop 250. At Wadley, a major northern cross street, I hit a red light. Sitting there, I thought about Ed and Steve, and how I was faced with a problem that had no easy solution.

Glancing at Mom, I started to ask for her advice, questionable as it might be, but stopped short when I noticed her eyes were wide and she looked shocked. "Mom? What is it?"

She raised her finger and pointed.

I followed the direction and saw a billboard across the street, rising up from behind Cattleman's Restaurant. On a white background, in huge letters shaped like little pink houses, it read, MARRY ME PINK.

"Who wants you to marry him?" Mom asked.

I sat through the green light and stared while people behind me honked. "I don't know."

* * * * *

There's more Silhouette Bombshell coming your way!
Every month we've got four fresh, unique and
satisfying reads that will keep you riveted....
Turn the page for an exclusive excerpt from
one of next month's releases

BEYOND THE RULES
by Doranna Durgin

On sale September 2005
at your favorite retail outlet.

"I need your help."

For an instant, words eluded Kimmer Reed. When she found them, they were blunt. "You must be kidding."

"You think I came all the way up here to kid you?" Hank, her long-lost, and not missed, brother threw his arms up, a helpless gesture. "You think I *want* to be here talking to you and your—"

"Ryobe Carlsen," Rio said in the most neutral of tones. "*Konnichiwa.* We can shake hands another time."

Hank's eyes narrowed. "You were there," he said to Rio. "Leo said there was a man involved."

"There were several, in fact. But I was one of them. I was certainly there when Leo mentioned how you planned to hand Kimmer over to him."

Relief washed through Kimmer. Rio might not truly understand what Kimmer's family did—or more to the point, *didn't*—mean to her, but he knew Hank had a lot to prove. She should have known…should have trusted him.

Of course, that wasn't something that came easily. Emotional trust was against the rules.

She took a deep breath, suddenly aware of just how much this encounter was taking from her. Tough Kimmer, keeping up her hard front when she just wanted to ease across the swing into Rio's arms. Except—

It was her own job to take care of herself.

So at the end of that deep breath, she made herself sound bored. "I can't imagine how you think I can help you at all."

"Leo said— Well, hell, you made an impression on Leo. He says you took down the Murty brothers when you were in Mill Springs. And he came back to Munroville spouting stories about terrorists. He said you'd taken them out."

Kimmer flicked her gaze at Rio. "I wasn't alone."

"He said they shot you, and you didn't even flinch."

She touched her side, where the scar was fading. It had only been a crease. She shrugged. "I was mad."

"He *said*," Hank continued doggedly, "that you were *connected*. That your people came into Mill Springs and did such a cleanup job that the cops never had anything to follow through on. Even those two guys you sent to the hospital— Homeland Security walked away with them."

"Leo talks a lot," Kimmer said. But she suppressed a smile. Damned if Hank didn't actually sound impressed. "And you still haven't gotten to the point."

"The *point*," Hank told her, "is that that's the kind of help I need."

"You want me to get shot for you?" Kimmer shook her head. "Not gonna happen."

"You gotta make this hard, don't you?" Hank shifted his weight impatiently, coming precariously close to Kimmer's freshly blooming irises.

Yes. But she had the restraint to respond silently, and he barged right on through. "Look, I'm in over my head. I let some people use a storage building for...something. They turned out to be a rough crew, more'n I wanted to deal with. An' I've got a wife and kids—bet you didn't even know I had kids—and I wanted out. Except I saw a murder, damned bad luck. They know I want out, and they don't trust me to keep my mouth shut." He closed his mouth to look at her with a defiant jut to his jaw, daring her to react to the story. To judge him.

Kimmer sat silently, absorbing it all. Hank on the run from goonboys. Hank scared enough to track down a sister he'd abused and openly scorned. Hank here before her, asking for help she wasn't sure she could or would give him. *Assuming I believe a word of it in the first place.* Wouldn't it be just like her brothers to send one of them to lure her back home, where they probably thought they could control her?

Out loud, she said thoughtfully, "'Bad luck' is when you're on your way to church and someone runs a red light in front of you. Witnessing nastiness at the hands of the goonboys you've invited into your home is more under the heading of 'what did you expect?'"

His face darkened with something between anger and humiliation. "You gotta be a bitch about it? I'm asking for help here, Kimmer."

"I'm not sure just *what* you're asking," Kimmer told him. Except suddenly she knew, and she spat a quick, vicious curse. "You want me to kill them. You actually want me to *kill* them."

Hank hesitated, startled both by her perception and her anger, and put up a hand as though it would slow either. Rio looked at her in astonishment—Mr. Spy Guy, somehow not yet jaded enough to believe this to be something brother would ask sister. And Kimmer, so mad she could barely see straight, still caught the implication of the unfamiliar sedan traveling too fast as it passed by her street. And as it stopped and backed up to hover at the end of the street.

"Dammit, Hank, did you tell anyone you were coming to see me?"

Startled, he looked as if he'd resist answering just because he didn't like her tone. By then Kimmer was on her feet, now bare. Rio, too, had come out without shoes. Sock-foot. He never wore outdoor footgear in the house out of respect for his Japanese grandmother's early teaching, even if he didn't use the proper slippers while indoors.

Family. She wanted to snarl the word out loud. She didn't take the time. She uncurled to flow off the swing, and by then Hank had followed her gaze and blurted, "Just a few people, but they didn't know why—"

"They didn't have to," Kimmer said, and by then Rio was on his feet beside her—and the sedan had turned sharply onto the narrow back street of wide-set houses, the acceleration of the engine clearly audible. "Keys, Hank!"

"What—"

She turned her gaze away from the car long enough to snap a look at him. "Your damn car keys—hand them over!" She didn't wait for compliance, but headed for him. No time to run inside for any of her handguns, no time to hesitate over anything at all.

"They're in the—hey!"

"They've already spotted it," Rio said, close behind her.

"You don't have to come," she told him—no sting to her words, just simple assessment of the situation as she hauled the door open and climbed into the driver's seat.

"Coming anyway," he said, just as matter-of-factly. And then gave Hank a little shove toward the back door on his way past; in a moment, he sat beside Kimmer. Hank—still baffled—got in the back.

"Where's the shotgun?" Kimmer asked, cranking the engine. It hesitated; she gave it a swift kick of gas and it caught, rumbling unhappily.

"I don't—"

"You *do*. Where?" She wrestled the gear shift into reverse, giving the approaching sedan a calculating glance. *We're not fast enough.*

"Under the seat," Hank admitted, and Rio ducked down to grab it. "Why—"

"What did you think?" She snorted, backing them down the driveway. "We'd have it out right here in my neighborhood, with all these innocent people going about their lives? In my own *house?*"

"I didn't think you'd run!" Hank snapped. "But then, that's what you're good at, isn't it?"

"When the moment's right." Kimmer cranked the wheel to catapult them out into the street, looking back over her shoulder through the rear glass of the big utility vehicle. *Too close. They're way too close.* She couldn't make herself feel any particular concern about her brother's safety—but this moment didn't have to be about Hank. It was about the goonboys, who were now chasing not only Hank, but Kimmer and Rio. Rio, whom she wouldn't allow to be hurt again. With the vehicle still whining in reverse, she locked her gaze on the rearview mirror. There they were. Goonboys, to be sure—guns at the ready, assumed victory molding their expressions.

She wasn't in the habit of letting the goonboys win.

Kimmer jammed down the accelerator and watched their eyes widen.

TO HELL WITH THE TRAINING DIVE.

Aleesha kicked into trauma-surgeon mode. Possible crushed ribs. Punctured lungs. Contused heart. And blood. Oh, God. There were sharks in these waters.

Well, she'd wanted adventure. She had to give Uncle Sam credit for delivering.

Meet Aleesha Gautier, medic for the Medusas, America's first all-female Special Ops team, in the next story of pulse-pounding military action from author

CINDY DEES

MEDUSA RISING

Available at your favorite retail outlet.

On sale September 2005!

If you enjoyed what you just read,
then we've got an offer you can't resist!

Take 2 bestselling love stories FREE!

Plus get a FREE surprise gift!

Clip this page and mail it to Silhouette Reader Service®

IN U.S.A.	IN CANADA
3010 Walden Ave.	P.O. Box 609
P.O. Box 1867	Fort Erie, Ontario
Buffalo, N.Y. 14240-1867	L2A 5X3

YES! Please send me 2 free Silhouette Bombshell™ novels and my free surprise gift. After receiving them, if I don't wish to receive any more, I can return the shipping statement marked cancel. If I don't cancel, I will receive 4 brand-new novels every month, before they're available in stores! In the U.S.A., bill me at the bargain price of $4.69 plus 25¢ shipping & handling per book and applicable sales tax, if any*. In Canada, bill me at the bargain price of $5.24 plus 25¢ shipping & handling per book and applicable taxes**. That's the complete price and a savings of 10% off the cover prices—what a great deal! I understand that accepting the 2 free books and gift places me under no obligation ever to buy any books. I can always return a shipment and cancel at any time. Even if I never buy another book from Silhouettte, the 2 free books and gift are mine to keep forever.

200 HDN D34H
300 HDN D34J

Name	(PLEASE PRINT)	
Address	Apt.#	
City	State/Prov.	Zip/Postal Code

Not valid to current Silhouette Bombshell™ subscribers.

Want to try another series?
Call 1-800-873-8635 or visit www.morefreebooks.com.

* Terms and prices subject to change without notice. Sales tax applicable in N.Y.
** Canadian residents will be charged applicable provincial taxes and GST.
  All orders subject to approval. Offer limited to one per household.
  ® and ™ are registered trademarks owned and used by the trademark owner and
  or its licensee.

BOMB04   ©2004 Harlequin Enterprises Limited

Something is stirring again...

CAST IN SHADOW

MICHELLE SAGARA

Seven years ago Kaylin fled the crime-riddled streets of Nightshade, knowing that something was after her. Since then, she's learned to read, fight and has become one of the vaunted Hawks who patrol and police the City of Elantra. But children are once again dying, and a dark and familiar pattern is emerging. Kaylin is ordered back into Nightshade and tasked to find the killer and stop the murders. But can she survive the attentions of those who claim to be her allies along the way?

LUNA™

On sale August.

Visit your local bookseller.

COMING NEXT MONTH

#57 TOUCH OF THE WHITE TIGER by Julie Beard
An Angel Baker Novel
Times were tough in Chicago in the year 2104. As a Certified
Retribution Specialist, Angel Baker had the responsibility of
making criminals pay for their crimes. But now she and her
fellow specialists were the targets—of smear campaigns, lies,
even assassination. Not even her cop boyfriend trusted her. Only
Angel could bring the mastermind of this twisted plot to justice
before she became the next victim.

#58 THE GOLDEN GIRL by Erica Orloff
The It Girls
Real-estate heiress Madison Taylor-Pruitt had it all—money in
the bank, the looks and labels to die for and her pick of eligible
bachelors. But when her own father was named prime suspect
in her coworker's murder, Madison's reversal of fortune seemed
like a done deal—until the elite Gotham Rose spy ring asked her
to find the real killer. Could the savvy socialite stay on the A-list
and keep her father off the Most-Wanted list?

#59 BEYOND THE RULES by Doranna Durgin
For once in Kimmer Reed's life, all the pieces were falling into
place. She had a dream job with the Hunter Agency, and a man
she actually trusted at her back. Then her deadbeat brother
showed up on her doorstep with a sob story and gunmen in hot
pursuit. Now a major crime organization had Kimmer in its sights
and her love life was on the rocks. It was enough to make this
undercover gal bend the rules one more time....

#60 MEDUSA RISING by Cindy Dees
The Medusa Project
When terrorists hijacked the *Grand Adventure* cruise ship
and took all the women and children on board hostage, the
all-female Medusa Special Forces team quickly infiltrated
and made plans to take back the ship. But Medusa medic
Aleesha Gautier soon found out that one of the hijackers wasn't
who he seemed to be. Could she trust his offer of help, or was
she bringing a viper into their midst before the final showdown?